Blood Runs True

E L Armstrong

Cover design by E L Armstrong
Cover art by Bronte Dixon

Paperback ISBN: 978-1-7391722-1-3
E-book ISBN: 978-1-7391722-0-6

Revised First Edition

For Holly, Hollie, Lucy, and Monty

1

The King is Dead

It was a bad day for the squirrel. Maybe even its worst day, barring the possibility it had seen its parents fall from a tree or some other squirrel tragedy. Still, its misfortune was my benefit.

Crouching down, I unwound the snare from the bushes before working it from the squirrel's fur. Two days it had taken me, to come up with this one measly prize. Orion and Ishmael would have been ashamed. Then again, given my ineptitude for snares during our lessons, they wouldn't have been surprised.

They'd intended the devices to be used for ambush attacks, fending off my objections that someone else would be able to set them for me. I still wasn't sure I saw their worth. I could have caught a squirrel with my bare hands quicker. But the experiment had given me an excuse to linger. It took time to set up a snare, even longer to wait to see if it would be sprung. I hadn't moved any closer to home for three days.

Looking from the limp squirrel in my hands to the sky overhead, I knew I wouldn't be going anywhere today either. By the time I cleaned the animal, lit a fire, and cooked it, it would be almost dark. Another day of freedom. But how many more could I steal? How long would my excuses last?

I jerked my hand, which had been creeping up towards my right shoulder, back down, flexing my creeping fingers to appease them.

Returning to my camp, which was nothing more than a natural hollow between two trees where I'd cleared space for a fire, I gutted the squirrel, burying the entrails then wiping my hands on its fur, scrubbing as much blood as possible from below my fingernails. Giving up, I scoured the forest floor for a suitable stick to continue the job when I heard it. The choked, fluttering alarm call of a disturbed pheasant as it took to the wing, somewhere west of me.

Frozen, I listened as my eyes darted between the trees. It might have been nothing. Just a bird, startled by another animal.

For over a month I'd haunted this patch of the woods and seen nothing more worrying than the claw marks of a bear gouged into a tree over my head. No hint of the threat Hamma had suspected lurked here.

The trees were now silent. No birds sang. Nothing rustled in the undergrowth. The quiet pressed on my bones.

A warbling song. The alarm call of another bird. Then the breaking of a branch, the snap and rustle of leaves.

Something was coming.

My hands leapt to the twin blades strapped to my legs, drawing them free with a rasp of metal. Closer now. The sound of breathing, fast with exertion, reached my ears. My head turned from side to side, trying to catch a glimpse of the newcomer through the army of tree trunks.

There! A flash of movement. Thorns, they were moving fast!

I crouched, shifting sideways to stay behind a tree as they approached, drawing hard upon the power held under my skin. Warm tendrils flowed down my left arm and across one side of my back. My breaths came faster, matching theirs, my muscles clenching.

When the foreign footsteps were too close to bear, I leapt, my tension escaping me in a shriek. The sound was echoed in a clash of metal as my blades were deflected. A foot connected with my thigh. I cried out as my leg went numb, turning my fall into a clumsy roll, and came up to a lopsided crouch with a snarl on my face, finally getting a look at my opponent.

A leather vest covered his torso, leaving his arms bare, and dark

2

woollen leggings reached down to his mid-calf. A year older than me, with short hair that fell over his forehead and deep, close-set eyes above a wide nose and stoic mouth, he was as familiar to me as my reflection.

"Nate!" I gasped, my focus slipping, and there was a sudden chill over my skin as the dark warmth receded. The air seemed to press closer to my bare arms in its absence.

"Tamara!" His face wore an expression of shock mirroring my own. He lowered his sword, twice the length of my blades, to his side.

"What are you doing here?" I stood, massaging my tingling leg.

"Looking for you," he replied sourly.

I frowned. "Here?" After leaving the Hollowed Tree, I'd followed the eastern branch of the Baerston Mountains south before descending into the forest to their east. Even the hunters who would spend seasons roaming the high peaks would rarely venture into this territory. I was so far east I'd been worried about avoiding demons, yet he had found me. "How did you know I'd be here?"

"I didn't," he said, sliding his sword away and running a hand through his hair, the colour of wet sand. "But you've been gone a long time. You clearly weren't on the traditional route."

"That's not an answer."

"Call it luck then."

I rolled my eyes, putting my blades away. His black eyes tracked the movement. Even after ten years of seeing them, the darkness of his eyes still caught me unawares, like a drop of cold water striking the back of my neck.

"Where have you been?"

"I... ah... nowhere." I turned away from him, striding back to my camp and crouching down beside the piece of scorched earth. My hands shook as I raked together a new pile of leaves.

"Nowhere?" The word was as flat and cold as the ground beneath my feet. "Four months, you've been gone."

I wanted to be angry, to snap that I didn't answer to him. But I

3

couldn't summon the emotion. "Is that why you're here then? Father sent you?"

Of course he had. He had no idea what had happened, either at the Hollowed Tree or six years ago when my future had been destroyed in one single moment. He wouldn't understand why I'd stayed away. No one would. I hadn't even intended to, but days had passed into weeks into months, and it had been so easy to delay over and over again. To steal another hour, another day, of freedom.

I'd taken too long. Father had given me these four months. But now my time was up. And even as King, with the forces of an entire city at his disposal, Father had only sent one person to bring me home. The one who would never have given up.

"No."

There was something in Nate's voice, beyond just the meaning of the word, that made me look up. He avoided my gaze.

"You *left*?" I knew Nate's loyalty to my father was far from absolute, but this was a step too far. He'd sworn an oath.

"No… it's…" He took a breath but seemed unable to speak.

Something dark and insidious stirred within me as I stood up. "Nate. Why are you here?"

He looked at me at last. "The king is dead."

I breathed.

In.

Out.

No. It wasn't possible. Surely some mistake. Or a misunderstanding. A cruel joke even. But there was no humour in Nate's expression, no sign of the little smirk that would sometimes appear when he was laughing silently at me. And he would never joke about something like this.

"Dead?"

He nodded. "I'm sorry."

I turned away. My breath lodged in my throat, choking me. I kept my eyes clenched shut against the tears.

The king is dead.

4

Four little words, shattering worlds.

Nathaniel was a silent presence behind me, reassuring rather than intrusive as thoughts ran through my mind.

Blue eyes like the summer sky, crinkled with amusement or hard with displeasure. Memories, advice given long ago, promises made and kept and broken.

Eventually, I opened my eyes again, shaking my head as I turned back to face him.

Like a fool, I'd searched for some kind of escape by staying away. But there was nothing to be found out here. Not now, not ever. Instead, all I'd done was lost the chance to say goodbye.

"What happened?" My voice was hoarse and rough.

He didn't answer me straight away, and part of me didn't want him to. I would rather remember my father as he had always been—proud and strong, rather than ravaged by some terrible sickness he'd been unable to defeat.

"There was an attack," Nate said.

"What?"

He was silent for a moment, and I gritted my teeth at the delay, my body trembling as I waited.

"It was quiet," he said. "We'd been along the valley, visiting the herders on the slopes. Then there were farmers on the way back. It was getting dark, but you know what he's like."

I did; my father wouldn't have wanted to rush a conversation or bypassed someone who wanted to talk with him. Not for such a mundane reason as time.

"We were almost back, just coming to the edges of the city. We could even see the gates, but…" Nate's face tightened. "They came out of nowhere. We were all there—the whole Guard—but it was like they were shadows. There could have been twenty extra soldiers for all the difference it would have made. I killed one of them; Hamma took down another. But Ishmael fell, Osanna went down. Rian died right beside me.

"Mara, I swear, I did everything I could. But I turned around, and I… I saw your father fall, and standing over him…" He broke off,

5

looking away.

"You saw who it was?" The words shook. Of course, I knew what they were, but I had to know, had to find the one who had...

Nate nodded. "He looked right at me," he said, his voice barely more than a whisper, "and his eyes... his eyes were like mine." He turned back, looking at me with eyes dark as charcoal, framed in white. Eyes that could not cry. Demon eyes.

His eyes were like mine.

I swallowed.

"He smiled at me," Nate spat, "and then they were gone, all of them, as if they'd never been there."

"He was like you?" I asked, staring at his eyes, focusing not on the dark iris—indistinguishable from the pupil—but the white around it.

In my mind, Nate's eyes were unique. The idea there was another half-blood, old enough to fight, old enough to kill, and we'd never known, never heard a whisper of their existence... Surely it couldn't be true.

"Justifies what everyone thought of me, doesn't it?" he said, bitterness seeping into his tone.

"How many of the Guard survived?"

Nate flashed me a quick look.

"None?"

He shook his head.

I sank to the ground, staring blindly ahead. Was the loss of my father not enough? Hamma as well? Ishmael? All of them?

Nate was the only one I had left.

I froze as the thought sank in. How would it have appeared to everyone, to find their King dead, slain by demons, and the only survivor a half-blood himself? Nate's nomination to the Guard had been contentious, despite all he'd done to prove himself. What rumours must have spread after this?

"What happened afterwards?"

Nate looked away, and I knew I wasn't going to like what came next.

"I hid."

I didn't respond. Would that make it better or worse? Would Nate gain more sympathy as a lone survivor, or as someone who was missing? My heart sank at the comparison. Neither option was good, but I wasn't convinced Nate had picked the better choice.

"You know what would have happened, what they all would have thought," he said. "I didn't have a choice."

"So no one knows who it was?"

"People found the bodies; they know it was demons."

"But the half-blood got away?"

He nodded.

My fists clenched, old leaves crunching in my palms. My father's murderer had survived, had escaped unpunished. The knowledge burned, tongues of flame rising in my chest.

Yet that fact was also the only thing that might save Nate's life. If it had been known that the killer was like him, I wasn't sure what people would have done. As my father had once said, the history of half-bloods was not pleasant. Those pages were splattered with blood.

Maybe Nate had done the right thing by hiding. This way, with my backing, at least he might have a chance to explain.

This was it. For all my running and hiding, it was inevitable. Despite my Thorns's rejection, despite my impairment, I would Claim the throne, just as my father had intended. To avenge his death, to ensure Nate's safety, I would do it.

"Right," I said, trying to sound decisive. "We'll leave at first light. It'll be okay. We'll get back and sort everything out."

That would be the easy part. Father had always made it clear he expected me to succeed him as he'd succeeded my grandmother. The only point against me would be my affiliation with Nate, but that would be a tenuous objection compared to my father's training.

I would have to send envoys to our allies in Charhelm and Lambridge, spread the news, and reassure them that all would continue normally. The Lambridge Council would scoff and reply with hidden implications that we should have 'dealt' with the demons a long time ago. Somehow, I doubted I would find the energy to be as patient with them as my father had been. I wondered with a scowl if he would have been as polite if they hadn't held such a stranglehold on trade from the Southerners.

"How long did it take you to find me?" I asked, my mind already several steps ahead of me. Nate wasn't the most reliable comparison—no one could run like he could—but he should be able to provide a rough estimate for how long it would take us to get back.

"Mara, it's not a case of..." he gritted his teeth, then forced the words out. "The throne has already been Claimed."

"What?" I stared at him. "By who? When?"

"The same day. Before anyone else even got back."

"So fast?" I drew back a little, not liking where my thoughts were going. "You don't think he could have known..."

Nate spread his hands. "I thought the same thing. But I don't see how, unless he was in contact with the demons."

I shook my head, dismissing the possibility. The demons didn't work with anyone. This usurper must have discovered my father's death some other way.

"Weren't there any objections? No one who raised arguments against him?"

"Oh, there were people who objected. Their bodies were left on the steps outside."

My body went cold. "Who is he?"

Nate shook his head. "His name is Djet, but no one seems to know much more about him. There were lots of rumours; he lived in the slums, he worked in the hall of records, he only kills with his bare hands, he's got wards all over his body, he can hear when someone is lying..." He looked at me. "Do you want to hear the rest?"

I shook my head. Djet... an old name. Very old. Double consonants had gone out of fashion before my grandmother's time. And as for the rest...

8

My fingers rose to stroke over the skin of my shoulder where one of my wards sat, untapped but always waiting. I deliberately didn't think about my back. Nate's arms were bare, his leather vest sitting high on his shoulders in the same style as mine, though he had no wards to display.

"How did you hear all this without being seen?"

Nate shrugged. "Turns out I haven't outgrown all my old hiding places."

The image of Nate, taller than me, long-limbed and round-shouldered, squeezed into a tiny nook, invisible to anyone passing, made me want to laugh. But knowing why he had needed those hiding spots in the first place sobered me at once. I settled for a shake of my head.

"Right. Well, we'll deal with this Djet when we get there." I sighed, picking at my fingernails as I thought aloud. "If he's kept up that attitude, people will be itching to get him out. Are they waiting for me to come back?"

"They think you're dead," Nate said bluntly. "Pilgrimage normally takes five, maybe six weeks, Tamara. You've been gone for months."

I stared at him, unable to say anything.

"There were whispers even before anything happened, people getting worried, but Djet actively spread the idea, and with no evidence to the contrary, everyone believes it." He shook his head. "I don't know if you told your father you planned to be gone for so long, but he never said anything to the Guard or anyone else. We didn't know what had happened to you."

"But you found me. You came looking."

He gave me a flat look. "Like you'd die without coming back to haunt me."

I smiled despite myself, though the expression died quickly. "I didn't mean to be gone for so long," I said quietly. "I just... needed some space."

"There's more," Nate said, taking a deep breath. "Djet has woken the Figures."

There was no light, no air.

I couldn't breathe. My nose was cold, my eyes stinging.

The world was dark, a flash of memory assaulting me in the blackness. A voice. Young, female, twisted with pain. 'Kill me,' she had whispered. Begged.

And standing over her, impassive and uncaring… grey skin, hard as stone, carved with wards beyond counting… blank white eyes, glowing faintly from within. The Figures.

"You're sure?" I whispered, with what might as well have been my last breath.

Nate nodded. "I heard that one enough to be sure of it before I left." His eyes met mine, then darted away.

So this is the truth, I thought. You didn't know I was alive; you just knew they would come for anyone who could oppose him. And that meant you as well as me. There was no bitterness in the realisation.

"We're dead." My voice was flat and empty. It was nothing more than a statement of fact. Undeniable, inescapable.

"We don't know they're coming for us."

I gave a bitter laugh at the feeble suggestion. "Why else would he have woken them if not for us?"

"The demons?" Nate suggested. "A show of strength? Or to get justice for your father?"

I shook my head. Though they were fair ideas, we both knew they were wrong. "They're coming. They're going to kill us."

Nate crouched down. "And are you going to sit there and let them?"

I blinked a couple of times before looking up. He was scared. It was written in the wideness of his eyes, the tension of his jaw. The mere mention of the Figures had always been enough to make him go pale, and though I could still see that same terror in his face now, it was controlled. He'd had time to think, aware of the threat but he hadn't given up.

His question ran through my mind again, and my stomach tightened. Was I just going to sit here? My father would be ashamed of me.

I raised my head a little more, my jaw clenched. Nate nodded approvingly.

"We should move," I said, my voice rougher than I would have liked as I looked around. Each sliver of darkness rippled with uncertainty. A flash of moving limbs or an idly waving branch? A patch of light hitting an errant stone or a pair of glowing eyes? I swallowed. For the first time since I'd entered these woods, the demons weren't the only threat stalking the edges of my thoughts.

To my surprise, Nate shook his head. "I think I got a good start on them, and I didn't exactly pace myself. You need to eat, and we both need to rest."

I hesitated. I'd rarely heard Nate admit to fatigue, but part of me still wanted to be moving, to be running. And despite the bags under Nate's eyes, the droop of his skin, I knew he would do so if I asked it of him… but I couldn't. If he said we had time to rest, I believed him.

The silence persisted as I struck a small fire, then left Nate feeding it little twigs while I retrieved the squirrel I'd snared earlier, spitting it and propping it over the flames. The simple tasks helped, focussing my hands and leaving my mind to pick over everything.

"So," Nate prompted, once the fire was crackling away by itself, casting a small circle of light around us, defying the oppressive darkness that was settling fast.

I watched it flicker, picking at my nails. "We need to get home," I said. The throne commanded the Figures; if I could lay even a single finger upon it, I could counter Djet's orders and stop them. "We can't do anything before that."

"Okay. But I'm not going to follow you if you plan on running straight back. There are potentially twelve Figures on our trail already. I vote that we don't go towards them."

"He wouldn't need them all," I said without thinking. Just one would be more than enough. The thought sent a chill through me, threatening to return me to a hopeless ball of fear, but I pushed it aside. I needed to think now. "And I wasn't suggesting we go straight back."

"So, what then?"

"The scenic route?"

Nate gave me a look. I matched it.

"I'm serious. If they're tracking us, they'll be following our trails, won't they? I went along the mountains on my way out so if we go south fast enough, we could slip around them and get back before they find us."

"That's assuming they have to follow the trail rather than tracking us directly."

My eyes flicked to his face, the firelight casting bruises across his skin. "That's not possible. They're not... I don't know... draw-stones for people, homing in on us or whatever you're thinking of."

"Are you sure? You've seen them at work. Is there anything you think they couldn't do?"

Looking away from the cooking squirrel, I took a deep breath, the sight of its charred flesh horrifically similar to the memories his question brought to the forefront of my mind.

"They can't do that," I said, trying to sound sure. The truth was, I had no idea as to the limits of the Figures' abilities. If there even was one. They had so many wards... Who knew what powers they granted? "We're going to get back, and once I've got control of the throne, I can stop them." That much, I was sure of. The Figures answered to the throne, bound by the will of the one who Claimed it.

I leaned forward and pulled the steaming squirrel off the fire, holding it away from me as hot fat dripped onto the ground. "Do you want some?" I offered.

He shot the meat a look, then shook his head.

"You can. There's enough."

"You need it. I'm fine."

I didn't object further, ripping the meat to pieces and burning my fingers as I checked for bones before eating. On the other side of the fire, Nate rubbed his face and tried to hide a yawn.

"You're exhausted. When was the last time you slept?"

He gave a dismissive jerk of his head. "Before you left?" he guessed.

I looked at him, not bothering to hide the emotions from my face. The way we'd parted had been haunting me.

"Sorry, that was…" He waved the comment away. "I shouldn't have said it."

"Even you need to sleep," I said. "Go on. We'll decide what to do next tomorrow."

His eyes flicked into the darkness around us before he shuffled back to lean against a tree trunk, pulling his sword close and keeping a hand on it even as his eyes closed. I watched him for a moment, then returned to my meal. I knew he would wake instantly if anything happened.

I sighed as I pulled apart the bare skeleton, toying with the bones, my mind still turning over the possibilities ahead of me. The Figures. Everything hung on them, and I didn't know enough. I suspected my father, as king, had had more information about the mindless warriors. Glumly, I wondered if Djet now had access to that same knowledge. The idea burned like a red-hot stone in my chest, and one of the slender bones snapped in my fingers. Taking a breath, I put them aside and picked at my nails instead.

I didn't believe Nate's paranoid suggestion that the Figures could home in on us directly, so they would either have to follow Nate's trail or mine from when I'd left, which was hopefully old enough that they would have trouble tracing it. For a moment, I considered waking Nate to ask him again how long it had taken him to find me, how much random searching he'd done, zigzagging through the forested hills, but I decided against it. Better to let him sleep for now. The fact we'd intercepted each other at all was astounding. With a bit of luck, the Figures would have to follow the same convoluted path, and then... what? They would find a place where Nate had turned back, find a trail where two people had walked, not one. It would be as good as confirmation they were on the right track, and they'd be able to come after us both.

Unless there weren't two people going in the same direction.

Unless two separate trails were leading away from this spot.

I closed my eyes, hating that I was considering the idea but also wondering if Nate had reached the same conclusion yet. It wouldn't matter if we were together or alone when the Figures caught up with us, but by splitting up, maybe we could keep the chase going for a while longer.

The potential advantage didn't make the idea any easier to stomach.

With another sigh, I kicked my legs out to the side and lay down, one hand lightly resting on my blades, and stared into the fire for a moment before closing my eyes. I pretended I was going to try and get to sleep, but in reality, I let my memories take over, flooding my mind with images of my father. I remembered him strong and weak, laughing and grieving, and had to grit my teeth against the pain that twisted my chest, but not one single tear hit the ground. I could not grieve yet. First, I had to make him proud.

2

Onward

"Another sighting?" My father crossed his arms, leaning back in his chair, speckled black and white hair catching a sliver of sunlight.

We were all sitting around the table in the room next to his office, a small space with bare stone walls and a single window facing west. Father sat at the head of the table beneath the window, on the only chair. Mother and I occupied the bench to his right. Hamma and Titan, two members of the Guard, sat opposite us.

"Three in a week," Father continued. "That's too many to be a coincidence. And the descriptions match?"

Hamma, Captain of the Guard, nodded. The portion of his face not hidden by a wiry beard was set into grim lines. "Mother and child, both blond, moving fast. The reports all come from the same area along the southern borders. This one said the boy might have been a little older, maybe twelve. They got a good look at him. They're certain about what he is."

Mother drew in a sharp breath, the noise loud next to me. "Twelve? So old."

My father grimaced, emphasising the creases already embedded around his eyes. "Too old." He didn't look happy.

I dropped my gaze, swinging my legs back and forth under the bench. Father said I had to pay attention. Everyone else certainly seemed to be very focused and serious, huddled in the little room off my father's study. With the door shut, the dark stone walls felt close and stern, but

15

the open shutters of the window helped, sunlight floating in.

A rhythmic tapping danced in my ears despite my attempts not to make any noise. I lifted my feet higher to stop them from knocking, but it persisted. I frowned, peering down in an attempt to find what I was hitting without alerting the adults to the fact I was less than attentive to their words. As I leaned forwards, I realised my mistake. The tapping wasn't coming from my feet at all but something further away.

Two dark-skinned fingers were tapping the wood of the bench across from mine in perfect time with the swinging of my feet. Scowling, I looked up. Titan wasn't looking at me, but there was a slight grin on his face. He winked when he noticed me watching him. I swung my legs faster, sticking my chin out as I turned away.

"…to have been able to keep him hidden for so long?" my father asked the room at large.

"Are we sure there hasn't been any sign of them before?"

"Jenna's searching the records again. If there was something, it was overlooked."

My chin jutted forwards at the mention of my father's assistant and scribe. She never had much time for me.

"So why would the mother have become so sloppy now?" my mother asked.

"You think she meant to be seen?" Titan asked, a frown creasing his brow, the wrinkles extending back along his bald scalp. His fingers were still tapping.

Everyone looked at Father. I swallowed. Everyone always looked to him. No doubt it was part of being king. The thought put a twist in my stomach. One day they would look to me, or so Mother said.

"It makes no difference if she planned this or not. We know about the boy now. He's just as much a danger to us out there as he would be here."

"I'm not sure Elissa's foster family would have agreed with that," Titan muttered.

My mother's hand shot out, gripping mine as my father and Hamma *both stared at Titan, who pulled a face but didn't apologise. I looked up at my mother, who forced a smile, releasing my hand. Elissa... The name was unfamiliar to me, but it clearly meant something to them.*

"Would you rather leave him running around out there? Doing who knows what, going who knows where?" Father asked, and Titan grimaced.

"Good point."

"We have to find him." My father looked at Hamma. "This is too important to be passed on."

Hamma inclined his head, his bushy hair bobbing. "I'll take the twins. Ty, you're in charge here whilst I'm gone."

Titan nodded, his fingers falling silent, and I looked up in time to see them all exchange glances laden with unspoken words.

The sun was falling, its brightness making my eyes water. Blinking, I wiped away the tears blurring my vision and wished my thoughts could be cleared so easily. All day they had spun and twisted, tightening into knots I couldn't unpick.

I was an orphan now, both my parents gone. The symmetry of their deaths might have made me laugh if it wasn't for the burning ache inside my chest. I'd been born into an era of peace lasting for two decades. It had cracked with the series of attacks culminating in my mother's death almost five years ago. After my father's retaliation for that atrocity, the attacks had quietened again. Now, after my father's murder, any illusion of peace was shattered for good. There would be war for what the demons had done.

For too long we'd held back, defending by not attacking, watchful but not aggressive. And now my parents were *gone*, stolen from me. Even with sunlight falling across my face, I could feel the darkness of my expression.

I didn't want to lead people into fights, into a war resulting in yet more deaths, but the demons had murdered my family. No more. We would wipe them out of existence. Every black-blooded one of them.

A pair of dark eyes framed in white flashed before me, and my angry pace slowed, the unconscious snarl dropping from my face.

Even the children? my conscience asked. The half-bloods?

Nate said it had been a half-blood who'd killed my father. But Nate was a half-blood too. I'd thought—everyone had thought— he was the only one. Apparently not. This other one had come from nowhere to rip away everything I'd thought was sure and certain. If they were so violent, so bold, as to attack the king, why hadn't we heard of them before? None of it made sense.

With a rough curse, I rubbed my face. I wished Nate was there with me, that we hadn't split up. In theory, it had been the right thing to do. In practice, I worried the memory of turning away from him would haunt me. He'd listened to my reasoning, my justifications, and said nothing. The nod of agreement, when it came, was palpably reluctant. It was more civil than the last time we'd parted but that hadn't made it any easier to walk away from him. Now I had no idea where he might be, and no hope of finding him again.

I turned my thoughts away. It was pointless to speculate on his path when I didn't know my own. I didn't *want* to guess where he was, in case things got nasty. There was no way to know exactly what Djet had ordered the Figures to do. I could still remember in far-too-vivid detail the aftermath of the one time Father had awoken them.

Trees splintered, roots ripped from the ground, fires burning. Total destruction. And the bodies… Fingers missing, skin peeled from limbs, bones broken, joints ripped apart. The heads untouched, every expression of pain and horror left hideously clear, every pair of eyes staring unblinkingly forevermore, not even a single drop of blood marring the faces, each one standing upright on the stump of its severed neck.

And a voice, pleading for death.

I shuddered, speeding up as if I could outrun the images. Half-jogging down a slope, I dodged a large boulder at the bottom and looked up.

18

He stared straight back at me with black eyes.

Demon.

Shit.

No time to think, I leapt forwards, drawing on my wards in a rush of warmth that enveloped my arms. I couldn't let him get away to carry the knowledge of my presence to his brethren. One, two, my blades flashed. The demon stepped backwards, twisting to avoid them. Too slow.

Metal sliced cloth and skin. Black blood splattered on the ground. A gash across his left forearm. But the wound wasn't as serious as I'd intended it to be.

He hissed, retreating. I ignored the noise, lost in his dark eyes, drowning in the endless pool of anger. Mother, dead. Father, dead. Now I had a chance to strike back.

I lunged again, aiming for his legs, a debilitating wound. Faster this time, the demon avoided the blows, jumping towards me to counter-attack. I flinched back, the warm patch on my left shoulder burning with heat as my balance ward flared. The demon was already moving, using my recoil to turn and sprint away.

Swearing again, I ran after him, tugging on my wards for more power. I couldn't let him get away from me. It was more than just my burning thirst for revenge. If he had enough time, he could transform, shed his human skin for something more sinister. I was willing to face the odds one-on-one against him like this, but if he transformed… Those odds were somewhat less in my favour.

I still bore the scars, four thin brown lines across my forearm, from the last time I'd faced down a transformed demon on my own. And that time, I'd been standing against my best friend.

The demon dodged sideways behind a tree trunk, and I saw a flash of red as the sun caught my eyes. My stomach clenched and I stumbled, roots grabbing at my feet.

No. He mustn't get away.

I sped up. If I could get there fast enough…

I swung around the tree, nearly losing my footing again as I skidded to a halt, weapons raised. There was no one there. The space was empty, the only movement the gently swirling leaves on the ground.

Damn it.

Thorns, please… I spun, eyes searching as I offered up the desperate prayer to the sky. *Please. Let him still be here. Let him not have gone far.*

My prayer was answered. The demon stood halfway up the slope I'd just come down. He wasn't even looking at me, his head turning as he scanned the trees.

I blinked, shocked. After the cold silence of rejection at the Hollowed Tree, *now* Thorns was listening to me?

I started towards the demon, but before I'd gone two paces he turned, looking down at me. His face pulled into a grimace, and he glanced around once more, still searching. Not finding what he was looking for, he darted away, retreating behind another tree. Another flash of red light.

I slowed. He was gone. Gone to get reinforcements? I wasn't going to wait around to find out.

My wards cooled quickly as I released the draw upon them, backing away. Slipping my blades back into their sheaths, I turned and fled.

This forest, east of the Baerston Mountains, had long been considered demon territory. Ever since I could remember, Hamma insisted they must have a home hidden somewhere within these trees. But the twins scoffed at the idea, and Father had shrugged it off as well. There was never any proof, no evidence of a camp. I hadn't seen any sign of them as I'd passed through the trees. Yet now, the day after learning of my father's death, I find a demon staring right at me. I doubted it was there by chance.

A bird swooped overhead, and I flinched, jerking away from the flutter of feathers. I watched it alight on a branch high overhead before moving on.

The rest of the trees remained motionless and silent, devoid of life, both natural and black-eyed. It was only a matter of time before the demon returned, though. Why else would he have fled if not to get others, return, and kill me with better odds? But with every minute that passed, it seemed less likely. If he was going to come back, he would have been here by now, surely. I glanced around as I jogged ever onwards.

Every step took me further from the place he had last seen me, the distance making me safer. As the threat of another attack diminished, a different concern grew. Why had he been watching me in the first place? Could they know Nate had delivered his awful news? Maybe they had been watching me even before then. The suspicion haunted me through the trees, whispering against the back of my neck, a chill that had nothing to do with the breeze.

No, I would have noticed if I was being followed. I had no evidence that was the case.

I tried to put it all together. What had changed recently? The demons murdered Father. I was expected to take the throne after him. They could have been plotting to kill me as well, to… what? To throw our people into chaos? They'd already done that by making their move whilst I was away from the city. Something else then. Were they trying to prevent my return to Alderth? Were they in league with the pretender who had Claimed the throne? That didn't seem likely either.

It had to be linked to Father's death. I wished I'd asked Nate exactly when he had died. Had his body been burned yet?

The unexpected thought hit me like a solid punch in the gut. I slowed back to a walk, gasping for breath as I gritted my teeth against the pain. Surely, he would have been given a true send-off, under the charred, Thorn-touched tree, but my doubts remained. If this Djet who was sitting on my throne was willing to kill those who defied him so freely, he could have dispensed with the tradition just as easily, and with the Guard dead…

For a moment, I let myself imagine how it should have been.

A few feet higher on the slope than the spot where Mother's pyre had been, I would have helped arrange the wood under the spindly shadow of the blackened tree. The Guard would carry Father's body, Hamma leading the procession. Nate would be walking with his five other comrades, and no one would question it.

Jenna would pass me the torch, included as she deserved to be after so many years of service. We would exchange a glance and then she would step back, leaving me alone with my father's body. I would stand strong and tall, and everyone watching would know they could trust me to rule with the same grace he had. I would light each of the four corners of the pyre, and fire would leap into the sky. Throwing the torch into the middle of the pyre, where my father's body would be covered in purple cloth, I would step back from the heat, and the Guard, *my* Guard, would fall into place around me, and I wouldn't need to look sideways to feel Nate's presence.

With smoke rising above us, releasing Father's spirit back to the sky, I would be the first to utter a cry of grief. The whole city would take up the call with me, and our tears would water the ground as our voices filled the air.

The vision shattered as I caught my toe on a tree root and stumbled. Gritting my teeth, I shook away the dream and the moisture it had brought to my eyes, breaking into a jog again. After my mother's funeral, it was easy to imagine my father's, only the barest adjustment needed to complete the fantasy. But it would never happen that way now. All I could hope was that it *had* happened.

Father deserved to be set free, not confined to the earth. The six members of the Guard would have been burned with him, seven pyres to light the skies, the smoke mingled together, honouring their sacrifice for their monarch.

As the day closed, my pace slowed, and I looked back over my shoulder less often. I found a stream as the sun was sinking, cutting through the ground as it made its way to the sea. Standing over the running water, I gazed down, taking in deep breaths as my stomach gurgled, reminding me I hadn't eaten today. It wasn't an urgent hunger yet, just a constant awareness. Finding food would take time, time I no longer had, now I knew the Figures were after me.

I rubbed the black tattoo high on my right shoulder. Growth, as we called it, was the ward I drew upon the least, the most dangerous of the powers I held under my skin. Many cautioning stories had been impressed upon me before I received it. Tales about those who had used it too often or for too long, collapsing as they went about their lives. There were only so many things the wards could provide, and extended periods without proper sustenance was not one of them.

I wasn't going to be reckless, though. I had eaten yesterday evening, and it wasn't like I intended to make it all the way home without eating again. I merely needed to extend the time before I had to stop for food.

I hopped down to the bank, scooping up water in my hands and slurping it before looking down at my rippling reflection. The water rushed by, blurring the image, but I caught glimpses of my copper-brown hair, loose strands burnished red by the setting sun. My father once told me I looked like a candle in the right light, tall and pale with fire on top. With a painful smile at the memory, I shook the cold water off my hands and turned away.

My thighs ached as I climbed back up out of the gully, but I ignored them, setting off again into the gathering darkness and drawing lightly on my growth ward to chase the hunger away from my stomach. I pushed on until the sun had set completely, plunging the world into darkness. I could have continued further, drawing on my sight ward to illuminate the world in red, but the mere thought of the headache that would cause was enough to make me reconsider. And like Nate, I needed to sleep. Neither wards nor demon blood could overcome that limitation.

Huddling down against a tree trunk, I tucked my hands into my armpits for warmth before closing my eyes. In the blackness, I thought back to my desperate prayer when I'd been searching for the demon. I'd prayed that he wouldn't have gone too far, and he hadn't. What did that mean? Had it been a coincidence, or had Thorns reached down and touched us in some way to make him linger?

Shifting on the uneven ground, I remembered the vicious storm that had finally prompted me to begin my pilgrimage. The force of the thunder that night had scared me. Thorns had been angry at my years of delay. So I had gone.

I'd made my way to the Hollowed Tree, the huge trunk blasted out by lightning. I'd stood in the ash at the centre, feels its softness under my boots, and waited. Waited for hours for something to happen, something to change. But nothing did. Thorns had rejected me. And the thunder since had held no words for me. Just empty noise. How could I rule without Thorns's approval, without their guidance?

Of course, I knew why they had rejected me. As I stood there like a fool, waiting with vain hope, I'd known. I was too weak. And Thorns knew it.

After that, I hadn't been able to face returning home. So I'd stayed away, and in my foolish absence, my father had been murdered.

I shifted the other way, trying to find a comfortable position against the tree. It took a long time for me to fall asleep.

The following day passed much as the previous had, full of circling thoughts and hilly forest but empty of other life. The sun was beginning to dip when the world brightened around me, and I came to a halt as I looked up.

The trees had ended. Ahead of me was a world of shimmering gold hills. The undulating land, painted with yellow grass gilded by the afternoon sun, rippled entrancingly in a gentle breeze. I stepped cautiously out of the trees as if my presence might shatter the beautiful illusion, but the image remained, the grass tickling my fingertips as I moved out across the plain.

On the other side of these plains, the sea waited. I should reach it tomorrow. Once I struck the coast, I could turn west and make my way to where the Griambrian River met the sea. Following its banks would lead me north, back home to Alderth. It was on those shores that Nate and I had agreed to meet again. Once I was closer, I would be able to gauge what was going on, to get a feeling for the state of the city and the mood of the people. Then I'd decide on the best course of action, whether that was walking straight up to the city or sneaking in.

Either way, the first step was to reach the coast. I strode forward, climbing a gentle slope to the top of the first small hill. From this vantage point, I could see the tops of mountains off to my left. I must have drifted east again whilst in the forest, the peaks closer than I'd expected.

Turning, I took one last look behind me, eyes running across the swaying sea of the closest treetops, splashed with yellow and orange as they began to turn with the season. The forest ended so suddenly it was like a wall across the land, as though the trees had spread until they hit some invisible barrier and could go no further.

Something else caught my eye. A flash of movement not made by an absently waving branch. My hands drifted to my weapons as I focused on the spot, thinking of dark eyes. When the shape stepped out from the forest and began moving up the hill towards me, my heart froze in my chest.

It wasn't a demon.

I wished it was.

It was a Figure, advancing towards me as if it wasn't sealing my death with every step.

Humanoid but so very far from human. Smooth, bare, grey skin broken only by an endless pattern of wards covering its body, from its feet to its luminous white eyes.

I met that dead gaze and knew I wasn't going to stand there and wait for it to come and kill me.

Whirling around, I sprinted down the other side of the hill. My breaths came in pathetic whimpers of terror, but I didn't look back. The very idea of it gaining on me was enough to make me run even faster.

Skidding at the bottom of the hill, I splashed across a rocky stream. Sharp stones jabbed the soles of my feet and the cold water rushed over my toes. I ignored it all. The ground fought me as I gained the opposite bank, ankles twisting as pebbles skittered away underfoot, taking my balance with them.

Barely managing to stay upright, I surged through the grass, listening desperately to hear the sound of another body disturbing the water behind me. None came, and a small, treacherous spark of hope ignited in my chest. I veered towards a large clump of bushes, thinking to shield myself from the Figure's gaze. As I reached it, the creature stepped calmly out from the other side.

I'd failed. Why couldn't Djet have let me come back to stake my own Claim as any honourable person would have? Why had he sent these things after me? Why had my father *died*?

I was too close and going too fast to stop or turn away.

My fate already decided, I let out a scream of fury as I took the only option left and threw myself at the creature, drawing my twin blades as I surged forward.

There was a metallic clang as the blade in my left hand rebounded off the Figure's grey skin. My other blade jolted, jerking from my right hand as the creature clamped its hand above my left elbow, spinning us both to the ground. The impact knocked the wind from me, but I had no time to stop and breathe.

Ripping my arm from its grasp, I rolled away, scrambling desperately along the ground. My arm seared with pain where the Figure had grabbed me as I scrabbled at the slope, getting nowhere. Determined, at the very least, not to die by a sword through the back, I rolled over, left arm clutched to my chest and right hand raised in front of me, the most ineffective shield imaginable.

The sky above me was empty.

Blinking, I lifted my head, looking back down towards the clump of bushes. Lying spread-eagled on the ground was a grey body.

For a second, I couldn't move, couldn't breathe, couldn't think. The whole world stopped. What I was seeing was impossible. It wasn't dead, *couldn't* be dead. Figures couldn't be killed. My blade had rebounded off its arm as if the limb was made from metal, but I could see the hilt of my other weapon, sticking out of its chest at

26

a sharp angle.

Swallowing, I made to get up but gasped in renewed pain as I moved my left arm. For the first time, I looked down at my elbow, examining the wound. The cut was deep but clean, a neat line across my arm that missed my speed ward by the barest of margins.

Shaking, I wrapped my right hand over the wound, my grip slipping in the blood trickling down my arm. My head spun as I rolled forwards, and I lurched to my feet. My side throbbed where I'd slammed into the ground but I stumbled forward, pausing a couple of strides away from the motionless body, still wary of a trick. This couldn't be real.

The Figure looked much like me, two legs, two arms, a head, but its glowing white eyes, now closed, and its metallic silvery-grey skin covered in patterns of white made it instantly identifiable. I'd seen the markings up close before, the one time I'd been down to the vault where they slept, and recognised some of them as the same wards adorning my arms and back. But there were so many more on their bodies, etched deeply into their grey skin as if carved there by a cruel blade.

Shuffling slowly forwards, I prodded an out-flung arm with my foot. It shifted a little but nothing more. Taking another half-step closer, I nudged the side of its body, the grey skin cold against my toes. It still didn't move.

I sank to the ground, staring blankly at the impossibility in front of me. My eyes were drawn to the place where the hilt of my dagger was sticking into the air. Letting go of my elbow without thinking, I reached out to run my fingers over the grey skin, leaving streaks of red. It was hard, unyielding. Yet my blade was right there, piercing its chest.

Numbly, I gripped the hilt and tugged it upwards. There was a moment of resistance, then it jerked free, slipping from my bloody fingers to tumble to the ground. Other than the dark liquid coating the blade, colouring it a red so dark it was nearly black, it might never have happened. I automatically reached out with my left hand to pick it up, but pain stabbed up my arm again, and I froze

27

with a hiss.

The shot of pain cleared my head. I had to keep moving. If one of them could find me, more could as well.

I stood up, nearly losing my balance again. My hands, painted with rivulets of blood, were shaking, and I took a deep breath, forcing myself to relax.

Warmth drained away from my right shoulder. My vision narrowed, black spots blooming before my eyes. I staggered but didn't even have time to register what I'd done before I fell, the darkness claiming me.

3

Leydford

The throne room thronged with people. I knew Father had hoped to have the room empty before the newcomers got to the city—he'd said as much to Jenna before the session, but it hadn't happened.

Peering through the door in the north wall, invisible in the dark passage, I could see petitioners milling around at the far end of the hall, either waiting for an audience or watching someone else's. Eight pillars of carved stone cut through the crowd, drawing a path from the double doors to where the throne sat atop its dais of three steps.

Sat in the middle of the citadel, surrounded on all sides by corridors and further rooms, the throne room had no windows. Instead, two huge skylights looked upwards, affording a view of the rest of the building, rising two further stories above, and a patch of sky beyond. With the sun almost directly overhead, the light was streaming down, painting two blazing rectangles onto the floor, the northern one positioned to bathe the throne in golden warmth.

From my vantage point, I could see my father's arm where it rested on the arm of the throne, his skin gilded by the sunlight. His sword, Mercy, stood propped against the throne, sheathed in white leather.

Next to him, Jenna sat on her usual wooden stool, a stack of papers balanced on her knees. She took notes at furious speed.

Straightening my back, I smoothed my expression, then stepped through the open door and walked around the back of the throne.

Edric, the shortest member of the Guard, with jet black hair, was standing between the throne and the back wall. He nodded to me as I passed, though his eyes didn't deviate from their planned path, sweeping back and forth across the hall for any threats. At the far end of the hall, from her position beside the doors, Miriam was doing the same.

Father looked away from his discussion with Jenna as I climbed the steps to stand on the left side of the throne. He gave me a small smile, and I returned it nervously, distracted by the hovering crowd.

Father straightened up as Jenna searched for the name of the next petitioner when a figure strode in through the double doors. All eyes turned to her at once, going to the two signal flags at her waist, one white, one black. A Watcher. There would be another stationed on the road outside the city, flashing their flags in a series of movements to convey messages to the ones stationed here. It was faster than sending a runner through the streets.

The Watcher approached and knelt at the bottom of the steps, tilting her head back to the ceiling.

"Rise," Father said.

She stood up and took a step closer. "Signal from the East Gate," she said, her voice low, foiling the people who pressed forwards to eavesdrop. "They're here."

My father nodded, his expression grim. He glanced at Jenna, who immediately gathered her many notes. The rumbling of the crowd peaked, a mixture of complaints at the session being cut short and speculation about why. The soldiers stationed around the edges of the room to augment the Guard chivvied the dawdlers out. No doubt most of them would dawdle outside in an attempt to get a glimpse of the impending arrivals.

Father didn't speak, and I took my silence from his. My heartbeat pounded in my ears as Jenna closed the main doors. Only the soldiers around the edges of the room remained, along with two members of the Guard standing at either end of the hall. The room looked eerie in its abrupt emptiness.

To my right, another door opened and my mother swept in. Titan and Helena followed, the former shadowing Mother towards the throne, stopping a few steps to my left. The latter headed off down the hall to join Miriam, passing Jenna as she hurried back up the room.

Father was still brooding. The silence, like a weight pressing down upon us all, only made my heart pump even faster, my hands flexing at my sides. I wondered if anyone would notice if I picked at my nails behind my back.

"Have I told you the one about the conker and the chestnut?" Titan said from beside me in a carrying whisper, and I had to bite my lip to hide my smile. On the other side of the throne, Edric groaned.

"Aren't conkers and chestnuts the same thing?" I muttered. I could see him out of the corner of my eye, looming dark and tall behind me.

"That's what they thought," Titan said, leaning towards me conspiratorially.

"Enough, Titan," Father said, rousing from his musings, though from the tilt of his mouth, I knew he wasn't actually annoyed.

"Just trying to lighten the mood, sire," Titan said, snapping his heels together as he stood stiffly straight again, the very picture of discipline.

"I wasn't aware it needed lightening," Father said, a hint of amusement in his tone now.

"You weren't aware of the mood at all, sire," Titan replied instantly, and I had to stifle my laughter.

"Alright," Father said, shaking his head. "Let's leave off the attitude for a little while, shall we?"

"Of course, sire. No attitude to be found here."

I snorted with amusement and disbelief.

A booming knock echoed through the room, and the levity was gone instantly. All eyes were fixed on the doors. The Guard checked their weapons.

"Enter." The voice of Rygorn, my father, was gone; it was the king who gave the command.

The door opened, and Hamma strode through followed by a woman and a boy who couldn't be much older than I was, barely into double digits. Orion and Ishmael flanked the pair. As always, the twin brothers were eerily similar, walking perfectly in time.

I looked doubtfully at the pair in the middle of the group, thinking perhaps three members of the Guard had been a little excessive as an escort, but then I caught a flash of dark eyes and swallowed. I was suddenly glad for the presence of the elite fighters. It was an effort to relax my shoulders and let out the breath that had lodged in my chest. Hearing of the boy's existence was somehow different to seeing him in front of me.

The woman had golden hair that caught the light from every window, glistening around her pale face, which was set in lines from her clenched jaw. The boy at her side had slightly darker hair, the colour of wet sand rather than sun. His face was wary, dark eyes flitting restlessly around the room.

Hamma came to a halt a few paces from the throne and bowed, the brothers following suit from behind him. The woman made no deferential movement, and after a glance at her, the boy also remained motionless.

"Alicia, and her son," Hamma announced. Father nodded once, and the Guardsman stepped to the side.

"Alicia," the king began, his voice serious but not stern, "you've been accused of harbouring an enemy of the people."

I blinked. With all the rumours and speculation surrounding the boy, I hadn't realised his mother was the one who'd been accused of a crime. I recalled my lessons, lists of crimes and punishments drilled into me from hours of rote learning. Harbouring an enemy of the people, suggested punishment: ten lashes across the forearms and imprisonment with labour for a period lasting no longer than one year.

Milder than the consequences for collaboration or aiding an enemy.

"Do you have a response to this accusation?" the king asked.

Alicia raised her chin, addressing the wall behind us rather than meeting my father's gaze. I frowned.

"I haven't harboured an enemy of anyone. I raised my son as best as I could. As any parent would do for their child."

"You raised him hidden."

"With good reason," Alicia replied, looking pointedly at the Guard standing around us.

She had a point, I thought. It was highly irregular for all seven members of the Guard to be present at once. Normally, at least two of them were off duty at any moment, often more.

I looked at the boy in question. I'd been expecting a terrifying creature, some sort of monster. But he looked like any of the other dozens of children who played in the streets outside. A little skinny, perhaps, but there was nothing extraordinary about him. His dark eyes moved from my father to the members of the Guard, flicking dismissively over me in the process.

That was where the truth was, I decided. It was in his foreign eyes. If Father viewed him as a threat, then that must be what he was.

My father sat back, tapping his fingers on the arm of the throne, and Alicia finally looked at him.

"We've done nothing wrong," she said; the quiver in her voice was barely noticeable.

My father looked at her for a moment more before turning his attention to the boy. "What's your name?"

The boy looked at him for a second before answering. "Nathaniel." His voice was steadier than I'd expected.

"Hm. My grandfather's name," my father commented. "You know what you are?"

"Yes," Nathaniel replied with a touch of defiance.

"You know what it means?"

The boy's eyes slid around the room, flitting across the Guard before he looked back at my father. "Apparently, it means this."

I frowned. What did he mean by that?

"The history of half-bloods might be sparse, but it's not nice," Father told him gravely. "There's a lot of blood splattered across those pages."

"I didn't know the past wrote the future," Nathaniel said, a slight tremble detectable in his voice at last.

I blinked, taken aback by his response.

"I haven't hurt anyone," he continued.

I believed him, though I had no reason to.

From my father's silence, I could tell he was also reassessing the boy before turning back to his mother.

"And the father?"

There was a heavy silence.

"You haven't seen him again?"

"Seen him?" Alicia choked out. She swallowed. "No," she said, her voice firm though her shoulders were shaking. "We haven't seen him."

"Lucky for him," Nathaniel growled, his whole body tense as he glared at my father with undisguised anger.

"Easy, kid," Titan said from behind me, and the boy switched his focus at once, staring past my shoulder. He remained tense for a second, then his shoulders dropped as he took a slow step backwards. His eyes found me again before flicking to the floor.

"Of course not," Father allowed, ignoring Nathaniel's outburst. "I apologise. What about other demons?"

"No."

My father sat back, still tapping his fingers on the arm of the chair. "Tell me how it happened."

"How it—" Alicia broke off, turning her face away. "You know how it happened," she said, her voice trembling with emotion.

Did they? I snuck a glance sideways, taking in the identical grim expressions on the faces of Jenna, my mother, and Helena. Yes, they all knew what was going on. I would ask Mother about it later.

Father paused, considering them both. Alicia continued hiding her face, but the boy looked up, meeting my father's gaze without flinching.

"You must be tired," Father said eventually. "Miriam will show you to rooms where you can rest. We'll speak again soon."

Miriam, a woman with a pinched face and dark hair in a long braid, stepped away from her post by the doors at once. Opening one of them, she waited in silence as Alicia backed away a couple of steps before turning and walking back down the hall. Nathaniel held my father's gaze for another second before following her.

Once the doors had closed behind them, my father dropped his elbows to his knees, rubbing his hands together slowly as he stared at the floor.

"He's not what you expected," my mother said, and he laughed wryly.

"To put it mildly."

"And if he can transform?"

I looked between them as my father dismissed the warning with a shake of his head. "He's too young. None of the other cases mention transformations until the child is older."

"He'll grow," my mother pointed out. "And you don't know what to do with him."

Father smiled as he sat up and took her hand. "Not yet, no. But he'll show us who he is, and then we'll decide, long before that issue arises."

I looked at the place where Nathaniel had stood so firmly. Stoic, reserved, but fiery. He might look like a child, but he didn't act like one. I thought he'd already shown us who he was.

Father turned to Titan, who was still staring down the length of the hall at the closed door. "So... conkers and chestnuts?"

The world pressed upon me in a cocoon of cloying heat and hazy voices. My face burned. Sweat trickled down my back. My breaths came in pants, muscles working against the weight of too many blankets. But it wasn't the stifling heat that had woken me.

I wasn't alone.

The voices were distant and indistinct, a stream of hissed whispers that teased at my ears without bringing any clear words. Keeping my body still, I cracked my eyes open.

Squinting through my eyelashes, I scanned the room. It was dim, the only light filtering in through an archway, silhouetting three people in a tight huddle. The walls and the floor upon which I lay were of a rough, golden stone. Nothing but slight ripples in the stone marred the bare surface.

The trio blocking the archway continued their whispered argument, oblivious to my consciousness. I opened my eyes fully. With the light behind them, I could see nothing of their features.

One seemed to be a woman, and she was the angriest of them, leaning toward the other two as she jabbed a sharp finger at them. The other two, both men, had their arms crossed, unswayed by the woman's assertions.

My stomach gurgled so loudly that I expected the trio to look around, but they did not.

My right side was a mass of throbbing aches. I shifted slightly, trying to gauge the damage. A sharper stab of pain from my left arm drew a gasp from my lips.

Memories rushed through my mind. The Figure… The fight… Then… nothing.

My stomach grumbled again, and I understood. I must have released my growth ward. Without it to sustain me, I'd fainted. Stupid, stupid mistake. Titan would have given me such a lecture for making so obvious an error. But I wasn't going to think about Titan.

I wracked my brain, searching for any flash of memory that might explain my current position, but found nothing. How had I gotten here? Wherever here was. Were these people friend or foe?

The voices grew louder, loaded with anger, carrying their words clearly to my ears.

"We are *not* going to make decisions based on fanatical nonsense and a few black swirls!" someone declared. One of the men. "Sire, you must see that this is madness."

"It's not madness; you've seen the words, the same as I have!" the woman snapped back.

Lying here would gain me nothing. There was only one way to find out what was going on here. But before I could move, someone else did. Someone much closer than those standing in the open archway.

I reacted instinctively. Snapping my legs up and out, I kicked off the suffocating blankets, launching them towards the fourth person in the room, the one I had overlooked. They gave an indignant yelp as the mass of fabric flew at them. I jerked the other way, rolling onto my stomach and lunging to my feet, wards flaring under my

36

skin. Beneath the ink, I could feel the bruises where the Figure had thrown me to the ground.

Upright, I whirled around, my hand jumping straight to my hip. There was nothing there. My weapons were gone.

My disorientation was suddenly tinged with anger. That was *fine*. I would face them without my blades. But something in me trembled at the loss.

Teeth clenched, I glanced between the four strangers, my good arm half-raised in front of me. Out the corner of my eye, I could see the stark white of a bandage around my other arm, covering the skin from just above my elbow to halfway up my speed ward. If the wound had broken the ward… The fear that shot through me was like ice. I tried to draw upon the ward, but the emotion froze my whole body, thwarting my attempt. Had it activated when I'd jumped up in the spike of adrenaline? I had no way to know.

The four strangers seemed shocked to see me upright and glowering at them. The three in the archway were still backlit, but all had turned to face me now. The fourth person, the one closest to me, had also frozen at my sudden movement. He'd caught the blankets I'd kicked at him and was now holding them awkwardly in front of him. Barely more than a boy, he was still easily the tallest in the room, towering over me by several inches. With gangly limbs, it looked like he'd been stretched. Even his face was long, with a pointed chin and tall forehead surrounded by a short tangle of brown hair. His expression didn't help, mouth ajar and eyebrows raised.

The three by the door broke out of their stupor first.

"Saviour," the woman breathed. She made to step forwards, but one of the others grabbed her arm, holding her back.

I blinked against the light, struggling to pick out their features. The woman's face was taut, the skin pulled too tightly, leaving lines around her features, but her eyes were alight with a feverish glow. The man who'd grabbed her was older, his dark hair fading to grey.

The third one, standing in front of the pair, had a deep forehead, set with a few faint lines. Dark brown hair teased at the top of it and around his ears. He had a strong jaw, wide chin, and a perfectly straight nose, but it was his eyes that caught my attention: a brilliant, fierce blue that seemed to gaze into my very soul.

He stepped forwards, a casual confidence in his movements, deliberate and unhurried.

I let him cross half the distance between us, everyone else frozen in tableau, before I tensed, raising my hand a little higher and shifting backwards slightly.

His steps slowed. "Hello," he said.

I blinked, my eyes flicking from him to the boy next to him, to the two still hanging back by the open doorway. It would be easy to get past them. Their arms were bare of ink, and none of them appeared to be carrying weapons. Even with one arm injured, I could take them all down. But I had no idea what might be waiting beyond the archway.

"Can you understand me?" the man tried again, enunciating every word.

Maybe it was better to wait for now. "Yes," I said, not relaxing a single muscle.

The man smiled, his blue eyes full of mirth. "What's your name?"

I hesitated.

"I'm Set," he offered, his tone still relaxed. "This is Noah,"—he gestured to the boy beside him, who hadn't stopped staring at me—"Mary,"—he glanced over his shoulder at the woman—"and Doctor Lucius. He's the one who treated your wound."

I took the opportunity to glance down at the bandage, trying to draw on the ward again. Nothing happened. My heart quickened, panic rising again. I forced myself to breathe slowly, pushing the horror down. I pulled more gently and nearly collapsed with relief when the ward responded. My skin warmed, a pool of heat centred around the middle of the swirl of ink. The blackness shifted slightly, undulating under my skin, ready to act if I called upon it further. The ward hadn't been damaged.

"Give us the room," Set said, with a glance back towards the others.

"No." I took another deep breath, trying to calm my racing pulse. "I'm fine. Thank you. I appreciate your assistance." I looked at Set. "Where am I?"

"Leydford. The city by the sea."

Leydford? I wracked my memories, pulling up mental images of the maps I had learned as a child. The lands to the west of Alderth were well documented, with roads showing the way to Lambridge and then north to Charhelm. But to the east, where I was now… The plains had been marked, with the mountains on their far side, but there had been no indication of any settlements I could remember. Certainly not a city.

"How?" The word slipped out. I raised my eyes, finding comprehension in Set's face. He understood the question, but it wasn't enough. "Why?"

Set glanced sideways at Noah, but the boy seemed to have no desire to speak, so Set answered me. "You were found injured on the plains and brought back here."

So they had found me after the fight with the Figure, after I had so foolishly released my growth ward. I waited, but it seemed that was all the explanation Set was going to give for my presence here.

"I told you our names," Set prompted. "Won't you tell us yours?"

I wasn't overly concerned with introductions. "There was another," I said.

A muscle flickered in Set's jaw. Again, he glanced at the boy beside him. I followed his gaze, meeting Noah's hazel eyes, full of disquiet.

"What was it?" he asked.

"That doesn't matter."

"Doesn't it?" he challenged me.

My foot twitched. I wanted to leap at him. Who was he to refuse to answer me? "Where is it?"

"I left it out there. I could only bring one of you back, and my horse didn't like going near it."

My jaw clenched. The thought of the Figure lying out on the plains was not comforting but somehow better than knowing the cold body was nearby.

"What was it?" Noah repeated.

"A monster."

"You killed it?"

I looked away. Had I killed it? It was my blade that had pierced its chest. There hadn't been anyone else there. Still, the concept didn't seem to fit. I *killed* it? They couldn't die. But I had killed it.

Set turned away from me, glancing at the others. "Thank you. That will be all."

The doctor bowed to him before leaving. The woman, Mary, followed suit, though she continued to gaze at me until she disappeared.

Noah stepped closer to Set. "Come on. I was telling the truth! And I'm the one who—"

"No," Set cut him off. "Wait outside."

Noah's jaw clenched. He looked at me as if expecting assistance, but I said nothing. Noah flung the blankets he'd been holding aside and stomped from the room.

Set waited until Noah was out of sight, then ambled over to the pile of crumpled fabric, picking it up and shaking it out. Extracting one blanket from the jumble, he folded it roughly before tossing it back down.

"Why won't you tell me your name?" Set asked as he began folding a second blanket. His soft bluntness made me smile. Asking, not demanding. His blue eyes pinned me in place.

"Mara," I told him. Not the name my parents had gifted me with, but people had been calling me by it for long enough that it felt right.

"Mara," Set repeated. "What happened? Noah comes back talking of men with metal skin, and then there's you with those markings on your arms. We all wanted to dismiss what he said as a boy's imagination, but..." His eyes flicked down to the bandages on my arm. "I have to consider all possibilities."

He waited, but I said nothing, looking past him.

"You called it a monster," he pressed. "What happened?"

"It doesn't matter now. It's dead." The words felt wrong.

"Are there more?"

"Yes." My heart dropped as I realised what that meant. "I have to leave. Now."

"Because they're after you?"

I didn't meet his gaze, looking around for my weapons.

"Why?"

I bit back an irritated retort.

He tilted his head, eyeing my expression. "It's part of my responsibility to keep this city safe," he said. "If dangerous people are trying to find someone we're sheltering, I need to know."

Pausing, I considered his words. Who exactly was he? A soldier? I guessed he was older than me, twenty-five, maybe thirty. Rather young to be in charge of protecting this city, Leydford, wherever it was. Regardless, he had no idea what he was talking about.

"They're not people," I corrected him. "And I didn't ask you to bring me here. I'll leave, and then you won't need to worry about it anymore."

"There's no chance they'll come here looking for you after you've gone?"

I hesitated, and that was answer enough. Nate had been right; I had no idea how the Figures tracked people.

My stomach twisted at the thought of Nate. One of the Figures had found me. Had any of the others ambushed him as well?

The one on the plains had caught up with me much faster than I'd expected. If they were following my path, it would bring them here. That was the last thing I wanted, to put these innocent people in danger. I'd seen the aftermath of the Figures' work before.

"If I leave, there's a chance they'll come here," I admitted. "But if I stay, it's guaranteed. I have to go."

"It's not that simple."

I raised an eyebrow. "Are you going to be the one to try and stop me?"

"You have to meet with the king first."

The king. The words were like a slash across my chest, leaving my

41

heart bleeding. It was a physical effort to push aside the image of my father.

"No, I don't. I'm leaving. Where are my weapons?"

"Strangers aren't allowed to carry weapons here."

I looked at him, standing impassively by the opposite wall. His forearms were soft, his shoulders wide but smooth and unmarked by any ink. I could break him with only my hands.

But there was no malice in his actions. He was merely doing what he thought was best. On a more practical note, I had no idea of the layout of this place and how many other warriors might be waiting outside the door.

"They shall be returned to you," Set said, "on the understanding that you don't keep them on your person. The rest of your belongings as well. But you do have to meet with the king. After that, what happens will be up to him."

I thought it over. It was only one meeting, and then I would be on my way again. "How long will it take?" I asked.

Set shrugged. "Not long. I'm sure he will make time for you tomorrow morning."

"Tomorrow?" My fists clenched. He had to be joking.

"It's late, and there are many other demands on his time."

Late? I blinked, side-tracked. "How long have I been here?"

"A few hours."

I relaxed a little. At least I hadn't lost a whole day. "Is there no way I could meet with your king this evening?" I forced some politeness into my tone.

"I'm afraid that's not possible."

"Make it possible."

Set raised an eyebrow slightly but otherwise didn't react to my tone. My irritation rose, as did my respect for him. Not one to be intimidated, it seemed.

"The doctor said you lost a lot of blood. You need to rest and have some food. Then you can meet with the king tomorrow."

My eyes flicked from Set to the archway, thinking of the infinite possibilities beyond it. Maybe there was a company of fighters

42

waiting outside. But maybe I would be able to get my weapons and run this very evening. It wouldn't hurt to cooperate until I could find out.

"Fine," I said. "But the longer I'm here, the greater the threat becomes. And that's on you."

Set gave a deep nod of acknowledgement. "I will ensure the king makes time for you early tomorrow." He stepped towards the archway. "Shall we?"

"One more thing," I called him back. "What were you talking about with the others? That woman… she called me 'saviour'. Why?"

Set tapped his fingers on his leg as he considered. "A bit of personal advice: don't get caught up in that. It won't help anyone."

"That's not an answer."

"No. But it's all you're going to get. Now, are you coming or not?"

I held my position for a moment before moving to follow him. If that was how he wanted to play it, that was fine by me. Whatever they had been discussing was irrelevant anyway. Let Set arrange a meeting with the king for tomorrow. I was going to find my weapons, and then I'd be gone.

Beyond the archway, a second room stretched away, much bigger than the one I'd awoken in. A flood of light coming from an archway to the right lit the walls of golden stone. Two rows of beds filled the space. Half a dozen of the beds were occupied, with more people talking to or crouching over the people who lay there. An outburst of coughing drew my attention to the left; the small girl afflicted was pale, and her bony chest heaved.

Noah had planted himself on the nearest bed but leapt to his feet as Set and I emerged. Around the room, other eyes honed in on us as well. On me. Hands paused in their tasks and feet hesitated mid-stride as heads turned in our direction.

I was used to stares, to attention. At home, people would nod at me as I passed them, move out of my path, watch where I walked.

But they knew me, knew my father, knew my place. They knew I was *someone*.

These stares were different. Unjustified. I was a stranger here. I should have been no one. Instead, I was being ogled like a piece of meat set before starving dogs.

Set seemed oblivious to the tension, striding off towards the other archway as if there was nothing unusual afoot. The other people slowly returned to their tasks, though many continued to glance up at me as I followed Set.

Noah fell in behind me. His presence so close made me tense, missing the weight of the blades at my sides more than ever, but I said nothing, focusing ahead as we passed through the second archway and emerged into full sunlight on the other side.

We were standing a little way up a hill, looking out over a city. Buildings dotted the landscape below us, but behind them, dominating the view, was a huge wall that reached from the coast on our left all the way around to join the mountains stretching away on the right.

My stomach sank at the sight. I looked above and behind us, at the cliffs rising to the sky. Maybe slipping away without meeting the king wouldn't be as easy as I'd hoped.

A breeze brought a taste of the sea, and my hopes rose again as I looked out at the sparking water. The sea meant ships, and ships meant trade. I could make it onto one of those boats and be gone in a matter of hours. Guilt twisted my stomach as I thought of the Figures trailing me here but leaving was the most I could do. Staying wouldn't help any of us.

"Oi!"

We all looked around at the call and found another man jogging up the slope towards us. He was younger than Set, closer to my age, but they shared the same brown hair, the same jawline. The newcomer had blue eyes too, though their colour was softer than Set's and there were no lines on his forehead. A slanted scar ran across his right cheek, a line of puckered skin stretching from the junction of his eye and nose to the corner of his jaw.

44

He slowed to a walk as he drew closer, his eyes dropping to my shoulders, examining my wards as I inspected his face. "So, it's true," he mused.

Set made the introductions: "Warren, this is Mara. Mara, my brother, Warren." Set made the introductions.

Warren offered me a lopsided smile, his scar pulling slightly at the side of his mouth. "Charmed."

"Likewise."

"What is it?" Set asked his brother.

"We've been summoned," Warren said, his eyes lingering on me. "Father wants us."

Set nodded, then turned back to Noah, fixing the boy with a stern look. "Mara's weapons are with Bardok, see they are returned to her along with the rest of her belongings. Find her a room for the night where she can leave them and take her to a mess hall. She will be meeting with Holt tomorrow."

"Of course, sire."

Offering me a cursory nod, Set turned and strode away with his brother, not down towards the buildings below but along the side of the cliffs. My eyes traced the path ahead of them to a large, blocky building built onto a plateau high above the rest of the city.

"Sire?" I repeated, watching the pair go. "Why did you call him that? Who is he?"

"Set's the Commander of the Scouts. And the king is their father."

My eyebrows rose. 'Commander of the Scouts'—an impressive title, though any nuances of its significance were lost on me. But it was the latter part of Noah's explanation that lingered in my mind.

If the king was their father, that meant, assuming I judged their ages right, and there wasn't another, older, sibling, Set was Heir, the same as I was. Or rather, the same as I had been.

"Ready?"

I jumped at the question, turning away from the departing brothers and nodding. Noah led me down the slope, towards the city proper.

The buildings were all made of the same sandy stone as the cliffs behind us, where the medical space was carved. Standing two or three stories high, with narrow alleys between each one, they made for a patchwork landscape, stretching up and around us. Windows filled with small panes of glass loomed overhead, but I only saw a couple with wooden shutters. Most were open or covered from the inside with sheets of fabric or leather. Likewise, the doors stood open and empty. Only the darkness within prevented me from making out the interiors, but I caught glimpses of tables and chairs or workbenches and shelves. Some of the buildings were silent, but others spewed forth sounds. Snatches of conversation, a clacking sound of wood striking wood, a rhythmic scratching, all came and went as Noah and I moved onwards.

Even with the distraction of the noises, it was the people who held my attention. As in the room adjacent to where I'd woken up, every person we passed stopped their business. Hands were raised to cover whispers as I walked by, eyes locking onto my wards. Some peered after me around the corners of buildings.

I fought to keep my expression calm, though I itched to bare my teeth and snarl at those whispering and staring. At least my leather vest hid my back, though none of these people would understand the significance of what was concealed there.

The wall loomed above us as I trailed Noah through the streets, and I fixed my eyes upon it, trying to tune out the mutters rising all around me. As we moved closer, I could make out engravings on its surface, but they were too distant for me to make out details. I tried to imagine how they had been carved at such a height. Maybe a harness of ropes lowered from the top. I looked even higher and wondered if there was a way to get to the top.

With the sinking sun behind it, the wall threw a huge wedge of shadow across the city, a slight chill in the air as we crossed into the shade. Noah turned before reaching the wall, heading south towards the sea, and I followed. I glanced sideways down each alleyway we passed, catching further glimpses of the base of the wall. The carvings existed down here too and were much larger than I'd realised. Wide strips of stone were chipped out, leaving deep channels. It wasn't until I happened to see the centre of a spiral, perfectly framed between two buildings, that I understood what I was looking at.

"Hey!"

Noah's cry was lost behind me as I veered off, marching towards the wall. I could hear his footsteps slapping on the stone as he struggled to keep up.

Bursting out from between the buildings, I skidded to a halt, staring at the wonder in front of me. I expected the illusion to shatter at any second. It wasn't until my outstretched fingers met the engravings in the stone that I believed it.

The wall was warded, spiralling lines forming patterns both familiar and foreign.

My fingers traced over the bold, blocky design of *strength*, repeated many times over the flat surface. *Balance*, identical to the tattoo high on my left shoulder, was there too, though less often. I stepped back, craning my neck to scan the rest of the wall. Amongst wards I recognised, there were others I did not. One immediately caught my eye.

It was the most common ward present, a spiral framed by a much thicker outer edge with stylised points reaching upwards like tongues of flame. Even the inner turns had smaller fronds reaching outward. The ward was far more intricate and detailed than any of the ones I bore on my skin.

The swirls here weren't separate from each other either, some transitioning from one ward into another. This wasn't just functional; this was art.

It was beautiful. It was terrifying.

How many different symbols were carved into this wall? It was like looking at a map of all we might once have known.

I let out a string of disjointed words under my breath, half-formed prayers to absent storm clouds.

"Who did this?" I rounded on Noah. The knowledge here surpassed that of the Warders at home. These new wards, the ability to link them… How much might the people here know? Would they be able to repair that which was broken? My chest tightened at the very thought. Could this be the answer?

"No one," Noah said, taking a step back from the intensity of my question. "It was here before our people arrived."

"You didn't do this?"

He shook his head.

As quickly as they had ignited, my hopes died. I turned back to the wall, reaching out to trace the link between two wards. There had to be a way. I couldn't make a discovery like this and have it mean *nothing*.

I looked sideways along the wall, eyes following the expanse of carved stone. No, this wasn't nothing. I wouldn't *let* it be nothing.

The knowledge was here, and whilst I lacked the ability to read it, I knew who could. My hand pressed more firmly against the stone. If our Warders could see this wall and study the secrets held on its surface, what could they learn?

Suddenly, the meeting with the king didn't seem like such a waste of my time. If I could come to an agreement with him whereby the Warders could journey here and study the wall, maybe that achievement would be enough to make my people overlook how broken I was.

4

Saviour

The stream of petitioners was never-ending. Two neighbouring farmers with a dispute over the ownership of a herd of goats, a report of a lack of maintenance on a stream, the resulting clog leading to a flood upstream that had ruined a crop of potatoes. When I was younger, listening to them had seemed like a chore, but now the cases began to hold my attention, and my father's judgements even more so. He would sometimes quiz me afterwards on what I had learned from the session. When one of the mountain trappers brought news of a group of poachers from Lambridge hunting on our side of the mountains, Father kept his expression neutral, thanking the trapper for their report before turning to Jenna, who was dutifully jotting the details down.

"Make a note to mention that with our next envoy. When do they leave?" he murmured.

"Two days," Jenna replied promptly.

My father made a noise of acknowledgement. "If the council doesn't deal with this group, we will."

The next ones to step forwards was a group of twenty fighters returning from Charhelm, having been relieved of their posts by those who had left a few weeks previously. The tales they told, of icy mountains that dwarfed the Baerston range, of the raiders who dared to scale them, both scared and fascinated me in equal measures.

As the group concluded their report and retreated, eager to reunite with their families, Miriam leaned forwards from her position behind us.

"He's here," she murmured, and Father straightened up at once, scanning the room. His mouth broke into a smile, and he climbed to his feet, descending the steps from the throne as he beckoned to a tall man standing by the wall.

The man, thin and pale but with an easy smile, approached, followed by a girl a couple of years older than I was.

"Master Atticus," Father greeted him.

Unlike the other petitioners, Atticus did not kneel but grasped the hand my father extended, shaking it firmly.

I looked him over eagerly, recognising the name and title. This was the man in charge of the warders. My back straightened as I watched the pair.

"Staying strong?" Atticus asked my father.

"Always." Father smiled, the question and answer clearly familiar to them both. "It's been a long time since you were up here. What can I do for you?"

"I wanted to introduce Bronwyn," Atticus said, waving to the girl who had followed him forwards. Her eyes went wide as my father's gaze moved over her.

"Another apprentice. Congratulations." He fixed the girl, Bronwyn, with a firm stare. "Your work will keep us all safe."

"Yes, sire," she murmured, peeking glimpses at my father from under her wild brown hair, the tangle of curls pulled back from her face in a ponytail.

"I'll be sure to check on your progress next time I'm passing," my father assured her, which seemed to scare more than encourage her.

"You're welcome anytime, as I've said before," Atticus said. "Not that you take me up on it."

"Demands of the job. I expect I'll be seeing you before too long again anyway," Father replied, looking back towards me.

I stood up straighter, trying to appear tall and grown-up. Atticus gave me a brief nod that I mirrored back at him.

"A few years to go yet," he said, and my shoulders slumped. Atticus laughed. "Your time will come," he assured me, turning back to my father as I sighed.

I didn't want to wait. Certainly not years. Eyeing the wards displayed proudly on the arms of all the adults in the room, I pushed down a rising wave of envy. I wanted my tattoos now.

Before I could brood any longer, Orion came striding up the hall from the main doors, his expression grim. Father excused himself from Master Atticus and went to meet him, his face darkening as Orion whispered in his ear.

He turned to look at me, his eyes flicking towards one of the side doors, and I knew I was being dismissed.

There was no resentment in my departure as I slipped out of the hall, turning right and hurrying towards the stairs beside the kitchen. One day, when I was older, I would be allowed to stay, no matter what business was brought before him. But, like my tattoos, that was still a long way off.

Climbing to the next floor, I turned back on myself, reversing the path I had taken on the floor below. To my left, windows opened onto the open space above the throne room. Through them, I could look down through the skylights and into the throne room. I had spent many a day with my nose pressed against the glass, peering down and trying to guess at the purpose of the discussions being had below. Today, however, I wasn't interested in snooping.

Stopping at the last door, I lifted the latch and stepped inside, inhaling the smell of dust and parchment. Inside was my haven, a small room stuffed with old books and records. Most of them had already been here when my father had first shown me the room, but some I had squirrelled away from the darkest corners of the Hall of Records in the city, and now the four sets of shelves were bowing under their weight. Three of the shelves protruded into the room from the northern wall, allowing access to both sides, and the fourth stood against the southern wall. Opposite the door, to the right of the only window was just enough room for a chair, the back and arms padded with a thick woollen cover.

Somewhere here, I remembered, was an account of how my grandmother's predecessor had arranged with Charhelm's King that our fighters would travel to defend their borders. It was an old account and a dull one, but it was stuck in my mind after the fighters' return, and I wanted to read it again.

The warriors we sent to Charhelm were the strongest link we had to the northern city. The raiders from over the mountains didn't have wards, but they were reported to be unnaturally fast, and the unwarded citizens who lived in the area were vulnerable. Charhelm needed us for our fighters, we needed Lambridge for their connections to the traders from the Southern Isles, and Lambridge and Charhelm needed each other to argue with.

I grinned at my joke as I stepped into the room. Father would tell me it was more complicated than that, that we were all connected, but he wasn't there to chastise me right then.

I was trying to work out which shelf the record was most likely to be on when a sound made me pause and glance around the room. The window in the eastern wall was propped open, and light shone in, but the spaces between the shelves were dark at the far end.

Gripping the hilt of my double-edged dagger, I peered down each one, looking for any sign of movement.

"Show yourself," I demanded, borrowing my father's best authoritative tone. There was another small sound, and my eyes snapped towards the window. Someone was standing on the other side of it, in the very corner of the room.

A patch of shadow moved, and I quickly shifted my focus down, frowning as the small figure resolved out of the darkness. I recognised his sandy hair, his wary expression, his black eyes. For a moment, we stared at each other suspiciously, but just as I was about to demand that he leave, another voice floated in through the open window.

"Come out, you little bastard. You can't hide forever."

My eyes flicked back to Nathaniel, who was half-turned towards the window, his face stiff, jaw clenched.

"What's the matter? Too cowardly to face us?"

Nathaniel's hands clenched into tight fists.

"I don't know about this..." another voice, low and nervous, chimed in. "We shouldn't be here."

"And he should?" the first one replied in a hiss. "This is the bloody citadel! If he can run around in here unchecked, what's next?"

"But what if we're caught?"

"Fine. You want to run back home, go ahead. Maybe this time when that thing goes wild, it will be your brother who's torn to pieces!"

"I didn't mean—"

"Then pull yourself together, for Thorns's sake."

The voices moved away, words becoming indistinct. Releasing my dagger, I strode over to the window and poked my head out. Below, the ornamental gardens were full of spring foliage and the first of the season's flowers. There was a flash of movement from the left, but the pair vanished around the corner of the building before I could get a proper look at them. Their voices faded completely as I turned to Nathaniel.

"You're hiding from them?"

He gave a half-shrug. "I'll go," he muttered, not looking at me.

"Who are they?" I demanded, and his dark eyes flashed in my direction. I expected him to look away again, but he didn't.

"Everyone," he said, only the bitterness in his tone making the word audible. He moved towards me, and I backed away, my hand still tight around my dagger. He watched my retreat without comment, turning away as he reached the window, bracing his hands on the sill.

"This is my room," I said before he could disappear. "No one comes in here."

He hesitated. "Sorry," he said, still staring at his hands.

"It's a good place to hide. If you need to."

He looked back, searching my face for a long moment before hopping out the window. I moved over and looked down, but there was no sign of him. Not even a rustle from the bushes.

Slowly, I turned away, sinking into the chair as I looked around. This was the place I could come to be on my own, the space that was mine and mine alone. Except now it wasn't. And I found I didn't regret it at all.

Moving faster now, Noah stuck to the edges of the streets as we left the wall behind, taking little alleyways and sharp turns wherever possible, avoiding the main streets and people. The sounds of the sea grew louder as we headed south, the crashing of waves tantalising in my ears as Noah crossed a larger thoroughfare and ducked into a building. I followed, slowing my pace until my eyes adjusted to the dimmer light. A sudden clang of metal made me jump and turn to the side, where a huge man was outlined by flickering flames.

"Hey," Noah called out.

The man's head turned briefly. I caught a glimpse of metal, glowing white-hot, then a hiss and a billow of steam.

"So," he said, putting his hands on his hips as he turned to look at us. He had huge shoulders and a red face, both justified as I made out the shape of an anvil behind him. With another grunt, the man stumped over to the wall and threw open some shutters, letting a breeze chase out some of the stifling heat. The light revealed a crooked nose and dark, wide-set eyes.

"I suppose you're here for them," he said, jerking his chin towards a back corner of the room. I looked, and my heart leapt.

"'Cos there couldn't possibly be another reason for coming," Noah grumbled.

I barely heard him, already striding over to a wide bench where familiar shapes gleamed silver in the gloomy room. My twin blades fit my hands the same way they had the first time I'd held them, as though we'd never been apart. My fingers sang at the reunion.

"That's good metal," the large man said from behind me. "It would be wasted on someone who didn't know how to use it."

"They were a gift," I said, spinning the blades. "And they're not wasted."

He grunted as I checked over my other knives, which had come from my pack.

54

"You're a fool."

I looked around, thinking the man was still talking to me, but his gaze had now shifted to Noah.

"So you've told me," Noah replied, leaning back on another of the many workbenches and crossing his arms. "Many times."

"Don't play games with me, boy," the man snapped, though his face had flushed redder. "You know what people are saying about her?"

I found myself leaning forwards, my breath catching in my throat. Despite all the people staring, not one of them had dared to say a word to me. What were they whispering behind their hands? Did it have something to do with how my tattoos matched the carvings on the wall? I bit my tongue, eyes flicking between the pair.

"Oh, they've been making it clear," Noah said, and the older man paused, looking at the tall boy.

"You've got no idea what you're doing, do you?"

"Not a clue," Noah admitted with half a grin, and the man shook his head though he was fighting a smile as well.

"Fool," he repeated firmly.

Noah's grin widened, and he gave a sheepish shrug.

"Your parents should have left you with someone else. Maybe they could have talked some sense into you." He walked back towards the glowing forge.

Shaking his head, Noah turned to me. "Satisfied?" he asked, nodding to my blades. "That's yours too," he added, pointing to the side. "We can take them to your room and leave them there."

I glanced to where he gestured and found my pack sitting on the floor. "My room?"

Noah shrugged. "If you're meeting the king tomorrow, you'll need somewhere to sleep tonight."

I grimaced, remembering Set's declaration that I couldn't meet the king this evening. With my blades back on my hips and my own motive for wanting to meet the king, it was harder to accept the delay.

I stowed my other knives in my pack and turned to follow him out when something on the wall caught my eye.

"What's that?" I asked, staring up at the slash of darkness suspended on the wall over our heads. It was too prominent to be a shadow, but I couldn't resolve the sight into anything else.

Noah turned, following my gaze, and let out a noise that was half amusement, half disgust. "That? That's Bard showing off."

"I heard that, boy!"

The shout from the other end of the shop made Noah grin, but I continued gazing upwards, part of me entranced, another part, for some reason, afraid.

"He calls it 'black steel'," Noah said, "but I've never managed to get out of him what it really is."

Stepping closer, I finally recognised the shape. It was a sword, easily as long as the one Titan favoured, its blade so dark that not a single speck of light reflected off it. Shadows played around the edges, blurring their form. Even the hilt and guard were black, though not to the same extent as the blade. They were a normal black, from dyes or inks, as opposed to the smooth depth of the blade, like night itself.

"He named it 'Darkness'," Noah said wryly. "As if it's not dramatic enough already," he added, though not loud enough for it to carry.

"He named it?" I frowned at him, thinking I'd misunderstood.

"Yeah." Noah shrugged. "It's not that uncommon. I'm pretty sure Warren has named all his swords, though he's a little less open about it." Reading my expression, he raised an eyebrow. "You don't do that?"

"Only the monarch can name their weapon," I told him, and he snorted.

"Let me guess. Your king had a sword called Wisdom. Or Honour."

"Mercy," I corrected him, the image of the blade sitting across my father's lap flashing through my mind.

"And is he merciful?" Noah asked as I turned back to the black sword.

56

An image of a body crumpled on the floor of the throne room, my father standing over it, his face hard and remorseless, flashed in front of me.

"He was. When it was justified."

"Was?"

"He's dead," I said, and my voice didn't even shake.

Noah didn't say anything for a second, and I wondered if my tone had been more transparent than I'd realised.

"Well, I guess you'll have someone else to name their sword now then," he said eventually. The words went through me like a gust of icy wind.

Djet was the one who had that right at the moment. If I could successfully depose the usurper, I would be the one to name my blades. Somehow, that thought hadn't occurred to me. I stroked my thumbs over the hilts of my weapons.

"Come on," Noah said, interrupting my musings. "Let's go find somewhere for you to stay."

If anything, the staring intensified as Noah led the way back towards the mountains and then began to climb up a winding path only a couple of paces wide. We now had no way to keep our distance from curious people who were more than happy to gawk, even stopping and blocking the path to watch us go past, now staring at the weapons on my hips as well as the wards on my shoulders. It was hard to tell, which made me more uncomfortable.

I was glad when the path levelled out and Noah led the way into a dark tunnel, my relief at the escape from watchful eyes enough to overcome my discomfort at the rock pressing down over our heads. A few dozen paces in, Noah turned right, heading along another tunnel. Faint light was visible from openings on the right, but it was barely enough to see by.

Noah stopped by one of the openings and gestured me inside. Slipping through the gap, I shuffled sideways around a sharp switchback in the rock and found myself in a small, square room.

No door. I would be sleeping with one eye open tonight.

A palm-sized hole in the opposite wall allowed light from outside to stream in, illuminating a bed carved into the rock, stacked with blankets. Otherwise, it was empty.

There was a hint of chill in the still air after the warmth of the evening outside, but not enough for it to be uncomfortable.

"All the rooms are pretty much the same," Noah said, having followed me in. "You can leave your things here, no one will come in, and I'll show you the food hall."

I turned back, about to question him further, but he was already slipping back through the sharply turning passage and was gone from view.

I laid my pack on the bed but hesitated with my hands on the weapons at my hips. Set had been clear that I wasn't meant to be armed—as if that would make any difference in a fight against these people—and Noah said my things wouldn't be disturbed, but I still didn't want to leave them here. Did I have any other option, though? My stomach, rumbling at Noah's mention of food, decided for me, and I placed the blades gently next to my pack. Grabbing a small dagger instead, I shoved it into a strap on my calf, out of sight, before following Noah back out to face whatever this city had to throw at me next.

I felt the absence of my twin blades with every step back through the city. Noah led the way to a large, single-story building, its long stone walls broken by a narrow window on either side of an open archway. A tangle of light and sound spilt out, hitting me like a barrier as I approached a wide archway to the interior. The smells sharpened as we stepped inside, the welcoming aroma of something rich and savoury followed by a sharper hit of smoke to the back of my nose. The noise died instantly as heads turned and eyes found me.

I didn't freeze. Titan had trained me too well for that. But my pace slowed, shoulders drawing in and fingers flexing as I looked around. No one moved, not a single hand raised in violence, but the room was charged, crackling with energy.

Every muscle in my body tightened under the scrutiny. If my stomach hadn't been twisting eagerly at the smells wafting towards me, I would have turned and left, if only to spite their curious stares. Unfortunately, after my injury, I needed to eat. I'd already proven that I couldn't trust myself to use my growth ward without making disastrous mistakes. I had no other options. Elbows clenched to my sides, I stepped forwards, wishing once again for my weapons.

Listening to the silence, I followed Noah to the side of the room, where the combined smells of food and fire grew stronger. I accepted a bowl with a careful measuring of dark stew, half my attention still on the room behind me, then trailed him over to one of the long tables. The space on the stone bench grew as we approached, those already seated there bunching up to make more room, eyes on me.

Noah flung himself down and attacked his food immediately, head down. I sat opposite him, relieved to have my back to the wall. No one would meet my gaze, looking away or dropping their eyes to my tattoos. My arms tensed even further, and I wished I had longer sleeves on.

In Alderth, leather vests like the one I wore were common. Wide straps ran over my shoulders to keep it in place, but the two wards on each arm were left exposed. It had always felt so *right*, displaying the tattoos that we all shared. Visible proof that we were all the same, that we could protect each other, that we would stand together. The same power, the same people.

Not here. Here, I was alone.

Hunching over the table, I took a bite of whatever was in the bowl. It was warm, though not hot, but I barely tasted it, my eyes still flickering around the room. Whispers began to break out in the corners, people leaning close to their neighbours to mutter secret words. Soon it seemed that Noah was the only silent person left, the buzz rising with every second. I ate distractedly, listening to the words floating past me, picking out one more than any other.

"…saviour… markings… like the wall… saviour… her arms…

just look… saviour… don't be stupid… ridiculous… saviour…"

Saviour, saviour, saviour. Set had warned me not to get involved with the idea, but he'd given no indication as to why.

I looked up at Noah. Was this what he and Bardok had been referring to when they'd spoken about what 'everyone was saying' about me? Was it all hidden in this one word? Why 'saviour'? What did they need saving from? And why me? Knowing what they were saying didn't answer any of my questions.

Noah refused to meet my gaze, staring determinately at the last dregs of his food. I felt a sudden stab of loneliness, more acutely aware of Nate's absence than I had been since waking in this city. He wouldn't have avoided my eyes. He would've raised an eyebrow in a silent question, daring me to follow this new mystery, with that steadiness in his expression that promised he would have my back if I did.

As soon as I finished eating, Noah pushed his bowl away and stood.

"Done?" he asked over the rising noise. I nodded, standing as well. The room went quiet again, but the stillness did not return. People were craning their necks, some even rising from their seats to get a better look at me as I strode towards the exit, craving the open air and quiet. When one of them stepped out to block my path, I didn't hesitate. A sharp tug on my wards, and I was past them, speed and balance carrying me out the door before they had a chance to open their mouth. The murmurings rose as I darted sideways along the street, out of sight of those still within.

Noah shuddered as he looked back. "That could have gone better."

I stepped in front of him, blocking his path, my eyes locked on his. He was taller than I was, probably taller even than Titan, but he hunched away, seeming to shrink as I glared at him.

"What was that?" I asked, watching his face closely. "Why is everyone staring? What were they talking about?"

My hand rose to brush protectively across my tattoos as if the stares could have leached the ink out of my skin.

Noah glanced behind him. The street was empty, but I could still hear the noise from within the crowded room. "It's… they…" He squirmed, shuffling his feet.

"Tell me."

"There's a prophecy."

"Excuse me?"

"I don't know, okay? It's… it's just a carving of a verse. And people think it tells of a saviour who's going to come." Noah waved a loose hand up towards the cliff above us, somewhere just to the side of the looming building Set and Warren had headed for when they left earlier.

"What does it say?"

Noah hesitated, shifting on his feet as he glanced around. Checking for witnesses, or hoping for someone to save him? When neither appeared, he sighed. "It says 'they will come with the darkness, bringing the light, dark strength on their arms. Death shall know fear.'."

I waited, but he said nothing more. "That's it?"

He shrugged.

"And people think it means me?"

Noah looked very deliberately at my wards. Black ink on my arms.

Black ink, dark strength…

I frowned as I looked away from his piercing gaze. That didn't fit; the strength wards were on my back, not my arms.

"A prophecy," I mused. I'd seen fortune tellers on the docks at Lambridge when I'd visited with my father. They'd called out to sailors, merchants, and anyone else who passed them by, offering foresight into prices or winds. Father had laughed when my gaze lingered curiously.

'The future's not for them to tell or us to know,' he'd said, steering me away.

"Prophesied by who?" I asked.

"An angel, apparently."

I gave Noah a curious look.

"A divine messenger," he expanded. "Though the divinity part is questionable. All the original stories say is it was a message from a being with white eyes."

White eyes. I took a step back from him. I might not know anything about angels, but I only knew of one being with white eyes. And I may or may not have killed one of them earlier that very day.

It was impossible, surely, for him to mean one of the Figures. For a start, what would they have been doing here? The Figures were bound to the throne of Alderth, to obey the orders of the monarch. Could one of my father's predecessors have sent them here to deliver the message? But to what end?

Historically, the Figures were a last resort, woken only when the need for defence was extreme or the desire for bloodshed high. They were warriors. Strong, hard, fast, but limited as well. Able to carry out orders but nothing beyond. Hardly the most obvious choice of messenger. They couldn't even speak; it couldn't have been one of them.

"This prophecy... the carving... where is it?"

Noah eyed me dubiously. "You don't want to get involved in this. Trust me."

Set had given me the same warning. "Oh? *You* seem to know plenty about it."

"I made some questionable choices, okay?"

I scowled, tired of the half-answers. "What does that mean?"

Noah shifted, moving away from my anger. "I wanted answers once I was old enough to understand that Bardok isn't my real father. And I thought I'd find them there, but the older I got, the more different versions of the story I heard, the more interpretations there were, but none of them made any sense. And none of them ever helped. Yeah, there are plenty of people who fawn over it, who will believe anything Mary tells them, who think that it's foretelling some great saviour, but there are far more who think it means something else."

"Something else?"

62

Noah finally stopped avoiding my gaze, meeting my eyes without flinching for the first time. "You can't have a saviour without having something you need saving from. So I don't think it's that difficult to understand why most of us aren't so eager for one to turn up."

I was silent for a moment, letting his words sink in. "I mean no harm to anyone in this city," I said.

"Sure," Noah said dismissively. "But intentions don't normally count for much in the end. My advice: stay away from the prophecy. It won't help anyone." He glanced around, rubbing his hands on his legs. "It's late. I'll show you back to your room."

He was right, full darkness had fallen whilst we ate, but I wasn't ready to sleep yet. Shaking my head, I took a step back. "I can find my own way."

Noah hesitated for a moment, then shrugged. "Fine." He turned and stalked away, disappearing quickly into the darkness.

I watched him go, surprised by his easy acceptance of my declaration. Maybe he just wanted to escape any further questions. Still, I wasn't about to object to the lack of supervision at last.

Stepping off the main street and into a smaller passage, I leaned against the building, feeling the rough stone under my palms. Letting the sensation slip away, I turned my thoughts inside, reaching with my mind towards my right elbow. My sight ward sat there, a tight, unadorned spiral surrounded by two concentric circles. Waiting.

I pulled on the ward. Warmth spread under my skin around the tattoo, a comforting heat. At the same time, the world descended into hues of red. The shadows were suddenly irrelevant, their depths yielding to the ward's power. The wall opposite me was a field of soft pink, the ground underfoot a deeper, poppy red. Edges were sharper, shining in my vision with a secret illumination. Lessening the draw, I let the colours fade a little, muting to softer tones whilst still affording me a clear sight of my surroundings. Then I stepped out of the alley and set off into the city.

It was easy to avoid the few people lingering on the streets.

Blinded by the darkness, they were oblivious to my presence, and it was easy to slip into shadowed corners when anyone passed. By the time I'd reached the northern edge of the city, where the wall curved around and met the cliffs to the east, the familiar headache accompanying my use of the sight ward was making itself known.

Ignoring the pressure on my temples, I surveyed the swath of open land dedicated to crops. Divided into rough rectangles, each in a different stage of growth, it made a patchwork upon the ground. Bare soil, dry and sandy, abutted rows of tiny, leafy shoots. At the bottom of the wall, several wooden cubes kept watch over the area, each one emitting a slight buzzing noise. Venturing closer, I spotted the occasional insect crawling over them and bid a hasty retreat. I looked over the small area with a frown. Surely this wasn't enough space to grow food for all the people here.

Turning away, I followed the wall south, eyes roving over the wards upon it. My heart pounded at the thought of my meeting with the king the following morning. Would he be open to the possibility of allowing our Warders to return here and study the wall? I imagined I could feel them, a reflection of the power under my skin. But older. Deeper. Stronger.

I continued further, barely looking where I was going, until shouts reached my ears. Dragging my eyes away from the wards, I looked ahead to where red-tinged shadows were visible, darting back and forth. I hesitated for a moment, then ducked between two buildings, winding my way through the narrow spaces until I reached a much larger thoroughfare. There, I halted, peering cautiously out.

This wider street, unlike most of the others, was paved with wide slabs of a different stone, grey and smooth. The squares abutted their neighbours neatly, though some of them were cracked, jagged lines zigzagging through the otherwise orderly picture. To my left, the street ran through the city towards the mountains, curving gradually out of sight. To my right, however, it widened further to an empty plaza before the warded wall. And at the base of the wall, directly ahead of the street, was a huge pair of wooden gates with thick braces and two huge drop bolts at the bottom. A beam fitted into stout metal brackets, but it had been lifted out of place by four of the men who swarmed around the courtyard, crying out instructions to one another other that were lost in the creaking and groaning as the huge gates, easily twelve feet high at their curved peak, began to open.

I'd taken three steps out into the street before I realised what I'd done and forced myself to a halt. Through the crack in the gates, I could see grassy plains stretching away, each strand of grass highlighted in red, a rippling field of fire. Freedom. An easy escape. With my speed ward, I could be past the guards and out the gates before they even realised I was here. In seconds, I would be on the move again, making my way home to take back my throne. Just how my father would have wanted me to.

I didn't move. I had the meeting with the king tomorrow morning. How could I walk away without exploring the potential that meeting held? If I left now, it might ruin any chance for me to return and seal an agreement in the future. Then there was the matter of the two blades Nate had given me. The rest of my pack, I would have sacrificed in a heartbeat, but the thought of those weapons curled around my chest like arms, holding me in place. I couldn't leave without them.

Where would Nate be now? Assuming he had done a better job of evading the Figures than I had, he might even have reached the banks of the Griambrian River south of Alderth, where we were supposed to meet. Even allowing for me to have taken a longer route, surely he would start to wonder where I was before long. What would he do then? Would he come looking for me once again, or guess the Figures had found me? Whilst I was stuck here, the latter might as well have been true. He would have to wait for me a little longer, however.

Hurried footsteps from behind made me glance over my shoulder, expecting to see someone coming to see what was going on, but instead, I caught a flash of movement as someone darted away, disappearing between two buildings. Eyes narrowed slightly at their retreat, I turned my attention back to the gates as a horse and rider burst through, hooves clattering on the stone. The guards reversed their motions at once, shoving against the creaking gates until they boomed shut again.

The rider dismounted, unwinding a scarf from around their head. They were about three-quarters of my height, their shortness exacerbated by the fact they were ridiculously out-sized by their mount, whose shoulder was as high as my head. The huge animal seemed perfectly placid, lowering its head to nuzzle at its tiny rider. Their scarf fell away, revealing locks of short, blonde hair pushed back from a sharp face, all cheekbones and pointed chin. Patting the neck of her horse, she looked around and her eyes fell on me.

We stared at each other, the warmth of my ward intensifying as I drew a little deeper on it, illuminating the details of her face. A narrowing of her eyes, a twisting of her mouth. Expression almost a sneer, she turned away, flicking her hair dismissively. Clicking her tongue, she disappeared between buildings, heading north, the horse striding after her.

I resisted the urge to scowl after her. Leaving the rider to her business, I turned south instead, towards the smell of the sea, now tantalisingly close. The ebb and wash of waves lured me in, and I made my way through the last tangle of buildings to emerge onto a stone wharf.

The lapping ocean reflected the stars above, a pool of night contained with a harbour formed by the mountains on one side and the warded wall, stretching out into the sea, on the other. There was only one pier, populated by half a dozen small fishing boats. Otherwise, the water was empty.

Taken aback, I halted at the edge of the wharf, looking out over the water. My initial thought of being able to sneak onto a ship and leave that way was unrealisable. But why were there no larger boats or trading vessels?

There was something strange about this city. Too small to sustain itself but sealed off from the outside world. Holding wards unknown to my people, but none of its residents warded. Plus, a prophecy some seemed to think referred to me.

A chill built around me as a breeze swept in from the sea. I looked down. The dark water was no doubt freezing, but it still called to me like the thumping of a distant heart.

Swim, it crooned. Run. Fly. Get out. Go home.

I knew the voice it spoke in and closed my eyes as it pulled on my soul.

I wanted to obey. I wanted to go home. But the water was cold, the wall high, the guards innocent. And there were too many questions here. Too many possibilities. Mysteries layered upon secrets. I wanted answers.

So I tuned out my father's voice, no matter how much it wrenched on my heart, and stayed, poised over the water like a statue, forever on the point of falling.

5

The Other King

After our first encounter in my library, I kept my eyes open for Nathaniel. I looked for him around the citadel, on the training ground, in the streets and markets, but I never so much as glimpsed him. It was as if he only existed in my thoughts and in my library.

He wasn't always there, but occasionally when I closed the door behind me, he would emerge from the shadows like a ghost and retrieve a book from the shelves. The first time, he sat on the floor beside the window, hidden by the shelves. I hesitated, then took my book to my usual chair on the other side of the window, watching him out the corner of my eye.

I made a note of which books I saw him with, trying to discern what he was interested in, but it quickly became clear that he was simply working his way along the shelves, steadily consuming every book I had stashed away, from recountings of epic battles to dreary accounts of trade contracts with Charhelm and Lambridge. I brought in another chair, heaving it through the corridors and pushing it into the corner where he liked to lurk. He pulled it away from the wall a little, leaving a dark space behind it, but conceded to sit in the chair rather than on the floor. I didn't mention it, and neither did he.

We barely said a word to each other for a whole year, aside from the occasional 'hello'. From there, we progressed to discussing whatever we were each reading at the time but always politely, a careful distance between us. If I sometimes thought he was moving more cautiously than normal, or when he was absent for several days, I wrote it off, pretending it was nothing but natural stiffness or that he was busy elsewhere. It wasn't until the truth was right in front of me that I finally acknowledged it.

Four years had passed since he'd first arrived, and it would only be a few more months before I got my wards. Titan said it would be several weeks, months even, before I could draw on them reliably, but even the thought of having the ink under my skin was enough to make my stomach tight with anticipation. Soon, I would be as strong as any of them. Soon.

My head full of dreams and my hands full of books, I grappled with unlocking the door to my library and pushed it open with my hip, glancing across the room as I always did, but the chairs flanking the window were empty. I turned away and began returning the books to their places on the shelves in the dim light of the dying sun until soft movement behind me made me jump, the last tome falling to the ground with a crash as I sprang backwards. Someone moved in the corner. I squinted, a familiar profile resolving from the shadows.

Nathaniel was taller than he had been when he'd first hidden in that same spot. He had several inches on me now, though I stubbornly hoped I'd be able to reclaim them in the future. He stayed leaning against the wall, avoiding my gaze as I let out a shaky laugh at myself. Retrieving the book from the floor, I returned it to its place, then ducked outside and grabbed a torch, placing it carefully in the bracket on the wall to illuminate the room.

I turned back to him and gasped. The whole of his right cheek was almost the same shade as his eyes, and a split in his forehead trickled blood down the bruised flesh.

"What happened?"

"Would you like three guesses?" he asked coolly, failing to hide a wince as he limped out of the corner, holding his torso stiffly.

I stared at him and felt my insides turn cold and hard. "Who was it?"

"Does it matter?"

"Yes!"

He smiled humourlessly and said nothing.

Scowling, I stomped over to a shelf and straightened the books to hide my shaking fingers. "How often does this happen?" I asked, glancing over in time to catch his shrug.

"Whenever they get the chance," he said. "Not that often," he added after seeing my shocked expression. "I stay out of their way as much as possible. Just got unlucky today." He took a breath, wincing.

"How many?"

"Three, four, sometimes more. It changes."

"How many in total?"

"I haven't kept track," he snapped. "However many are out there." He waved a hand towards the window and the city beyond.

I turned, taking the book I was currently shuffling with me, grasped in white knuckles. "There are good people here," I said.

He shook his head. "Not to me."

"It can't be eve—"

"Look at me! What am I?"

I looked into his black eyes. "Half-blood." The words radiated a chill through my chest.

"Half-blood," he repeated darkly. "Bastard. Freak. Monster. All they have to do is look at me. I can't hide it."

"That doesn't give them the right to—"

"Right?" He gave a bitter laugh but stopped quickly with a grimace of pain. "They don't care about what's right."

"So leave!" I said, gesticulating wildly with my book. "Run away."

He looked at me. "I can't. Your father has forbidden it. The Guard hunted me down once already; I'd rather not have them do it again."

I stared back at him. My father hadn't forbidden him to leave… had he? "No, he hasn't," I said, but there was no conviction in my voice, and he looked away from me. Hot anger curled in my stomach. "And your mother?"

He nodded grimly. "Same for her. She's living down the valley. As far out as your father allows. I don't go there."

"Why not?"

He snorted. "She at least has a chance without me. People don't know who she is until I show up. She doesn't need me there to mess things up for her. So I stay away."

"She said that?" I couldn't believe it. After everything Alicia had done to protect her son when he was younger, why would she have abandoned him now?

"She doesn't have to. She's better off without me. She doesn't want me there."

"Grow up," I snapped. "If she didn't want you, she would have drowned you when you were born."

He drew back so sharply it looked like a flinch. He stared at me, and I glared straight back.

"I'm going to talk to my father," I said," and this—" I gestured to his bruised face, "—is never going to happen again."

He looked at me, his dark eyes tired, and said nothing, so I spun on my heel and strode straight out of the library. I got halfway along the corridor before I realised I was still clutching a book in my hands. Looking down at it, I flipped it open to read the words written in dark ink. The Life and Reign of Anatoly Gentle-heart. I snorted at the irony.

You never went to war, I thought wryly as I stared at the name of the king who'd been dead for more than a century. You never battled the demons, and they never attacked you.

But how had that been achieved? The writer suggested peace, some secret treaty, but I doubted that. The demons didn't deal with treaties or negotiations. The only language they understood was that of blood and death. Shaking my head, I snapped the book shut. The demons of a hundred years ago weren't my problem. The half-demon hiding in my library was, and it was a problem I could do something about.

Morning came before I was ready for it. Misty light floated in through the palm-sized hole in the wall, dust sparkling in the air. There was a dull throbbing in my temples, a familiar pain from using my sight ward.

When I'd finally made the connection between its use and the ache that followed, I'd spent almost a week examining the tattoo, trying to compare it to everyone else's without letting on what I was doing. I'd even gone back to Master Atticus and asked him to check it. Neither of us found anything wrong. The design was flawless. Since then, I hadn't told a soul about the headaches and their source. One broken ward was enough to hide. I couldn't have anyone doubting my capabilities, especially if I wanted to take my father's place.

Sitting up, I rubbed at the epicentre of my headache, trying to massage the pain away as I turned my thoughts to the more immediate future. After finding the harbour completely bereft of ships, my best hope for a peaceful departure was the meeting with the king Set had promised me. Then there was the possibility the meeting held for reaching a deal about the wards as well.

Between everything else going on yesterday and the supposed prophecy, I hadn't asked what the unfamiliar ward did or if the people here were even aware of its potential, but this would be an opportunity to ask those questions. It would need to be done quickly, however. Set seemed sensible enough, but he didn't understand the danger the Figures posed or how the threat transferred onto them because of my presence here. Hopefully, the king would be more tractable.

After digging quickly through my pack and pulling on a loose shirt with sleeves reaching down to my elbows over my leather vest, I made my way outside. The sun was hidden behind the mountains to the east when I emerged from the tunnels, but the sky above was a bright, sparkling blue, studded with clouds. It was well after dawn. Set had said the meeting would be early this morning, but how early was early?

I made a brief detour into the city to grab a warm roll from one of the mess halls and ate it as I made my way back up the mountain, towards the blocky fortress Warren and Set had been heading for yesterday. People murmured as I passed, the word 'saviour' ringing in my ears, but my determined stride deterred any further interaction.

The palace, lacking the grace the word implied, was surrounded by another stone wall, probably ten feet tall, though this one was unwarded. Four soldiers, armed with long spears, guarded a large archway leading within. Brushing the crumbs from my breakfast off my hands, I slowed my pace. The quartet exchanged glances, shuffling their feet. One, who looked to be the oldest, lowered his spear slightly.

I stopped well out of reach. Were they not told to expect my arrival? Before any of us could say anything, the soldiers looked away, to something behind me. I turned.

A short woman was approaching, her steps sure and quick. I recognised her diminutive stature and messy blonde hair from the previous evening. There was no sign of her huge horse now, but the slight sneer as she returned my gaze was unchanged. She passed me without a word, the soldiers not even blinking as she continued unchallenged.

I looked at the older one, his spear still held at the ready.

"Can't let you through."

I blinked, staring at him. I hadn't even opened my mouth. His face was hard, but his eyes looked almost smug.

"Excuse me?" I glanced from him to his three companions. They looked uneasy, but from their youth and deferential demeanours, the speaker outranked them.

"You're not authorised to enter," the soldier said, enunciating each word. He was definitely enjoying this.

I fought down a wave of anger. "I have a meeting with the king," I explained, trying to keep the fact that I wanted to punch the smug expression off his face from colouring my tone.

"I could go and check…" The younger soldier who made the offer trailed off as his superior glared over his shoulder.

"I've not been informed of this," he said, turning back to me. "And the king will not be accepting audiences for another hour at least. Therefore, we cannot let you pass." The satisfaction at holding this power over me was palpable, rolling off him in waves. The younger soldier who had spoken up looked distinctly uncomfortable now, glancing back over his shoulder towards the palace.

I was considering whether or not it would be worth removing this particular obstacle by force when a familiar figure arrived from inside the palace.

Set raised a hand as he spotted me. I didn't respond, my eyes flicking from him to the soldier. Set's welcoming smile turned to a frown as he drew closer, his expression going hard as he noticed the tense stances of the group. The oldest soldier jumped as Set clapped a hand on his shoulder. With his other hand, he pushed the soldier's spear upright, stepping close to him. I couldn't hear what he said, but I watched over Set's shoulder as the soldier's face went pale, his gaze dropping to the floor. He didn't say a word, not looking up even when Set turned to face me, his smile back in place.

I raised an eyebrow.

"My apologies," he said, all smooth charm. "If I'd known you were an early riser, I would have come sooner. Please, come with me. The king is ready to meet you."

"Uh-huh," I said, still watching the soldier who refused to meet my gaze. With an effort, I stopped glaring at him and refocused my attention on Set, fixing a polite smile on my face. "After you." I gestured him ahead of me, shooting one last look at the soldier as I passed through their midst. He didn't look up, but his upper lip twitched into something like a sneer.

The courtyard beyond was small and bare, the monotonous stone broken only by a few plants in carved troughs. Set didn't dawdle, and I dragged my eyes away from the splashes of green as he moved through a second archway to the interior of the palace.

Inside, we made our way down a wide passage of yet more sandy stone, though this was carved with delicate lines that danced and twisted around each other. Doors, real doors of solid wood, stood closed at intervals on both sides of the hall. Small alcoves dotted the walls, each filled with a plinth, topped with various objects. A piece of twisted grey driftwood was succeeded by a slim, undecorated vase that had been broken and then repaired with some dark substance, the jagged black lines standing out against the surface. On the other side of the passage, two halves of a sphere of grey stone lay next to each other, not quite touching. And between each item, a wooden door.

After the uniformity of the stone buildings in the rest of the city, I'd wondered if the gates were the only wood here. I reached out a finger to brush over the grained surface as we passed, just to confirm that the material was real.

We turned left into a smaller passage, right, then right again before Set stopped beside a door and cracked it open, stepping inside and holding it for me. The hall beyond was larger than I'd expected, supported by thick stone pillars, with wide, south-facing arches overlooking the mountains and the sea, letting light flood inside.

There were several other people already inside, gathered around the edges of the room. Most were focused on the open space in the middle of the rows of pillars. A cluster of four stood on a balcony on the opposite side of the room, talking intently amongst themselves.

"Wait here," Set murmured, then strode off to the left.

Ignoring his instruction, I moved forwards. Using the columns as cover, I tracked Set to the end of the hall, where an ornate wooden throne stood.

Set took up a place to the left of the throne. Warren stood on the other side. The man on the throne between the two brothers shared their pronounced forehead, straight nose, and dark hair, though his was threaded with grey. Warren, having noted his brother's return, looked up, scanning the hall. When he spotted me skulking off to the side, he inclined his head slightly before returning his attention to a frizzy-haired woman before them. Her voice shook as she addressed the trio.

"—a good boy really. He would never have meant to get caught up in anything. He made a mistake, that's all." She took a deep breath, swallowing a sob. "Please. He's all I have left. My only son. Please..."

I fought a scowl. So much for the king not taking audiences yet.

The king looked at her with a serious expression, and when he spoke, his voice was deep and tight with annoyance. "Your son did not have permission, or just cause, to be beyond the wall," he said. "I cannot risk more lives to go looking for someone who so recklessly puts themself in danger. I hope Malcolm will return, but I cannot justify sending anyone after him. That's my final word."

I looked away, feeling slightly sick. Not at the king's words or the woman's plea, though. The room itself made my head spin.

A king on a throne at one end, flanked by his children, the columns leading away from him... It was too similar to the throne room back in Alderth. I looked to the right, already knowing that I would see two large doors, and there they were, a cruel mirror of my home. Four guards stood around them, holding the same long spears wielded by those outside. Other than the rows of arches along the opposite wall and the materials—sandy stone here, grey blocks at home—it could have been the same place.

Swallowing down the nausea, I turned back to the woman in front of the throne. She had dropped to one knee, a sob rising then stifled. "If your wisdom decrees it so," she said, an undertone of steel in her shaking voice.

Mutters swept the room.

The mother rose, turned, and walked away, her steps unsteady but her chin raised. Tears left wet tracks down her cheeks, but she made no attempt to wipe them away. She was halfway along the open space when she spotted me; a brief glance at first, then she looked again. Her stride faltered, feet scuffing on the floor as she stopped. She looked from my face to my shoulders, as if she could see through the fabric covering my wards.

"Saviour." The word was a gasp, forced out through an indrawn breath. She surged towards me, arms outstretched.

I tensed, ready to knock her away, but there was no anger in her

76

face, no weapon in her hands. She stumbled, toppling forward. Her hands were still raised, no way for her to break her fall. Lunging from behind the pillar, I grabbed her arms, saving her from landing on her face. It was only after I caught her that I realised she wasn't falling at all. Her weight was too far back, the movement too controlled. She landed on her knees in front of me, hands gripping my forearms. The cut across my left arm stung.

"Saviour," she breathed again, eyes glowing with a feverish brightness. "I know why you're here. Please, you must help me!"

"Enough!" the king snapped from the other end of the room. I looked up. He'd risen to his feet, a scowl on his face. "Get her out of here. Now."

"Please."

I looked back down at the woman's whisper.

"Please, you're my only hope. You must help. You must save him!"

"Who are you?" I asked, keeping my voice low.

Two of the soldiers from by the door were advancing, faces weary as they grabbed the woman by the shoulders and dragged her upright.

"I'll wait for you!" she called out as she was pulled away. "By the sea. Find me, Saviour!"

The doors closed behind her with a bang, and I was left standing alone.

Someone cleared their throat behind me and I looked back. The three men clustered around the throne were watching me, the king's eyes narrowed.

I know why you're here…

Swallowing, I pushed the woman's words out of my head as I turned to approach the king, slipping back behind my mask. *Why* I was here was irrelevant.

No one had told me of the customs here, what indication of deference I was expected to make before their King. The woman had knelt. I would not kneel. I would never kneel to anyone again. So I bowed, a graceful motion with an adequate content of respect.

None of the observers scattered around the room gave any indication if it was enough.

How strange, to be on this side of the interaction. I couldn't recall the last time I'd stood before my father like this. Yet the resemblance in the locations was uncanny. Even the three steps up to the dais on which the throne sat looked the same.

"It's a pleasure to finally meet you," the king said, and I dug my fingers into my palm to pull myself out of my spinning mind. "My name is Holt."

"Mara," I replied. "It's an honour."

"Likewise. I apologise for Rhianna's behaviour. That was unseemly." Holt's eyes flickered first to my shoulders, then to the wound over my elbow. "I believe you have an interesting story."

"Not that interesting," I said lightly, hoping to move the conversation away, or even better, to a quick conclusion.

"I disagree. The whole city seems to have been stirred by your presence."

"Quite unintentional, I assure you."

"Oh, of course, but still..." He let out a sigh a little too deep to be plausible. "They are fascinated by you." His eyes were fixed on my shoulder now, and I didn't like it one bit. "Will you show me?" he asked with false politeness.

For a moment, I wondered what would he do if I refused. I pulled up the sleeve covering my left arm, twisting my body towards him so he could see the two wards inked under my skin, though the lower one was partially obscured by the bandage over my wound.

His nostrils flared. "I never set much store by prophecy," he said, sitting back in his ornately carved throne. A spate of muttering swept the hall, but Holt ignored it. "Though one does have to wonder..." The words faded into an expectant silence. "What do they mean?"

I let my sleeve drop, smoothing the material down before answering. "They're a custom among my people."

"But what do they *mean*?" he repeated.

78

"Balance, speed—"

"Strength?" he suggested.

"No." I smiled, trying to soften the snap that had crept into the word.

It wasn't exactly a lie. My strength wasn't held on my arms.

"You have your own archive of wards as well, it would seem," I said, inclining my head towards the open archways and the city beyond. I couldn't see the wall from this angle but I hoped the meaning would be clear.

Holt's eyes narrowed, his hand tightening on the arm of his throne. He turned, looking up at his eldest son. Set's face was tight as he exchanged a look with his father before returning his eyes to me. I didn't like what I saw within them, the way their fierce intensity pierced me. Suspicion. Doubt. Wariness.

Under that gaze, my own emotions took on a similar tinge. Had I just made a mistake? Why had my asking about the wall caused such a reaction?

On Holt's other side, Warren was glancing between them, as much in the dark as I was, excluded from the look that passed between his father and brother.

"Noah?" Holt called out.

My heart sank further as sharp footsteps echoed through the room. I glanced sideways at the tall boy as he knelt beside me then rose, his hands held in fists at his sides.

"What happened yesterday?" Holt asked.

"I'd gone west in the afternoon," Noah began cautiously, eyes on Holt's feet, "looking for signs of the herds on the plains. I was close to the forest when I heard a noise."

My head swivelled between them. "What does this matter?" I asked.

"A noise?" Holt pushed, ignoring me.

Noah twitched. "A scream," he clarified.

"Like someone was scared?"

Noah shook his head. "No, it was more... angry, or... I don't know. Just angry, I guess."

I looked away, remembering my roar of fury when I'd thought death was only heartbeats away.

"And then?"

"I went towards where I'd heard it," Noah continued. "At the bottom of a hill, I found two... people lying on the ground." He glanced in my direction for the first time.

"Who were they?" Holt prompted him.

My jaw clenched. What was this? An interrogation? A trial? What was he doing?

"One was Mara," Noah said. "She was unconscious, bleeding from her arm."

"And the other?"

Noah hesitated, chewing his lip. "It *looked* like a person, but... its skin was grey, almost shiny. It was just lying there, not moving."

"This man, he was dead?"

"It wasn't a man." Noah turned slightly pink. "It didn't have..." He hesitated again, fumbling for the words. "Anything. Down there. Not a man, not a woman. It didn't even have hair. It was smooth, all over. Except..." He frowned. "There were carvings on it."

"What sort of carvings?" Holt was leaning forwards now, more intent.

Noah glanced sideways at me. "I don't know," he said doubtfully. "I didn't really look at them."

I kept my face deliberately smooth. From his glance, it was clear what his suspicions were, so why was he holding back?

"If you had to guess?" Holt pushed.

"I don't know," Noah insisted, his voice firm for the first time. "They were just... patterns."

Holt made a humming noise in his throat, but behind him, Set frowned. Warren's face was expressionless, though his eyes were fixed on me with unnerving focus.

"What then?" Holt asked.

"My horse didn't like the... the grey one. Wouldn't go near it. So I bound Mara's wound and brought her back."

I looked away from him again, away from all of them, out between the pillars to the south and across the sea. What would have happened if he hadn't found me? I might have been halfway home by now. Or I might never have woken up, bleeding out with no one to know, no one to burn my body, no way for me to return to the sky. Maybe that was Holt's motive—to remind me that I owed these people.

"Keera?" Holt called out, breaking my reverie.

I looked around as someone else approached us from behind. It was the tiny woman who'd passed me outside. Her short hair was lying flatter now, but her features remained just as sharp. She looked straight past me, chin raised, coming up on Noah's other side and kneeling briefly. She looked even smaller next to his lanky frame.

"I found the place Noah described," she said without prompting.

My jaw clenched.

Was this the reason I'd had to wait until today for an audience? So she could confirm Noah's story last night? That must be why she had been returning so late. My fingers tingled as I resisted the urge to clench them into fists.

"There was blood on the ground," she continued, "but no body. If it had been there, it's gone now."

"Gone?" I echoed.

Keera turned to me with sharp eyes. "Gone."

A tremor went through me from head to toe, the bruises all down my side aching. If the body was gone...

"I have to go," I said numbly. The wards could wait. The Figure's body was gone. Someone, something, must have moved it. One of its fellows, perhaps? They might have already tracked me here, already watching from outside the wall. They might already be *inside*.

I shuddered. The wards would have to wait. I had to get out. I had to *run*.

"No." Holt's objection was so unexpected that I looked up, sure I must have misheard. His expression was hard, full of suspicion.

"You don't *understand*," I growled. "My presence could put you all at risk."

"Or maybe it already has," Set said, and I glared at him. His face was apologetic rather than angry. "You said it yourself; even if you leave, it might still come here looking for you."

"So instead of taking a risk, you want to make it a certainty?"

"You say that as if letting you leave wouldn't be its own risk," Holt said.

I blinked, shocked. What did he have to fear from my departure?

"Nothing is certain," he continued. "But you..." He shook his head, raising a finger in my direction. "Something about you doesn't add up."

"This place doesn't *add up*!" I snapped, reaching the end of my tolerance. "You have a port but no trade. No ships to bring goods, no markets! You have a forest within sight of your walls but nothing made of wood! What are you doing? Cowering in a cave around some random words, hoping they'll give you the answers?"

There was a heavy silence. Holt's face darkened. His sons exchanged looks behind his back. It was their discomfort that told me how close to the truth I'd come.

"You're not hiding in a cave," I said slowly, studying their expressions. "You're hiding behind a wall." The silence was enough to tell me I was right. "Why? What are you so afraid of?"

"Monsters," Warren answered, the harsh word clashing with his simple tone.

"Monsters." The same word I'd used to describe the Figures. "Like..."

"No, not like that... thing," Noah answered the unfinished question. "They're like us, except—"

Holt stood up before Noah could finish. "Enough."

Noah fell silent at once, his shoulders hunching inwards under the king's anger. My eyes narrowed, triumphant at having finally found the secret that would galvanise Holt into action.

"Except what?" I asked, my eyes on the king. For a second, I didn't think anyone would answer, but I was proven wrong.

"Their eyes," Warren said.

His father turned on him with a hiss.

I looked at the young prince, who stared right back.

Monsters that looked the same as them, but their eyes were different.

It wasn't difficult to put together.

"Their eyes are black," I stated. Every face turned towards me; the three on the dais, Noah and Keera, the rest of the hall behind me.

I was the one to look away.

Demons. They were hiding from demons, and it couldn't be an idle decision if they were at the point when they wouldn't venture beyond the city limit or accept ships into their harbour. They stayed where they knew it was safe.

But surely nowhere was safe...

"The wall..." I muttered to myself. My head snapped back up. "The wall keeps them out?"

Holt stared at me, seemingly unable to bring himself to answer, but behind him, his sons both nodded. Warren looked eager, intense, leaning forwards. Set just seemed resigned.

My head echoed their motion as I thought. Simple stone wouldn't keep the demons out; they'd proven that many times over. There must be something else, some other force at work...

It hit me in a sudden blow, the knowledge stealing the air from my lungs and the ground from under my feet, leaving me breathless and floating. The wards that I didn't recognise. They were keeping the demons out. Wards that could repel demons.

Was this where it had all started, where our wards had come from? Everything we were meant to be, preserved in stone in a hidden corner of the world.

Once again, everything switched. The Figures could all go die underground. My life was irrelevant. If I could just get the knowledge of those wards back home...the demons would no longer be able to attack. I would carve the symbol into every rock in the city myself if I had to. We would be safe at last. We would win.

It was so simple to me, so obvious. I turned on my heel, walking away.

"Stop!" Holt's voice was like a thunderclap, but I barely heard it, lost in whirling implications.

A sudden movement in front of me brought me to a halt. Guards blocked my path, their spears held low and ready. I blinked at them, unable to fathom why anyone would stand in my way when my path was so clear. Turning, I looked back down the hall.

"The wards on that wall are keeping the demons out," I said, my voice low.

Holt's eyes flashed as he took a step forwards. "And why is that a concern of yours?"

"You think you're the only people the demons hurt?" I snapped back. "Those wards could help! I need to see them again."

"Absolutely not!" Holt strode forwards, closing the gap between us.

Warmth flowed down my arms as I drew upon my wards. If he wanted to come at me, I'd be ready for him.

Set jumped forwards, catching his father by the arm and pulling him back. Holt barely seemed to notice, not taking his eyes off me.

"You don't go near the wall," he snarled.

"That knowledge isn't yours to keep!"

"I think this meeting is over," Set said, his voice far leveller than mine or Holt's.

The king said nothing, eyes not leaving mine as his son drew him back towards the throne. I glanced at Set, whose bright blue eyes flicked pointedly towards the door. I hesitated for another second, but he was right. There was nothing more to be gained here. Lingering would only make the situation worse.

So I turned away, ignoring the wide-eyed expressions of those watching as I stalked out of the room, leaving a tense silence behind me.

6

In Search of Escape

It was a short trip from my library to my father's study. Out the door and straight along the dark corridor running along the northern edge of the citadel. There were no windows—it would have been bad luck. At the end, I turned left and found Titan and Hamma on duty outside the door, their postures relaxed, but their eyes vigilant.

"Little one," Titan acknowledged me with an easy grin.

I gave him a mock scowl. "I won't be little for long," I said, sticking my chin up. It was true; my eyes were level with his shoulders.

"Well, when you're as tall as me, I'll stop calling you that."

I frowned. He was taller than either of my parents, taller than the rest of the Guard as well. "Fine," I said, and he chuckled. "Is he busy?" I asked, looking at the door between them.

"He's working on the papers," Hamma said, his eyes skating over my face. "Everything alright?"

I nodded, unable to summon a smile with the image of Nate's bruised face still fresh in my mind. I took a step forward, then hesitated, glancing at the book in my hand. Grimacing, I placed it carefully on the floor opposite the door.

"Want us to keep an eye on that for you?" Hamma offered, a twinkle in his eye.

"Only when you have an eye to spare."

Titan let out a dramatic sigh. "Reduced to guarding books," he moaned. "What will become of us next? Holding doors and polishing floors, no doubt."

"Well, if you're offering…"

Titan grinned and opened the door for me with a deep bow, winking as I swept past him.

"You can't help yourself, can you?" Hamma asked before the door closed behind me.

The room beyond was dominated by a large desk with a high-backed chair on the other side. Two lesser chairs waited before the desk. Around the walls, boxes, piles of paper, and odd knickknacks overflowed from shelves and spilled into piles on the floor. The desk itself was meticulously ordered, each piece of parchment neatly aligned, pens cleaned and waiting, ink bottles stoppered. I knew the cleanliness was only possible because any errant items without a place would be relegated to the shelves, doomed to gather dust until they were covered over and left to suffocate.

I looked to my right, where another door stood open, showing a sliver of the smaller room beyond. Crossing the study, I stopped in the doorway. The afternoon sun was shining directly through the window and onto the table that ran the length of the room. Two benches on either side filled the rest of the width of the narrow space. There was a single chair at the far end, under the window, but my father had scorned it for one of the benches today, parchment spread over the table in front of him. His sword, Mercy, leaned against the end of the bench beside him, the silver-white blade reflecting the sunlight.

Dropping to my knees in the doorway, I tilted my head back, staring up at the ceiling as I bared my throat to my king and my father.

"Rise, my child," he said. I rolled smoothly back to my feet, lowering my gaze to meet his eyes as he set down the sheet of paper he'd been holding. He sat back on the bench as he watched me. "Under what circumstances would the Guard bow to me, rather than kneeling?" he asked.

"When they are on duty and perceive a possible threat, to which they may be less able to respond if they kneel," I said promptly.

"Good. And the rest of the population?"

"When they're insulting you."

"*Tammie.*" *He tutted, but the disapproval was lightened by the twinkle in his eyes.*

"*It's true.*"

"*Regardless.*"

I sighed. "*Bowing would be employed for less formal occasions, often in private meetings, or when the subject feels that kneeling is unnecessary, or doesn't want to convey the implied respect.*"

"*When you are queen, who will you bow to?*"

"*Other monarchs, if I deem them to be of equal or greater authority than myself.*"

"*Who will you kneel to?*"

"*No one.*"

"*And why, as my expected successor, would you kneel to me?*"

I took a breath. "*When I approach you as my king, rather than my father.*"

"*Ah.*" *Locking his fingers together on the desk, he looked at me with a mixture of pride and regret.* "*And for what reason do you come before your king?*"

"*Nathaniel.*"

"*The half-blood.*" *He made a low noise without taking his blue eyes from my brown ones.* "*What of him?*"

"*I found him in my library just now.*"

Father sat upright, his jaw clenched. "*Thank you for bringing this to my attention,*" *he said, a chill in his tone now.* "*I will deal with him.*"

I shook my head. "*I gave him permission to go in there years ago.*"

Father's eyes narrowed. "*And he has made use of that permission.*"

"*Yes.*"

"*What was different about this time?*"

"*Half of his face was the same colour as his eyes,*" *I said.*

He took a breath but didn't say anything, his gaze drifting away from me as he thought.

"*Did you forbid him to leave?*" *I blurted out.*

His eyes snapped back to me. "*I did.*"

"*And his mother too?*"

"Yes. Though she's been pushing the boundaries of that restriction recently."

I laughed bitterly. "I can't imagine why."

"Tamara..." he began, a frown on his face, but I disregarded it.

"Why do you keep them here? She'll be shunned the minute people find out what happened to her, and he refuses to visit her for fear of making it worse, but he's not safe here! Why not let them leave, live their lives somewhere else?"

"Think, Tamara, think!" my father said, his palms slapping the table. "Why do I keep them here?"

I paused, looking into his sharp eyes. "You don't trust them."

"No, I don't."

"Why not? What have they done?" I demanded.

He gave me his most disapproving look, and it still had the power to make me look away, far more effective than the loud slap of his hands earlier. "Because she hid him," he said. "For years."

"And him?"

He gave me another look. "I cannot disregard his blood," he said.

"You could have given him a chance."

"I am giving him a chance."

"A chance to be beaten? To be hunted, to be hated?"

"He has the option of defending himself."

I gave another harsh laugh. "Does he? What would you do if someone came to you with bruises and said Nathaniel caused them?"

"No one has come to me," my father said, and my fists clenched for the first time since I'd entered the room. "Someone has come to you."

I went still, staring at him.

"So," he raised an eyebrow, "what are you going to do about it?"

"Put a stop to it."

"How?"

"However I can."

He smiled. "Well, you'd better get to work then."

"You're giving me permission?"

"I am King," he said. "You are my daughter and—Thorns

willing—you will be queen one day. You have the power to change things, and you don't need my permission to use it." Our eyes met.

I nodded slowly. "Thank you," I said, turning away.

"Tamara," he called me back, his voice grave. "I know you'll make me proud."

Encouragement or warning? I wasn't sure which, but I nodded again before slipping out of the door.

Heart still pounding in my ears, I blundered through the corridors, taking turns at random. I knew I'd noted objects on plinths earlier, but my hands were shaking now, my face flushed with heat, and I couldn't recall the details. Was that chunk of rock familiar? That bowl?

At an intersection, I finally stopped, flexing my hands. That meeting couldn't have gone much worse. Not only had I failed to even begin to properly attempt to convince the king to let me leave, but my interest in the wards had goaded such anger from him that any further discussion seemed impossible. Why though? Why had my questions goaded such suspicion from him and Set?

What was I meant to do now? I hadn't gained permission to leave, and even worse, Holt had ordered me to stay away from the wall. Not that he could stop me.

The idea festered in my chest. Go to the wall, make a rough copy of the wards somehow, and then get out. Whatever the cost.

What a proud moment that would be. A triumphant return with news of powerful, previously unknown wards... and an enemy in those who held them. Angering the king and then cutting down who knew how many to escape. That would make a wonderful start to my time as queen. What if these people had more wards hidden away somewhere? My actions could destroy any chance we had of gaining that knowledge.

Thorns, what do I do? I prayed, but as always, there was only silence in response. And footsteps. Someone was coming.

I darted to the left, hoping whoever it was hadn't seen me.

"Wrong way." The voice was light with amusement.

I looked back. Warren, the king's youngest son, gave a lopsided grin.

"Assuming you're looking for the way out, that is," he continued. "Easy to get lost in here. It's hard to keep track of the direction when there are no windows."

I didn't reply, but neither did I walk away. Whilst he hadn't spoken during our last argument, Warren had gone against his father's wishes in the throne room to give me answers to my questions. He was the only member of the royal family who hadn't been concerned by my questions. Maybe he would answer some more for me.

"It's that way. Just so you know," Warren said, pointing to a different corridor.

I walked slowly back towards him. Didn't I owe it to my people to try to find a diplomatic way out of this? Warren could be the answer. Unless he was only here on his father's orders, sent to make sure I didn't go against his last decree to stay away from the wall.

"Why did you follow me?" I asked. Testing, probing.

"Like I said, easy to get lost." Warren shrugged. "And I wanted to talk to you."

"Alright," I said. "There's something I've got to do, though."

"Walk and talk?"

"Okay."

"So…" Warren began, as we walked together down the passage he'd indicated. "You put that together pretty quickly."

"Which bit?"

"The demons. You've encountered them before?" He turned right.

"Yes. Not in a good way."

"No, I doubt any encounter with them is good. Some people say their hearts are so black with hate that it shows in their eyes. They say they have nothing but darkness inside them."

I followed him around another corner. *Darkness.* The words of the supposed prophecy Noah had recited came back to me. The

90

mother who'd been in the throne room when I arrived had called me Saviour. *I know why you're here,* she'd said. But what did she mean by that? The king had dismissed her concerns about her son and said he couldn't risk sending anyone to look for him. But he'd sent Keera out to corroborate Noah's story of how he'd found me.

"Mara?"

I looked up. Warren had stopped a few steps ahead and was staring at me. I hadn't even realised I'd stopped walking.

"Is your father always that prickly?" I asked.

Warren was silent for a moment, his face suddenly cold. "He's been worse since we lost my mother," he admitted, "but he doesn't normally go off like that. I guess I wanted to apologise. I didn't want you running off after that and doing something rash. And it saves him having to send anyone else to keep track of you."

"So you *are* here to keep an eye on me." Though I would be shocked if Holt hadn't sent others after me as well.

Warren spread his hands, a winning smile suddenly blooming across his face. "I'm just here to keep you company. Maybe even provide some entertainment. If you want me to leave, I will."

"I didn't say that."

Warren grinned but didn't respond as I strode past him towards the door that led outside. We emerged through it, Warren a few paces behind me, into the courtyard Set had led me through, though on a different side. Warren was right—I'd been completely turned around inside.

Without looking back, I strode across the open space towards the gates where the soldiers I'd encountered earlier still stood. They watched us pass without comment, though I noticed the belligerent one Set had reprimanded drew back a little.

Warren remained silent as he followed me to the cave where I had slept the night before. Inside, I picked up my twin blades and slotted them into place at my hips, enjoying their comforting weight.

Having waited outside, Warren eyed the blades when I emerged.

"You know the rules about that," he said mildly.

91

"You know I don't care," I replied, echoing his tone. "Besides, your father says everyone's talking about me already anyway. What's one more thing for them to gossip about?"

Warren opened his mouth, then sighed and closed it again. "Fine. Please don't stab anyone."

My mouth twitched.

As we emerged from the caves, I paused, staring across the roofs of the city below to the wall beyond. The sun had risen over the mountains now, and I could just about make out some of the wards coiling over the stone. Warren said nothing as I stared hungrily at them. I should have just made a copy last night and then left immediately. What would he do if I were to head to the wall now? Or any of my other followers. I was sure they existed.

Not yet, I decided. Between the man beside me and the woman who said she would wait for me by the sea, I still had options.

With my weapons at my sides, I received even more stares as we descended into the city. Warren's presence by my side didn't prevent mutters from adults as we passed. The gangs of children running wild through the streets watched us with wide eyes as we headed south.

"You don't trade anything," I remarked as we passed an intersection with a wide courtyard that would have been perfect for a marketplace. "Even within the city."

"No. Not on a large scale, anyway."

"What about things you don't have enough of? Like wood." I didn't mention the entire *forest* within sight of their wall. "Who decides where that goes?"

"People petition to Father," Warren explained. "He decides where it's most needed and sees that it's distributed fairly."

"What if people disagree with his decisions?"

"He's king. What are they going to do? People might grumble a little bit, but that's as far as it goes." Warren gave a tight smile. "The thing about having an outside enemy is that it pulls people together. Why waste energy fighting amongst ourselves and do

92

their work for them?"

We emerged onto the main thoroughfare through the city at almost the same spot where I'd seen Keera returning last night. I couldn't stop myself from hesitating briefly, looking towards the gates to freedom and the secrets of the wall around it.

Behind me, Warren shifted. I blinked, looking away quickly. I wondered if I should ask him about the wards now? After the reaction I'd gotten from Holt and Set, even though Warren hadn't shown the same emotions, something told me to hold my tongue. At least until I had more of an idea about *why* my enquiry had caused such suspicion from the other two.

I continued walking, Warren shadowing me silently between the last few buildings to emerge onto the wharf. A little way to the left, the mother with frizzy hair was waiting, her head turning as she scanned the area.

I know why you're here… Her whispered words in the throne room returned to me and my heart jolted. This woman had answers.

Her eyes lit up when she noticed me, and she took a step forward. I stopped her with a swift shake of my head and held up a finger to tell her to wait. I could hardly interrogate her with Warren beside me. She nodded, though her eyes never left me as I turned to follow Warren already walking the other way along the wharf.

Ahead, the harbour ended in a smooth curve. Beyond it, between the water and the warded wall, was a strip of land. Along the base of the wall were more planting beds for crops, obscuring the lowest edge of the wards. But in front of them, a large, roughly circular area covered in fine yellow sand was kept clear. On the edge closest to the buildings, I recognised the blacksmith, Bardok, standing beside two racks of swords. He was holding up one of the weapons, the metal glinting in the sun, as he spoke to two younger boys.

It was towards the opposite edge, however, that Warren was heading, where a larger group had gathered. As we approached, I saw the short blond woman, Keera, making her way over to join them. My steps slowed.

"What's this?" I asked Warren's back.

He turned, a wild grin lighting up his face. "Training," he said triumphantly. "I thought you might want to join us."

I jerked to a stop at once. He wanted to see what I could do with my wards, to pass that information back to his father. Did he think I was so naive as to give away my secrets like that? Not that my abilities themselves were a secret, I begrudgingly admitted.

"Training for what?" I asked, unable to stop the coldness seeping into my voice.

Warren, having noticed my sudden halt, had already turned. His grin didn't fade, unaware of my suspicion. "To fight against the demons," he announced.

I said nothing, my head cocking sideways as I stared at him. He was human. Nothing more. No wards, no way to match the demons' powers. How could he be so deluded as to think he, to think *any of them*, could stand against the demons?

"It can be done," Warren continued, misinterpreting my silence. "They're not invincible, Mara. I've seen them bleed."

I've seen them die, a part of me wanted to retort. But I had wards. He didn't.

"How?" I asked. He couldn't mean *he* had taken up arms against them, surely. Maybe he'd witnessed an argument?

Warren glanced over his shoulder, to where the group was watching us. Waiting for him, I realised. Regardless, he took a step closer to me, leaving them waiting.

"It was a couple of years ago," he began. "My grandfather died. Father's father. We carried him out to the pyre, me and Set and Father."

They burned their dead as well. The knowledge twisted something inside me.

"Out?" I repeated. "Outside the wall?"

Warren nodded. "We would always hold the service on the plains. We thought they understood what was going on because they never came when we were out there for that. Not once." His jaw tensed, eyes shifting past me, staring into the past. "Until then. It

94

was right when Mother lit the pyre. Everyone was screaming, trying to run, but it was like they were everywhere. No one knew where to go. And you wouldn't even know one was there until they turned around and looked right at you."

I didn't need to read the haunted anger on Warren's face to guess the outcome. Isolated, confused, without the means to fight back... It must have been carnage.

"But there was one," Warren continued, his voice still low but rich with intensity. "He got me—" he gestured fleetingly to the scar across his face "—but I got him too. If they can bleed, they can die. So that's what we're going to do."

At my continued silence, Warren's shoulders slumped.

"You think it's a stupid idea, too."

My eyes narrowed. "Who has said that?"

Warren crossed his arms, eyes dropping to his feet as they scuffed at the ground. "Father," he admitted in a mutter. "And Set. But it's like you said! We can't just hide behind the wall. We have to do *something*. For everyone we..." His sudden return to animation faltered.

"Everyone you've lost?"

He nodded.

"How many people died that day?"

Warren's eyes fell again. "Fifty-six."

I sucked in a breath. This wasn't a large place. That must have had a significant impact on their population.

"That was when Father shut everything down," Warren continued. "Since then, almost no one goes outside the city. No one even objected to it. Last year, there were more guards than woodcutters. The hunters and scouts still go out, keeping track of the herds, but Father doesn't like it. He's always really tense until they come back. It's only a matter of time until he orders that to stop too. And I've tried to tell him that we could make a difference, but he won't even acknowledge that we've been training!"

Shoulders heaving, Warren ran a hand through his hair, a gesture that reminded me of Nate, and let out a deep sigh, as if breathing all the pent-up emotion out of himself.

"You know, the worst part isn't even his dismissal; I'm used to that," Warren continued bitterly. "It's that he thinks it's working, keeping everyone shut up in here. It's like he doesn't understand what it's costing us."

"Is it working?"

Warren hesitated at that, clearly not having expected the question.

"How many people have you lost since the order to stay inside?" I pushed. I couldn't blame Holt for the decision. For all Warren's passionate words, it was still madness. There was no way they could realistically stand against the demons.

"Three," Warren admitted sullenly. "Well, four now, with Rhianna's son. But that's different."

"Why?"

Warren shrugged, looking away. "There's no one to blame but him. He's been seen in some rough circles. People who can be counted on to do anything."

"What do you mean?"

"Poachers. We barely have room to grow crops inside the wall. We can't keep animals for meat too. When herds move through, we take some of them, but there's a limit to what's sustainable. People want more, and where there's demand, people will find a way to fill it.

"We never catch anyone at it, so we can't prove anything, but it's no secret some people will sneak out and hunt in the forest. It's madness, but no one is going to turn the food away. We traded the ability to farm outside for the safety of staying inside, but it's driven some people in a dangerous direction."

"Why doesn't your father put a stop to it? If he's so opposed to anyone else going out, why are they an exception?" I asked. Internally, I was picturing the gates and all the soldiers I'd seen guarding them last night. Surely these poachers weren't 'sneaking out', as Warren put it, through that way…

"He doesn't *allow* it, as such. But no one will name those who are involved, whether because of the threat of repercussions or the risk of losing their source. Plus, there's the group aspect. If one person talks and the hunters are stopped, everyone who is currently benefiting will be furious. They keep each other in line. We have suspicions, but Father doesn't want to move too heavily against them in case it causes unrest. Malcolm, Rhianna's son, had been spending a lot of time with a group we're fairly sure is behind most of it and now…" He spread his hands hopelessly. "He's gone."

"So, you think he went outside the wall and the demons killed him. And Holt doesn't want to risk any more lives by sending more people out to look for him."

"Yeah, that about sums it up."

"But he was willing to send that other woman, Keera, outside to check Noah's story. Oh, sorry—*my* story."

Warren met my accusatory gaze. "That's different."

"Is it?"

"Either Malcolm's dead, or he'll find his own way back. There's nothing for us to do about it either way."

"What if he is still alive?"

"If he's injured or something—which is a slim probability—he knew what he was doing, the risk he was taking. He's on his own."

I looked away, crossing my arms as I stared across the harbour.

"There's nothing to be done for Malcolm," Warren said again, more gently this time. "Look, why don't you come and meet everyone?" He took a step backwards, towards the group still waiting on the edge of the sandy area.

I snorted. "And what do you imagine that would accomplish? My participation is hardly going to persuade Holt this is a worthwhile activity. In case you didn't notice, I don't think he likes me much."

"Maybe not," Warren agreed. "But it might encourage other people to take an interest."

Other people… Why did I suspect he had a certain, specific group in mind when he said that?

"Maybe later." I took a step back.

"Come on. What else are you going to do?"

"I thought you said you didn't follow me to babysit me," I

challenged him.

Warren hesitated, then shrugged. "As you like it." With that, he turned and walked away, towards the huddle of people who were all staring at us.

I held their gaze for a moment, then glanced back over my shoulder. Along the wharf, Rhianna was still waiting.

I know why you're here, she'd said. What information did she hold? Did she know something about what Noah had seen out on the plains? Or was it something different?

She'd also called me Saviour.

Set had warned me away from those who did so. Noah had echoed the same sentiment. I turned and made my way back along the wharf towards her.

7

A Darker Time

Nathaniel was gone. I froze just inside the door, staring at the spot where he had stood, his face bruised and battered. After Father dismissed me, I rushed back to my library as fast as I could. Not fast enough. He had already slipped away. For a moment, I wavered, rubbing my short fingernails and considering my options.

I know you'll make me proud.

Back straightening, I turned on my heel and, for the first time, went searching for the half-blood.

Over the next two days, I learned my knowledge of the city was not as extensive as I'd thought. There were plenty of places where I knew someone could hide, and I found many more of them, but all were equally devoid of the one I was searching for.

I didn't ask anyone if they'd seen Nathaniel, not wanting to give away who I was looking for or face questions about why, but the end of each day left me firmer in the knowledge that either he was outside of the city or could hide far better than I could seek. In the end, it was more by luck than skill that I found him.

A flash of sandy hair disappearing through a shadowed doorway into an old storeroom ignited a flare of triumph in my chest. My strides lengthened as I hurried after him, dodging around the last few traders packing up their goods for the day.

I was halfway to the door when another group beat me to it, piling through the doorway and out of view, so intent on their goal they didn't even look around. Frowning, I jogged across the market square and ducked into the dark passage.

Out of the bright light, the group seemed to have relaxed, and I could hear them jeering ahead of me. Their taunts and calls in the darkness lit an angry fire in my chest, flushing my face with its heat as I closed in on the pursuers.

"Come out, come out, you little bastard!"

The shout from ahead spurred me faster. I could see the light of a torch ahead of me, the flames flickering around the cavern at the end of the passage.

"Nothing here, Nic."

"Keep looking. It's in here somewhere."

By the time I arrived, they had spread out, tossing the contents of the storeroom aside in their search. Sacks, both full and empty, were now strewn over the floor, crates and barrels shoved aside, teetering dangerously at the limits of their balance.

"Hey!"

They all whipped around at my shout, stunned to see me planted in the middle of the passage. All were significantly older than I was, probably in their late twenties, but none of their faces were familiar to me.

The one furthest away, holding the flickering torch aloft to peer behind a stack of crates, recovered first.

"Tamara," he said. He turned to face me but didn't move away from the spot by the wall, addressing me across the rest of the group. "You shouldn't be here. It's dangerous. Go back to the citadel. Don't worry—we've got it under control."

He had a wide face and a harsh jaw softened by the shadow of a beard. There was anger etched around his dark eyes at my interruption, though his voice was light and soothing. It stirred a memory in the back of my mind, but I couldn't place where I had heard it before.

"Really? Dangerous enough to need seven of you to deal with it?" I asked, raising an eyebrow as I gestured around at them all. I crossed my arms. "Nathaniel, won't you come and join us?"

For a moment, there was silence. Would he do as I'd asked, or would his wariness take precedence?

There was a rustle from the far corner of the ceiling, then Nathaniel dropped into view, landing on a stack of crates that wobbled under his weight. He hesitated then jumped down, looking past the seven men to meet my gaze. His face, still bearing fading bruises, was doubtful, but he held his ground under the weight of hate-filled stares.

"I see no danger here," I said calmly to their leader, whose hand had tightened on the torch he held. "Certainly nothing requiring you to keep it 'under control'." I twisted his words, sneering them back at him. His fellows shifted nervously as they glanced between us.

The leader smiled, the expression sitting well on his face, crinkling his stubble-covered chin. "You don't understand—"

"Don't I?" I cut him off.

"How could you? You have no idea what he's capable of." The smile was gone now, his tone hard. "You're just a child; you don't even have your wards yet. Leave this to the adults to sort out."

My arms twitched, the muscles where my wards would one day be contracting at his words. I didn't move my eyes from his. "You know who I am. You know who I'm going to become. And I promise you, I'll remember you." I let my eyes flicker sideways, making a point to examine every face. "All of you. So, unless you want me to be even more displeased than I currently am, I suggest you get out." I stepped to the side of the passage, leaving the exit clear.

None of them moved. They looked to their leader, watching to see what he would do. Even Nathaniel was focused on him, his dark eyes narrowed. The ringleader was still watching me, weighing up his options.

"Leave," I ordered, my voice cold. "Now."

He looked once more at Nathaniel, then turned away, taking a step forward. I let out a relieved breath, my shoulders dropping just as he whipped back around. The head of the torch painted fire through the air before it smashed into Nathaniel in an eruption of angry sparks.

Furious words were born and died on my lips, insignificant against *the roar that split the world.*

A shape flew across the room as a dark creature lashed out.

The leader hit the far wall with a thud and slumped to the floor. His companions let out shocked cries, one of them taking a step towards him.

A second roar froze them in place. All eyes were fixed on the creature standing where Nathaniel had been only seconds before.

Taller than any of us by an easy head-and-a-half, the light from the dropped torch reflected off the shiny surface of its inky-black skin. Twisted horns made its head look too big for its body, casting elongated shadows over the wall.

I took an instinctive step backwards, eyes wide. I'd been told about how the demons could transform into monsters like this, beasts of raw rage and power, but never dreamed there could be one lurking under Nathaniel's skin. It suddenly dawned on me that I didn't really know the boy at all.

The creature snarled again. Another arm lashed out, smashing a crate, sending shards of wood flying through the air towards us, grain pouring onto the floor in a steady hiss.

I ducked as a fragment of wood flew past me and heard a yelp from one of the men who hadn't been so lucky. In the brief silence that followed, I risked a glance up as I straightened. At the movement, the creature's eyes, as dark as its skin, fixed on me. There was no recognition in their gaze, no hint of mercy.

One of the men started whimpering. The monster's head swivelled around, unsure who to focus on. I squared my shoulders. Much as I despised what these men had been intending, they were still citizens of this city. And I had called Nathaniel out of his hiding place. This was my responsibility. My fault.

I cleared my throat. The black eyes snapped to me and a low growl rumbled through the room, vibrating in my chest.

"The three of you further back, get out. Slowly," I said, advancing cautiously closer to the creature.

"Tamara... don't," one of them whispered.

"Go now," I said. Out of the corner of my eye, I saw them make their shuffling escape. Black eyes glinted in the firelight, and I moved forward again, bending to pick up the dropped torch.

The growling intensified. Black lips peeled back from pointed teeth.

"The rest of you," I said, retreating a step. "Get him—" I flicked the fingers of my free hand at the unconscious figure "—and take him out."

They obeyed without question, flinching as the creature swayed, its focus flicking between the men and myself. My palms were sweaty as they gripped the wooden torch, the fire dancing to the tune of my trembling hands.

Down the dark passage behind me, I could hear a distant commotion. The other three must have raised the alarm. From the way the monster hissed, tensing its arms, I knew it had heard it too. Now it was moving, it seemed unable to stop, prowling from side to side.

I swayed on the spot, mirroring its pacing. My mouth was dry. I resisted the urge to cough and held my ground until the trio was behind me, grunting with the effort of dragging their co-conspirator along the passage. Then I was alone with the beast.

With nothing else to distract it, it turned its full focus to me, planting its feet and hissing angrily.

I took a step back, not running away but trying not to pressure it either.

"Down there! It's down there!" someone shouted, and the sound of running footsteps approached.

I flinched, spinning to look behind me. The movement took the flaming torch closer to the beast and there was another roar, another flash of dark movement. Pain raked across my forearm, the torch dropping to the ground as I cried out.

"Tamara!" Titan burst into the room, at my side in an instant, blade gleaming in the firelight. "Are you alright? What happened? How did it get in? Where is it?"

My left hand clamped around my bleeding right arm, I looked past him. At first glance, the room appeared to be empty. Where had the *creature gone?*

"There," I croaked, pointing with my shaking hand at the patch of darkness in the furthest corner.

"It's going to be alright," Titan said grimly, swooping down to pick up the torch I'd dropped and holding it aloft in his free hand. "You need to lea—"

He fell suddenly silent as the light slid over the creature in the corner, who hissed at us both.

"Is that Nate?" Titan asked, shocked.

I blinked, gaping at his back.

"How..." My voice trailed off. I could find no resemblance between the black-skinned beast and the sandy-haired boy. How could Titan possibly have recognised him?

"What happened?" Titan asked, his blade lowering as he stared across the room. The creature stared back, teeth still showing, but now silent.

"There were people going to hurt him, and I followed—to stop them. And I tried to get them to leave, but they wouldn't, and one of them hit him with the torch and..."

Titan glanced from the creature to the burning torch he was holding, then turned to me, showing his back to the creature.

"Hold this," he said, thrusting the torch at me.

I took it instinctively with my right hand. He caught my wrist, looking at the four gashes across it and the blood smeared over my skin before he turned away with a grimace. Sheathing his sword, he stepped forwards, his shadow casting a patch of darkness over the creature who bared its teeth again as he drew nearer.

I wanted to shout out a warning, to tell him not to, but I bit it back, unwilling to risk spooking the creature with Titan so close.

"Hey, kid," Titan said softly, his words barely reaching my ears. "Rough day, huh?"

The beast growled again, a warning. Titan disregarded the sound, taking another step forward. It was one step too far. The thing that had been Nathaniel lashed out, impossibly fast.

Titan was faster. In a blur of motion, he stepped past the blow, slapping the muscular arm aside as it sailed past him before dodging in close. One fist snapped out to deliver a sharp blow to the creature's forehead. They stepped apart, the creature shaking its head, eyes closed. Titan had one hand on the hilt of his weapon, but he didn't draw it.

"Don't make me do it, Nate. I know it's you. Come on now."

There was another growl in lieu of a response, but I imagined the sound held less anger. The creature turned aside, shoulders hunched over.

"Come back, Nate. It's not worth it. You know it's not."

The creature retreated further, shivering as Titan cautiously released his sword again.

"Nate? Come on, come back."

It happened all at once.

The skin lightened, the horns shrank, the claws retracted into fingers, and Nathaniel slumped sideways, falling to the floor, his eyes open but unseeing. Titan crouched over him as I stepped cautiously closer.

"Aww, kid," Titan muttered, turning Nathaniel's limp head, the torchlight falling on his bruises, "what happened to your face?" Twisting around, he looked back up at me. "Are you okay?"

I nodded, too stunned to speak.

"Let's get out of here," Titan said grimly. He heaved Nathaniel up and pulled one of his arms over his shoulders.

I dropped the torch and slipped under his other arm, taking some of his weight. I held my right arm held aside, blood dripping off my fingers.

We were almost at the exit when we met Orion and Ishmael, both with their weapons drawn. The twins stopped abruptly at the sight of us.

"Ty?" Orion asked in bewilderment, but Titan shook his head, and we kept walking, Nathaniel slumped between us.

Stepping out into the light after the gloomy passage felt like waking from a nightmare. But the blood was still sticky on my fingers, Nathaniel was still unresponsive beside me, and the nightmare was seeping into the real world.

Rhianna came to meet up. I didn't stop as we met but kept walking along the wharf, waving for her to join me.

"Saviour," she breathed, shadowing my footsteps.

"You said that you know why I'm here," I said, not looking at her. I was scanning the buildings next to us on the wharf, peering down the alleys between them for eavesdroppers.

Rhianna stopped. I continued for a couple of paces before turning to face her. "There has never been a darker time," she said, her eyes fixed on mine. "My partner was lost. Now my son. *She will come with the darkness, bringing the light.* You're going to save him."

For a moment, I just stared at her. Was that it? She knew nothing. Nothing except her own twisting of the situation, thinking I was useful to her. But she could still be useful to me too.

"Please," she continued. "I can't lose him too."

I gave her a gentle smile. "Of course, I will help you. I'll do everything I can to find him."

"Oh, thank you, thank you!"

I took her arm, drawing her forwards again. "I need to know everything about the last time you saw him. When was it? What was he doing? Where was he going?"

"It was two days ago, in the evening. He didn't mention where he was going, just left and never came back."

That was worthless. I didn't have time for subtlety. Pulling us both to a halt again, I gave her a serious look. "Warren told me they suspect Malcolm has been meeting with a group of poachers."

"He's a good boy. He wouldn't mean to get into any trouble, I swear."

"I believe you," I hushed her. "But I need you to tell me who he was meeting."

She withdrew slightly, her eyes dropping.

"They might know more about where he was last seen or have seen him more recently," I pushed. They also knew how to get out of the city without the king knowing about it, but there was no

106

reason to mention that.

"I... I don't know."

"Anything at all. Anyone he was hanging around with? Any new friends? Anywhere he started going recently?"

"I *can't*," she whispered, her eyes flicking up towards me, laden with more than doubt. She was scared. "I shouldn't... Maybe the king will send out a search party."

She tried to step back, pulling away from me. I tightened my grip on her arms. "You know he won't," I said, lowering my tone to a growl. I turned my shoulder towards her releasing one of her arms to push up my sleeve at the same time, so my wards were right in front of her face. "You know what these mean."

She didn't, of course, not really, but I drew hard on the markings, letting the dark tendrils unfurl under my skin. Her eyes went wide, breath catching as she stared. I could imagine how it would look to someone who hadn't seen it before, the edges of the black wards blurring like smoke under my skin, writhing to be free.

"I am the best chance Malcolm has," I said. "The longer we wait, the less likely it is that I can help him."

Rhianna wasn't trying to pull away any longer. I let go of her arms, stepping backwards as I released the draw on my wards, feeling the warmth fade.

Rhianna's jaw was clenched, her eyes on my wards, but the fear lingered on her face. Scared, but not desperate enough to break. Not yet.

"You have to decide," I said. "I can't do anything for your son unless you're willing to help me."

She remained silent, eyes flickering.

Pursing my lips, I turned and walked away.

I didn't look back as I retraced my steps along the wharf. Once Rhianna realised that Holt wasn't going to help her, she would surely be willing to tell me exactly who her son had been meeting with. But until then, my options were limited.

I *could* return to the wall and try to make a copy of the wards. I

107

might even succeed before anyone could stop me. But the unknown design was painfully intricate, with seamless swirls and whorls expanding from the main spiral. If it had been a simple design, like the strength ward, it might have been possible.

But such actions would have consequences. It was hardly surprising that Holt was reluctant to give up such secrets. From his reaction in the throne room earlier, it was obvious he was uncomfortable with my interest in the wards. Who knew what retaliation he might deem acceptable for any attempted theft of the knowledge? Whilst I hadn't spotted anyone following me, I doubted Warren was the only one who had pursued me from the throne room. The king's eyes would be watching me, whether I saw them or not. I could only hope they hadn't been close enough to overhear my conversation with Rhianna.

I needed something now to distract them, to lull them into thinking I'd abandoned my quest for knowledge or freedom, in favour of obeying Holt's orders.

I blinked. I'd reached the end of the stone wharf some time ago and now stood staring blankly across the open space, not realised what I was looking at. Warren and his group were training almost directly in front of me, half of them engaged in pairs, striking at each other with wooden practice weapons, the other half watching, shouting suggestions or encouragement. An idea stirred inside me.

Holt wouldn't be fooled by complete compliance. I'd already shown him I wasn't to be cowed. But there was a chance I could divert his attention with a different form of rebellion, and here was Warren, having already invited me to participate in an activity Holt disapproved of. Maybe Warren wanted to use me to gain favour among those who called me 'Saviour' but that didn't mean I couldn't use him too. The flash of guilt I felt was only momentary.

Focused now, I watched the group for the first time.

They were slow. Without wards to draw on, their arms and legs were sluggish, as if they were wading through water. Compared to them, Nate would have been a trail of smoke, dancing on a breeze.

My jaw clenched. Holt was right; there was no way they could stand against the demons. All the training in the world was pointless. They would never be good enough.

But they're still trying.

I paused, some of the tension seeping out of my jaw as I examined the thought. It was surely a special level of courage to be willing to face those odds and keep on trying. Warren knew the danger and knew his limitations, but he wasn't shying away. He wasn't hiding in the woods, avoiding his responsibilities. Fingers of shame clenched around my stomach, twisting.

Maybe Warren wanted to use me, and maybe I wanted to use him. But that didn't mean I couldn't help at the same time.

Warren didn't immediately notice me approach the sandy training ring. He was facing away, watching Keera fighting against an older man, his arms crossed. It was the others who turned, shifting nervously at the sight of me, waiting.

Only when Keera caught sight of me, dancing backwards to disengage from her opponent and turning towards me, did Warren look around. Behind him, Keera did not lower her weapon as I moved toward them.

Warren turned to face me, arms falling to his sides. The rest of the group, probably a dozen in total, hovered around us, pressing closer without daring to approach.

"You're right," I said, directing the words at Warren. "They can be fought. They can be killed. I've done it."

Warren's eyes blazed, his shoulders tightening as his head lifted.

"But you can't do it like this." I glanced around now, inviting them all to listen. "The demons are faster than you. Much faster. You only have two options; outnumber them or take them by surprise."

"You mean trick them?" a woman with bushy brown hair pulled back from her young face asked with a frown.

I nodded. "Tricks and lies can be your best weapons."

"And that's all you've got to offer, is it?" Keera's words were blunt and cold. Behind Warren, she still held her wooden practice weapon half-raised in front of her. "No, thank you."

I didn't bother moving aside, just stared at her over Warren's shoulder. She stared right back.

"You think you can do this alone?" I challenged her.

She gestured with her sword. "We've been managing just fine without you."

"Yes. Against each other. Do you want to know how much that will help you against them?"

I didn't wait for an answer.

Heat bloomed down my arms and across my back as I darted around Warren, lunging across the space between us to snatch her weapon from her grip. I was two steps away before she flinched, jumping backwards as if I couldn't have caught up to her in a heartbeat.

The rest of the group recoiled from my sudden movement as well, several retreating. Warren had spun on the spot, eyes wide as he stared at me, but didn't pull away.

"I'm sure you're great against each other," I said to Keera. "But you can't be ready to face them unless you practice against someone comparable." Gripping her weapon by the blunted tip, I held it out to her. "But if you'd rather carry on by yourselves…"

Keera said nothing, eyeing the weapon I offered suspiciously before glancing at Warren.

"Can you teach us to move that fast?" Warren asked.

I waited until Keera reached out and took her weapon back before I answered. "No. There are some things I can't pass on. But I will do what I can."

"Can't or won't?" Keera asked.

"Both," I said, without looking at her.

"What did you mean about tricking them?" one of the others, a young man with a wide face and a strong jaw, shaded with ginger stubble, spoke up from the back of the group.

I took a moment, gathering my thoughts before I answered. The group breathed in the silence, their focus pressing in on me. "Your best chance will always be in numbers," I began. "To work

110

together in groups to overwhelm one of them. But there might be instances when that's not possible. You might be cornered or alone. You might not even have any weapons."

The faces around me were grim as I set out the scenario.

"Sounds pretty hopeless, doesn't it? And it could be. So act like it. Cry, cower, beg. Be as pitiful and non-threatening as you can. Then, at the first opportunity you get, strike and strike hard."

"You just said we didn't have any weapons," Keera pointed out.

"I did. But that doesn't mean you're unarmed. If you punch someone in the nose, demon or not, their eyes are going to start watering. That could give you a chance to get away."

"You want us to go hand-to-hand with them?" The young woman with bushy hair looked sceptical.

"If there's no other choice, yes. Preferably without them realising what you're about to do."

"And that's what you do, is it?" Keera sneered.

"I have."

"And what happened?"

"I'm still here."

She scowled as she looked away.

"It will not be easy," I said, raising my voice. "These are demons you're facing. They're faster than you. Stronger than you. But that doesn't mean you can't win."

I looked around at the group, watching doubt and fear harden into determination. Beyond them, over by the building lining the wharf, a small crowd had already gathered. Some watched with interest, others impassively, as if our actions were nothing more than a mildly entertaining spectacle. It would be one of those, or more, who would report back to the king. I forced myself not to smile as I turned away.

"So," I said to the group. "Have any of you fought hand-to-hand much?"

There was a brief pause.

"I broke Aaron's nose last year," one of the men said with a quick grin at another who scowled back, but without anger. Now I

111

looked for it, his nose was slightly crooked.

"Anything more than brawling?" I clarified. I wanted to look at Warren, to question this lapse in their training, but I resisted. Maybe they thought it wasn't effective or useful enough to bother.

At the back, one hand went up. It was the bushy-haired woman, her fingers barely above her head, looking around as if searching for another volunteer to spare her. I was half tempted to do the same. If I had guessed which of them would be most likely to respond, she would not have been high on the list.

Regardless, I moved through the group toward her. She was shorter than I'd estimated but not as tiny as Keera, her eyes roughly level with my mouth. The rest turned to watch, huddling around.

"What's your name?" I asked.

"Rosita."

The word was so quiet I almost missed it, the sound of the waves snatching at the whisper.

"Alright then." I stood facing her, sideways on to the rest of the group and raised my right hand, my palm extended towards her.

Her eyes went wide, darting from my hand to my face, shoulders hunching further in towards her body.

"Haven't got all day," I said gently, so the others couldn't hear. "Go on." I tapped my palm with the fingers of my left hand.

Rosita glanced sideways to where everyone was watching her, then drew in a deep breath. She took half a step backwards, putting her right foot behind her left as she raised her hands in front of her face. Eyes focused now, fixed on my palm, she struck.

It was a good hit, the knuckles of her fist connecting firmly with my palm. I yielded to the hit, letting it push my hand back towards my shoulder.

"Good." I smiled at her, and she flushed slightly. "Again."

She obliged, another smack echoing around the group. Nodding to her, I dropped my hand, turning to face the others.

"What do you notice about Rosita's form? What does she do?"

"She's fast," Keera spoke first, and Rosita ducked her head,

112

blushing further.

"Yes, absolutely. There's no point dawdling. Commit and act. What else?"

"Right foot is further back."

I didn't spot who spoke this time, but I nodded anyway. "Excellent. Swap places with me," I said to Rosita, quickly spinning around so she was on my left. "Give me a target."

She obliged, raising her hand as I had done. I sank into the same stance she had been in, right foot further back, hands raised in front of my chin. My left arm stung where the Figure had cut it, and I spared a moment to be grateful the wound wasn't on my right arm.

"You want the foot that corresponds with your dominant hand to be further back," I said, stamping my right foot to draw their attention to it. "And when you punch, you *twist* your hips, giving you the most power possible." I demonstrated, giving a much slower punch than Rosita had so they could see what I was doing. "You're not just punching with your arm. Turn your shoulders, turn your hips, use your feet—you can even twist on your toes to get some extra power.

"You'll also notice," I said, gesturing for Rosita to return to the group, "that when we give each other a target, we're using the same hand, so it's on the opposite side from the other's perspective. We're punching *across* our bodies, using that twist of the hips as much as possible."

There were nods throughout the group, acknowledging my words.

"One more thing: where are our hands before we punch?"

"Up. In front of your face," Warren said from his spot on the far left of the group.

"Exactly. Doing so allows us to protect ourselves, our face, neck, chest, and also maintain good form when we're punching. But think about what I was saying earlier, about being cornered by a demon. Why could having your hands up be a bad thing in that scenario?"

113

"The demon might guess what you're going to do," Rosita said from where she'd slotted herself back into the group.

I smiled at her again. "Exactly. Your best bet is to try *not* to look like you're going to, and then don't hold back. Alright. Line up in height order and then get into pairs. We'll start practising with your hands up first, then work on the best way to get in a good shot without letting on what you're about to do."

They were willing students, listening to my coaching and putting it into practice without hesitation. I started them off with one out of each pair giving targets for the others to hit, then swapped them over, letting them all feel the difference in the power delivered by having one foot further back.

When they stepped apart again, I walked down the middle of the group, watching absent hands massaging palms or knuckles.

"It hurts," I said, nodding at one man's hands.

He immediately dropped them back to his sides.

"There's no point pretending otherwise." Reaching the other end, I turned, making sure every pair of eyes was focused on me. "This is dangerous in itself. Your hands hurt now, when you've been working together, giving a yielding surface. It will hurt a lot more if you manage to hit a cheekbone or a rib. You could break a knuckle." I looked into every face, holding their eyes. "I don't tell you this to put you off or make you hold back but to warn you that this should be used only as a last resort. If you have weapons, use them. If you can retreat, do. But if you can't, don't ever forget your hands. You are never without the means to fight back."

I looked up and down the lines one last time, my eyes lingering on the prince. "Any questions?"

Only when more than half of them were too tired to hold their stances any longer did I call a halt. They gathered around, faces weary but pleased. They'd done better than I had in my first lesson and had improved fast, following not only my instructions on how to appear scared and unthreatening, then suddenly attack, but

114

exchanging tips between themselves as well.

I'd learnt things too. A few names had stuck to the images of their faces. Aaron, with the broken nose under sharp eyes that never strayed far from me. Jory, who'd admitted to breaking Aaron's nose. Andy, the oldest of the group, with grey hair but steady hands and a quick tongue. I had yet to learn any other names, but they all looked to Warren for guidance and acknowledgement.

"You've done well," I said, looking around at them all. "Remember what we've done here. You don't have to go around punching things to practice but think the movements through in your head. Let your mind know what to do, then your body can follow.

"Don't get overconfident, though. This isn't going to take a demon down. This is what you'll use to distract them, to make them pull back, to make them pause, to surprise them." I looked around the group, seeing a mix of expressions, ranging from apprehensive to excited to unreadable.

"Alright," Warren said, stepping out of the group and clapping his hands, the knuckles of which were red. "Same time tomorrow."

They left slowly, murmuring among themselves. I looked beyond them, at the silent crowd gathered along the wharf. They'd been there the whole time, constantly moving as people joined or left the group. I'd lost track of them as I'd focused on teaching but thought I recognised a few of the faces who had remained all afternoon. As if they had nothing better to do. Or as if they had a reason beyond curiosity which invited them to linger.

When I looked at them directly, most of the crowd scattered, falling over each other in their haste to look busy. A few held my gaze, rapt.

I turned away, walking to the edge of the circle where I'd left my blades. I strapped them on before picking up my loose over-shirt and pulling it over my head, covering the dark ink on my shoulders as Warren came up beside me.

"Thank you," he said.

"I'm going to regret this, aren't I?"

"No," he said, his voice firm. "You're helping us."

Exactly, I thought to myself. And you're not going to want me to leave while I'm useful to you.

8

Diplomacy

The walk back to the citadel seemed to take a long time. I felt lost, the familiar surroundings blurring into cold indistinct shapes. Everyone we passed stopped to watch us, their eyes roving over the purple band tied around Titan's arm, the blood dripping down my hand, and the limp boy between us.

I'd never been more relieved to climb the steps to the large doors into the citadel. We passed the throne room and turned left, then immediately right, shuffling into the medic's room. Large windows along the back wall overlooked the medicinal gardens. The room was smaller than the bustling hub in the city but far more private.

Five empty beds sat along the wall opposite the windows. We lowered Nathaniel onto the one furthest from the door, where he instantly curled up into a ball, arms inside his knees. I stood, staring at him, my arm throbbing, the dull pulse echoing with the memories of what just happened.

Lucia, the woman who ruled the medics with an iron fist, came striding in from the open door leading directly to the gardens, soil-encrusted hands on her hips. "What's this?" she demanded, her eyes flicking between the three of us.

The snap of her voice made me flinch. I looked away from Nathaniel, taking what felt like my first breath in hours.

A gaggle of medics, armed with various gardening implements, swarmed around the open doorway.

Lucia moved forward, but Titan stepped between her and

Nathaniel.

"Take care of her arm," he said firmly.

Lucia glanced at me, her eyes finding the blood smeared across my arm. She threw another angry glance at Titan. He didn't budge. She bustled away, calling one of the girls over before leaving through the internal door. I suspected I knew where she was going.

"Sit down," the girl said, pointing at the bed adjacent to Nathaniel.

I opened my mouth, but Titan gave me a look, and I sat, letting the girl prod at my arm. Titan grabbed a chair from the other side of the room and sat next to Nathaniel, watching us.

"You don't have any of your wards yet?" the girl asked.

I shook my head mutely, but then a thought occurred to me, and my head snapped up. "This won't stop me from getting them, will it?"

"Are you scheduled already?"

"Not yet. At least a few months away, Master Atticus said."

"Then it shouldn't be a problem as long as they don't get infected. Keep them clean, and you should be okay."

We didn't say anything else as she washed the four long gashes across my forearm, dabbed various herbal pastes onto the wounds, and then bandaged them.

"What's going to happen?" I said as she retreated.

Titan looked at me, then back at Nathaniel, who was still folded in on himself. "I don't know."

We were both silent for a few minutes. It felt like hours.

"How did you recognise him?" I asked eventually.

Before he could answer, the door exploded open, and my father came striding in, his face darker than I'd ever seen it before. Hamma and Miriam hurried along in his wake.

His steps slowed as he approached us, the scene in front of him apparently not what he'd expected. Father's eyes went from Titan to the mound that was Nathaniel, to the bandage around my arm, and then back again.

"What happened?" he growled.

I looked down at the floor.

"He transformed," Titan said. He was staring at my father with an odd expression on his face, his jaw clenched.

Father took in a long breath, then sighed, his eyes hovering on Nathaniel's still form before turning to me. "You're hurt," he said.

"It was my fault," I said at once, but he held up a hand, cutting me off.

"You were there?" he asked. I nodded. "Come with me. We need to talk."

I hesitated, looking at Titan and Nathaniel, but stood and moved to his side.

"Stay with him," Father ordered Titan, who remained uncharacteristically silent. "I'll want your report later." Then he turned and walked away. I followed.

Shut in my father's study with both my parents, I fixed my stare on the desk as I told them every detail of what had happened. I could feel my mother's warmth at my side, though she made no comment. When I'd finished, there was silence. The dark grey walls loomed judgmentally in my peripheral vision.

"What did it look like?" Father asked, and I glanced up at him. He was staring into the distance, not looking at me.

"It was... big," I said, lacking any better words. "Tall, black skin, claws, horns. Fast, strong." Scary. I kept the last thought to myself.

"And Titan recognised him? You're sure you didn't tell him who it was?"

"I'm sure." I watched as he stood up and paced across the room to stand before the window, staring out.

"You think this might have happened before?" my mother asked.

I glanced between them, from my mother's shrewd expression to my father's back. My fingers were numb where they were clenched in my lap. Could she be right? Had Nathaniel transformed before, in front of Titan? Surely, Titan wouldn't have hidden that. He would have told someone. He would have told Father, at least.

Father sighed and shook his head, turning back to face us. "Let's not *jump to that conclusion."*

"What's going to happen now?" I asked.

Father paused before answering. "Someone was hurt," he said, "might even have been killed. And you were hurt."

"They hurt him first!"

"He hurt you," Father spoke over me.

"This is my fault. I thought I could help."

"It's no one's fault," Father corrected me, coming back to sit in his chair on the other side of the desk. "But there will be a trial. I know you don't like it," he said, his voice rising as I opened my mouth, "but even without you being hurt, the outcome would have been the same. Someone else was hurt. There has to be a trial."

A trial. I stared at him. Nathaniel, a half-blood, being judged. I could imagine what the testimonies of the other men would be like, the false accusations they would make. I was shocked by the surge of anger and protectiveness the images invoked.

"I'm the one that asked him to come out," I tried to explain again. "He was hiding. He didn't mean for any of this to happen."

"As you've already said. Yet, he chose to reveal himself. You called him out, and he came." For an instant, all I heard was the blame in his words, and I felt awful, but when I looked up, there were too many emotions on his face for me to separate them. Maybe some resignation, a little pride, a bit of worry, but no blame.

"It was always inside him," he continued, looking at my mother. "It would have emerged eventually. Maybe tomorrow, maybe in a month, but it would have happened, and there's nothing anyone could have done to cause or prevent that."

I closed my eyes, hands clenching even tighter. A hand touched my chin gently, pulling my face around, and I opened my eyes to meet my mother's gaze.

"We cannot unmake the past," she said gently. She released my chin to take one of my hands instead, worming her fingers into my vice-like grip. She turned to my father. "What needs to be done?" she asked, and his eyes shone as he looked at her.

"We need to find out what happened to the other man, the one who was injured, and find out how bad his injuries are. We'll need to talk to Nathaniel, hear his perspective. Send for his mother, too. And I need to talk to Titan."

"I'll send a messenger to Alicia," my mother said, squeezing my hand before standing. "Then I'll find out what I can about the one who was hurt." She swept from the room.

"Go and rest," my father suggested, but I shook my head.

"I'll stay with Nathaniel."

He gave me a sharp look. "I can get someone else to do that," he said as I stood up.

"No. I'll do it."

He looked at me for a moment. "Be careful."

I looked away, remembering the monster bursting out of the boy, and I nodded.

We retraced our steps back to the medical room, neither of us speaking, Miriam and Hamma accompanying us. Orion and Ishmael stood just inside the small room, and Titan was still sitting beside Nathaniel, his elbows on his knees. He looked up as we walked in, jerking upright at once. His face was hard and grim as he stepped away from Nathaniel, but he spared me a glance as we passed each other. He was still taller than me, but it didn't feel like he wasn't looking down at me anymore.

Titan walked past his fellow guards with his head high, but my father paused to speak quietly to them before leaving. The twins followed him out, but Miriam and Hamma remained, taking their places beside the door, their watchful gaze trained on the immobile half-demon beside me. I turned away from them, sitting in the chair Titan had vacated. From this vantage point, I could just see Nathaniel's face, pressed up against his knees. His eyes were open and unblinking. Their black irises seemed larger than normal. I suppressed a shiver, sitting back and pulling my bare feet up onto the chair, wrapping my arms around my legs as I watched him.

"It's going to be okay," I whispered, more to myself than to anyone *else. I couldn't think of anything else to say. The lie felt heavy on my tongue.*

How could it be okay? There was going to be a trial. I knew Nathaniel had acted in self-defence, but how much would his blood skew the outcome?

I'd thought I could help him. How very wrong I had been.

I followed Warren through the city to one of the mess halls in silence. At the doorway, I caught his arm, stopping him before he could enter.

"I need to talk to your father again," I said. "Alone."

I'd been thinking about it all afternoon, and it was the best option I had come up with. Maybe now we had both calmed down, and without the pressure of any witnesses, Holt and I would be able to have a reasonable conversation.

Warren's eyes sharpened. "Why?"

"Please."

He hesitated for another moment. "I'll pass on the request, see what he says. I can't promise anything though."

"Thank you."

He nodded, glancing over his shoulder at the light spilling from the food hall. "Go get some food. I'll come back here."

With that, he moved past me, quickly disappearing into the city.

I faced the doorway he had indicated and squared my shoulders. Despite the roll I pilfered before I met with the king, I was hungry. After my last disastrous use of my growth ward, I was reluctant to draw on it again, and with my injured arm, I knew I had to eat. Even if it meant facing the stares and whispers once more.

From gossip about the other cities we traded with, I knew most people had to eat far more often than we did. I assumed these people were the same. I wondered, not for the first time, if it was a side effect of our wards that allowed us to go comfortably without food for so many hours at a time. Even if we weren't actively drawing on the growth ward, did it affect us anyway? I had eaten more as a child, but that was justified by the fact I was still growing. I'd never asked any of the Unmarked about their eating habits. Nate didn't fit that theory; even though he didn't have any wards, he didn't have to eat at all. Of course, he'd never fit into anything.

Smiling briefly at the memory of pushing him to try as many different foods as possible, I walked into the food hall, trying to ignore the hush and flicker of turned heads as people registered my presence. I turned away, joining the back of a small queue waiting for food. A name behind me caught my attention, and I paused, listening hard.

"—to Holt," someone was saying.

Another person snorted. "Don't even bother. Go see Set. He'll listen."

The queue moved on, and though I strained my ears as I accepted the portion of stew measured out, I couldn't pick out any more of the conversation through the noise. I remembered the way Set had grabbed his father's arm, stopping him advancing toward me. Maybe Set took a greater role in the governance of this city than I'd realised. But from the snippet I'd overheard, it didn't sound like Set was an accomplice in Holt's regime. More like an alternative to it.

Food clutched in my hand, I turned, surveying the room quickly. A hunched figure in the corner caught my eye, and I made my way toward them.

"May I?" I asked, coming to a halt opposite Noah.

He just shrugged, not looking at me. Sliding onto the bench opposite, I watched him eat determinately, his gaze fixed on his food. I waited, not touching my food.

"What?" he grunted after several moments of silence.

"Have you had a good afternoon?" I asked in my most falsely pleasant voice.

"Not as busy as yours," he snapped, then dug up another spoon of food, his knuckles white from the tightness of his grip.

"You don't like what Warren's doing??" I pushed my bowl aside, setting my forearms on the table between us as I leaned forwards.

"I'm just trying to help."

"Well. I didn't realise your 'help' was quite so selective."

I frowned. So that was what he was bitter about.

"I didn't choose who was there. Warren's hoping for more people to take part. If you want to join in, talk to him about it."

"Sure." He dropped his spoon, sending angry splatters over the table. Reaching out, he grabbed my left arm and pulled it across the table so that my bandaged elbow was between us. "I saved your life. You could at least have remembered that."

I twisted my arm out of his grip, quashing the impulse to break his wrist at the same time. He let me go without resistance.

"What do you want me to do?" I demanded in a low hiss.

"You could start by telling the truth! Why are you here? What do you want?"

"Why am I... You're the one who brought me here!" I pointed out, furious. "I'd be happy to leave right now if Holt wasn't being so awkward about it. And speaking of telling the truth..." I leaned toward him, lowering my voice. "You're one to talk. You didn't tell him about the wards on the Figure."

Noah's jaw clenched. "That's different. I didn't know what they were."

"Oh, yes, you did."

We stared at each other for a moment, then he stood up. "Maybe you're right," he said coldly. "Maybe you should just leave."

I spread my hands, exasperated. "No argument from me. But Holt's diplomacy could use some work."

"So could yours." And he left.

I turned to watch him go, my mouth open, though I had no idea how to respond. Alone, I turned back to my food and began eating without tasting a single mouthful. My spoon scraped the bottom of the bowl when Warren sat down opposite me.

I straightened at once, staring expectantly at him. He met my eyes and shook his head before starting on his own supper. I watched him for a moment, then stood up and followed Noah's path out of the room.

124

So Holt refused to meet with me. Well, if he thought he could avoid me that easily, he was in for a surprise.

Later that evening, I sat with my back against the wall of my room and listened to the city grow quiet outside. A final set of footsteps passed the door and faded, leaving a persistent silence. I opened my eyes.

It made little difference, the darkness enduring. I got blindly to my feet and took off my shirt, leaving my leather vest exposed. Taking a long breath, I drew on the ward of sight on my right arm. The room blossomed into view, tinged red, as the familiar warmth spread out around my elbow from the inked design.

Moving through the switchback door, I paused, looking carefully both ways. To the left, I could see the slight illumination from outside. To the right, the dark tunnel extended away under the earth. Before I looked away, I noticed a flicker of movement. The outline of two people, one male, one female, was just visible, standing within a recessed doorway further along the passage. The man had yawned, raising his hand to cover his mouth, and it was this motion that alerted me to their presence. His companion elbowed him, and he scowled at her, shifting slightly where he leant against the wall, head drooping again. The woman was more alert, her eyes trained on the entrance to my room. Her gaze was so intent, I thought for a moment she had seen me looking back at her, but then her eyes wandered away, flicking across the tunnel before returning. I recognised her from the harbour earlier in the day. She had watched me teach. Now here she was, watching me again.

I stood, my thumb tapping the hilt of my weapon on my hip as I watched the pair. I needed to get outside without them noticing. Although the man seemed bored and ready to fall asleep standing up, the woman was unwavering in her attention.

Releasing my sight ward, I blinked, squinting through the sudden darkness. The pair were almost invisible. Only knowing they were there let me pick out the faint outline of a pale hand as it covered

125

another yawn. If this was all they could see of me, maybe I had a chance of slipping away from them.

I looked the other way. Whilst there was some light filtering in from outside, it was dim and fragile, the entrance to the tunnel visible as purple against black. Not enough for them to see me, but sufficient to show up my silhouette if I stood in the wrong place.

Drawing on my ward again, I looked up and down the stretch of tunnel between me and the outside. The opposite wall was in deeper shadows, visible as a darker red under the power of my ward. If I could cross to the other side of the tunnel, I could slip outside unnoticed.

Turning my attention back to the pair of watchers, I waited for an opportunity, drawing on my other wards in preparation. Speed and balance, the warmth of both enveloping my left arm from elbow to shoulder. My head spun, the effort of drawing on three wards simultaneously making me nauseous. I swallowed convulsively, staring at the vigilant woman, wishing her to look away.

The man yawned again, grumbling slightly, and the woman scowled, half-turning to jab him with her elbow once more.

I leapt across the tunnel, flattening myself against the opposite wall, not daring to breathe. There was silence. I had no doorway to hide in here; if either of them stuck their heads out from their hiding place, they would be able to see me. For several seconds, I remained immobile, waiting. There was no movement from down the tunnel, no call of alarm. Slowly, I crept further up the passage, glancing back every few steps until I reached the entrance. Keeping myself flattened to the wall, I squeezed around the corner and hurried away.

Free of the tunnel, and the spies it contained, I looked across the cliffs to the left. Lights flickered high above me, and I smiled through painful nostalgia, remembering another king who'd stayed up late every night.

The delay in getting outside meant it was now later than I'd anticipated, but I wasn't going to turn back now. I was going to find Holt and talk to him again—whether he wanted to see me or

126

not.

After one more glance over my shoulder, I jogged up the path, squinting along towards the blocky fortress as I climbed. When I reached a fork, I paused, crouching low to the ground as I peered through the darkness. The gate in the fortress's wall was closed, but with the help of my sight ward, I could make out the shape of four soldiers standing guard. There would be no entrance for me that way.

I turned to scan the slope above me. The scree was barren and treacherous, a steep gradient of loose stone with no cover. The left-hand fork of the path wound upwards, and from there, I thought I would be able to find a way across the gradient.

Turning away from the fortress, I followed the path higher. A small track led to a plateau in front of a large opening through which I could see part of a shallow cave. Was that the place where the supposed prophecy was carved? Something to investigate another time.

The track faded into obscurity as I climbed higher, but I pushed onwards, picking my way across the scree, using the larger boulders to steady myself. Small pebbles skittered away down the slope, obnoxiously loud. Wincing, I glanced at the soldiers guarding the gate. Two of them were frowning up towards me, nudging their companions as they did so. I froze, watching their eyes track over the place where I stood and then move on. Briefly, I released my ward of sight. The darkness closed in like a shroud, rendering the soldiers invisible in the gloom. Which meant they wouldn't be able to see me either.

Reactivating my ward, I waited until the soldiers turned away before moving on. One of them continued to shoot glances up the slope, and I cringed at every clatter and grind of the stone under my feet.

Once I was directly above the fortress, out of the sight of the soldiers, I began to descend. It was harder than the climb. Every step threatened to unleash an avalanche. Permanently hunched over, I slid downwards, my balance ward battling gravity. Four feet from the wall surrounding the fortress, I paused, finding my balance, then leapt, a blaze of heat smothering my back as I drew on my strength ward. From its base, the wall was at least ten feet high, but from partway up the slope, with my ward burning, my fingers reached the top.

My body slammed into the sandy stone, driving the air from my lungs, but my grip held. I hung there, catching my breath for a few seconds before heaving upwards. My left arm wobbled, searing with pain, and I dropped back down with a gasp. I'd forgotten about the wound the Figure had given me. Gritting my teeth, braced for the pain this time, I pulled myself up again, flaring my strength ward as I did so. My right arm flexed, lifting me towards the top of the wall, but my left arm buckled before I could get an elbow over it. The fall jarred me, my fingers slipping. I clung on but barely. This was not good. The soldiers, already suspicious, could have heard my descent and be coming to investigate even now.

Closing my eyes, I focused on the ward centred over my shoulder blade. The warmth was already uncomfortable, but it wasn't enough. I needed more. My skin grew hotter as I drew more and more power, the heat shifting from discomfort to pain. Surely my skin was cracking, charred and blackened with the heat. I clenched my teeth to hold in a whimper. My eyes snapped open, and I heaved myself upwards once more, ignoring the tremor in my left arm as I swung my right leg up.

My ankle caught the top of the wall, and I released my strength ward at once, the searing heat dissipating as I shimmied my leg over the wall.

I heaved myself up the rest of the way and rolled off the other side. My feet slammed into the ground, knees bent, hands out to steady myself.

I straightened up slowly, reaching back over my shoulder to feel the skin on my back. It was smooth and supple, a slight lingering warmth the only sign of my use of the ward there. No burnt or blistered skin. I let out a shaky breath. I'd never drawn so deeply on a single ward before.

The courtyard was full of shadows but empty of any signs of life. I was inside. Now I just had to find Holt. I hesitated. What if he wasn't here? What if he slept in the same tunnels I just left? I could be in completely the wrong place. Yet the presence of soldiers guarding the gate suggested he was here.

Taking a breath, I pushed the doubts aside. I was here now. I had to try.

Moving swiftly, as if I could outrun my misgivings, I made my way to the door and slipped inside. The corridor beyond was quiet as I hurried along, trying to remember the route Set had taken to the throne room. That would be as good a starting point as any.

I still hoped Rhianna would put me in touch with the poachers, who would reveal the hidden way out, but if I could persuade Holt his city was better off without me in it, that might not be necessary. Since he refused my request for a second audience, this was the only way I could see him alone. Maybe without an audience judging his every word, he could be prevailed upon to see sense.

A few people were moving around the castle, some soldiers on roving patrols and a couple of other people I assumed worked here. My speed ward lent wings to my feet, and I darted down corridors to avoid them, hiding around corners or in doorways.

I managed to retrace the way to the throne room, slipping through a door into the long room. I couldn't stop my eyes drifting to the carved wooden throne. In my mind, I saw a different seat, far away, with a dead man sitting upon it. Jaw set, I turned aside.

Just as I was contemplating which way to go, a door opened.

I dove behind one of the pillars and folded myself into the shadows, not daring to breathe as I listened to two familiar voices moving through the room.

"—don't understand what you think this will achieve," Set was saying.

"How can you say that?" Warren shot back, frustration colouring his tone. "She knows about the demons, she's fought them before."

"You sure about that?"

"Excuse me?"

Their footsteps paused, and I risked a glance out from behind my pillar. Warren's hand was on Set's arm, the same irritation I'd heard in his voice apparent on his face, his brows furrowed over angry eyes.

"Don't give me that look," Warren continued. "What did you mean by that? Go on."

"Just remember that we don't know why she's here or where she came from. She can say anything she likes, but we have no proof it's true."

"You think she's lying?"

"I didn't say that," Set replied. He reached out now, returning the grip on Warren's arm. "But I can see what's going on. You need to be careful."

"Of what?"

"Of which head you're thinking with," Set snapped.

"Oh, shove off," Warren scoffed, pushing Set away.

I suddenly realised what Set had meant and I recoiled back behind my pillar, gagging.

"Fine. But remember that she wants to leave."

"Not if Father gets his way."

"Does this mean you actually agree with him? Wonders never cease. Where are you going now?"

"To talk to him," Warren said, and I poked my head back out to see him striding determinately across the room away from me.

"No, don't!" Set called after him. "It won't—" But the door had already swung shut again. "Help," Set finished with a sigh. He stood staring after his brother for a moment, then made his way to a different door and left.

Once the door closed behind him, I slid out from behind the pillar. I had to follow Warren. If he was going to see Holt, he would lead me straight to him.

But at the same time, after what Set had implied, I wanted to run in the opposite direction. Even if that meant jumping right off the balcony behind me. Of course, Warren hadn't confirmed it… but he hadn't denied the accusation either. I shuddered, swallowing down more bile before squaring my shoulders. It was a problem to deal with later. Right now, I had to stay focused.

Crossing the room, I eased open the door Warren had departed through. On the other side, a narrow, dimly lit passage extended away from me. There was no sign of Warren. As quietly as I could, I slipped through and hurried along to where the hallway met another one, extending away to the left and right. I slowed, peeking around the corner.

Warren was walking away down the passage to the right. I waited for him to turn the corner, going right again, before I followed, walking quickly to make sure I didn't lose him. I needn't have worried, for when I reached the end of the passage and peered around the next corner, I found him standing immobile in front of a door. His hand was raised, but he didn't knock, just stood there, poised on the edge of movement.

I watched him, wondering what the issue was. I had never hesitated to approach my father; he had always been willing to listen to a problem, whether trivial or serious. Yet here was Warren, holding back. Did he think Holt would reject what he had to say, or be angry at being disturbed by it? Set's parting words, which Warren had not slowed to hear, certainly implied something of that sort.

After several more seconds, Warren lowered his hand. He turned and walked away, head lowered.

I stepped around the corner as he left, staring after him. I remembered the way he had chosen to answer my questions in the throne room earlier, when Holt had been silent. Set's words echoed in my mind as well.

The way Warren had looked at me when I'd said I fought demons, when I'd demonstrated what I could do with my wards… the awe in his eyes.

My stomach clenched. If Warren did look at me like *that*, he might be a valuable ally, easily swayed to my side if I needed him. But it would also make him more reluctant to help me leave.

Beyond that, it was an attachment I had no interest in. I liked Warren; he had a fierceness to him, and he was determined to stand against the demons. People here seemed to respect him, though without the deference I'd seen them offer Set. Warren could be a friend and a useful ally, but he would never be anything beyond that. I would have to make sure I discouraged him before it got any further. Besides, Set was right; I was going to leave, one way or another.

With that thought, I gritted my teeth and strode towards the door where Warren had stood. I didn't hesitate but pushed it open and walked straight in.

Luckily, it was an office I'd barged into, not Holt's bedroom. Holt himself was standing on the other side of a desk stacked with thick, clunky objects, illuminated by a single candle. The window beside him was wide open, and he gazed out at his city.

At the sound of the door opening, he turned, raising a single eyebrow as I moved to stand in front of the desk.

"Good evening." Any surprise he felt at seeing me was hidden well.

I blinked. The courteous greeting was not something I'd planned for. At the very least, I'd expected him to ask how I'd gotten in. Beyond that, the calm tone was so far removed from his wild anger earlier that it threw me.

"It's polite to reply," he said when I didn't respond.

"There are many polite things we seem to have dispensed with," I said. I could hear the hardness in my tone, too level to be angry but missing politeness by several shades.

"Indeed," he replied, his voice dropping to mimic mine. "Honesty. Truthful introductions..."

"Temper control?" I suggested, and his serene facade twitched as his eyes narrowed.

"Respect," he finished firmly.

"You refused my request to talk to you again."

132

"I made my position clear. There's nothing more to say."

I sighed. We'd done this dance before. Much as I was loath to admit it, if there was one person in this city who should know the truth, it was Holt. My father always said having good information leads to making good decisions. I desperately wanted Holt to make a good decision.

"Well, I have more to say," I said, squaring my shoulders. "My name is Tamara, rightful Queen of Alderth."

"Rightful Queen," he repeated. "Meaning there is an un-rightful one?"

"There is another currently Claiming the throne," I admitted, trying not to show how the words cut me.

"And the previous ruler?"

"Rygorn; my father."

Holt returned to his seat behind the desk. "Well. That was more in three sentences than you've told anyone since you got here. I assume you have a reason for offering up this information all of a sudden?"

I resisted the urge to scowl. "I need to get home."

"Hmm." His face gave nothing away.

"Why am I still here?"

"Because I don't trust you."

"You don't know me."

"Exactly. I don't know who you are, why you're here, what you want."

I frowned. "I was brought here," I reminded him. "I didn't walk up to the gates and demand entrance."

"No," he said. "If you had, you'd still be outside them. Yet here you are. You got in and did it very cleverly. So... did you stage the whole thing?"

"Did I..." I broke off, staring at him. Where had this idea come from? "You're joking."

"Am I?" he asked. "There's no trace of your supposed monster, nothing but blood on the ground, and you, inside my city."

"One of *your* people saw the Figure."

He didn't say anything.

"I don't want to be here," I said, enunciating every word. "If you don't trust me, then let me go home, and you never have to think about me ever again!"

"Or I let you outside the walls, and you go straight to the demons and tell them everything you've seen in here."

I blinked, opened my mouth, closed it again, and tried to remember to breathe. How long had it taken him to come up with all these paranoid theories? That must be why he had reacted so badly to my interest in the wards. He probably suspected I wanted to examine them for any weakness to report back to my supposed allies. I immediately resolved not to mention them again.

"You're delusional," I said, almost to myself. He just looked at me. "Do you know what I spent the afternoon doing?"

"Teaching some of my fighters how to punch each other," he said. "And encouraging them in their fantasy that they will somehow be able to fend off monsters. It's almost as if you want them to throw away their weapons during the next attack."

"Oh, Thorns," I snarled to myself. "So you don't want me to leave because you think I'm in league with the demons, but you don't want me here because apparently, I'm sabotaging your fighters?"

Holt twitched one eyebrow in silent acknowledgement of the magnitude of his dilemma.

I took several breaths. I needed this to work. Forcing my shoulders to relax, I uncrossed my arms. Open, soft, inviting body language.

My fingers brushed against one of the blades I carried on my hip. Holt hadn't mentioned their presence. Half-formed ideas flickered through my mind, each more sinister than the last. I dismissed them all. Threatening Holt was unlikely to open the gates out of the city. And I wasn't prepared to break this already tenuous relationship so soon.

"Your son is rather enthusiastic about the possibility of fighting the demons," I said.

Holt's face twitched, his brows coming together in confusion for a second as he opened his mouth, then closed it again. His face suddenly cleared, and his jaw tightened before he spoke. "Warren can be over-eager. He hasn't thought through the outcome of this ridiculous idea."

My instinctive response was to jump to Warren's defence, but I clamped it down. I needed to be calm now, to consider my words. Something about Holt made that difficult for me.

"What do you suggest as an alternative then?" I said, resisting the urge to cross my arms again. "What will you do? Sit here, hiding behind the wall until it crumbles? Can your people survive like that?"

"My people are not expendable," Holt said, his face calm and steady. "I've seen what happens when we stand against the demons; it's death, every time. Parentless children, empty homes, friends lost. My son might think of this as inspired… it is madness."

"He doesn't believe that," I said. "Neither do the other fighters. It gives them hope."

"Hope can be a dangerous thing."

"Or it could be what saves you."

Holt stood up. "No. They may call you *saviour* out there, but I know exactly what sort of salvation you would bring: lies and betrayal. I will have no part in it. Now get out."

I couldn't hold back my smirk at the irony of his words, spreading my hands as I took a step back. "Just give the order, and I'll be gone."

He continued glaring at me.

"Fine." It was clear I would get no further with him. I turned and walked away. There were other avenues I could pursue anyway.

At the doorway, I stopped and looked back. "Just so you know, I've been fighting demons my whole life. They killed both my parents. I would never work with them."

Holt said nothing, and for a second, I understood. He wanted me gone but didn't know what I might do if I was set free. He wanted to keep his people safe but wouldn't risk letting them be trained to fight the demons for fear of the resultant confrontations.

Holt was afraid. And against his fear, I had no hope of persuading him to let me leave. Shaking my head, I walked out and slammed the door behind me.

9

Potential

I sat alone with the catatonic Nathaniel for what felt like a long time, broken only by the intermittent glances that I threw around the rest of the room, the patches of light from the windows jumping across the floor each time.

At some point, Edric and Miriam arrived to relieve the twins. Not long after, Titan returned. He exchanged a glance with his two fellow Guards but didn't say anything to them. Instead, he walked over and sat on the bed behind me.

I pushed the chair back, turning to face the man. He refused to meet my gaze. I'd fully intended to interrogate him, about how he'd known the monster in the storeroom was Nathaniel, about what he and my father had just discussed, about what he thought would happen now. His expression made me rethink that plan. There was bleak anger painted around his eyes and mouth, etching his dark skin into an unfamiliar pattern.

"Bad decisions all around, then."

I opened my mouth and then closed it again, confused.

"Do you want to tell me what you were thinking?"

It was an effort not to flinch from the frustration in his tone, the disappointment and anger emphasising his accent.

"I… I was trying to help him."

"Why was that your responsibility? You're still a child and—"

"I'm not just a child!" I sat up straighter, my scowl matching his. "My father said I should do something."

"Oh, believe me, I've made my opinion on that very clear to him. You don't even have your wards yet!"

"What difference does that make?"

"What if those men hadn't listened to you? What if they'd decided to do to you what they'd done to him?" Titan nodded at Nate.

"They wouldn't dare!" The ice in my veins didn't quench the fire in my words.

"They could have! And you wouldn't have been able to stop them."

I didn't have a response to that.

"Why did you have to go looking for him? Why couldn't you just wait for him to come back to your library? Now look what's happened."

I looked.

I looked at the boy curled up on the bed. I looked at the bandage on my arm and remembered the swipe of a powerful arm, the sight of a body flung through the air. My face was wet. More tears rolled down my cheek every time I blinked. I wasn't sure when I'd started crying.

Titan sighed, running a hand over his shaved head, his anger melting away. "Come here."

I almost fell out of the chair, stumbling over to sit on the bed beside him. He wrapped an arm around me.

"I was just trying to help him."

"I know," he said wearily.

He let me lean on him as I wept.

"How did you know it was him?" I asked when my tears had run dry.

I felt the movement as Titan lifted his head to stare at Nate. "Because I looked," he said, squeezing me gently.

"But... but it was..."

"He," Titan corrected me. "It was him. Is him."

I swallowed, trying and failing to avoid the memory of the black-skinned creature. There had been nothing of Nathaniel left on its features... had there? Titan claimed to have recognised him. But how?

I was saved from having to respond by movement on the other bed.

We were both still, holding our breaths. Nathaniel's spine cracked as he shifted, his black eyes blinking, closer to awareness than they'd been in hours. They were fixed on the man beside me.

"Titan?" Nathaniel whispered, the sound hoarse.

I wiped my face quickly.

"Hey, Nate," Titan replied just as softly, taking his arm from around my shoulder to lean forwards. "How are you feeling?"

"I don't know," Nathaniel said. "What happened?"

Titan didn't reply at once. Nathaniel blinked, raising his head an inch, his eyes flicking to me.

"What happened?" he asked again, his voice a little louder.

Miriam and Edric, stationed by the door, looked up as they realised he was awake.

"It's okay," Titan tried to soothe him. "Just relax."

Nathaniel's eyes found the bandage on my arm.

I could see it happening, the memories falling into place inside his head, his face taking on a new shade of horror with each one.

"No. No, no, no, no."

"Nate," Titan began, half rising to his feet.

The movement seemed to break whatever cycle Nathaniel had been stuck in. He launched himself backwards off the bed, scrambling away across the floor. Titan and I leapt to our feet, as Miriam and Edric stepped forwards, their hands going to their weapons.

Trapped in the corner, Nate turned away from us, pressing his face into the wall as if he could push himself through the surface to be entombed within the stone. An awful sound escaped him, a keening, groaning wail of horror and despair.

I flinched, the sound scaring me more than the roars of the creature, though the earlier sounds hadn't made my eyes prickle or my nose sting.

"Nate," Titan said, failing to cover the desperation in his tone as Nathaniel fell silent. "Nate, listen to me. It's okay. You're alright."

"I'm just like him," Nate said, the words muffled by the wall.

"No!" Titan snapped, apparently understanding more than I did,

stepping closer to the boy. "Nate, c'mon. You're not, you know that."

Nathaniel turned, looking up at him, and there was a darkness in his face I'd never seen before.

"You're not," Titan repeated firmly.

Nathaniel's eyes closed again, and he leaned his head sideways to rest on the stone.

With a sigh, Titan shuffled closer and sat with his back to the wall, an inch of space between them. "It's going to be okay," he said.

It took a minute, but eventually, Nathaniel rolled around, without opening his eyes, to press himself against Titan's side. It was only with the comparison of their bodies I realised Nathaniel was shaking. Slowly, I sat on the bed he had vacated, facing them both.

"Nathaniel," I whispered. "Nate."

He responded to the latter, opening his eyes and looking up.

"I'm sorry," I said. "I'm so sorry. I shouldn't have called you out. I should have just made them leave. This is all my fault. I'm so sorry."

He blinked, his bleak gaze sharpening. "I'm sorry that I... that you got hurt. And it's not your fault."

I grimaced, hating the lie everyone seemed so eager to tell me.

"How do you feel?" Titan asked Nate before I could argue.

Nate closed his eyes again. "Hot. Cold. Like I've been sleeping for days. Tired. Like my skin's about to explode. Like I'm empty inside."

"Well," Titan said, "at least that's nice and simple."

When I awoke the next morning, it took several seconds for me to remember where I was. After my late night, I was exhausted. Despite the bright sunlight funnelled into my room through the tunnel in the rock, I remained lying on the bed. Curled atop my blanket, I relived my angry exit from the palace.

With frustration boiling in my veins, I hadn't bothered to hide my presence. By some stroke of fate, I hadn't encountered anyone on the way out. Though the soldiers outside were shocked by my abrupt exit, none followed me down the mountain, unwilling to abandon their post. Even their questioning shouts faded, leaving me to descend with nothing but my frustration for company.

Inside the tunnels, I'd waved sarcastically to the two watchers who were supposed to keep track of me before disappearing back into my room. They were useless, all of them. The watchers shouldn't have been so far from my room. The soldiers shouldn't have let me pass in the night or leave unchallenged. Such carelessness would never have been tolerated at home.

I closed my eyes against the morning light. *Home.* The word was edged with pain. Where was home? My people thought me dead. The throne of Alderth was Claimed by another. Was that my home?

My eyes snapped open, and I rolled off the bed, landing on my feet.

Yes. It was my home, and I was going to get back there. That meant getting out of this city. It meant facing the day. No more lamenting. I had failed to convince Holt to let me leave, but that wasn't my only option. I had another plan in motion.

I glanced at my over-shirt, thrown into a corner, but turned away and left the room with my shoulders bare. People would recognise me by now; there was no need to hide my tattoos. I would accept their stares. Let them see my difference. Let them see I didn't belong here.

Emerging from my room, I was immediately confronted with two impassive faces staring at me. The two who had been watching my room last night had been relieved, and their replacements weren't as subtle. The new pair, both men this time, had been leaning against the wall directly opposite my door but now stood upright, eyes fixed upon me. They said nothing, waiting.

I laughed, unable to stop myself. Apparently, Holt had decided to keep a closer eye on me after last night. Still grinning, I shook my head and turned away, heading outside. They followed silently.

The sun was already high when I and my followers emerged from the tunnels. The city below was busier than I'd seen it before. Watching from above, it was as if I observed a colony of ants, a web of chaos and disorder. Yet, somehow, each one knew their place and purpose, moving with the turnings of those around them rather than being crushed.

Hesitating, I considered the many hives of activity. Where was Rhianna likely to be? I needed to speak to her again, to see if she had considered my proposal. She was my best chance of getting in touch with the group who dared to venture beyond the wall without Holt's approval. But I had to find her first. And, I thought wryly as someone shifted behind me, I had to get away from Holt's two agents. That, at least, shouldn't pose too much of a problem. It would simply be an issue of timing.

I was just about to descend into the city when something made me pause and look back up over my shoulder. High above, I thought I could see the very top of the opening to the cave I'd spotted the previous evening. Was it, as I'd suspected then, where the prophecy was carved? Rhianna had called me 'Saviour'. She might be there, praying to the cold, unfeeling, stone. And if not, maybe there would be clues about where the message had come from and if it was indeed from one of the Figures.

Changing direction, I began to stride up along the path, my shadows scrambling after me, caught off guard by my sudden movement. I let them follow, setting a steady but forgiving pace up the slope. They stayed close on my heels until I reached the plateau in front of the gaping maw of the cavern. There, they hesitated.

I stepped forwards.

The cave was shallow, and though the direct sunlight reached no further than the entrance, it was enough to illuminate the rest of the space inside. The curtains caught my eye first. Deep purple fabric reached from floor to ceiling in thick folds on either side of the unnaturally flat back wall. With the slightly shadowed interior, it was hard to be sure, but it looked to be almost the same colour as the bands the Guard wore back home.

My jaw tightened. First the similarities of the throne room, now this. Why?

Something moved, and I lowered my gaze. Five people sat on the floor of the cave, grouped around the middle of the back wall. One of them had turned and, seeing me standing there, gave a soft gasp, drawing the attention of the others, who also looked around. Rhianna was not there. I glanced over the faces barely long enough to ascertain that fact, then looked up at the wall again, to where they had been staring before my interruption.

A grey plaque was set into the wall, the dull colour standing out against the surrounding sandy stone.

The people were getting to their feet, one of them moving towards me, but I didn't seem to be able to take my eyes off the rectangle of metal.

"Saviour."

I jerked, finally looking away at the vaguely familiar voice. It took me a couple of seconds to recognise the woman who had approached me. Her skin was pulled tightly across bony cheeks, peeling away from her eyes and leaving them overly large. She had been arguing with Set when I'd first awoken in this city. I was sure he had said her name, but I couldn't remember it.

"I'm so glad you've come to us," the woman continued breathily.

Something in her tone made me want to turn and walk straight back out. Rhianna wasn't here. I had no reason to linger. Yet my eyes returned once again to the plaque.

The woman noticed, following my gaze. "Please," she invited me, sweeping a hand towards it. The serenity of the movement was somewhat reduced when she immediately began flapping her hand at the other people to move aside. They did so without protest, practically stumbling over their own feet as they retreated, several with heads bowed.

I hesitated for another second, then stepped forwards, crossing the distance to the back of the cave. The woman shadowed me every step of the way.

The metal was cold under my fingers, dancing somewhere between silver and grey, and I realised what it reminded me of. It was the same colour as the Figures' skin. I drew back at once, pulling my hand from the metal as if it could infect me.

143

"Beautiful, isn't it?"

My eyes drifted to the four lines of script carved into the polished surface. Unlike the wards etched into the Figures' skin, the indentations showed only more grey metal, not white.

they will come with the darkness
bringing the light
dark strength on their arms
death shall know fear

Exactly as Noah had recited it.

"Where did it come from?" I asked, my voice slightly hoarse.

"It was a gift," she breathed. "From—"

"An angel?" I finished, remembering what Noah had said.

"You have encountered them before?"

"Tell me about them."

"What would you like to know? It was a long time ago, but we do have accounts from that time, stories of those who were privileged enough to be here."

"Whatever you know," I said. "What did they look like? Why did they come? Was this verse spoken, or written here, or delivered already carved?"

"So many questions," the woman said, smiling, though the expression didn't meet her eyes.

"Please," I forced out. "Any detail may be critical."

"Very well." the woman pursed her lips, thinking. "Several hundred years ago, this was, but accounts tell of a silver man who came from above, bearing a message of great hope." She gestured to the plaque. "He pressed the metal into the stone, and though he spoke no words, his eyes held all the light of the world within them."

The last sentence was breathy and recited from memory. She gazed at me, her eyes bright. I looked away, back at the silver-grey metal on the wall. A silver man with light in his eyes. The Figures were neither male nor female, but the rest fit too closely for

144

comfort. The part about coming from above, though…

Whilst I wasn't sure of the precise limits to the Figures' powers, I was absolutely certain they could not fly. Or mostly certain, at least. Maybe 'above' simply meant the Figure had come over the mountains. It would be a treacherous path for one of the unwarded people who lived here, and I doubted I would be able to make the climb, but such a descent probably would be within the Figures' capabilities.

"Dark strength," the woman murmured from beside me.

I glanced sideways in time to see her hand reaching toward my tattoos. I jerked away before she could touch me, and she pulled her hand back at once.

"My apologies, Saviour," she said, head bowed as she took a step backwards.

Dark strength? My eyes returned to the prophecy. That didn't fit. My strength wards were on my back. I could remember the pain as the needle made its steady progress over my shoulder blades.

"Please, tell us how we may be of assistance?"

My immediate instinct was to tell her that if she could convince Holt I wasn't here to sell them all out, that would be highly useful. I glanced back over my shoulder to my two followers, wondering how they would react to such a statement. One of them was watching out of the cave, checking if anyone else was approaching. But the other was looking around the cave with narrowed eyes, his face tight with discomfort and covered with a sheen of sweat. Did this place make him uncomfortable, or was it being among people who viewed me as an ally rather than an enemy?

Maybe it wasn't such a bad thing for them to be reminded of what the implication of their actions could mean to others.

"I thought we should talk," I said, without looking away from the man. His face paled further at my words. I turned back to the woman as he swallowed. "I'm afraid I was not at my best when last we met. Remind me of your name?"

"Mary," she informed me, with a slight bow. She looked from me to the two who had been following me that morning. "Will your…

friends be joining us?"

Now the others who had been waiting in the cave also looked up, heads flicking between us and the two men hovering at the entrance. The second one had noticed what was going on as well. Five against two, assuming those here chose to rally around me, and from their stances, it seemed likely they would.

"They have been assisting me," I said, deliberately meeting the two pairs of nervous eyes. "But no, that will not be necessary. I'm looking for someone. Rhianna."

"Of course, of course," Mary said. "Her poor boy. But there is so much to be done, Saviour, I wouldn't want you to feel pressured into focusing your efforts too closely. We all feel for her distress, of course, but there are many such sad stories to be heard here. Those who stray from the safe paths may sometimes place themselves in peril, or even risk other's lives along with their own."

It seemed Holt wasn't the only one who was less than concerned about Malcolm. I wondered briefly which of them would be more likely to help the boy if the opportunity were to arise.

"Certainly," I cut in before Mary could ramble on any further, trying to formulate a reply she would accept. "But sometimes unexpected paths must be walked to remove greater evils. Rhianna has information that may be of assistance to me. It's vital that I convene with her as soon as possible."

The meandering, flowery words seemed to placate her, and she nodded seriously, her eyes locked on mine as I spoke.

"Of course," she said again, nodding eagerly. It seemed to be her favourite phrase. "I understand. We merely hope you will not lose sight of the larger issues present here."

I didn't reply to that, lowering my head and allowing my eyes to narrow slightly.

"I'm sure you will not, of course. Let me think…" She frowned, her eyes drifting away from me. "I believe there was a group of hunters due to return today. Rhianna is likely to want to speak with them, to see if they discovered any evidence of her son."

"A group," I repeated. "Who have been outside the wall."

146

"Yes. They left a couple of hours before you arrived, I believe."

It was an effort not to scream. So there were people outside the walls, people who'd left two whole days ago, yet Holt wouldn't let me leave in case I told the demons secrets about the interior of this city. Did the extent of Holt's hypocrisy know no bounds? What if the demons captured one of the people who lived here, ripping the information from them with pain and blood?

"I see," I said, and I could feel the tranquillity of my mask cracking. Mary recoiled slightly. "Thank you." I forced my face into a smile with a semblance of calm. "Your assistance will not be forgotten."

"Of course. Whatever you require," Mary said.

I was already turning away, striding out of the cave entrance, throwing a smug glance at my shadows as I passed them. One recoiled from the expression, both silently following me back down towards the city. I was tempted to draw upon my speed ward and leave them behind, but if I then took too long to find Rhianna, it would give them a chance to catch up to me. Better to wait for now, though their crunching footsteps echoing mine set my teeth on edge. I couldn't bring myself to regret confronting Holt despite their watchful presence now. I'd needed to see him again, to give him another opportunity to reconsider his stance.

At the bottom of the steep path from the cliffs, a large crowd had gathered, blocking the main thoroughfare. I tried to peer over their heads but couldn't see any cause for the huddle. From the raised voices and gesticulating hands, they seemed to be arguing. Not wanting to be drawn into anything, I headed in the other direction, looking for a way around the obstruction.

My alternate path took me past the edge of the patch of open land at the northern edge of the city. It was teeming with workers, all moving carefully through the closely packed rows of crops. Several smaller figures caught my gaze. Children, some looking barely past their first decade, worked alongside adults. When I looked again, I saw most of them were around my age or younger. Only a few looked as old as my parents had been. I didn't see anyone with hair whitened from age.

They're manual labourers, I reminded myself. The older ones couldn't bend down to work the soil. The elderly must be working elsewhere.

Turning away, I found an unblocked path south and hurried along it, heading for the gates.

They were as firmly closed as ever. I stared hungrily at the slabs of wood for several seconds before turning in the other direction, scanning the street. It only took a couple of seconds to spot the one I'd been searching for.

Rhianna was standing on the other side of the thoroughfare, hands clutched together, her red-rimmed eyes staring unblinkingly at the gates.

I made my way to her. Her face tightened at my approach, chin trembling slightly, but she did not look away from her vigil. Beside her, I turned, glancing back. As I did so, there was a shout from above. I looked up at once, catching a glimpse of someone hanging over the top of the wall, shouting something down. Rhianna gasped beside me, a wet sound. The soldiers in front of the gate sprang into motion, scurrying back and forth in a tangle of bodies and limbs.

The gates shuddered, groaning loudly, then cracked open.

The reaction was much the same as if had been two evenings previously when Keera had returned to the city. Everyone in the vicinity melted away into the shadows. The street was suddenly deserted. Faces flashed from doorways, cautious glances followed by hasty retreats. The two men who'd been following me backed away, hands clutching at their weapons as they edged closer to the nearest alley, ready to flee.

There were two exceptions to the abrupt retreat.

Rhianna remained locked in place beside me, her eyes never leaving the gates. And a set of confident footsteps, approaching from behind.

I turned just as Keera drew level with me, meeting my gaze briefly before continuing. She disappeared into the group of

148

soldiers just as people came in through the gates.

The group that spilled into the courtyard was larger than I'd expected. I counted ten people, all with bulky bags over their shoulders.

"Keera!" the woman at the front, with brown hair pulled up behind her head, exclaimed in surprise and pleasure, holding out her hands and seeming to summon the shorter woman from within the crowd. They grasped hands, voices lowering to normal volume while the rest of the group filed in, the gates reversing their motion to swing closed again behind them.

Ten people. Ten lives Holt risked outside the wall, but he objected to people wanting to fight the demons. Hypocrite. My hands clenched.

Beside me, Rhianna took a step forwards, her whole body vibrating. One of the last people through the gate, a young man, caught her eye. His face tightened as he shook his head.

Rhianna's shoulders slumped as he turned away, his expression pained as he hoisted his burden higher on his back. It was easier to guess what news she had been hoping for. But it was to my advantage that Malcolm had not been found.

I moved up beside the older woman.

"I can find him," I promised. We were too far from the gates to be overheard by them, but I kept my voice low, aware of my shadows who had halted their retreat now the gates were closed again. "But you've got to tell me everything you know."

Rhianna drew in a shuddering breath and nodded.

I pushed down the flare of triumph in my chest, moving around to stand in front of her, leaning in close.

"He was meeting someone by the waterfront. One of the warehouses. I don't know which one. And he mentioned a name. Ava."

"Ava," I murmured to myself.

"I can show you where she might be," Rhianna offered, but before I could respond, she stiffened, looking past me.

I turned to see what had caught her attention.

It was Set. He stood with Keera and the group who had returned to the city. His eyes were on us, a slight frown on his face. Had his father told him about our conversation last night?

I stepped away from Rhianna. "No, that's okay. I'll find them." I wanted to accept her offer of assistance, but Set had already seen us together. I didn't want to be observed leaving with her as well, reinforcing any connection I had with her in his mind. "Thank you."

She nodded, her eyes filling with tears. "Please find him, Saviour."

"I will," I promised. I glanced past her at my two shadows, who were edging closer with every second, the guilt apparent on their faces as they realised they might have missed overhearing key information.

Looking back over my shoulder again, I found Set still watching me. I glanced at the two men, then looked back at him, raising an unimpressed eyebrow. He lowered his chin slightly as if to ask me what I'd expected.

That answered that question. He definitely knew what I had done last night.

Narrowing my eyes slightly, I turned to face him properly, allowing a slight smile to play around my mouth as the two wards on my left arm began to grow warm.

Speed and balance, an amused voice whispered in my head. There's a reason we have both.

Set almost seemed to guess what I was about to do. He had time to take half a step forwards, and then I was gone, running so fast there was no way any of them could follow.

10

First Blood

The stubby candle in my hand flickered as I stumbled through the gloomy underground passage. Full of cobwebs and dark corners, the spaces underneath the citadel were rarely used, either left empty or filled with relics of darker times. There was one particular set of curios I was keen to avoid.

The Figures, servants of the throne, had never been awoken in my lifetime. Not long after Nate's arrival to Alderth, Father brought me down here to the chamber where they slept. The row of grey bodies, stiff and silent, left me distinctly uneasy. With a huge array of wards across their skin, the Figures were nigh-on invincible.

Father hadn't told me the details of how to awaken them, but I gathered that it was a long and possibly dangerous process, and putting them back to sleep again even more so.

Personally, I hoped they stayed asleep.

I brushed my hand along the wall and tried to recall Titan's directions. I'd passed two doors already. It couldn't be much further…

The wooden door appeared, and I hesitated, wondering if I should knock. It seemed ridiculous to do so, but at the same time, I couldn't bring myself to just open the door. What if I'd misremembered the route? What if this was the wrong door, and cold grey bodies were waiting beyond…

Pushing the paranoia aside, I rapped a knuckle twice against the door. The sound didn't carry as much as I'd expected it to, but it still made me look around again, searching the shadows for any hint of grey skin. I couldn't suppress the fear creeping under my skin.

There was no response to my knock, but I pushed the door cautiously open. It creaked loudly, catching on the floor after only a few inches. I shoved it with my shoulder, and it jerked open.

The candle's flame illuminated an almost empty room with an unidentifiable lump of material piled in one corner and a person sitting against the back wall.

Without the candle, it must have been pitch black, but Nathaniel looked at me without wincing. His dark eyes remained as unreadable as ever, with no distinction between pupil and iris.

"Are you sure you couldn't have found a gloomier spot?" I whispered as I crouched down.

"Wasn't planning for visitors."

"Titan told me where you were."

"Of course, he did." He looked away, letting out a breath that was almost a sigh.

"It's going to be okay," I said, but he gave me a flat look. I tried again. "You were defending yourself. The law is on your side."

"It's not going to matter though, is it?"

I stood up, and his eyes followed me. "Yes, it is. Let's go."

He remained seated for a moment, then sighed again before standing. He swayed. I raised the candle a little higher, the light falling more directly on his face. He eyed the flame with distaste. He was pale and had dark circles under his eyes.

"Have you slept?" I asked. "Or eaten?"

He shrugged as he followed me out into the dark corridor, and my jaw clenched. No one had sent him down here in the run-up to the trial, but he'd found his way to the deepest tunnels under the citadel. Whether Titan had found the half-blood or Nate had told him where he was hiding, I wasn't sure.

In some ways, his absence had been a blessing with all the rumours flying around. It had only been a week since the incident, but stories had been running wild since the very first day, opinions flaring on both sides. I'd been pleasantly surprised by those who hadn't called for

Nate's blood, though they weren't as rigorous in their arguments. Most simply pointed out the lack of trouble he'd caused in the past.

At my father's insistence, I avoided the debates. That didn't stop my stomach from contracting into a hard mass when I heard the angry discussions. Even if my father ruled in Nate's favour, would it deter the rest of the population from forming their own judgement and acting upon it?

I drew in a steadying breath. My chance to speak would come soon. Whether it would be enough was yet to be seen.

Nate stayed silent, leaving me to my thoughts as we returned to the rest of the world. Just outside the large doors to the throne room, I paused to glance sideways. His colour didn't look any better for being in daylight, but he stood straight-backed, annoyingly tall, eyes fixed ahead. He'd always seemed so small before, head ducked down, hunched over in corners. I'd underestimated his true height. He'd crept up on me.

I pushed the doors open.

The throne room was packed. People were crammed on either side of the walkway, the occasional elbow or foot intruding onto the empty path. Glares from Helena and Miriam, flanking the throne, stopped people from straying too far. I wished this could have been dealt with without the audience, but the people would never have stood for that. Nate's judgement fell to the king, but he was judged by the rest of the population. No doubt there was a large crowd outside as well, impatient to hear the outcome.

I'd taken two steps before I realised Nate wasn't keeping pace with me. It was too late to stop. Nate needed me to be in control. If I hesitated or showed discomfort at having him behind me, all could fail. I kept walking, pausing in front of the throne to bow to my father. He nodded as I straightened up and moved to his side but didn't smile. As I took my place in front of Helena, his calm gaze returned to the doorway. Beside him, I could finally turn back without it looking suspicious.

Nate stood where I'd left him, framed by the doorway. His eyes swept from the crowd to my father and back again. His throat bobbed as he swallowed.

"Enter." It was the king's formal tone that rang out, cutting easily through the murmurs, though the word was light and pleasant, almost welcoming.

Nate stepped forwards, moving past people who watched him in equal silence, though many eyes shouted their owners' opinions. The whole hall seemed to have tensed, waiting for an explosion. My shoulders hunched in response.

A few steps away from us, Nate paused, his dark eyes darting to me for a split second before he sank to his knees, head tilted back to the ceiling as he exposed his throat.

Rising to his feet, Nate moved to the left side of the hall. I saw his mother, at the front of the crowd, give him a hard smile. Looking away from her, his eyes found Titan, on the opposite side of the hall. They looked at each other for a moment before Nate's eyes dropped back to the ground, hands hidden behind his back as he waited.

Nate's list of allies was short. My chest tightened. I took a steady breath through my nose, trying to dispel the feeling of suffocation.

I looked at his mother. Alicia had arrived the day after the incident, her face pale when my mother brought her to the hospital where Nate, Titan, and I had still been hiding. Nathaniel had leapt to his feet as his mother marched in but then froze. It had been she who'd swept forwards, pulling him into a tight hug. The surprise in his face had been painful to see as he'd returned the embrace. Titan and I had followed my mother silently out into the hallway, giving them privacy.

I blinked the memory away as a new group of people appeared at the doors. The seven men approached us in silence. I recognised them as the ones from the storeroom. Their leader had the remnants of a bruise on his temple, matching his dark expression. Nate stiffened as they knelt before my father, then moved to the opposite side of the hall. The injured one stared at Nate with enough intensity to burn, and I felt my jaw clench.

"Tamara," Father said, his voice gentle but loud enough to carry across the crowded hall. I took a breath, pushing down my emotions, and strode forwards, turning on my heel to stand before him. Our eyes met briefly before I dropped smoothly to my knees, tilting my head back to the ceiling for a moment, then rose back to my feet.

"Tell it all," Father said, and my stomach clenched at the ancient words. "Tell it true." He gave me the tiniest nod of encouragement. "From the beginning."

Taking a deep breath, I told him. I told them all. I went back years, speaking about finding Nathaniel in my library, about the voices I'd heard outside the window, and then about the more recent time when his face has been covered in bruises. It was easy to skim over how he hadn't had permission to be in my library in the first place. Instead, I painted the most vivid image I could of an innocent child, unjustly abused and mistreated. I told them about finding him in the city, about the group of people chasing him, and how I'd followed them to put a stop to it. I took another breath, willing myself not to glance at Nate, and then I told them everything that had happened in the dark storeroom.

I bowed again when I finished, listening to the mutters from behind me. As I returned to my place at my father's side, I couldn't stop myself from glancing sideways, and Nate's black eyes met mine for a long moment before we looked away from each other.

My father looked the other way. "Titan."

The tall man left his post against the wall, next to the seven culprits. Edric was waiting to take his place. Titan stopped on the same spot I had and knelt, the dark skin of his throat flashing in the light.

My father spoke the ritual words again as Titan rose to his feet. "Tell it all," Father said, his voice a little harder than it had been when he'd addressed me. "Tell it true."

"I was in the city," Titan began, "and I heard a commotion. I went to investigate and found people panicking. There were three men, shouting about demons. I asked where, and they pointed to the entrance to an old storeroom. I went inside and passed four more men coming out, one of them unconscious. When I reached the room, I found

Tamara, apparently alone. I checked that she was okay, and she pointed me to a back corner." Titan hesitated, took a breath, then continued. "There was a demon there." He stopped again, glancing sideways, but Nate's eyes were fixed on the floor.

"What did you do?" my father prompted, and Titan looked back at him.

"I picked up a torch from the floor, to see if there were any more. There weren't. It was just one. I recognised Nathaniel, and I knew he wasn't a threat."

There was an upsurge in the level of muttering, to the extent that my father swept a look over the hall. I caught the phrase 'not a threat' repeated in dubious tones. Titan waited for the noise to die down before he continued.

"He changed back and collapsed. Tamara and I carried him out."

My father nodded, and Titan moved aside. Father tapped his fingers lightly on the arm of the throne, eyes swinging from one side of the room to the other.

"Nathaniel," he said gently, and Nate's head came up at once. "How much of what happened do you remember?"

"Most of it."

"How did you feel?"

"Angry," Nate said after a moment, his voice low but audible. "Like everything I'd ever felt suddenly came to the surface."

"How many times have these men attacked you?" Father asked, his voice steady.

For the first time, Nate looked at the group.

"I don't know," he said. "It's different people, different numbers."

"How long has it been going on?"

"Ever since I got here," Nate said, his voice harder now.

"Have you ever made any attack on them or anyone else?"

"No."

"Have you ever threatened them or their loved ones?"

"No."

"Have you ever gone looking for them, sought out a confrontation, or

156

initiated contact with them in any way?"

"No."

The rest of the hall was silent, averting their eyes. I was sure, at that moment, even if they hadn't been the ones to lash out at Nate, none of them would have stood up to object to it. For the first time, I wondered if the abuse had ever happened in public. How many people had walked past, looking aside rather than stepping up to stop it? My stomach clenched as I looked back at Nathaniel. Sensing my gaze, he looked up at me, his eyes steady, his face tight. Something passed between us, like a fleeting movement caught from the corner of an eye, like a whisper of a promise not yet made.

Emerging onto the waterfront, I skidded to a halt, looking left and right. I'd run the other way from the gates, hoping to throw off any pursuers, then circled back, but there was no way to know how much time I'd bought. To the right was the sand circle where I'd held my lesson yesterday, and beyond it, the wall. The wharf in that direction was busy, with people moving back and forth. A fishing boat bobbed beside a pier in the harbour. A stream of people scurried from it, carting the catch towards the buildings. It would be possible to hide a rendezvous point amongst all that chaos, but it would be risky. Turning away, I jogged left, where the wharf was quieter. I only had so much time before someone came looking for me. I had to find Ava before they found me.

One of the warehouses, Rhianna had said. The large buildings here, with their lack of windows, would indeed be a perfect meeting place for a group that wanted to remain unobserved. That was assuming this 'Ava' she mentioned was part of the group of smugglers, not a different sort of secret rendezvous. It looked promising, though. Any of these warehouses could be the one. Maybe with a little bit of security to deter any eavesdroppers...

I slowed, looking over the people within sight.

Ahead, a group of four women stood together in the shadows cast by the cliffs, talking animatedly. Closer to me, a man and a woman sat together by an open doorway, making repairs to a fishing net. It was possible they were keeping guard, but the open entrance behind them didn't offer much security. I turned to look over my shoulder. Several paces behind me was a teenage boy, sitting cross-legged on the floor. His attention focused on a pair of dice he threw across the ground, observing the outcome, then throwing again. Immediately to his right was a wooden door, one of the first I'd seen here outside of the palace. The rest of the wall was solid stone, unbroken by windows. Private, secure, safe. I looked again at the boy.

It was the first time I'd seen anyone here older than an infant who wasn't working. A young, strong man, sitting idle, playing a game. He didn't fit.

I backed up until I was standing in front of him. The stone dice clattered across the ground.

"A'right?" The boy's voice replaced the song of the dice. He squinted up at me through a flop of dark hair.

Every second I stood there solidified my certainty I was in the right place. And I was done with caution.

"I'm looking for Ava."

The boy sniffed, the dice cracking together in his palm. "Don't know her."

He dropped his gaze, raising the dice, ready to throw again.

Something inside me clenched. I trembled with an anger that had been building ever since I awoke here. All I wanted was to *go home*. Why was everyone in this city determined to prevent that? Holt with his cowardice. Set by collaborating with him. Warren with his misguided affection. Mary with her infatuation. Now this boy, like all the others, was in my way.

I was done with being polite. I was not going to be so easily denied anymore.

Stepping sideways, I planted myself in front of the door, eyeing it critically. Hinges on the right, latch on the left. The boy hesitated, shoulders tensing, dice silent in his frozen hand as he glanced at me again. My eyes narrowed.

158

Drawing sharply on my wards of balance and strength, I spun, putting my back to the door and leaning forwards as I kicked out behind me.

The mechanism holding the door closed splintered as my foot connected. The door burst open, slamming against the wall with a sharp crack. The boy scrambled to his feet, a cry ready on his lips, but any warning he might have given was too late. I was already inside.

The large space was bright, despite the lack of windows facing the sea. The opposite wall was pock-marked with long slits, letting shafts of diffuse light permeate the cluttered warehouse. Sacks were piled high against the walls. Uneven pyramids of barrels climbed haphazardly from the remaining floor space, leaving thin, winding paths between them.

At least twenty people were scattered throughout the room. Far more than I'd expected. The closest group was three young women and one man, who had been lounging at the base of a pile of barrels. They lunged to their feet, raising blunt cudgels and staves.

The anger inside me roared hotter. Yet more people standing in my way, trying to deny me. If that was what they wanted to do, they could face the consequences of their choice. Maybe that would help convince Ava it was in her best interests to help me.

One of the women took a step forward. Too slow.

I moved through them like a storm without bothering to draw my swords. Titan's lessons flowed through my mind and down my limbs, my wards dark and writhing under my skin. The one who'd stepped forward opened her mouth in an angry query that never came. My fist snapped her jaw closed from below. Her eyes went wide as her hands flew up to her mouth, dropping her cudgel to the floor. She staggered backwards, colliding with the barrels, several of which crashed hollowly to the floor. The man hit the floor next, the victim of a collision between my knee and his groin that he was too slow to block. He sank without a sound as I moved past him. The last two women stood a few feet apart. I feinted towards the one on the left, who flinched back as I lunged to the right. A punch to the gut and the woman folded, choking around my fist. I hooked my foot around hers and shoved, sending her sprawling.

By now, the rest of the people were beginning to catch up with what was happening. Shouts echoed through the space, flurries of movement as those around me tried to decide whether they should approach or retreat. The final woman of the unlucky quartet had also recovered some of her wits. The end of her stave connected with my left thigh, just above the knee, and my leg buckled.

Hissing at the sharp pain, I hopped back a step, weight on my right leg, and drew one of my swords, the blade whistling through the air.

A flash of silver and red. Sudden stillness, rippling outwards.

The woman and I stared at each other, neither of us blinking. Blood welled in the cut across the back of her hand, shining on the edge of my blade where it was now pressed against her throat. The rest of the people fell silent, apart from the man on the ground behind me, coughing and wheezing.

I was breathing hard, anger and adrenaline pulsing in my chest. At the edge of my vision, I could see the wards on my outstretched arm. The ink was alive under my skin, moving with a mind of its own. My eyes flickered to the wound on the woman's hand. The first blood I'd drawn in this city.

And I'd accused Holt of not keeping his temper.

"Your boy outside wasn't very helpful," I said, pitching the words to the room at large. It was too late to take back my actions now. The only way to go was onwards.

No one moved.

"I'm looking for Ava."

There was a pause, a silent in-drawn breath.

"You've found her."

I looked sideways. The woman who'd spoken was halfway across the room, partially hidden by the barrels between us. Judging by the lines on her face, Ava was at least as old as Holt, possibly a little more. Older than either of my parents had been. Wisps of

160

pale blonde hair floated by her cheeks, having escaped from the plait curled around her head. She moved forwards with a lurching gait, picking her way through the room towards me. As she approached, I saw she was leaning on a wooden cane, limping heavily. She stopped beside the woman I'd punched in the stomach, who was climbing back to her feet, hands over her abdomen and glaring at me. Ava's expression was shrewd as she studied me.

I stepped back, removing my blade from the throat of the woman in front of me, who was still clutching her stave, unsure whether or not to use it. "We need to talk," I said to Ava.

She glanced at my victims. "Are you giving me a choice, Saviour?"

There was a moment of tense silence. I was sure her use of the title was not casual. There was an indrawn breath from by the wall, a slight movement. I glanced over, my eyes catching on a familiar face.

Rosita, one of my pupils from yesterday, stood at the front of a group of ten people, all of whom looked ready to attack at the slightest hint of a threat to Ava. Rosita blushed, dropping her gaze to the floor as I raised an eyebrow. What was she doing here?

Turning my gaze back to Ava, I slipped my sword away, holding my empty hands out to the side.

Ava's hand tightened on her cane, her eyes flitting around the room, pausing on people as if counting. Weighing the odds? Eventually, she nodded.

"Come with me." Her eyes left me again, repeating their circuit of the others, but with more focus this time as she let out a ream of instructions. "Someone get the door. Gennifer, help these guys up, then join us. You know who to bring. Rosita, you come too."

Orders given, Ava turned away, limping back through the maze of barrels. Softening the draw on my wards, I followed her. Rosita hurried along behind me.

"So." Ava halted beside a large wooden table, covered in tablets etched with tallies and notes, like the ones I'd seen on Holt's desk.

Leaning her cane against the table, she braced her hands upon the surface, eyes piercing me. Queen of a different sort of domain.

I walked on a little further into the small space, like a tranquil pool squashed between the trees of barrels and crates surrounding us.

"You wanted to talk."

Turning back to face Ava, I leaned against one of the stacks of barrels, comforted by the barrier at my back. They swayed precariously but remained upright.

Rosita hovered a few feet away, wide eyes flicking from myself to Ava.

Adrenaline was still making my heart race, my hands itching, but I tried to match Ava's composure. I wanted to advance on her, demand to know how her people got out of the city, to force her to share the secret with me. The memory of the blood on my blade was still vivid in my mind - blood I spilt, provoked or not. It made me feel uneasy for a reason I couldn't quite explain.

"It has been brought to my attention," I said, "that someone is missing from this city."

Ava gave no reaction. Behind Rosita, three more people approached two women and a man who joined the periphery of the group.

"Appeals have been made for my assistance in this matter."

"I'm aware of Rhianna's requests," Ava replied, her eyes flicking to the newcomers.

I followed her gaze. The man was vaguely familiar, looking back at me steadily. The woman I had punched in the stomach was glaring, her breaths still laboured. She had reclaimed her wooden cudgel, gripping it tightly as if longing to use it. The third woman was completely unknown to me.

"I was *not* aware that you had any inclination to assist her."

"She's not the one who requires assistance," I said, looking back at Ava. "There's a young man outside the protection of the wall. He's the one who needs... saving."

Ava's mouth twitched at the word. "And why exactly would you

162

be interested in saving him?"

That, unfortunately, was a good question. One for which I did not have an adequate answer. Then again, I hadn't expected this to be easy.

"Maybe I'm not," I said, holding her gaze. "But there is more than one life at stake. The people in this city need help, help I can provide. But not as the relations currently stand. Holt thinks I'm in league with the demons."

Rosita drew in a sharp breath, her face full of horrified outrage.

"If I can find Malcolm and bring him back, I hope that will go some way to persuading him he is wrong. Or at least to convince others of that."

"Holt is stubborn. He won't be swayed by popular opinion."

"Holt won't be King forever."

Ava raised an eyebrow. "I'd advise you against saying that in any other company. I expect he has had even less subtle thoughts about you, however."

"It wasn't a threat," I said mildly. "And whatever thoughts Holt may have, I hope he's not stupid enough to act upon them."

"Stupid, he is not," Ava agreed.

"But whilst he may be content to wait and see how things develop, there's still a boy in trouble."

"And what, exactly, do you want from us?"

"I want you to show me how you get out of the city."

The woman I didn't recognise let out a sharp bark of laughter. "Why would we do that?"

"What do you have to lose?"

"Everything!" the woman exclaimed.

"You," Rosita said at the same time. She looked afraid.

Ava nodded. "She's right. All you have done since you got here is to try and leave."

"What makes you say that?" I asked, trying and failing to keep my voice light. I hadn't actually tried to leave… yet.

Ava lowered her chin, giving me a very direct and unamused look. Did she know what had happened in my first audience with

Holt? There had been other people there. With a jolt, I realised where I recognised the man standing next to Rosita from; he had been on the balcony. And he must have reported all of what he'd heard back to Ava. What other spies did she have positioned around the city?

"If you were to learn of a way out," she continued as if I hadn't spoken, "you would simply disappear."

I looked at Rosita again, deliberately letting my gaze linger. "That's not *all* I've done. There are other things I've started here that are not finished." I turned back to Ava. "I would offer to let one of your people accompany me, but they wouldn't be able to keep up. I could give you my word I would return, but..."

"But it wouldn't mean much," Ava finished for me, nodding again.

"Rhianna asked me to save her son," I said. "I intend to do so, but I need your help."

"Malcolm is not your responsibility," the unknown woman said shortly.

"That's true," I agreed. "I'm not the one who left him out there."

Her jaw tightened, hands clenching into fists. "You don't know anything about it."

"And how many people do you have out there looking for him now?"

There was a telling silence, glances shot back and forth.

"We didn't want to leave him." The words were barely more than a whisper, Rosita's eyes on the floor as she spoke.

'*We*'.

My chest clenched at the pain in her expression.

"Maybe we can make a deal," Ava said. "Something in return for showing you the way out."

My heart leapt at her words, throwing off the momentary pity that gripped it. I kept my face blank, raising a calculated eyebrow. "I'm offering to search for your man for you. That is what you get in return."

"Or you leave, and we're left with nothing. I require something more to mitigate that risk."

I looked at her. Despite the limp in her stride, there was no weakness in her expression. "What do you want?"

Her eyes darted to my arms. "The markings. Tell us how to use them, and we'll show you the way out."

I didn't have to think about it. "No."

"No?" Ava cocked her head. "Do you want to leave or not?"

"Not for that."

Ava's jaw clenched, the challenging smirk sliding off her face. "Very well then." She straightened up, crossing her arms. "We have nothing more to discuss."

My mind raced, desperately trying to find another angle to work, but the hardness of her expressions rebuffed any ideas I had. She had set out her terms, and whether she was serious or merely testing my resolve, they were not terms I would ever agree to.

"Apparently not," I agreed.

Our eyes locked, neither of us blinking, both waiting for the other to break.

I gave up first, turning away from the older woman, pushing my way past Rosita and the others.

"Please!"

The desperate word made me hesitate and look back, but it wasn't Ava. The stricken plea had come from Rosita, her face distressed.

"I thought you were trying to help us," she continued, her voice quieter now I was looking at her. "Why help us to fight if you're not going to do this?"

Ava's face was visible past Rosita's shoulder, but I ignored her, keeping my gaze fixed on Rosita.

"I am helping you. But I can't give you the wards."

"Can't, or won't?" the other woman asked.

"Both."

"Then we'll do it without you," Ava spoke up. "You can't stop us trying ourselves."

My stomach twisted in fear. She was right; I couldn't stop them from experimenting with the wards. How long would it take before their imitations, copied from glimpses of my skin or straight off the wall, were accurate? Every angle, every measurement, would have to be perfect, but when they were...

"Then people will die," I said to her. "You don't know what you're doing, and people will get hurt. I can't make you believe me, but it's true. If you choose to disregard that warning, anything that happens will be your fault."

I turned to leave again, and this time, no one stopped me.

Outside, in the sunshine, I stalked away from the warehouse. The boy guarding the broken door glared at me as I departed. I wanted to snarl back but resisted. I'd let my temper get the better of me too many times in the past few minutes. Coming to a halt at the end of the wharf, I stared across the harbour, oblivious to any activity around me.

I had never lost control like that before, never been so unconstrained. Where had my mask been when I'd forced my way into the warehouse, the veil behind which I'd always been able to hide my emotions? The abandonment had been liberating. And dangerous. I remembered the cut across the back of the woman's hand, a wound I had dealt. If I had kept control of my temper, that might not have happened.

Would it have made any difference to the outcome of my conversation with Ava though? Would she have been more inclined to help me if I'd offered calmness instead of intimidation? I doubted it. She knew what she wanted from me, and it was something I couldn't give.

I knew some of the requirements involved in getting the wards. The recipient had to be a teenager, normally between 14 and 16. I'd been 14 years and 11 months, and for the weeks leading up to it, I'd visited Master Atticus every other day, waiting with bated breath each time as he looked me over and declared me to be "not quite" ready. Exactly what it was he'd been waiting for, I had no idea.

166

Then there were the secrets of the tattoos themselves, of the ink which was kept locked away until needed, guarded at all times. The composure and method for making it was known only to the Master Warder and his two senior journeymen.

Even once I'd received my wards, the pain of their activation seared forever into my memory, it had taken months of tutorage before I could draw on them reliably.

I vividly remembered the story of two boys who drew crude imitations of the wards on each other with burnt sticks for a game when they were ten. By some tragic miracle, one of them managed to get the speed ward right. The boy, delighted at his new ability, only managed a few paces with his newly increased speed before he tripped. He had broken his neck and died.

Wards created in a medium other than ink would be less potent, but the power they contained was no less dangerous.

Similar things would happen here if Ava encouraged her people to experiment with the wards themselves. Any warnings I gave, however, would likely be brushed aside as evidence of me trying to hoard the power of the wards for myself.

Staring across the rippling water, reflecting the scudded grey clouds and blue sky above, I felt uneasy. Surely, as the one who understood the risks, it was my responsibility to prevent such tragedies from occurring here, but how?

My first thought was to go to Holt and reveal the identity and location of the hunters. The information might even be enough to persuade him I was not in league with the demons and to let me leave. But even as the brilliance of the idea occurred to me, something held me back. I thought of Warren's words, about how no one else would give up the hunters because they didn't want to anger everyone who benefited from their activities. And whilst they seemed determined I wouldn't benefit, what would the rest of the people do if their so-called 'Saviour' outed the people who had been risking their lives to feed them for years? Did I want to make that many enemies?

Was there anyone else who could stop Ava's plan? Maybe

Warren? Or Set? Set might be a better choice. Heir to the throne, Leader of the Scouts, he seemed to command more respect than his younger brother. Would it be enough to curb Ava's ambitions?

"Mara?"

I looked back. It was Rosita, one foot scuffing at the ground.

"Are you… I mean, can I…" She glanced away, towards the wall. I waited, giving her nothing.

"The lessons," she managed to force out. "Can I still come?"

Glancing behind me, I followed her gaze. Across the other side of the harbour, I could see a small group of people waiting. Even with the distance between us, I recognised Keera's diminutive stature and Warren's profile as he joined the group. It must be later in the day than I'd realised.

I frowned. Holt had made it clear last night that he didn't want me training with the fighters. But, now I thought about it, he hadn't explicitly said I wasn't to continue the lessons. And it seemed he hadn't passed his sentiments on to Warren or any of the others. An oversight or a deliberate risk?

I turned back to Rosita's hopeful face. "I'm not going to stop teaching you," I said.

She relaxed at once.

"Tell me something; does your involvement here," I nodded subtly back towards the warehouse, "have something to do with you being the only one who's got experience with unarmed combat?"

Rosita gave a brief, self-conscious grin. "It might."

I snorted with amusement. "Go on. I'll be there in a moment."

She hurried off, but I lingered for a few moments, staring across the water again as my humour faded. My plan to persuade Holt to let me leave had failed. My attempts to get Ava to reveal her secret way out had failed. It seemed like every moment was forcing me closer to my final option, the one I'd hoped to avoid; violence.

I'd tasted it already in the warehouse, and its residue was bitter in my mouth. It also carried its own risk. I'd never seen any less than a dozen soldiers on the gate, all of them armed. Against the four in the warehouse, one of them had managed to get a hit on me. And whilst I hadn't been aiming to hurt anyone in that instance, I didn't like the scaling up of the odds.

I needed a new plan, but at that moment, I didn't have one, and people were waiting for me. Turning away from the empty expanse of the ocean, I made my way toward my students and tried not to feel like I was turning away from my own people, waiting so much further away.

11

Pressure

Father turned away from Nathaniel, towards the group at the other side of the hall, half of whom cowered under his gaze.

"Nicholas," Father said. His voice was calm, but there was a hard edge to it. "Step forward."

The leader of the group turned his head, looking away from Nate at last. He eyed my father for a few seconds before moving away from the rest of them and stopping in front of my father. He did not kneel.

"Did you follow this boy into a storeroom with violent intentions?" *my father asked.*

Nate twitched at the description, but it was true. He wasn't technically old enough to be considered an adult. That could work in his favour.

"Yes," Nicholas said, his eyes snapping back to Nate, who held the gaze without flinching.

"Why?" the king demanded.

"Because he shouldn't be here. You risk people's lives by letting him live here."

"You risk everything by thinking you have the right to change that."

"He's a half-blood," Nicholas said. "It could kill everyone in the city!"

"And did you stop to think that you might be the one to make him want to do so?" Father shot back. "If you had concerns, you should have raised them with me rather than taking matters into your own hands and attacking a child."

"That thing is not a child!"

I couldn't help glancing at Nate. His eyes were narrowed, but he remained in place, not moving a single muscle that might give credit to the wild accusations.

"You should never have allowed him into the city! Or..." Nicholas broke off, dropping his gaze as he reconsidered the wisdom of his words.

"Or?" my father prompted.

Nicholas looked up with fire in his eyes. "Or you should have just killed him," he hissed. There was a sweep of muttering, though who it was in favour of, I couldn't tell.

"Something you have failed to do."

I drew back at my father's words, a sharp breath searing its way down my throat.

"You clearly weren't going to do anything to protect the people of this city," Nicholas said.

"And despite your delusions, you clearly can't. Again."

Nicholas's jaw snapped shut with an audible crack, his hands balling into fists.

'Again'? I frowned internally. What did Father mean by that?

"You would condemn an innocent," my father said, leaning forwards. "One who has never threatened you or anyone else in this city. Who has acted only in self-defence. I have heard nothing to justify your actions, which display a consistent lack of moral judgement and empathy."

"Lack of judgment!" Nicholas exploded, the shout cutting through the muttering of the crowd. He took a step forward, but Edric was faster, instantly blocking his path to my father. Nicholas ignored the Guardsman, staring past him at Father. "You're the one who let him in here, even after what happened last time! You didn't see what he turned into; it's only a matter of time before someone else is killed, and that will be on your hands! If you're not going to do what is necessary, you're too blind to lead us!"

The noise of the crowd peaked, then died away.

Everyone stared at my father. It wasn't the words for an official challenge, not quite. My father could still order them taken from the room. He did not. Instead, he raised his eyebrows, as if inviting Nicholas to continue.

My hands shook.

He couldn't possibly… Surely Nicholas would reconsider, would think better of the idea. That must be what my father was waiting for. He was making sure everyone saw Nicholas back down.

Nicholas's chin came up. My stomach dropped.

"Rygorn, you are not fit to lead."

The words echoed in my head, over and over. Words without regret. It was done. The challenge was issued.

I let out a slow breath. Father would have to face it. He had the choice of when to do so within a maximum of three days. He could also dictate the weapons used. The trial would have to be delayed until afterwards. Maybe that was Nicholas's goal, to cause a setback, though I couldn't see how it would benefit anyone. It wouldn't help him anyway. He would die. Father would win the challenge. He had to.

My father hadn't moved, staring at the younger man, his face unreadable. Then he stood and drew his sword, Mercy, in one swift movement.

Edric, still standing in front of Nicholas, glanced back.

Father turned, laying his sword down across the arms of the throne. There was a tightness around his eyes. I thought I saw the sides of his mouth twitching, but then he turned back to face the audience, and the expression was gone.

Breath raced in and out of my lungs. I waited for Father to declare when the challenge would take place. But he descended the steps without saying a word.

A wave of whispers swept the hall. Nicholas swallowed.

"I accept your challenge," the king said.

To the side, Titan's jaw was clenched, and his hand tensed on the hilt of his sword, but he said nothing. Did nothing. I took half a step forward, about to cry out, but Helena grabbed my arm from behind, pulling me back. Her grip was painfully tight.

My stomach trembled, shudders rippling up into my chest. The room was suddenly cold.

"Edric," my father said.

The dark-haired man stepped aside, removing the barrier between Nicholas and my father. A tiny squeak escaped my lips.

Nicholas didn't wait, striding forwards at once, building momentum as he crossed the empty space.

My father watched him approach without making a single move to defend himself. When Nicholas was almost running, my father made his first move. He bowed.

My mouth opened, but the ability to make any noise had deserted me, and my shriek curdled in my throat, sticking there, choking me.

The move surprised Nicholas. His strides faltered, but only for a moment. He sped up, letting out a yell as he launched himself at my father, who was still half-bent over, unprepared, defenceless.

It was over almost before it began, a seamless blur of limbs. Nicholas's leg came up towards my father's face, but an arm was already there, blocking it. A twist and duck, and Father was behind him, one arm hooked around his foot, the other snaking around his neck. Nicholas flailed, off-balance. My father yanked him upright.

My jaw hung open. I'd never seen anyone move that fast, not even Titan. My father's upper arm was a mass of writhing black ink, his wards swarming under his skin like a pit of snakes. A hunger grew deep in my chest. The imagined pain of the needle was forgotten.

I wanted that power under my skin. I needed it.

Nicholas wasn't finished yet. The wards on his arms were alive as well. I flinched as he drove an elbow backwards into my father's side. Balanced on only one foot, his aim was off, but he still connected. My father didn't even let out a breath at the impact. He drove his knee into the leg still supporting Nicholas's weight. It buckled, and my father released his foot, letting Nicholas crash to the ground, his knees hitting the floor with two echoing cracks.

Nicholas abandoned the offensive, both hands now scrabbling at my father's elbow where it tightened around his throat. There was blood where Nicholas's fingernails gouged tracks in his arm, but my father ignored his efforts, looking sideways to where his companions stood, staring on in horror. One of them took a step forward, but another grabbed their arm, holding them back.

"Anyone else?" my father asked, his voice carrying over the gargling noises coming from Nicholas.

They were silent, faces pale, eyes wide. My father raised his gaze, surveying the rest of the hall.

Nicholas went quiet.

"Anyone else?!" his voice rose.

A ringing silence answered him, broken by the dull thud as Nicholas's lifeless body slumped to the floor.

I closed my mouth.

"Next time you think about taking the law into your own hands, think it's okay to hurt a child, regardless of who their parents are, think of questioning me... remember him." My father stood for another second, staring out at the crowd, who looked back with the same wide-eyed expressions. He turned to face Nate. "I hereby declare you innocent of any wrongdoing. Injuries induced were in self-defence. This session is over. Clear the hall!"

As the crowd hastened to obey, many glancing back over their shoulders, I looked at Nate. He was staring at my father as if seeing him for the first time, his expression unreadable.

Helena, seeming to remember herself, let go of my arm, which throbbed at the sudden release, and stepped backwards.

"Take them downstairs. You know where," Father said to Edric, nodding to the rest of Nicholas's conspirators. "I'll deal with them later." He wore a grim smile as he climbed the steps to the throne. I stared at him.

Titan broke the silence, letting out a string of words I didn't recognise. I glanced at him, shaken out of my numbness. I could count the number of times I'd heard him utter his native language on one hand with fingers to spare. He strode over, stopping inches behind my father.

"Hamma is going to kill you for doing that," Titan said so only Father and I could hear.

"Only if Zita doesn't do it first," he replied, picking up Mercy and slipping it away.

"You deliberately made sure he stayed with her, didn't you?"

"Call it a contingency plan."

"And you provoked Nicholas on purpose. What if you'd lost?"

My father gave Titan a sharp look. "Thank you for your confidence."

Titan held his gaze. "Not the point, Rygorn. Don't do that again. What were you thinking?"

"I was thinking about relative values."

Titan stared at him for a moment, then his eyes flashed past my father, towards Nate, and he frowned. He glanced at me then looked away again.

My father followed his gaze, turning to me. "Alright, Tammie?"

I opened my mouth, but nothing came out. I tried again. Nothing. Tremors still radiated from my stomach. It was all I could do to breathe. My eyes darted from the slumped figure in the middle of the floor to the wards on my father's arm, the black ink once more constrained within the swirling markings.

Reaching out, my father squeezed my shoulder, then turned, looking across the hall and beckoning with his other hand. I turned. Nate hesitated for a second before approaching, his steps measured. He stopped in front of us, eyes fixed somewhere around my father's elbow. No one spoke for a moment.

"You didn't have to do that," Nate said, breaking the silence.

"No," my father agreed, "I didn't. But I did."

"Why?"

My father glanced past Nate at the emptying hall. Alicia was hovering, halfway to the doors, but the rest of the crowd was well out of earshot. A quick nod told Alicia she could approach, and he turned back to Nate, beginning to speak without waiting for her to arrive.

"Some of us have been doing more productive things than sitting around in the dark," he said.

Nate didn't look away at the chastisement, though his jaw tensed slightly, and his eyes narrowed.

"Do you know who Elissa was?" Father continued.

"Another half-blood," Nate answered. "An orphan. She died twenty-five years ago."

"Do you know what happened to her?"

"She was taken in by a family, raised by them. And when she was fourteen, she killed them all and several others." Nate didn't look away from my father. "I assume she transformed."

Father nodded. "She did. It took five members of the Guard to stop her. Nicholas's parents lived next to the family that took her in."

I swallowed as I looked down at Nicholas's body.

"He wasn't there when she transformed, but they were. So was his little brother."

Nate's gaze had drifted aside, staring off into space. What was he thinking? Was he trying to imagine that day or perhaps reliving his own transformation? I pictured him as he had been, the inky black skin, the pointed teeth, claws and horns and growls. What must it have been like, to have a monster suddenly ripping through your home, through your family... Or to have it happen when you weren't there? Maybe imagining it would be worse than actually witnessing it.

Behind Nate's shoulder, Alicia's face was like the moon, pale and distant.

"Nicholas thought my mother shouldn't have allowed Elissa into the city in the first place," my father continued.

"Maybe he was right." Nate's words were very quiet. Alicia reached out, taking hold of his hand and squeezing it.

"Perhaps," my father said calmly. "When your existence became known, he requested an audience with me and gave a rather passionate speech about how you should be killed immediately. Needless to say, I refused to acquiesce. He has been gathering support against me ever since. To be blunt, I'm surprised he didn't just kill you himself. If he *hadn't been so scared of you, he probably would have."*

Dark eyes flicked up to his face. "There were times when I think he was trying," Nate said.

My hands balled into fists. Titan's had done the same.

"I'm not surprised. And I apologise for allowing it to continue as long as it did. But I needed him to make the challenge against me. I'm sorry for what you have been through."

Nate looked up at him, holding his gaze at last. Eventually, he nodded. "I owe you an apology too."

"Oh? What for?"

"That first day... I thought you'd judged me then, because of what I am."

"I did," my father said, and there was an odd smile playing around his mouth. "I judged you as someone who needed further judgement."

When I reached the sandy circle, all those who had been present for the session yesterday had arrived. Today, however, they did not begin practising amongst themselves but waited for me. Warren was at the front of the group, his eyes bright, an eager smile twitching at his mouth.

I didn't return it, glancing away. It wouldn't do to encourage him.

Once again, a crowd had gathered along the wharf. I scanned the group, wondering how many of them were spies for either Holt or Ava. As I looked, two familiar men pushed to the front, both red-faced and breathing hard. I smirked at them before turning away. What had they and Set made of my sudden disappearance? Would they report back to Holt that they'd lost me or try and hide it? I couldn't bring myself to care.

My thoughts still full of the encounter with Ava, I barely noticed what I said to the students. I let them split themselves into groups of three, which could coalesce into squads of six, giving them even better odds. I acted as the 'opponent' for them to train against, my wards letting me imitate the speed of a demon. Even when we were finished and I stood alone in the centre of the circle after dismissing them, the warmth around my wards—speed, balance, and strength—was slow to dissipate, lingering deep under my skin.

They had struggled at first, unsure of how to counter my swiftness, hindering each other as they tripped and stumbled around my whirlwind of motion. It had taken several frustrating rounds against each group before Warren, Keera, and the third member of their group - Jory, a man a few years older than me with sandy blond hair that reminded me of Nate - began to talk to each other. Their short, sharp instructions - 'there', 'mine!', 'back', 'go' - let them shift into a workable cohesion. I had aching bruises forming on my arm and lower back that told of their success. The other groups had followed suit and made quick progress.

Now, watching them leave, I was left with a curious mixture of hope, pride, and despair. I had no doubt I was doing the right thing. Though I couldn't give them my wards, I could give them the skills and confidence to stand against the demons. And I could no longer deny I cared for these people. Not only the individuals, Warren, Rosita, Noah, the faces I was coming to know, but for the others as well. The nameless masses who, despite their cowering and their prophecy and their secrets, had forged a place for themselves inside me.

Their story could so easily have been mine. If my people didn't have the wards, we would have been equally defenceless against the demons. How could I judge them for hiding behind their wall when it was the only defence they had? Did we not hide behind our wards? We would never expect one of the Unmarked to stand beside us in the fight. These people hid and waited for a saviour because it was all they could do.

Yet I despaired as well because I couldn't help them without forsaking my people. To leave no longer felt like a requisite but a betrayal. But to stay here and delay my return home would be a much greater one, a treachery so large I could barely comprehend it, let alone contemplate carrying it out. No, I couldn't stay.

The crowd that had amassed to watch our practice was breaking up, the curious faces drifting away like dandelion seeds in the wind. My two shadows from earlier had disappeared at some point. That made me frown. There was no way Holt would have called them off, so they must have been replaced by other, subtler watchers.

Free, to a certain extent, I wandered alone through the city to one of the mess halls and ducked inside. I ate alone, head down, practically inhaling the dark stew on offer. It was watery and over-salted, but I didn't care. Across the room, a child appeared to feel the same, griping at their smaller portion. Their mother tipped more stew into the child's bowl from her own before returning to her conversation. Once my hunger was satisfied, the guilt over the confrontation with Noah returned. It was too late to do anything about it, though, and I couldn't see any other answer I could have given him. I didn't want to upset the group Warren had already amassed, and I didn't have enough time to work with Noah on his own. Between training the group and juggling plans to try and get out of here, I was already stretched too thin.

That thought reminded me of my failure to convince Ava and her group of poachers to help me earlier, bringing a scowl to my face. After the disastrous meetings with Holt, they had been my best hope. Was there something more I could do to convince them? I remembered Ava's face as she'd made her counter demand for knowledge of the wards and felt my jaw clench. It was doubtful she would back down or settle for less. Which left me with one option: fighting my way through the soldiers at the gate and making a run for it.

I sat for a while, resisting the idea, as the dinner crowd thinned. I had yet to spot anyone following me. Either Holt had realised it was pointless, or the replacements he'd chosen were simply better at their job. The noise level increased, and I blinked, looking around properly. Despite the late hour and the food having been dispensed with, people lingered, splitting into groups from three or four to larger clusters of more than ten. The bigger groups let out raucous bellows of laughter. I could hear the clatter of dice between their outbursts. It seemed this was a time for socialising. I stood up before my presence could disturb their relaxation, or worse, one of the groups invited me to join them.

The streets outside were quieter, but the evening was still light enough for me to move through them without tapping my sight ward. Another beacon of noise and laughter drew me to another mess hall, and I loitered in the shadows outside, watching those within until a face caught my gaze.

Set, the elder of the two princes, was standing behind a group of four people playing a game that seemed to involve carved blocks of stone. He was smiling, making comments on the play. As I watched, a woman approached him from the side. He turned to her without a hint of hesitation, instantly as focused on her as if they were alone in the room rather than surrounded by talk and laughter on all sides.

The scene repeated itself several times as I watched, Set slipping in and out of the general inclusion of the game for each person who approached him. It put me in mind of Hamma, always willing to talk but still constantly alert to any danger that might present itself. It took a moment for me to remember Hamma was dead, along with my father and the rest of the guard. The knowledge hit me like a solid blow to the stomach, sucking the breath from my lungs and the purpose from my heart. I wanted to turn away, to find a dark corner to retreat into and never come out. But that wasn't how they had raised me.

I stepped out of the shadows I'd been skulking in and made my way into the large room. Set's eyes snapped to me as I stepped inside. I didn't break from his gaze, wending my way towards him through the people clustered around the benches. Instead of waiting for me to come to him, he met me halfway, skilfully manoeuvring us to a relatively quiet section of the room.

"Mara," he greeted me. "How are you?" His smile appeared genuine, but I remembered what I'd overheard between him and his brother; he thought I was playing them.

I jerked my head. "I've been better."

"Oh?" he tilted his head, the very picture of respectful interest.

"Be honest with me," I said, taking the more direct route. "What's it going to take for your father to let me leave?"

Set paused, his jaw clenching. It ruined his placid expression. "Let's sit," he said, moving further away from the crowds to a bench next to the wall.

I sat opposite him, waiting.

"It's not as simple as you might think," Set began.

I kept my face impassive, though I desperately wanted to object.

"You disagree."

I blinked, shocked he had been able to read me so easily. "I don't see why it's so complicated."

"You made it complicated when you antagonised my father."

"When *I* antagonised *him?*"

"Asking questions, challenging him in front of everyone, always pushing for more. Not to mention what you did last night. And that stunt this afternoon. Pleased with yourself after that, were you?"

"It made a point." It *had* felt good to use my wards and leave the pair who'd been trailing me behind, but I didn't have to tell him that.

Set snorted. "Indeed. Point received. You won't have to deal with them anymore."

I drew back slightly, surprised. Had it been Set, not Holt, who had called them off? Was that why I hadn't seen anyone else following me?

"Yeah, you're welcome," Set shot at me, guessing my unasked question. "Couldn't just keep your head down, could you? Now look at the mess we're in."

I considered him as he looked away. His voice was calm, but there was bitterness underneath. Maybe I could read him just as well as he could read me. And he'd said 'we', not 'you'.

"Mess?" I prompted him.

"You stuck in here, and one of our guys stuck out there."

"You want to find Malcolm."

"Of course I do," Set said, lowering his voice.

"Then why don't you do something about it?" I hissed, matching his volume. "You're the king's son, you're in charge of the scouts. There must be something you can do."

"I've already told the scouts to be on the lookout, but I can't do anything more without my father's approval, and he's not going to give it when he's so obsessed with you."

Obsessed? I wasn't sure whether to be exasperated or flattered.

"And what are you going to do if one of them comes back and tells you they found a sign that Malcolm is alive out there?"

Set's eyes jumped to mine, then dropped just as quickly to the table between us.

Guilty. Guilty, guilty, guilty.

I leant forward. "They haven't already…"

"No!" Set hissed back, gritting his teeth as he glanced around. "And if they do, I'll do whatever it takes to get him home. But at this point… it's unlikely."

I sat back again, unable to dispute that. I didn't know this place, how it worked, what went on, but surely if Malcolm could have returned, he would have done so by now. And if he had been detained for some reason… it was unlikely to be a good one. I understood Rhianna's desperation better with every passing hour. Had everyone in this city given up on her son?

I met Set's eyes. *Whatever it takes.* Maybe there was still one person who hadn't given up on Malcolm.

"Give me some time," Set said, leaning forwards, eyes flicking past me to the rest of the room. "I'll talk to my father, but it will take a while."

I glanced over my shoulder, both to check if anyone was too close and to give myself a moment to think. There was a promise in Set's face. He would do everything in his power to get me out of this city. In that respect, he was on my side, perhaps more than anyone else. In return, he was asking me for time, for patience.

I thought of all Nate had told me about what was happening back home; how Djet was murdering anyone who stood against him, about the rumours of missing children, the Figures he had awoken,

182

currently unaccounted for. I thought of Nate himself, undoubtedly worried that I hadn't arrived home yet. What was he doing now? Would he be searching for me again, putting himself on a direct collision course with the Figures?

Set wanted time. I couldn't give it.

"How long?" I asked, turning back to him. "A week? A month? People are waiting on me. You're not the only one with responsibilities."

"Then why are you still here? You know where the gate is; you could have tried to fight your way out. And from the reports about what you've been up to with my brother, you might even succeed. But you haven't. Why not?"

All the excuses I'd been telling myself flickered through my mind as I searched for one he might believe.

"Honestly."

Our eyes met, and I saw my own soul reflected back at me. Were we the same? We could read each other so easily.

"Alright," I said. "I'll tell you the truth if you answer a question honestly for me."

I knew what his answer would be before he gave it. It was the same response I would have given.

"Depends what your question is."

I waited, letting him weigh the risk.

"Fine," he said after a pause. "Ask your question. If I answer, then you have to answer mine."

I smiled, impressed, and nodded. Then I sat, letting him wait as I considered the evidence surrounding the question I wanted to ask. The tiny patch of land at the northern end of the city for crops. The watered-down stew, the careful way it was doled out, the times I'd seen adults tipping some of their portions into the children's bowls. The barrels in Ava's warehouse, which had fallen so hollowly to the ground, swaying when I leant on them. Because they were empty.

"How long before this city runs out of food?"

Set's nostrils flared as he drew in a sharp breath, eyes widening.

He hadn't expected me to know about that. Despite my evidence, I hadn't been certain of it myself until I'd seen his reaction.

He was silent for a couple more seconds before he answered me. "We'll make it through the winter."

I stared at him, waiting for him to say more.

Surely there must be more to say.

In the silence, I swallowed.

I had a hundred responses running through my mind. But none of them would help. They had been living with this problem for too long already. There was nothing I could suggest they wouldn't surely have thought of already.

"What are you going to do?"

Set looked past me, his eyes sweeping slowly over the rest of the room, over the people congregated there. The pain on his face was horrible to see. Eventually, he looked back at me and smiled, though there was no humour in the expression.

"I answered your question. It's your turn," he said. "Why are you still here?"

My jaw clenched, teeth grinding painfully, but I had made a deal with him, and he had answered me.

"The wall," I said. "The wards on it. I know some of them," I flexed my shoulders slightly so he couldn't miss my meaning, "and it's clear what some of the others can do. But there's more there. Some I've never seen. And I've never seen wards joined together like they are here. That wall holds knowledge, more than I can understand or take with me.

"Yes, I could probably get past your soldiers at the gate. But I couldn't do it cleanly. There would be deaths. And what then? I want to walk out; I don't want to have to run. And I want to be able to come back."

"Surely you could just make a copy of the wards."

"Not with enough accuracy. It would have to be perfect for them to activate."

There was more to it than just that. I didn't know if the wards were dynamic, like those on my skin, able to be drawn upon or

184

released as needed, or if they were only able to be used on a static medium, like the wall, fixed and unchanging.

"But the Warders, the people who know more about them, if they could come here and study the wall…" I let the sentence tail off. There were too many possibilities to put into words.

"It's the truth," I said when Set didn't respond.

"I believe you," he said, eyes on the table.

"Then what is it?" It was *something*. I could see it, sitting behind the mask he wore.

"Nothing," he lied, pasting a tight smile on his face as he sat back, stretching his shoulders as he looked away from me.

"I wouldn't expect it for free," I said, reaching across the table, though I stopped short of actually touching him. "Whatever you needed that I could give, I would."

I meant it. Food, fighters to stand against the demons, more training, I would negotiate any deal they wanted.

Set hesitated for a moment, then stood up, the tense smile not leaving his face. "I'm sure my father will appreciate that. Please excuse me; it's been a long day. Sleep well." He stepped away from the bench. He didn't leave the room but made his way across the room to a pair of women by the opposite wall, engaging them in conversation. I twisted to watch him go, but he didn't look back.

I turned away slowly, my fingers dragging over the rough surface of the bench. What had I done to make Set shut down like that? There had been something before then; I could still feel the residual tremors of it in my bones. Was it just the similarities of our circumstances—both children of a monarch—that had enabled us to see through the other's mask so easily, or was it something more?

The murmurs of the room behind me were becoming pointed. If I remained here any longer, no doubt the attention would only increase. Pushing to my feet, I wound my way towards the exit. I needed to think further about what Set had said.

"Saviour, won't you join us?"

I meant to keep walking, but something in the voice caught my attention. My eyes flickered to the side, and I saw something in my peripheral vision that couldn't be ignored. A familiar face. My whole body jerked, spinning so fast that I felt warmth under the skin of my shoulder as I drew on my ward to keep myself balanced, eyes searching for the face I'd seen. I found it at once and was instantly disappointed.

His skin was the same dark colour, and he had the same square jaw and shaved head, but it wasn't Titan. His eyes were closer together, his face older. My tense shoulders dropped with disappointment, but it was too late to hide my reaction.

"Sorry," the Southerner said, "I didn't mean to startle you."

"No, it's not…" I took a breath, trying to steady my racing heart. "I thought you were someone else."

"You've met some of my kinsmen," the man said. His accent was reminiscent of Titan's, though somewhat stronger, drawing out his vowels, stretching each word as if to feel it within his mouth for longer.

"Just one, really," I said, unable to deny it. I had also met the crew of a Southern ship whilst in Lambridge several years ago, but only briefly.

"Please," he gestured for me to sit down, pushing aside the tokens he'd been using to play a game with the rest of the group. They were all watching, eyes flicking from him to me, a mixture of interest and annoyance across their faces.

I hovered, not wanting to accept but unable to walk away.

"I'd welcome any news of the one you know," the man said, seemingly unbothered by my refusal to sit. "We don't often leave the Isles."

I knew that much from my lessons. I knew the names of the four Southern Isles that were populated and could identify their shapes on the maps.

"Yet here you are," I pointed out, playing for time.

The dark-skinned seafarers who dwelt on the Isles were notoriously close-knit, rarely accepting outsiders onto their land or leaving to settle elsewhere. Titan had, to my memory, never said a

186

single word about his homeland, no matter how many times I'd asked. He probably wouldn't want me talking about him with this man. I felt a surge of rebellious anger. Why did I care what Titan would want? Pushing aside my doubts, my guilt, the memories of all he had ever done for me, I took a step closer to the table.

The man laughed at my comment. "Aye, guess I had a change in perspective or something like that. Home wasn't home anymore. So I jumped ship. Somehow ended up here, don't ask me how."

"Because no one else would have you," one of the women put in, drawing laughs from them all.

"Oh please, you wouldn't know what to do without me," he shot back, grinning. "The name's Perrin," he said, turning back to me. "Won't you sit? I came here a few years ago, haven't heard much from the Isles since. Has your friend been away long?"

Guilt and daring warred within me, but I couldn't help taking another step closer. He might know something about Titan's past. Not that it even mattered anymore, but my curiosity was rising with every second.

"Yes, he left a long time ago," I said. "He was very young, only a teenager."

Perrin was frowning, his face thoughtful.

"His name's Titan."

Perrin's frown remained for a couple more seconds, then his eyes went wide. "Winds and waves," he breathed. "Titan? Zattan's boy?"

"You knew him?"

"Not personally, but the *stories*! I mean…" His eyes were bright with excitement as he licked his lips.

"What happened?"

"It was years ago, obviously, and I was away at the time, but apparently, Zattan got back from a voyage, and the very next day, he beat the kid half to death right in the street."

I gaped at him, speechless with shock.

"Someone tried to pull Zattan off him, got themselves a taste of his temper for their troubles, and the kid managed to get away. As

187

far as I know, no one from the Isles ever saw him again. Most people thought Zattan finished the job off later, in private. The family never mentioned his name again."

My jaw was still hanging open. It couldn't be true. The tale Perrin told of an abused, outcast child didn't fit with the Titan I knew, so strong, so funny, such a fierce fighter.

The Titan who had left his home at such a young age that he had been able to gain the trust and friendship of my father and grandmother in time to be able to receive his wards at Alderth. The Titan who never spoke of his home, or his family, or his past.

"Guess he never told you any of that," Perrin said, chest puffed out.

I shook my head, still wide-eyed, trying to remember how to speak. "Why?" I croaked out. "Why would his father do that?"

Perrin shrugged. "There were a million rumours. Anything you can imagine, it was speculated on. It was all anyone on Arcton talked about for months. Provided none of his family was within earshot."

Arcton. The south-westernmost of the Isles and the second largest. And apparently, the place Titan had lived. My guilt returned with a vengeance. What right did I have to pry into Titan's past? Weighing all he'd ever done, he deserved better from me. I stepped back, feeling slightly sick.

"It was good to meet you," I said faintly. "I have to go."

"Sorry," Perrin said, seeming to look at me properly for the first time since beginning his account. "Not the nicest of stories."

I gave a jerk of my head, not sure whether it was meant to be a nod or a shake. As I looked up, I met Set's eyes. He was watching me from the other side of the room. I turned away and hurried out.

The darkness outside was cool and welcoming. I made my way back up to the tunnels in the mountain, barely registering the journey. My thoughts were full of Set's face, the empty barrels in the warehouse, and Titan, whom I hadn't seen in almost four years.

12

To Fall

My toes ground into the dirt as I spun, the world blurring around me as I retreated from my attacker, the sword I still wasn't entirely comfortable with held firmly in my grip. But no matter how fast I moved, he was always there, poised, ready. Inescapable.

In one last desperate attempt, I drew awkwardly on the tattoo on my left arm, gritting my teeth with effort before the unnatural speed flowed through my limbs. I darted past his next attack, feeling a brief thrill of triumph before my feet betrayed me. I fell, sprawling spectacularly onto the dirt.

Above me, Nathaniel laughed, but there was no cruelty in the sound. Scowling, I rolled over, spitting dust from my mouth. He grinned, twirling his sword lazily before advancing on me. His weapon looked so natural in his grip, an easy extension of his arm.

Titan moved forwards as well, shaking his head. Nate reached me first, extending a hand and pulling me to my feet.

"Speed and balance," Titan said, his eyes on me. "There's a reason we have both. Your strength will help as well once you can use them all together."

I swallowed down a wave of nausea. My strength would never help me again. Not in the way it should. The wound on my back, though scabbed over now, seemed to sear with new pain.

"I can't even draw on one, let alone two," I said.

"It will get easier," Titan promised. "Are you practising?"

I said nothing, but the silence said enough. What was the point of practising? I would never be strong enough now. Once Titan realised that I had reached my limit, that I would be so weak forever...

Titan shook his head. "Well, that's your choice. If you'd rather trip over your own feet here, where we get to watch you..." He spread his hands. "I don't think Nate and I are going to object to the entertainment."

I forced myself to nod, avoiding his gaze as I jabbed the point of my weapon into the ground.

"Still no good?" Titan asked, gesturing to it.

Grimacing, I shook my head. "It just feels wrong."

It was true, but I was glad to be able to blame at least part of my limitations on the fact that I hadn't felt comfortable handling any of the weapons I'd tried so far. If it distracted Titan from my other issues, I wasn't going to discourage him.

"That's okay." He shrugged, holding out a hand. I surrendered the sword to him without resistance. "We'll have another look in a minute. But first..." He turned away from me, and Nate's smile vanished at once. "You. Sloppy footwork, too eager on the attack. Where's the control we discussed?"

Nate made no response, his expression wary.

"You know your problem?" Titan sighed. "You're getting overconfident."

Nate backed away as Titan raised the weapon I had rejected. He spared a moment to wink at me before stalking after the retreating half-blood. I pretended to share in his amusement as I walked back to the wall surrounding the yard and sat down, watching them circle each other. At least I wouldn't be the only one humiliated today.

I could just make out the tendrils snaking along both Titan's arms and over his shoulders as he drew on his wards. The black ink was hard to pick out under his dark skin. He had been older than most when he'd received his wards but seemed to use them effortlessly. Master Atticus knew his business well.

They clashed in a whirl of limbs and a clang of metal, their feet throwing up puffs of dust as they danced back and forth. I'd thought of

Nate as a natural predator, but he was outmatched by the more experienced Guardsman.

Titan didn't have to coach us, and I knew it ate into his time off-duty, but I felt more gratitude than guilt. I was sure no one else would have agreed to teach Nate. The 'incident' was almost a year behind us, but it hadn't been forgotten, and the consequences remained. My father had made official the proclamation that Nate wasn't allowed outside the city, a punishment to be brought up whenever anyone tried to question the injuries he had caused when he transformed. I'd tried to talk to Father about it, but he shrugged me off, saying nothing had changed. In some ways, he was right.

People would skirt around Nate on the streets, whispering as he passed, hiding their children away at the sight of him. As I hadn't spent any time with him in public before the incident, it was hard to say if this was any different to what he'd experienced before.

If it ever went any further than looks and whispers, Nate never mentioned it to me or Titan. Limited movement or not, I hoped the outcome of the incident with Nicholas had made it clear that Nate was not an easy target. There would be repercussions for attacking him. The fact that Nate was now learning how to fight properly, not just fists and fingernails, was no bad thing either.

Even as I thought of it, the flat of Titan's sword connected with Nate's elbow. With a cry of pain, he staggered backwards. His weapon fell from his limp fingers, and I came to my feet at once.

Nate's teeth were bared in a silent snarl. He shook his head slowly, eyes shut as he fought a more private battle.

It was several seconds before Nate breathed again, straightening up with a grimace and massaging his elbow as he glanced between us, giving a wry smile.

"Got him?" Titan asked.

"Yeah, I've got him," Nate groaned, squinting against the sunlight. I let out a breath, relaxing muscles I hadn't meant to tense.

'Him.' That was what we'd taken to calling Nate's other half, the creature living inside him. From Nate's guarded words and moments *like this one, it seemed that he was always waiting, just below the surface, for the slightest break in Nate's self-control.*

"Good lad," Titan said. "Come on. One more round."

Nate scowled, glancing away. "Now?"

"Yes, now."

Nate shook out his arm and picked up his sword from where it had fallen, twirling the blade before falling into a crouch. They sprang at each other again.

They were both panting when they drew apart, Titan turning back to me and gesturing me forwards with the sword I so disliked.

"Alright, let's see if we can find something else for you to try," he said with a quick smile.

I got up without enthusiasm. Nate glanced away as I approached, gazing out to the south.

"Got somewhere to be?" I asked.

He nodded but still hesitated.

"Your mother?"

He nodded again.

"Do you want company?" Titan asked.

Nate smiled now, but it was too tight to be reassuring as he shook his head.

"You will let us know if anyone does anything," Titan reminded him, and I bobbed my head in agreement.

"I will," Nate confirmed, sliding his sword away.

We both watched him leave the courtyard. Titan sighed before heading towards the armoury. The purple band of cloth around his arm gained us access, and he led the way through twisting shelves of weapons, setting aside the rejected sword for cleaning and sorting. Trailing behind him, I watched as he considered the racks.

"How come Nate found one so quickly?" I grumbled as he lifted a new sword and immediately replaced it. "Why is it taking so long? Am I doing something wrong?"

"Nate got lucky," Titan said. "And it's nothing you're doing. When

we find one that's closer to being right, it will at least give us a starting point to work from." He picked up another sword, slightly shorter and thinner than the previous one, and passed it to me.

"How long did it take you to find yours?" I asked as I took it, hefting it and making a face.

Titan reached down, touching the hilt of his huge two-handed sword. "Mine? Almost four years."

I gaped at him in horror, and he laughed.

"I found one that suited me well enough after a year or so, maybe a little less. Then I slowed down, taking longer with each one until I knew what it was that I didn't like so that I could move towards what I did."

"And you knew? When you found it?" I asked.

"The moment I held it," Titan said. "But don't tell Hamma I said that. Or the twins. They think this is all nonsense."

I grinned. "I wouldn't dare."

"What do you think?" Titan asked, nodding at the new sword in my hands.

I wove it through the air experimentally, careful not to knock any of the others on the racks around us. Switching from two hands to one and back again, I shrugged. "Not great, but not too bad, I suppose."

"Give it—"

"Seven days," I finished for him, resisting the urge to roll my eyes.

He used the sheath to smack me on the shoulder, then sobered, glancing around to check we were alone and lowering his voice. "Mara, is everything okay?"

My stomach twisted, the wound on my back searing with pain again. "Yes," I said, perhaps a shade too quickly. "Why?"

Titan held my gaze. "You know why. Something's bothering you. Is it your wards?" I tensed again, but he continued before I had time to panic properly. "I know it can be disheartening to start with, but it will get easier to draw on them, I promise. It just takes time and practice."

Forcing myself to relax, I smiled and nodded.

"Alright then." Titan clapped me on the shoulder. "Let's get out of here. I'm starving."

The smile slid from my face as I followed him back outside. Time, practice—neither of them would fix the wound through the strength ward on my back. I was broken and forever would be.

I didn't go to the mess hall the next morning. After Set's revelation about the food supplies here, I couldn't bring myself to consume a single bite of their dwindling resources. Instead, I drew on my growth ward to keep my hunger at bay as I sat in the cool shadow of an alley beside the wall. It wasn't a perfect solution, but it could keep me going for a couple of days until I figured something else out. Elbows on my knees, ankles crossed, I stared at the array of wards sprawled over the stone surface.

Now Set had called off the people following me, there was no reason not to come here. If someone spotted me and reported it back to Holt... well, what was he going to do? Besides, hidden in the shadows between two buildings, a dead-end behind me, it was unlikely I was going to be discovered. I was, finally, free to examine the wards.

I hadn't brought anything with which to make a copy of the wards. I was sure there would be something somewhere within the city that I could steal and use, but I couldn't bring myself to leave my vigil yet.

Admitting to Set that I wanted to be able to come back and cultivate this knowledge, saying the words out loud, had broken down a barrier inside me. Hunger gnawed at my soul for the power displayed here, so close yet infuriatingly out of reach. A story written in a script I couldn't read. Noah said that they hadn't built this city but found it.

What had happened to those who had been here before, the ones who had carved these wards? Had they allied with my ancestors to pass a fraction of their knowledge on to us? Or had something happened to force them to leave this place with its protective wall? Maybe they had travelled west and made a new settlement in a valley, built new walls there, despite having left behind the wards to adorn them.

Whatever the link, some of these wards were identical to the ones tattooed on my skin. I was staring at a piece of my history. No matter what it took, I would find a way to come back and reclaim it.

I arrived early at the sparring ground that afternoon. A chill wind blew off the sea. Waves lashed angrily in the harbour, throwing spray high in the air as they smacked against the wharf. Dark clouds were splattered across the sky, pushing northwards. I watched them rolling in as I warmed up, rising slowly up and down on my toes to work my calves as I stretched out my arms.

My students began to arrive a few minutes later, along with the usual group of watchers gathering to observe.

"Pair up," I called out when everyone had arrived. "Hands up, stay defensive, and try to step on your partner's toes. Not too hard. We're just warming up."

They did as I instructed, spreading out and facing off against each other. Aaron was left partnerless. I frowned. There had never been an odd number before. I looked around again, trying to work out who was missing.

"Where's Rosita?"

They paused, looking around as if to confirm her absence. Warren turned, glancing along the wharf towards the warehouse where I found Ava. My eyes narrowed, but he looked away just as quickly, scanning the rest of the wharf.

"Shall I go and find her?" Aaron asked.

"No," I said. "If she's not here, that's her choice." I pushed down my irritation, forcing a smile. "You can pair with me."

Aaron swallowed before taking half a step closer, raising his hands in front of him to protect his face. I mirrored him and struck out first, lunging forwards to tap the top of his foot with my toes. He jumped slightly but retaliated in kind. I pulled my foot back, avoiding him.

196

"Did you do this when you were training?" one of the others asked.

"Oh yes," I said, grinning as I remembered how viciously Nate and I had played this game. "The man who trained us said it was a good way to get us to keep track of our opponent's feet without looking at them."

Aaron, who had been staring at my feet, flushed self-consciously and raised his gaze. I took advantage of his embarrassment to land another hit on his toes. Face hardening into a scowl, he stepped towards me again. Refusing to look down, he was a little off target, but his foot grazed the side of mine.

I kept them going for a few more minutes, increasing the speed of my attacks until Aaron was flushed with exertion rather than embarrassment. Stepping back from him, I clapped my hands to draw the attention of the rest of the group.

"Alright, that'll do. Everyone grab a weapon."

Armed with wooden practice swords, they lined up around the edge of the circle. Claiming two for myself, I returned alone to the centre. A gust of wind tossed my hair into my face, and I shook it back over my shoulder with a scowl as I turned to look at them all, considering how best to test them. It was annoying that Rosita wasn't here; it messed up the teams they had chosen. But it did give me an idea.

"Okay, we're going to change the groups today," I said, "and get you fighting with different people."

"I thought we'd agreed you were going to let us choose our groups," Keera said, frowning.

"Oh, well, I'm sure if you explain that to the demons, they'll wait for you to go find the rest of your team if you've been separated," I shot back.

Keera's mouth thinned into a line, but she made no response.

"Maybe you've been split up. Maybe one of you is injured and out of the fight. Maybe someone's already dead." I looked along the line of pale faces, some openly shocked, others grim with acceptance. "You won't always have time to prepare, to plan," I said. "You need to be adaptable, to fight with whoever you find next to you, not just who you wish was there."

I clacked my weapons together sharply in front of me, the impact ringing out, making them flinch. "So. Jory, Keera, you come in first. Warren and Andy, give them a count of fifteen, then you can join in."

They nodded, the ones I'd called stepping forwards. My weapons held ready, I drew upon my wards, feeling the steady warmth as they activated. I was suddenly light on my feet, ready to dart in any direction, unable to fall. Fast, balanced, strong. My students moved in, and we began.

I 'killed' Jory before Warren and Andy were allowed to join in, but they were in time to save Keera from my onslaught, and I called a halt to the bout when Warren stabbed me just under the ribs. The rest of the afternoon continued in a similar pattern. I would call out groups in various configurations, with short breaks to drill them in particular moves or give them a chance to practise unarmed combat against each other.

Despite the short time I had worked with them, I could already see significant improvement. They were no longer taken aback by my enhanced speed and were far better at countering it. I had fresh welts across my legs and back to prove it.

The final bout began with me facing Keera, Aaron, Miranda, and Steren. They worked together well, immediately going on the offensive, forcing me to keep moving as I dodged their attacks. Steren spun the sword from my left hand, and I twisted away from her, retreating to gain some space. I'd only withdraw a single step when something streaked towards my head.

My shoulder blazed with heat as I drew instinctively on my ward, dropping to my knees and whipping my arm up, taking the fierce blow on my forearm rather than my head.

If it had been a real sword, it would have taken my hand off. As it was, there was a loud crack and I rolled backwards, clutching at my left arm, gasping with the sudden pain.

"*Thorns, Thorns, Thorns,*" I spat the words over and over to keep myself from saying anything worse.

My other weapon fell to the ground, forgotten. Everyone froze, Keera with her arm still raised, the guilty weapon suspended in the air.

"Mara! Are you okay?" Warren leapt towards me, the rest of the group spilling forwards in his wake.

Teeth gritted, I flexed my fingers. The pain radiating through my arm intensified, but everything seemed to work. I was lucky. Very lucky.

"Yeah," I said, climbing to my feet. "I'm okay." Looking past Warren, I met Keera's eyes. She was caught between horror and surprise. A reflection of my own emotions.

"I…" she began, then faltered, lowering the sparring sword.

"Well done," I said to her as everyone pressed in around us. "You saw an opportunity and acted on it. That's exactly what you all need to do." I broke Keera's gaze, looking around at the rest of them. "Good work from everyone. We'll leave it there for today. I'll see you all tomorrow… if my arm is still working."

There were some weak laughs at my attempted humour, and they began to drift away. Keera seemed rooted to the spot. It was only when Miranda took her arm that she allowed herself to be led away, still stiff and wide-eyed.

Warren hung back. "Are you sure you're okay?" he asked.

"Yeah. It's not broken," I said, still rubbing at the red spot on my arm. I could feel it starting to swell. "I've had worse."

"Do you want to come and grab some food with me?"

My eyes flicked up at the innocent question. Warren's face was open and inviting.

"I spoke to your brother last night," I said.

Warren's brow furrowed. "Oh?"

"Oh," I echoed back at him. Devoid of the lightness injected by his tone, the word sounded flat and harsh, full of scorn.

A flush crept up his neck, and he ducked his head, looking aside.

I realised my mistake. I'd been referring to the food situation.

Warren must have assumed Set and I had been discussing something more personal. Still, I needed to talk to him about that, so I squared my shoulders and mustered my courage.

"Warren, I think you're a good guy. You and your brother are going to do well here. But I've got other responsibilities, other places to be."

Warren's hands flexed. He shot me a sideways look. "You could stay."

I got the impression there were a few more words that he wanted to add at the end of that sentence, but he held them back. I bent down, retrieving the sparring swords I'd dropped earlier. Warren watched me, waiting, finding hope in my silence.

"No, I can't." I met his eyes. "And if I could, I wouldn't."

Warren flinched, shoulders jerking. I walked away, leaving him standing alone in the middle of the sandy circle. I might regret it tomorrow, but at least he understood the situation now. Like I'd told him about my arm, there were worse pains. But that didn't stop it hurting.

The weather worsened throughout the evening. Sitting in my room, I listened to the rain growing heavier outside. The small opening in the rock which allowed light inside started to drip water, fat droplets splatting onto the floor. The erratic *plunk-plunk-plunk* did nothing to soothe my mood. Vivid flashes of bright light broke the darkness, accompanied by a low rumble of thunder. Thorns, the all-seeing, painting pictures on the sky for those who could see, speaking for those who could hear. But not for me.

The guiding hand which had led every previous monarch was denied to me. I knew that. My pilgrimage had made it abundantly clear. I had been rejected.

Thorns knew. They knew I had a broken ward on my back. They knew I was unfit to lead. What other crimes had they found within my soul? What other shortcomings of character had cinched their decision to turn away from me?

I had tried so hard. Every lesson from my father, every task set
200

before me, I'd done it all. Even after Thorns's rejection at the Hollowed Tree, I had still intended to return home eventually, to serve my people in the best way I could. Despite the demons and the Figures and now the people of this city who tried to waylay me, I was doing all I could to get back.

And still, Thorns would not speak to me.

Another rumble of thunder reverberated in the air around me, buzzing deep in my chest. Nothing but meaningless noise.

I lay down, wincing at the pressure on my bruised arm, and closed my eyes. Thorns wasn't the only one who could reject.

A huge crack of thunder. Sharp and demanding. My eyes snapped open just as the flash of lightning illuminating my room faded. There was someone there.

I didn't hesitate. Launching myself off the bed, I was upright instantly, one of my twin blades held outstretched, keeping the unknown figure at bay. There was a gasp of indrawn breath, barely audible over the driving rain outside. The drip of water into my room had intensified, a regular patter on the floor breaking the silence.

"I come in peace," the intruder said.

A sharp tug on my sight ward flooded my arm with warmth. The room sharpened, visible to me in red-tinged light. I frowned as I recognised the lined face of the person in front of me, the lopsided stance, the cane braced against the floor.

"Ava," I said, lowering my weapon from her face as I stepped backwards. "What are you doing here?"

There was another flash of lightning, the intensity lessened with my sight ward active. The accompanying thunder was gentler, soft and calming.

I glanced towards the opening in the wall, distracted.

"I'm hoping you can live up to your title," Ava said, her voice cracking.

I examined her face again. Her jaw was clenched tight, and there was a sheen of unshed tears in her eyes.

"What's happened?"

"It's…" she choked, swallowing hard before continuing, forcing the words out with visible effort. "Genni, my daughter, left last night with one of her friends. They went to look for Malcolm. And they haven't come back."

My stomach twisted. "Are you sure? They're not just hiding somewhere else?"

Ava nodded. "Genni was in charge of the excursion when Malcolm was lost. She's felt guilty ever since. What you said to her the other day… I know my daughter."

I blinked. Genni must have been one of the other women in the warehouse when I'd confronted them. I couldn't recall exactly what I'd said.

"They might just still be looking." The words were weak in my mouth, any hope drained by the weight of inevitability in my chest and the shaking of Ava's head.

"Even if Genni had wanted to stay out there, Rosita's more sensible. She would have insisted they come back if only to maintain appearances."

I didn't think my stomach could drop any lower. "Rosita," I echoed dully. That was why she missed the lesson this afternoon. Because she wasn't in the city. She was risking her life on a misguided rescue mission.

Another rumble of thunder filled the silence between us, echoing the disquiet inside me. Three people outside the safety of the warded wall. And an opportunity.

I met Ava's desperate gaze. "Get me outside. Now."

After so many attempts at diplomacy, so much posturing, so many threats, it was almost too easy. There was no negotiation, no hesitancy. I grabbed my twin blades but left everything else. It would be suspicious to bring my whole pack. There was nothing in it I couldn't do without.

Ava led me out of my room and picked up a single candle that was sputtering on the floor, holding it in front of her as we walked

202

deeper into the mountains.

My heart pounded with anticipation. This was it. I was finally going to get out. I would be able to go home.

"Going somewhere?"

We both jerked to a stop, my twin blades rasping as I pulled them out, searching for the new threat.

A shadow unfolded itself from one of the doorways, its gangly limbs filling the tunnel ahead of us. I recognised his height as much as his voice.

"Noah! What are you doing here?" I hissed, stepping towards him.

"Just keeping an eye out. Good thing too, it seems. I bet Holt would be interested to know about this." I'd never heard his voice so cold.

"Oh please," Ava scoffed. I glanced sideways as she moved up to stand next to me. Any anguish in her expression was buried by impatience, the focus of the obstacle seeming to override her emotions. "If you think my brother doesn't already know everything going on in this city, you're an even bigger fool than everyone thinks. Go ahead, you won't be telling him anything new, and I doubt he'd appreciate being woken in the middle of the night just for this. Mara, let's go."

She made to move past Noah, but he stepped sideways, blocking the path. Ava hesitated, eyeing him.

"Move," I said, sliding my blades away as I took another step forward. "Or I'll make you move."

Noah's shoulders stiffened as he glared at me. "No."

My left arm grew warm as I drew on my speed ward, lunging forwards. I lost my grip on my sight ward, not having enough focus to maintain both, and the tunnel went dark. Blind, I kept moving, knowing Noah wouldn't be fast enough to dodge before I got to him.

I was half wrong. My left hand grabbed his shoulder, but he had already shifted his other arm, and I missed it in the darkness. Using the grip I had, I shoved him backwards, and there was a loud crack as he collided with the tunnel wall. I made another wild grab for his other arm but missed again and ended up driving my empty hand into his stomach. He let out a great huff of air, curling in upon himself. I released his shoulder and he sank, gasping, to the floor.

Ava strode forwards, grabbing my elbow and pulling me with her along the corridor.

I twisted my arm from her grip, matching her hasty steps as we left Noah behind, reactivating my sight ward as I followed her.

"Brother?" I hissed at her. "Holt is your *brother*?"

"Not by blood. My sister married him. Foolish girl."

"But…"

"Come on!" She strode further ahead, taking turns in the tunnel seemingly at random, one hand trailing along the wall to guide her.

"So Holt agreed to this?"

Ava tutted. "Of course not. He'll be livid when he finds out you've gone. But I can handle him."

I stopped in the middle of the passage, staring at her back. "But he knows about what you do—about going beyond the wall. That you're the one who organises it."

"Yes." She showed no sign of slowing, so I hurried to catch up.

"Does *everyone* know?"

"Most people do. But no one knows that everyone else knows. Everyone keeps it a secret because they think it's a secret. Even though it's not."

She turned into a room similar to mine, except without the fissure in the rock letting light in from outside. It was half full of loosely woven sacks stacked against the walls. Striding to the back corner, Ava felt around, pushing piles of sacks aside to reveal a dark hole about three feet wide, with rough, jagged edges.

My chest tightened as I looked at it.

"This will bring you out on the mountainside, outside the wall. It's a bit of a slope down to the ground, but not that steep. There's already a group out there looking for the girls, and I'll be sending another within an hour. I'll delay Noah for as long as possible too."

She stood up, turning to face me, eyes searching wildly in the dark but seeming to find the outline of my face and latching onto it. Her composure, brought on by Noah's challenge, was beginning to crack again.

"Please. Find them."

"I'll do my best."

"Thank you." She hesitated for a second longer, then stepped around me and hurried off.

I turned my gaze to the hole she had uncovered, some of my enthusiasm dimming. My palms were sweating. I reminded myself of the others that had passed this way. Dropping to my hands and knees, I inched forwards, increasing the draw on my sight ward to counteract the darkness of the small space. It didn't help. In the red-tinged light, the low ceiling seemed to press down upon me.

Releasing my ward and closing my eyes, I moved forwards, ducking my head when it scraped on the ceiling, concentrating on keeping moving, just keeping moving. There was a dull roaring in my ears and not enough air in my lungs. I found a corner, twisting my way around it, then another one. I saw a flash through my closed eyelids and opened them.

There was light ahead. Faint and dim, but it promised an ending to the blackness of the tunnel. I sped up, scraping my palms on the rough rock. The roar wasn't just in my ears anymore, but ahead of me too. The pounding of heavy rain. A rumble of thunder called me on, and I scrambled my way out of the tunnel, pushing through some bushes as I staggered to my feet. Rain fell relentlessly onto my hair and face as I squinted upwards.

The storm clouds above me flashed with a fresh bolt of lightning, but the thunder this time was gentle, curling around my chest approvingly. Basking in the wildness, I let a grin unfurl across my face. I was free.

13

The Worst It Can Be

Under Titan's continued encouragement, I spent many afternoons shut away in my room, practising drawing on my wards. Painful contortions in front of the polished mirror confirmed what I suspected; the wound on my back completely bisected the strength ward over my right shoulder blade, rendering it useless. The more I practised with my wards, the more I felt its loss. I was unbalanced, strength flowing down the left side of my body in a steady stream but only trickling across to my right arm. I kept working, drawing deeper and deeper, feeling the physical effort of spreading the single ward across the entirety of my body. But it did get easier. Titan had been right; the daily practice helped. I would never be as strong as I should have been, but everyone had limitations. Regardless of it having been imposed upon me, this was mine, and I mitigated it as best I could.

I made progress using the other wards as well. I rarely tripped over my own feet anymore and could reliably draw on two wards simultaneously, though not always very effectively. Using three at once was still beyond me, but I did at least believe it would one day be possible and was determined to continue my solitary training.

Several months after I'd begun my private practices, I took my starting position in front of the window in my room, taking a deep breath as I focused on my wards. Before I started to draw on them, a sudden noise broke my concentration.

Bong. Bong. Bong.

My stomach clenched at the bell's tolling, echoing its call across the city. I leapt across the room, grabbed the latest sword I was trying out, and wrenched the door open. The stairs were directly opposite, and I threw myself down them, crashing into the wall as I spun around the corner.

On the floor below, two people stood not far from the stairs, heads whipping around as they searched for the source of the noise.

Bong. Bong.

I didn't need to see Nate's face to recognise him.

"What's going on?" he cried as I leapt down the next flight of stairs. Behind him, his mother's face was pale.

"Demons attacking!" I shouted over my shoulder.

I heard him urging his mother to stay put, but two sets of footsteps echoed mine as I reached the ground floor and raced along the corridor parallel to the throne room. My father would be there, organising our defences. People would be fighting wherever the enemy appeared, but it would be from here that the best fighters would leave to crush them completely. Once the fight was over, there would be the injured needing aid, healers who could use an extra pair of hands. I needed to know how I could help.

Nate caught up with me quickly but didn't push past, following as I slammed open the side door to the throne room, stumbling into the chaos on the other side. It was not the sort of chaos I had expected.

My father stood in the middle of the room, his sword, Mercy, gleaming angry and bloody in his hand. My mother was beside him, every member of the Guard surrounding them, facing outwards in a circle of protection.

Around them ranged almost a dozen unfamiliar figures, their weapons drawn. I could see the black eyes of those facing me, standing out above the wild grins on their faces.

The warning bell tolled on.

Without thinking, I lunged forward, stabbing the closest demon in the back. It screamed as it fell, dragging my weapon with it, leaving me defenceless. The others turned at the cry of their fallen comrade, inky eyes fixing on me.

The Guard attacked. Swords flashed as they engaged the demons. But none of them were fast enough to intercept the one who leapt at me from the left, his face twisted with fury. Jumping back, I raised my hands defensively, lips drawn back as I snarled at his approaching weapon.

I dodged sideways, then lashed out, aiming my punch at the demon's extended elbow. It connected, stinging my knuckles, but I hadn't drawn on my wards. Without them, the blow wasn't powerful enough to have any effect. The demon's black eyes and dark hair filled my vision, its breath loud in my ears.

Then it was gone. Nate had thrown himself at the demon, taking advantage of its focus on me to push it back.

I ducked away, pulling my sword from the body on the floor with a sickening squelch, leaving a trail of black blood on the floor as I turned back to the fight.

The demon had regained his balance, looking at my defender for the first time. "Traitor!" he spat, eyes fixed on Nate's, and he attacked again. Nate lunged forwards to meet him.

Cries from behind me drew my attention. Orion and Ishmael were closest to me, fighting side by side against three demons, their identical faces eerily blank as they fought. I leapt forwards, thinking to help, but before I could, Titan blocked my path. His arms were blurred, sword flashing in front of him. Under the combined onslaught of two demons, he was losing ground.

I backed away, gripping my sword tightly. My wards felt like a physical pressure underneath my skin, brought to the surface by the rampant power being drawn by the Guard. It was my speed ward that I focused on, sitting just above my left elbow. Sparks flooded my body, sharp and tense. I darted around Titan and his opponents.

Past the twins, Helena was down on one knee, one hand pressed over a wound on her stomach. She was still fighting, but her moves were desperate.

I ran to help her, diving forwards to slash at the attacking demon. They parried, long hair swishing through the air as she turned to me.

The force of her next attack knocked my weapon from my hand. The sword clattered away across the floor.

I lunged forwards, latching onto her arm. The demon jerked back, trying to shake me off. I twisted under her arm, using my momentum to pull her further away from Helena. Her weapon fell from her hand at the strain on her wrist. Her other hand flashed between us, metal glinting between her fingers. I released her with a cry, stumbling backwards as the small blade drew a deep line of pain across my forearm.

I retreated, clutching my arm. Warm slippery blood coated my fingers. The demon grinned, but a hand grabbed me from behind before they could attack again. Hamma shoved me towards my parents as he surged past me.

Breathing hard, I retreated, glancing at my arm. The cut wasn't as deep as I'd thought. My mother reached out to me. I hurried to her side, horribly aware that I was unarmed again. In the centre of the protective bubble formed by the Guard, I glanced around, trying and failing to look everywhere at once.

Helena had taken advantage of my interference to get up, but she swayed on her feet. Edric, unarmed, faced an opponent at least a foot taller than he was. Nate was still engaged with the demon he'd pushed off of me.

My mother made the barest whisper beside me, a hiss almost lost in the sounds of battle from all around. I turned my head in time to see a figure leap past the Guard.

Mother raised her stunningly thin sword, ready to counter him. She was fast and deadly, but he was faster, slicing savagely across her stomach even as her weapon took him in the throat. He crumpled as she staggered backwards, both hands pressed over the long deep wound that dribbled trails of blood.

"Zita!" my father cried as I let out a wordless shriek of anger, catching my mother and lowering her to the ground.

"I'm okay," she said with a grimace. It was a lie. Despite both her hands pressing over the wound, blood ran in sheets down her stomach,

soaking her shirt and the top of her leggings. She raised one hand to grip my arm, and in the exposed wound, I saw the gleam of something that was not meant to be seen.

"Look up," she reminded me, squeezing my arm, leaving smears of blood. I did as she bid, swallowing down bile as I tore my eyes from her open stomach. Bodies lay strewn around, some twitching, others still, all surrounded by blood in various shades.

Directly ahead of me, the Guard continued fighting, my father among them. On the other side of the fighters, a demon was assessing the situation just as I was. I lowered my mother to the floor, standing upright and grabbing the closest weapon, a short sword barely longer than my forearm. The demon's eyes met mine, and he grinned.

My stomach dropped, and I watched, helpless, as his face darkened, his skin turning inky black as he changed, protected by those fighting against the Guard in front of him. Hamma let out a cry of warning, but with their path blocked, they could do no more than I could.

Within seconds, the demon had grown a foot taller, huge horns bursting from his head, curling protectively forwards to shield his eyes. His hands, complete with newly formed claws, flexed. He let out a roar like a laugh.

The other demons let out whoops, redoubling their efforts at the sound of their transformed comrade. The huge monster was still looking at me, our eyes locked until another figure stepped between us.

Even though he was taller than me, Nate looked pitiful against the towering monster. Then he began to grow.

I took a step backwards as his sword fell to the ground, his back broadening, hair disappearing into black skin, horns and claws bursting forth. His bellow shook the whole room, full of anger. A challenge.

Everyone flinched at the noise, the unexpected shift in dynamic making them hesitate. The demons' eyes widened in shock as the Guard glanced back, unsure if the newcomer was friend or foe. Titan was the only one unphased, taking advantage of the distraction to dispatch one of the attackers before anyone else recovered.

The two hulking figures seemed unperturbed by the fighting that resumed between them. They both snarled, low sounds that reverberated in my chest. Nate leapt, shoving through the other combatants. His impact knocked them both away. They rolled towards the doors, where I lost track of which was which in the whirling tangle of vicious limbs.

In front of me, Helena was on the floor again, clutching at her chest. Beyond her, Hamma and my father were being forced slowly back towards the spot where I guarded my mother.

The twins were still fighting together, but Orion was limping badly, unable to put weight on his right leg. As I watched, Ishmael lunged forwards, stabbing their opponent in the armpit. The demon dropped with a gurgling cry, thrashing on the floor. The brothers dropped back, Ishmael supporting his brother away from the fighting.

I jumped into the gap they left, stabbing at one of the demons threatening my father. He spasmed as my weapon cut across his back, then dropped as Mercy flashed across his throat. Another body fell at the same time, Edric finally finishing off his giant opponent. He didn't take so much as a breath of rest, immediately moving to support Titan.

The balance of the fight had changed. We were winning.

The demons fought to the last, not one of them running when they saw their comrades fall.

I was glad; it meant we got to kill more of them.

In moments, there was only one left, still wrestling fiercely with Nathaniel at the other end of the hall. Claws flew and teeth snapped. Drops of oily black blood littered the floor around them as they grappled. All eyes were upon them. The Guard stood frozen, weapons held ready. One of the beasts finally gained a hold over the other, legs wrapped around their waist from behind, trapping one of their arms. One hand gripped a horn, twisting the other's head, the other hand gripping their throat, squeezing mercilessly.

"Which one's which?" Hamma cried, weaving on his feet, sword raised. "Do we help?"

My eyes flicked between the two foreign faces, trying to identify them.

Which one was Nate? Titan had recognised him over a year before, but how?

The suffocating demon's free arm flailed backwards, sharp claws leaving bloody cuts. The aggressor howled in pain but hung on, refusing to release their hold.

Black eyes met mine, the one on top staring across the space between us, and I finally saw what Titan had seen. Black skin, and thick horns, and sharp teeth. None of it mattered. It was still him.

"No," I said, not breaking the eye contact. "He's winning."

I was right. Baring his teeth in pain or triumph, Nate's demon form tightened his grip, claws digging into flesh. Blood gushed across the floor. Two bodies shook, locked together in death and exertion. The victor ripped their hand away, leaving a jagged wound in the dying demon's throat. The room was silent.

Slowly, Nate unwound himself from the demon's corpse and stood up. Blood dripped from his hand and the wounds that littered his body. He eyed us warily, looking over weapons held at the ready.

There was a moment of silent trepidation, then I took a step forwards, drawing his attention.

We stared at each other for a moment, not blinking, before he relaxed, head drooping and shoulders lowering. He let out a gusty breath, eyes closing, and shuddered as the darkness faded from his skin. Messy blond hair reappeared, and Nate staggered, reaching out a blood-covered hand to steady himself on a pillar. His dark eyes, the white slowly returning around the edge, flicked to mine before returning to the floor.

"Sorry," he said into the deafening silence.

Titan laughed, his legs folding as he sat down to regain his breath.

I looked around. There was no direction to turn without seeing the destruction. Blood painted the floor, smeared with footprints, and splattered across the columns. Even my father's throne hadn't escaped the carnage. A body lay sprawled over the steps, face down, one hand flung out towards the great stone seat as if in beseechment.

Ishmael was sitting on the floor, his hand closed tightly around his brother's limp arm. His face was pale as he looked blankly at Orion's open eyes, staring equally dully up at nothing. Helena's breath was wheezy, blood pooling around her from the wound on her side. My mother's face was tight with pain from the slash across her stomach, still oozing blood and intestines.

It was to the latter that I went, pressing my hands over the wound, blood welling between my fingers. Looking up, my eyes swept the room again, settling on a halo of yellow spread over the floor under the opposite wall. Alicia's head was turned towards us, her eyes half-open, mouth twisted into a static grimace.

Swallowing hard, I looked back at Nate, whose eyes had found his lifeless mother. I turned away from his crumpling expression. I couldn't even imagine his pain.

By the end of the night, I wouldn't have to.

Somewhere outside, the bell was still tolling.

Freedom. It stretched out before me, visible in the empty, open plain, the grass whipping back and forth in the storm. It beckoned to me from the trees beyond, the shelter of their leaves and branches. And it spoke to me from the sky, where Thorns drew a jagged line of light through the clouds, sharp enough to draw blood.

Freedom. I could leave, at last, make my way home, back to my people. Thorns was showing me the way, their lightning pointing westward.

I didn't move.

Somewhere out here, three people were in danger. Malcolm, whom I'd never even met. Genni, who felt so guilty over his disappearance she put herself at risk. And Rosita, with her wild hair and surprising experience with unarmed fighting. She had been one of the first to speak up in my initial lesson. Now she was missing.

I hung my head, the rain dripping from my nose and chin. Eyes closed, I didn't see the next flash of lightning, but the accompanying roll of thunder lodged a word inside my chest. An instruction. A demand. *Home.*

My knees shook, wanting to move forwards but unable to. I couldn't do it. I couldn't just walk away. Two mothers had come to me, begging for my help. What if it was my children who were lost?

Opening my eyes, I blinked the water out of them. From my vantage point on the cliffs, Leydford's wall stretched away to the south. I wasn't going back. They couldn't make me.

The truth of that thought made me pause. I was out. I was stronger, faster, than they were. If they wanted me back inside that wall, they'd have to kill me first. But that didn't mean that I couldn't bring Rosita and her friends back before leaving.

My head came up a little more.

Of course, I might not find them. They might already be dead.

But that didn't mean I couldn't look. It didn't mean I couldn't *try.*

The weight holding me in place lifted. I would make my way west but look for the trio on the way. And if I found them, I would do anything I could to get them back to their home before I returned to mine.

Set's words returned to me; *whatever it takes.* It seemed he and I were too similar for our own good.

I imagined Holt's face after I brought the three home safely and then left again, and smiled.

Thunder rumbled overhead, but the sound held none of the anger I expected from my decision to delay. It was a warm caress of approval.

And I finally understood.

Thorns's silence, so absolute, even after my visit to the Hollowed Tree, was broken. They couldn't speak to me then because my journey was not yet over. My pilgrimage had not been to the tree; it had been *here*, to this city, to the secrets it held.

Now I'd completed my task, Thorns was here, with me, to guide me home, regardless of delays.

Another crack of thunder, even louder, sounded overhead. A manic grin split my face as the rain ran down my cheeks like tears. I joined my voice to the cry of triumph from the sky.

214

Thorns stayed with me until I reached the treeline, where they fell silent, but they had done their part, and I continued over the wet ground as the sky lightened overhead. I must have slept for longer than I'd realised before Ava had come to find me, for the storm clouds gave way to the greyness of pre-dawn. Water trickled down my arms, dripping off my hair, but I made no move to shake off the moisture. The rain had been a gift, a shield against watchful eyes as I crossed the open plain.

The forest was alive after the storm, full of dripping leaves and the fresh smell of bark. I kept to a steady pace, searching for any signs of other life, whether it be Malcolm, Genni, Rosita, or the other group that Ava mentioned was looking for them. It felt painfully slow. Stopping to investigate every rustle of a branch, every path through the undergrowth, took time.

The urge to speed up, to run home, was incessant, but I resisted. I'd resolved to take the time to look for Malcolm and the others. That was what I was going to do. Even when the time the sky was light enough for me to release my sight ward, I hadn't covered much ground. Behind me, the top of the wall was still visible. The city would be waking soon. How long would it take for them to discover my absence? Would Noah have followed through with his threat to go to Holt, or had Ava stopped him? Holt would be furious when he found out I'd left, regardless of the source of the information. He would probably be pacing the throne room, spewing hateful theories about how I was dangerous, that I was working with the demons. It was all irrelevant now. Hiding behind the wall, there was nothing he could do.

I paused, bending to examine what I'd thought was the imprint of a boot in the ground, but was nothing more than a pattern of moss coating some rocks. Another false hope. I hadn't found a single sign of the ones I was searching for.

But it wasn't only the citizens of Leydford for whom I was on alert. The Figures were also on my mind.

There hadn't been so much as a whisper of them since I arrived in the city but I knew they wouldn't have given up. If they could have tracked me there, they would surely have turned up by now. Maybe the wards preventing the demons from entering worked on them too. Or had they been waiting for me to leave?

I glanced around again but the trees were empty. Nevertheless, I sped up, matching my steps to the faint drumming in my ears.

There was also the matter of the one I'd killed. According to Keera, there had been no sign of the body when she got there.

For a moment, I considered going to check for myself but quickly dismissed the idea. Keera would have lied to me if she wanted, no question, but to Holt, Set, and Warren? I didn't think so.

The thumping grew louder, pounding under my feet as well as in my ears.

Buh-da-dum. Three beats. Buh-da-dum. Buh-da-dum.

I turned, looking through the curtain of tree trunks.

Horses. A line of riders, cresting the rise between myself and the wall, bearing down on the trees with alarming speed.

I swore, ducking behind a tree and peering out. What now?

Their current course would take them past me. If they entered the trees, they would block my path.

I could run. I was faster than their animals if I drew on my ward, but how long would they pursue me? Or I could hide and hope they would pass me by. Then I'd be stuck, cowering in the bushes. Or I could face them. I remembered my declaration earlier in the night. They couldn't make me go back.

The riders were closer now, and I could make out a couple of their faces, though none that I recognised. I counted eight, maybe ten, but it was hard to keep track as they flashed in and out of sight through the trees.

As I weighed my options, the riders split up, four cantering past me, the others slowing and turning to follow the tree line back the way I'd come. Ducking back out of sight, I let my head fall back against the tree trunk. Hiding here gained me nothing. At best, it would waste time. At worst, it would be rendered pointless when I was discovered.

Gritting my teeth, I stepped out and headed towards the open plain.

I was spotted before I got halfway there. One of the riders pulled their mount around to ride towards me, their eyes locked on mine. She brought a hand to her mouth and whistled loudly through her fingers.

More hoofbeats approached as I left the cover of the trees, blinking in the early morning sunlight. Three riders converged on us and this time, I recognised one of them.

Set swung his leg forwards over his horse's neck, leaping to the ground. His face was hard, jaw working furiously, his hair a mess. The other riders gathered behind him as he stalked toward me.

"My father ordered me to kill you on sight," he spat, stopping a few strides away.

I eyed him warily but he made no move to act on the instruction. He ran a hand through his hair, messing it up even further.

"Warren begged me not to," he continued. There was a tremble in his voice. "After watching Father give me a direct order. He *begged*." Set shook his head, jaw clenched. "You're damn lucky I love my brother."

Hesitantly, I let my hands drop from where they had been gripping my blades. "What was I meant to do, Set? I had an opportunity, and I took it."

"You were *meant* to give me a chance! I told you I was working on it, but that wasn't good enough for you, was it?"

"I guess not."

He turned away, pacing back and forth.

"So what now?" I asked. "Why are you here if you're not going to try and kill me like your father wants?"

Set paused in his agitated pacing and looked at me. One side of his mouth quirked up into a smirk. "How could I? We never found you."

"You…" I looked from him to the other riders. They were all staring determinately over my head. My shoulders dropped as I realised what he'd meant. The men here were Set's, the same way

Nate had always been mine, even when my father was still alive. If he asked them to lie for him, they would.

I looked back at Set and nodded.

He mirrored the gesture back at me, some of the tension between us dissipating.

"I've been looking for Malcolm and the others," I said by way of a peace offering.

Set nodded. "We're going to do the same, now we're here." He glanced back over his shoulder. The others, accepting the signal, turned and rode away.

"Tell Warren I'm sorry," I said, "if you get a chance. I'm not abandoning you, I promise. I will come back."

He didn't look at me, watching the other riders retreating. "It might not make any difference."

I frowned, remembering the way he had shut down the conversation the last time I had mentioned returning. "What do you mean?"

"Warren can dream about fighting all he wants, but it's not actually going to happen," he said, glancing at me as if daring me to challenge this statement.

I didn't. All the teaching in the world couldn't enable these people to stand against the demons. Without wards, they would only ever be able to mount the most desperate of defences.

"We need to stop fighting the inevitable," Set continued. "Our ancestors didn't build the city. They found it empty and stayed there. There's no mention of demons in our history until we settled here. So maybe it's not *us* they are attacking."

"Those walls are powerful," I pointed out. "They're keeping the demons out. If you leave, you'll be vulnerable."

"That won't matter if it's not us they're after."

"What else could they want? And what if you're wrong? What if they're just playing with you because you're easy targets? If you come out from behind those walls, you'll be slaughtered, every one of you. Isn't that what happened at your uncle's funeral?"

He gave me a sharp look. It seemed Warren hadn't told his

218

brother he'd shared that story with me. "That won't happen if they don't realise we're gone," Set said.

I frowned at him.

He jerked his chin back towards the city. And beyond.

"You'd go over the mountains?"

His silence was confirmation enough.

I looked at the peaks, high and sheer. Was it even possible to go over them?

One brother wanting to fight, the other planning to flee. Both trying to protect their people, neither knowing how. Could they balance each other out, or would they just clash so hard that nothing ever happened?

Set was the elder of the two. When Holt died, he would become King, and the decision would be his. I hadn't considered the possibility I might return to find the city empty, its residents having fled.

"Listen, I—"

"Set!"

My words were cut off by the cry. There was horror in the voice. We spun around. Further along the tree line, one of the riders was beckoning.

Set turned away, heaving himself back up onto his horse. Other riders were already heading toward the caller. I kept pace with Set as he trotted briskly along to where the other rider pointed at something in the trees.

I followed the line of his finger and drew in a sharp breath.

It was not a pleasant sight.

The body hung, naked and limp, suspended by ropes stretching from each wrist to the trees, legs dangling a few inches off the ground. His feet and calves were burnt, the skin black and cracked, flashes of white bone showing at his toes. His genitals had been torn off, streaks of dried blood encrusting his thighs. Blood coated his neck and chest as well, spilling from his mouth. His arms had been cut so many times they looked striped, an intricate pattern painted in red and white, ending at his wrists, which were chafed and swollen from the braided rope. His fingers were destroyed, every joint twisted out of place.

Behind me, one of the riders threw up. Another quickly followed suit. Set's breathing was uneven. I wasn't sure I was ever going to breathe again. My hands shook and I felt cold all over, despite the rising sun.

There were only two options, and I'd seen the work of the Figures before. They were brutal and merciless, but they were also quick. This wasn't them. This was demons.

"Is it Malcolm?" I asked. My throat was dry, the question cracking as it forced its way out.

"Yes." The single hoarse word seemed to be all Set could manage.

Beside us, one of the other riders drew their sword. We turned to look at them.

"I heard something," she said, staring into the trees past Malcolm's broken body.

We followed her gaze, my eyes flicking from one tree to the next, searching for movement. There was nothing. I was just about to look back at the rider to ask exactly what she had seen when I heard a faint tapping.

If we hadn't all been silent and listening, I doubted I would have noticed the sound at all. Set drew his sword, taking a step toward the trees. I grabbed his arm and hauled him back.

He frowned at me, but I raised an eyebrow. Lips pressed together, he nodded, falling back behind me. I glanced around at the other riders, glad to see them closing ranks protectively around their prince.

Drawing on my wards, hands on the hilts of my blades, I moved cautiously forwards. I ducked under one of Malcolm's outstretched arms, holding my breath against the putrid stink of his body. The leaves under my feet were squelching and damp. I didn't think the wetness was merely from the rain.

Away from the others, the air seemed heavy in my ears. Beneath my pounding pulse, there was another noise, a steady crinkling of leaves. A sharp crack, like rock on rock, made me flinch. Something was here with me.

My hands were sweating. Swallowing, I reaffirmed my grip on my blades.

I stepped past a wide tree trunk and found the source of the noise.

"Oh, Thorns," I breathed, horrified. I wanted to rush forward but forced myself to remain still, tearing my eyes away from the scene in front of me to scan the trees. It might be a trap.

There was no movement. I couldn't see anything lurking among the trees. Carefully, I moved into the small clearing, alert for anything suspicious. When nothing happened, I dropped my hands from my blades.

"Set!" I called over my shoulder as I approached the smaller of the two figures in the clearing.

Rosita's arms were bound behind her at the wrists. Another rope extended upwards, over a tree branch, leaving her suspended, shoulders strained backwards. Her head hung limply forwards, body twisting slowly in mid-air.

I grabbed her shoulder but flinched back from the softness of the joint under my hand.

"Rosita," I pushed her hair back from her face, touching her cheek gently. Her skin was chilly under my fingers. Not yet cold but no longer warm either. There was a trickle of dried blood over her chin. I took a step back as Set hurried into the clearing, flanked by several of his people.

He looked past me to Rosita's dangling body. I shook my head. His attention shifted at once to the other occupant of the clearing. In my haste to check on Rosita, I had forgotten she was not the first one I had noticed.

The other woman sat against a tree trunk, curled slightly sideways, her head turned away from us, long dark hair hiding her face. One hand was flexing slowly over the leaves, crinkling them on the ground. Her other hand twitched, shaking as it rose an inch into the air, then dropped back down. The pebble held in her hand

221

made a sharp cracking sound against the ground.

Set strode over to the woman, dropping to crouch beside her. "Genni?"

She made no response to Set's voice, just continued her incessant stroking of the leaves.

"Genni, what happened?"

I followed more slowly, hanging back as he reached out to touch her leg. *Genni*. Ava's daughter, the one who had blamed herself for Malcolm's disappearance.

Her hands clenched into fists, her body cringing away from Set.

"No, no more, no more." Her voice was hoarse and cracked, the words barely understandable.

"It's okay. You're safe now. I've got you." Set took hold of her hand, rubbing it gently.

She was still for a moment. "Set?"

"Yes, it's me."

The woman's head turned, her long dark hair shifting, and her face became visible for the first time. I leapt backwards.

Genni's right eye hung out of its socket, the bloody globule swinging halfway down her cheek. Blood dripped over her chin. Several strands of hair stuck to it, standing out against her worryingly pale skin. Her other eye seemed to be in place, but her face was so swollen around it that I couldn't be sure.

Set, to his credit, did not recoil, but the horror on his face was plain to see.

"I'm sorry. Set, I'm so sorry. I had to tell them, I had to…"

"It's okay, Genni. You're going to be okay."

"Tell them what?" I asked. "What did they want to know?"

"How to get into the city without going through the wall. I had to tell them. I'm sorry. I'm sorry."

The way into the city without going past the wards. The same way I had left only hours before. Now the demons knew about it.

Set spun on his heels to look up at me. "Will that work?" he demanded. "Will they be able to get in if they bypass the wall?"

I shook my head, horrified by the possibility. "I don't know."

"How can you not know?!"

"Because *I don't know!*" I snapped back. "I told you before that I don't know everything about the wards."

He looked away, eyes darting around the clearing, taking in Rosita's limp body, Genni's curled form, still babbling apologies, and the other riders, all looking to him for direction. He had the same look on his face I'd seen on my father's so many times before, jaw clenched, eyes narrowed. A face making a hard decision. I knew at that moment that I was looking at a king.

"Lucas, Jade, get Malcolm and Rosita, take them home, gently. Thomas, with me, let's get Genni out of here. Everyone else, back to Leydford. Check the tunnels, set up patrols and a curfew. I don't want anyone on the streets by the time I get back."

They leapt to follow his orders at once, scattering in every direction, and I was left in the middle of it all, surrounded by motion but totally adrift.

"Set…"

"Go home, Mara," he said wearily, bending down beside Genni, who let out a cry of pain as her legs shifted.

A distant low mournful sound echoed between the trees. A horn being blown.

Everyone froze.

Genni gave a shuddering gasp and began to sob.

"Back to the city," Set shouted. "Now!"

They obeyed, all scrambling back through the trees. I followed more slowly, leaving Genni sobbing alone on the ground, emerging from the trees as the horses thundered away.

I was left with the scent of fresh vomit and death. And my freedom.

There was nothing to stop me walking away. Set had even told me to go home.

I glanced back over my shoulder, but the sight of Malcolm's tortured body hadn't changed. I looked away. The same beings who had done that were attacking Leydford.

I could go back. Or I could go home.

As the sound of hoofbeats faded, I thought I could hear the screaming. I didn't need to imagine what the demons might be doing; an example was only a few feet away from me.

There was only one option.

I was running after the horses before I'd even thought it all the way through.

14

Broken Stone

The route onto the roof wasn't a secret, but it wasn't obvious either. In the north-western corner of the top floor, beside the Guards' Room, a door led to a small, windowless space, seemingly empty other than stacks of boxes and records along one wall. At the far end of the short space, out of sight behind the neat piles, was a second door. Behind it, a tight staircase ascended in darkness to the flat roof of the citadel.

I drew on my site ward as I climbed, lending a red tinge to the world, highlighting the edges of the cold stone steps. Predictably, the familiar headache began to make itself known. I grimaced but didn't release the ward. Hopefully, with more practice, it wouldn't plague me so much. One useless ward was as much as I could bear.

At the top of the stairs, I opened the door and stepped out onto the roof, releasing my ward. The sky above was black, but there were no clouds to hide the stars tossed across it. The waxing moon was almost full, casting a silvery light over the city. Ahead, a single figure stood precariously close to the edge, arms crossed, staring towards the blackened tree and the glow of the pyre still smouldering beside it.

I joined him silently, gazing at the spot where my mother's body had been consumed, the smoke rising through the branches of the tree above. I could still make out the glow of the two pyres lit at twilight. Orion had earned the right to be set free alongside the queen.

Alicia had been burned lower down the mountain, her pyre lit earlier in the day. I knew many had expected it to be even lower, but none dared to grumble within earshot of her son, who now stood beside me.

I had wept for Alicia and all she had gone through, but the majority of my tears had been saved for my mother. Combined with the rest of the crowd that had gathered for her send-off, we had watered the ground with our sorrow, bringing life to the tree atop the hillside.

Now there was an emptiness inside me, a hollow space I could not fill.

"When will we leave?" Nate asked, his hoarse voice breaking the silence between us.

"Leave?" I repeated.

"We have to make them pay!" he insisted, turning to face me. His black eyes were overly wide.

I didn't say anything.

"How can you just stand there?" he demanded. "Don't you want to get revenge?" He took a step forward, uncrossing his arms.

I flinched.

He stepped back at once, turning away from me.

"You're angry," I said.

"Of course I'm angry." There was a pause. "I should have protected her."

My brow furrowed. "You did protect her. You protected all of us, protected the king—"

"He's not my king!"

"How can you say that?" I cried, fired up at once. "After all he's done for you!?"

Nate gave a chill laugh. "Like what? Like having me hunted down when I was eleven? Or when he left me to fend for myself against Nicholas because it didn't suit his agenda to help me?" He shook his head. "You, and Titan, and her." He gestured angrily to the hill. "You three are the only ones who ever gave a damn about me. You are the ones I was protecting. And I failed."

I opened my mouth, then closed it again. How could I tell him he hadn't failed when his mother was dead?

"Exactly," he said bitterly, correctly interpreting my silence. "How are you so calm?" he demanded when I didn't say anything else.

"Calm?"

"Why aren't you screaming and raging? You just lost your mother! Don't you care?"

I drew back, feeling my face harden. "You didn't even cry!" I regretted the words as soon as I'd said them, but the feeling behind them was real. I had seen him standing in front of Alicia's pyre, his eyes completely dry. To attend a burning and not offer tears for the deceased was an outrageous insult and for a family member... It was unthinkable.

Nate was staring at me. I wondered if I'd finally hurt him the way he'd hurt me.

"I can't cry," he said eventually, his voice more even than it had been at any other point in our argument. He gestured to his face. "Demon eyes, remember?"

My jaw dropped.

"You... can't?"

He shook his head grimly.

"Oh, Thorns. Nate, I'm sorry. I was angry, I didn't mean—"

"I hope you did," he cut across me. "At least that would mean you feel something."

"You know I feel things."

"You never show it."

We stared at each other for a few more seconds before he brushed past me, heading towards the stairs.

"Father is thinking of inviting you onto the Guard." The words burst out, though I'd told myself that I wouldn't tell him. I couldn't bear to see him walk away from me like that.

Nate stopped, standing for a long time before looking back.

Maybe I shouldn't have told him. But when I'd overheard Hamma and Father bring up the empty position, and Nate's name had been mentioned as a candidate to fill it... my heart had felt like it would burst with excitement. It would be an undeniable declaration of trust on my father's part, but no less than Nate deserved.

"Orion is..." I swallowed. "And Helena might have to retire.

You're good enough. You can hold your own against Titan. You killed two of the demons yourself."

"But—" He glanced around. The roof was empty. *We were alone.* "What about what I just said?"

I didn't need to question what he was referring to.

"The Guard is sworn to protect the king," I said. "And his family."

There was a long silence.

"If he doesn't do it now, it would be the first thing I do when I'm on the throne."

"But I'm a—"

"So?"

"The rest of the Guard... they'll object."

"Titan won't. And you impressed Hamma. They'll bring the others around if any of them don't agree. Just think about it. Please."

He nodded silently, looking back up at the dying fires. I followed his gaze. He'd just lost one family, but he was about to be offered a new one. I desperately hoped he would take it.

With my speed and balance wards burning under my skin, it didn't take long to catch up with the horses. They tossed their heads as I drew alongside, unnerved at being outmatched. The top of Leydford's wall came into sight over a hill. A pillar of smoke rose above it.

As we crested the hill, I looked for the large gates set into the base of the wall. One was ripped free of its hinges, lying on the ground outside the city. The other hung at a crooked angle.

I glanced sideways at Set as we charged down the hill. His face was pale, eyes wide but determined. I sped up, my feet barely touching the ground as we flew onwards.

I reached the city first. Jumping the fallen gate, I skidded to a halt on the slick, rain-wet stone of the courtyard. It took a second for the sounds to pierce the thumping of my heart. My head turned this way and that as I tried to sort out the cacophony. Howls, screaming, the clash of metal on stone; the noise assaulted me from all directions.

Ahead, two figures emerged onto the street, wrestling furiously. One gripped the other by their hair and arm, dragging them closer to the gate. The aggressor looked up as clattering hooves announced the arrival of Set and his entourage. Black eyes narrowed.

With a wild scream, I drew my blades, throwing myself forwards. My speed surprised the demon, who struggled to untangle himself from his victim. He'd expected a human. Someone weak. Helpless.

I didn't feel human as I descended on him, knocking aside his blood-encrusted sword with one blade as I thrust the other through his stomach. He cried out, releasing his weapon as he looked up at me in shock. His eyes widened as they flicked from my wards to my face. His mouth opened just in time for me to put my free blade through it and out the back of his head.

I stepped back, withdrawing both weapons. They painted lines of blood on the ground as the demon's body crumpled. The woman he'd been dragging along was nowhere to be seen.

Someone moved behind me. I spun, ready to attack again. It was only Set, his face stunned as he looked down at the demon inside his city. The city we'd all believed to be protected, invulnerable.

I looked past him and gasped.

The repelling wards all around the gate were destroyed. The stone where they'd been carved, shattered. Their power gone.

Set looked back, following my gaze. His face paled. He drew his sword. "To the king!" he shouted to his group, taking off at a sprint, heading deeper into the city.

It wasn't Holt's face I saw as I followed.

Wards still alive under my skin, I tore through the city, Set left far behind me. A terrified scream from my right made me look around. I caught a glimpse of a man and two children, pursued by a silhouette with its weapon raised.

Part of me cried out in response, but I kept going, tuning out the sounds of fear and pain.

Reaching the base of the cliff, I shoved my blades away,

scrambling directly up the scree rather than following the winding path. When I reached the gates to the palace courtyard, they stood open, unguarded. My stomach clenched.

I slowed, crossing the space at a jog, drawing my blades again. Inside, the corridors were equally silent and empty. It was almost peaceful. The carnage outside might not have been happening. For a moment, I wondered if it had been a vivid delusion. But there was blood splattered up my arms and screams still echoing in my ears.

What was I doing here anyway? I had no allegiance to Holt. I could be helping the vulnerable people below. Holt might not even be here. But when Set mentioned the king, all I saw was my father's face. And now here I was. I remembered my declaration that I wouldn't re-enter this city and grimaced.

Clashing swords reverberated along the hallway, pulling me from my thoughts. I was surprised to find I recognised the door directly ahead of me. In my distraction, my feet had brought me to the throne room. And from the noises I heard inside, someone was fighting for their life.

I sprinted towards the door. Lowering my shoulder, I pulled on my strength ward and smashed into the throne room.

Bright morning sunshine spilt through the open balcony onto a cluster of people. Everyone turned to stare at my unexpected entrance. Two guards were lying on the ground, one dead, the other likely to join them soon. Another one stood grouped with Warren, Holt, and Noah, all with their weapons raised. Four demons circled the quartet, their grins fading at my arrival.

I dove towards them. Fury guided my arms, my wards burning as I moved faster than ever before. The first demon died from a single blow to the neck, powerful enough to sever halfway through to its throat. Blood spurted everywhere. The second had just enough time to raise his weapons, but they didn't help. I felled him with a vicious slash across the leg and a stab to the chest. The third one dropped his sword and tried to change. His skin darkened to pure black, his face distorting before I kicked him back against a pillar and slit his throat, letting a stream of black blood pour down over his chest. I turned to the fourth one, but there was a flash of red light, and the space was empty.

Shaking, I turned back to where the others stood. The guard stared at me in shock, unable to process what had just happened. Warren and Noah were lowering their weapons, the latter with a wary expression.

Holt looked neither relieved nor pleased by my arrival. He took a step forwards, gripping his sword tightly.

"You!" he spat, raising the weapon. "What have you done? Where's my son?"

I stared at him for a second, then turned resolutely away, looking at Warren instead. "Where are the others? Keera, Andy?"

"Out there," Warren panted, flicking his chin across the room to the open balcony and the city beyond.

I felt a brief flash of worry for my students but shoved it away. They had a better chance now than they did before.

"Set?" Warren asked me anxiously.

I held his gaze, remembering what Set said about Warren begging him to spare my life.

"He's on his way," I said. I turned away, looking at the bodies of the three demons I'd just killed. Titan would have been impressed. "What happened?"

"I don't—NO!"

I flinched, Warren's shout giving me just enough warning. Holt's sword flashed past my shoulder, inches from my skin. I danced backwards, away from Holt's attack. Snarling, I raised my blades to counter, but before I could strike, Warren leapt between us. I froze, stunned, as he faced down his father.

"What are you doing?!" Warren shouted.

"She's working with the demons!"

"She just *killed* three of them!"

"We don't have time for this!" I snapped.

They both ignored me.

"Move!" Holt demanded.

"No!"

Warren's shout rang through the otherwise silent room. Holt's face darkened as he stared at his youngest son. Behind him, Noah's eyes were wide as he watched the standoff.

"How dare you?" Holt growled. "Move. Now."

"No," Warren repeated, quieter but no less intense.

Something closed in Holt's expression, his brows lowering as his eyes narrowed.

"You are no son of mine."

Noah and the soldier beside him both drew in sharp breaths. That was clearly not an idle sentence. My stomach sank. I wished I could see Warren's face. He hadn't moved at his father's proclamation.

I took half a step forward, reaching out to brush his elbow with my fingers. "There's no time for this," I said, my voice low. "People are in danger. We need to help them."

Warren remained frozen for another moment, then took a step back from his father, his weapon falling to his side as he turned towards me.

"You're right," he said, the words cold and empty. "Let's…" His voice tailed off as he stared to the side.

I turned.

A demon walked through the door I had thrown open. They stepped calmly to the side, watching the five of us without a word. Another filed in after them. Then another. More.

I swallowed, meeting each pair of cold black eyes. Then the last one stepped inside, pushing someone else before them, and I couldn't look. Wouldn't look.

If I looked, I would have to see.

My wards went cold, the power fading from them.

Beside me, Warren lunged forwards. I grabbed him before he could go more than a step, hauling him back.

I did a quick head count. Eight demons. And one other. The one I couldn't bear to acknowledge.

One of them stepped forwards, and I recalculated.

Seven demons. One half-blood.

Something fluttered inside my chest, like a dying bird desperate for release. But I couldn't move. I couldn't do anything.

"My, my," the half-blood said, his voice soft and silky smooth. "What a surprise." He was young, younger than me, with high, prominent cheekbones and a delicate nose. "Hello, Tamara." He didn't smile, but there was a brightness about his eyes, belaying their darkness. "How did you end up here? This place is meant to be off-limits. But no matter. We're overdue for a little chat."

My hands shook. My eyes darted to the other one, the one who didn't belong among them, the one I wasn't meant to be seeing.

Don't look. Don't look.

But I had to look.

Blood ran down the side of Set's face from a wound at his temple, but he otherwise appeared unhurt. The demon behind him had both his arms pulled back, I could see the strain across Set's shoulders and chest, matched by the fluttering muscle in his clenched jaw. He didn't make a sound, his fierce blue eyes hard as they met mine.

"Let him go!" Holt snapped, taking a step forwards, his weapon raised.

Instantly, the demons drew their weapons, but they were not pointed at us. Set didn't react to the forest of weapons suddenly aimed in his direction. His eyes flicked from me, to his father, to his brother.

Holt lurched to a stop.

The half-demon tutted as if admonishing a child. "That was rude," he said, turning his intense gaze from me to Holt. "You are the one in charge here, I presume."

"I am."

I tried to calm my racing heart, to bring back the cool, collected focus that would allow me to draw upon my wards. It did not come.

"My companions are encountering more resistance than expected," the half-demon said, his gaze still on Holt. "You are going to tell your people to lay down their weapons. They will cooperate with us, fully and without question, and when the work is complete, you will all be released."

I felt a surge of pride through my numb terror. Either my students were doing an exceptional job of making a nuisance of themselves, or the rest of the population had taken a stand alongside them.

"What work?" Warren spoke up from beside me.

"I will not trade my people into slavery," Holt barked, ignoring his younger son.

"Oh." The half-demon frowned, turning to glance back among the other demons. "That's strange because the way *his* friends were all so eager to protect him, I assumed he was someone important. If not, however…" He took a nonchalant step towards the demon holding Set.

Warren, Holt, and I took simultaneous steps forwards.

The half-demon smiled. "That's what I thought. So… what will it be?"

"Don't do it," Set barked. He twisted against his captor's grip, wincing when they jerked at his arms in retaliation.

"Let him go," Holt repeated. There was no tremor in his voice.

My eyes darted amongst the demons, searching for a path, an opportunity. But whichever way I looked at it, I would never reach Set in time. There were too many of them, and unlike the demons dead around my feet, they were not going to be caught off guard. I met the elder prince's eyes and knew he'd seen my assessment and understood the conclusion I'd come to.

"Give the order for your people to surrender, and I will release him to you. Or keep bleating like that and see how long my patience lasts." The half-demon sauntered away, through the ranks of his fellows, towards Set.

"Stop this," I snapped. "You have no quarrel with these people. Let him go."

Maybe I could grab one of the other demons, threaten them as the half-blood threatened Set. But what if he was willing to

234

sacrifice his companions? It was too risky of a stand-off to create.

The half-demon turned, raising one eyebrow, and let out a laugh. "My, my, my. I did not expect that. Honestly, Tammie, don't tell me you've let yourself care."

It was as if I'd missed a step going downstairs. My world lurched, the sensation painful in my stomach and chest. There was a dull roaring in my ears.

"What did you call me?" I growled. Only one person ever called me that.

The half-blood met my gaze, seeming to realise his mistake.

I could feel my face twitching, the moisture prickling in my eyes, the hilts of my blades cutting into my palms.

I'd known. Ever since I'd seen his eyes, on some level, I had known.

What had Nate said to me when he recounted the tale of my father's murder? *His eyes were like mine.*

"Your father was a noble man, in his own way," the half-blood said. "But he wouldn't listen. So I did what had to be done."

"I'm going to kill you," I vowed. "Slowly. I'm going to hear you *scream.*"

The half-demon's face twitched, lips thinning to a sharp line. "Go on then." He took half a step towards me, arms spread in invitation. "I'm right here."

My teeth ground together. One foot edged an inch forwards. I wanted to do it. The *thing* that murdered my father, my king, stood in front of me, mere feet away. I wanted to claim my vengeance with pain and blood. I wanted it so badly that it hurt.

My eyes flickered to Set.

I didn't move.

"Why are you doing this?" Warren cried, trying to step around me, but I blocked him again. Having one of the brothers under threat was already too much. I couldn't let Warren put himself in danger as well.

"Because someone has to," the half-demon snapped, "and no one else will."

"Just let him go," I said, trying to convince myself I wasn't begging.

"Pathetic," the half-blood sneered, turning back to me. "I expected more from you."

"I'm not the one hiding behind a hostage," I shot back.

His eyes narrowed. "Alright," he said coolly. He drew a short knife from a sheath on his forearm.

We all stepped forwards, Warren and the other soldier letting out angry shouts of protest.

Set's nostrils flared as his breathing quickened, but he didn't make a sound as the half-demon turned towards him, playing the knife between his knuckles.

My hands shook, my breaths uneven, but with the unspoken threat held on the knife's sharp edge, there was nothing I could do.

The half-blood leant in close to Set, whispering something in his ear. Set's face hardened, his eyes on his father. He snapped his head forward, trying to headbutt the half-demon, but he was too quick, pulling back with a laugh before Set could make contact. He circled behind Set and his captor, still spinning the knife between his fingers.

"Stop it," I snapped, my heart pounding. "You have nothing against these people. Let him go."

The half-blood paused in his circling, shaking his head. "You're wrong," he said. "And besides, you just told me to stop hiding." His lips twisted into a cruel smile. "It's just one life. What does it matter?"

In one careless motion, he stepped forward and drew his knife across Set's throat.

Blood washed down Set's neck. His face went pale.

The demon holding his arms stepped back, and Set dropped to the floor, a puppet whose strings had been cut.

I wanted to sink to the floor with him, to release my scream like the blood now spreading inexorably across the floor, unstemmed by Set's pitiful grasping at his own throat. But I didn't have the luxury of time, of grief.

236

At the murder of the prince, the barrier between us was broken.

The demons attacked. The half-demon who'd so casually stolen Set's life leapt forwards. I raised my eyes from the dying man twitching on the floor and lifted my blades to meet him.

Once, twice, three times, our weapons clashed together. He was faster, a benefit of his demon blood, and my emotions were too loud for me to effectively draw on my wards. My cuts were thrown wild, but my anger lent me a different kind of strength, and I'd pushed him back a step when I heard Warren yell in pain behind me.

No. Not him too.

I whirled away, shoving through the tangle of fighting bodies. Anyone in my way was knocked aside, be they friend or foe. Warren was staggering backwards, nursing a deep cut across his arm. The sight of his blood sent a shock of icy fury through my veins, freezing all else in its path. In the chill emptiness left behind, I found my wards and *pulled*.

Warmth flared under my skin, the world around me blurring as I leapt in front of Warren, driving his opponent back with a ferocious slash. The demon hissed angrily, denied his easy target. He thrust his sword towards my chest. I swayed aside, ink and heat writhing along my arms. With the blade in my left hand, I knocked his weapon aside. I jabbed my right one through his ribs.

The demon's snarl turned static, his face draining of colour as he dropped to his knees. I turned away before he hit the ground, eyes searching desperately for the one who could not be allowed to escape.

A door burst open behind the throne and a squadron of soldiers raced inside, immediately throwing themselves into the fray. I spared a moment to mentally commend their bravery.

The demons let out howls at the new arrivals. I saw one of them trying to change, their skin darkening to a smooth, oily black. A soldier tackled them before the transformation was complete and they both disappeared in the mess of bodies.

I had no time for triumph. I spun, looking, looking, looking…

There! The half-blood was standing by the exit to the balcony, shouting something at one of his fellows as he casually dispatched a soldier with a long, fluid slash across the chest. Freed of an opponent, he turned, surveying the grappling fighters throughout the hall, eyes snapping from one body to the next.

With a growl, I launched myself across the room.

He spotted me as I broke free from the crowd, ready for my approach. He parried my lunge, dancing backwards out onto the balcony. Sunlight slid over him, making his dark hair shine. I followed, attacking in a whirlwind, feeling my wards writhing under my skin.

Sunlight shivered around us, winking off the metal of our blades as they smashed together. He twisted his sword, locking up one of mine, gripping my other wrist with his free hand. Inches apart, we grappled, neither able to overcome the other. I met those dark eyes, just like Nate's, and snarled. He smiled, that same cruel, careless smile he'd given me before slitting Set's throat.

I dropped my sword. It clattered on the stone floor, its ring echoing under our feet. My hand now empty, I twisted my arm in his grasp, my skin burning with the friction, and seized his wrist in a counter-grip. His eyes narrowed as he began to draw away. I didn't give him a chance.

Throwing myself backwards, I gripped his wrist with every ounce of strength I could rip from the single ward on my back. His mouth opened, eyes widening as he tried to pull free, but my momentum was too much.

My back whacked into the hard floor, head knocking against the stone as I flung the half-demon past me. He spun in the air and smashed into the low balcony wall with a crack that had nothing to do with the stone.

Gasping, head ringing, I rolled onto my side, feeling the bruises to come, and pushed up onto my hands and knees. The half-demon was upside down, contorted unnaturally over the balcony. His shoulders lay on the ground at a crooked angle, his legs curled over the wall, ankles dangling over empty space.

I crawled towards him. He was still alive, eyes huge, breaths coming in uneven, panting gasps.

Grabbing his shoulders, I gave a monumental tug. His lower body slithered towards me, flopping limply onto the balcony.

The sounds of fighting from inside seemed distant. Removed. Irrelevant. My blades glittered in the sunlight where I'd dropped them, calling to me. I restrained myself. I couldn't kill him yet.

Looking down at his helpless form beneath me, it was hard to remember why.

"You killed my father," I growled.

He was too dangerous to leave alive. It was inevitable. He deserved it.

He blinked, black eyes wide, then he laughed, the sound rasping and wheezy. "And I'd do it again," he panted, the laugh turning into a cough.

"You killed Set."

He coughed again, but I could hear the laughter beneath it, mocking me. My hands twitched towards my weapons again. He was at my mercy, something I found to be in short supply.

With a physical effort, I reined in my vicious thoughts.

"Why did you come here?" I forced the words out. "Why did you attack this place?"

He spat defiantly, a globule of his inky blood landing with a gentle splat next to his head. My grip on his shoulders tightened, my fingers digging into the joints. He grimaced, then lunged upwards.

I jerked back as something silver flashed past my face. There was a dull impact on the top of my shoulder. The pain came a moment later.

Gasping at the sudden burn, I recoiled, falling back to the floor. I looked down. His knife, the same one he'd used to kill Set, was buried an inch deep beside my left collarbone. Flinching, I twitched my arm, but the pain intensified, sending spasms through my shoulder. Gripping the blade, I ripped it free. Blood oozed out of the wound, seeping under the leather of my vest.

The half-demon laughed again, trying to use his arms to push himself along, legs dragging uselessly behind him. I stared at him for a moment, then reversed my grip on the knife and ripped it across his face.

His eye burst under the blade like an over-ripe berry and he screamed.

I basked in the sound.

He flailed in pain, but I turned the blows aside, kneeling on his closest arm. Changing my grip on the knife, I stabbed it into his other eye. His body shook with something akin to sobs, but it was dark blood, not tears, that ran down the sides of his face.

"Answer me!" I demanded. "Why come here?"

He bared teeth outlined with black blood. "Go die underground," he snarled.

The words struck me like lightning, my jaw snapping shut as I jerked backwards. Something burning and ice cold rolled through my veins. He wasn't going to give me any answers. I let him writhe on the stone for another few seconds.

Then I slashed the knife across his throat.

Dark blood sprayed everywhere.

The dying demon choked, trying to pull in a breath of air, bubbles forming in the blood pulsing out of his throat. He shuddered, twitched, then went still.

My heavy breaths seemed louder in the quiet of his death.

My hands shook. Clenching them into fists, I stood up. He was never going to cooperate. His last words made that clear.

Turning away from his body, I squinted into the relative darkness of the throne room.

Inside, the remaining demons had frozen, staring at the body behind me. There was a moment of stillness, then a flash of red light and, as one, they disappeared. The remaining fighters spun around, confused by their sudden exit. I staggered inside, my right hand pressed over the wound on my left shoulder.

The arrival of more soldiers had undoubtedly helped, but there were still bodies strewn all around the room.

240

The guard who had been present when I arrived was now collapsed against the base of a pillar, both hands clamped around his leg. Blood welled up between his fingers. Noah was upright but swaying, covered in so much blood, both red and black, that I couldn't tell if any of it was his.

Warren was on his knees between the bodies of his brother and his father.

Holt had fallen on his front, one arm stretched out towards Set, reaching for his elder son even in death.

Set lay on his back, one hand still over the wound at his throat, but there was no more blood to be spilt. His eyes, glassy and empty, stared up at the ceiling.

I closed my eyes rather than look at Warren's face. Another image flashed in front of my closed eyelids. An identical room, littered with bodies of people and demons alike. That time, it had been my family dying.

Running footsteps made me look up. Another half dozen people burst into the room.

"They've gone! They've all gone! Just left, and—" The woman at the front broke off at the sight of the silent room and the bodies that littered it. For a moment, no one spoke.

Warren was still on his knees, unmoving.

"The king is dead," one of the soldiers said. "All hail the king."

"All hail the king," Noah echoed, followed tentatively by the rest of the crowd.

The silence that followed the proclamation was absolute. The whole world paused, holding its breath. Waiting.

15

Survivor

"We are gathered here to remember those who came before and to decide on those who will come after." My father's voice was sombre, resonating around the circular stone walls.

He would have said the words before, but this was the first time I'd attended an initiation to hear them.

Congregated underground, the flickering torches threw shadows over us all. I watched with bated breath. My father stood beside Hamma. The remainder of the Guard arched around them on either side, all facing into the centre of the room. I hovered behind them, my back to the wall. The two initiates waited on the other side of the room.

My father stepped back, ceding the floor to Hamma. The broad-shouldered Captain moved forwards to the centre of the room, turning his back on the initiates to face his fellows.

"We remember Helena," he began, "who was injured in service and judged herself to be unable to continue in her post. We will remember her dedication and her loyalty. Whatever was asked of her, it was never too much. She will be with us, always."

"Always," the others echoed.

Hamma let the word fade away, the silence curdling for a few moments before he spoke again. "We remember Orion, who gave his life in defence of the king. We will remember his noble heart and his persistent humour. We will remember him as a devoted brother. He will be with us, always."

"Always."

The word was more subdued this time, barely a whisper from Ishmael, whose shoulders were tense. I swallowed, trying to clear the painful lump in my throat. Hamma stepped back into the line, meeting my eyes briefly before turning away. Father moved forwards again to stand behind his shoulder.

"Who can take the place of those you have lost?" he asked, the words echoing around us.

"No one," the five voices replied.

"Will you continue to serve without them?"

"We will," they chorused.

"Will you accept new members into your ranks, to enable you to better protect the throne?"

"Who should we accept?" Hamma asked. His voice sounded quiet after the layering of the other responses.

"Osanna, step forward," Father said, his voice softer now.

The woman, short with long dark hair, stepped into the middle of the circle formed by the members of the Guard.

"Nathaniel, step forward."

Nate moved up beside her, his face drawn but determined.

"Kneel."

They both did so, sinking to their knees with their heads bowed forwards.

"Members of the Guard, will you accept these initiates among you, as brothers and sisters, to fight and die together?"

"Aye."

Hamma answered first. The word was repeated five times around the room, and with each affirmation, my heart beat faster. In some ways, this was a formality. The Guard would already have argued and reasoned and debated about the two candidates, but until those words of acceptance had been uttered, a sliver of anxiety remained lodged in my chest. As Miriam completed the chorus, I let out a breath of relief.

"Initiates, will you swear to protect the throne, the city, and the people, against any threat?" The gentleness of my father's tone when *he'd called them forward was gone. These words were harsh and cold. A demand. A challenge.*

"I will," the pair intoned together.

"Will you swear to stand against any foe, to risk any injury, to sacrifice your life if necessary?"

"I will."

"Then swear it. By name, by blood, by honour," my father said.

"By name, by blood, by honour, I so swear," Osanna said.

"By name, by blood, by honour," Nathaniel repeated, "I so swear."

My father stepped past Hamma, approaching Osanna first, who held her left arm up in front of her. With a quick, practised motion, he looped a purple strip of cloth around her upper arm, tying it off. Moving sideways, he stood before Nate, repeating the gesture. My chest tightened, constricting bands of pride and excitement squeezing the air from my lungs.

"Rise and present yourselves."

They stood together, Osanna moving first to the barred wooden door in the wall to my right. She placed both her hands on the surface and remained motionless for a moment before stepping away.

I suppressed a shudder, glad I wasn't the one who had to make contact with that door.

Nate approached with more hesitation, pausing before reaching out with tentative hands and pressing his palms to the wood. He stayed for a heartbeat, then stepped quickly away from the door to where the Figures slept.

Hamma was the first one to approach the pair, a wide smile on his face. "Welcome," he said. There was such genuine warmth in his voice that the heavy atmosphere broke, the rest of the Guard moving forward to greet their newest members. I watched as Titan and Nate looked at each other for a moment before Titan pulled him in for an embrace.

My smile was so wide it hurt.

Stab. The needle entering my skin didn't hurt. It was a minor discomfort at most. Irrelevant. *Tug.* Fine thread pulled the wound at my shoulder closed. I barely registered the sensation.

All around, people were rushing past me. Cries of pain and grief filled the air, undercut by a constant weeping that echoed around the wide room.

Stab. Tug. I hadn't been back to the large cave serving as a hospital since I'd first awoken in the smaller room next to it, but I doubted it had been this busy in a long time. Every bed was filled. Those around me were occupied by people with lesser injuries like mine, tended to by harried medics, treating their patients and then chivvying them away to make room for the next.

The loudest screams emanated from the other side of the room, where the more seriously injured were being treated. The sharp smell of blood prickled in my nose with every indrawn breath.

As if I hadn't smelled, hadn't felt, hadn't tasted, enough of it.

'Just one life.'

I closed my eyes.

'What does it matter?'

I grit my teeth, trying to force the cruel words away.

He was dead now. I'd avenged my father and Set.

And it hadn't made the slightest bit of difference. Set's body still lay in the throne room. I hadn't been able to face Warren but had stumbled out of the palace without saying a word, leaving him with the corpses of his father and brother.

I turned away from the woman stitching up my shoulder, staring out the wide archway at the sky visible beyond. A small patch of fluffy white cloud was meandering across the blue sky.

Thorns… Thorns… I didn't know what to say. What guidance could I ask them for? What help was there to be given? It was all too late.

And all my fault.

I dropped my gaze back to the floor. If I hadn't challenged the half-demon, hadn't pushed him…

Then what? Did I really believe he might have released Set?

Why had he been here anyway? He'd wanted the people here to

do some sort of work. But, as Warren had questioned, what work? What would the demons have needed humans for? The half-demon had been quick to give up on that demand as well. Surely he had known that once he...

My thoughts faltered, shying away from the memory.

Once he'd lost his leverage, what had his plan been then? Was he going to threaten Holt directly, or had he completely abandoned whatever slaver ambitions he'd had?

Maybe I should have been more insistent in my questioning of him once he was crippled and helpless. But his harsh words—*go die underground*—had turned my blood cold. It was a horrible fate to wish on someone, to condemn them to be trapped beneath the earth forever, to never return to the sky.

He was never going to give me answers.

It didn't matter anymore anyway. He was dead, his conspirators had fled, and the people here were left with blood and sorrow in their wake.

"Keera!"

The sudden cry made my head snap up again. Bile rose in my mouth as I looked towards the entrance, dreading what I would see. Keera was standing there. Her hair was matted with red, and there was a wound across her arm, blood snaking down to her wrist. She looked exhausted and shaken but was standing unaided, arms open to catch the desperate embrace of the dark-haired woman who had called out to her.

The pair clung to each other, the dark-haired one pulling back and peppering Keera with questions, fussing over her injuries.

Keera shrugged her off, holding her away, speaking in low, urgent tones.

I was about to look away when the other woman nodded, turning to point at me.

Keera followed the line of her finger, eyes settling on me like a weight on my chest. I shifted, about to rise, but the woman stitching my shoulder stabbed the needle into my skin again, fixing me in place.

246

Keera threaded her way through the rows of beds towards me, her face closed off and serious. My mood turned darker with every step she took.

"What is it?" I asked before she'd even reached me.

"Need you," she said shortly. Her eyes flicked over my wound. "You okay?"

I nodded. "What's happened?"

"Hannah?" Keera addressed the woman standing over me, ignoring my question.

"I'm nearly done," the woman said, not looking up from her work.

"Keera."

"Not here," she said firmly.

I bit my tongue, holding back my insistences.

The woman who had clung so desperately to Keera had followed her over, now drawing her away from me with a gentle touch. I watched the pair, seeing the softness of the way they held each other, then looked away, craning my neck to see the wound Hannah was ministering to.

Held closed by her neat stitches, the cut looked innocent, like nothing more than a minor scratch. I could still feel the knife jabbing into my flesh, could still hear the squelch when I'd pulled it out. The blade had pierced through the shoulder strap of my leather vest but missed the ties that held it closed. I could feel eyes on the exposed flesh where I had undone them, letting front and back hang down whilst Hannah cleaned and treated the wound. The strength ward on my shoulder blade would be partially visible. At least it was the undamaged one on my left side. If the wound had been on my right, I wasn't sure what I would have done.

Hannah finished trying a tight knot and stepped back. "Wait here. I'll get something to strap your arm up."

"Don't bother," I said, standing up, already working to pull my vest closed over the wound. It rubbed uncomfortably against the stitches.

"You need to keep it immobilized," Hannah frowned.

247

"I'm sure there are other people who need your help," I said, turning to face Keera. "Let's go."

She did not object, stepping away from her partner and heading towards the door. My stomach sank at her quick acquiescence.

We walked out into the bright sunlight together, Keera setting a brisk pace as she led the way down towards the city.

"Where were you?" she asked before I could question her. "Steren tried to find you. So did Andy."

"I left." There was no reason to lie about it.

"Without permission?" Keera peered sideways at me and snorted. "So that's why he sent Set out."

The casual way she said his name sent a shock through my whole body. She didn't know what had happened in the throne room.

I couldn't bear to tell her.

"Where is everyone? Are they…"

"They're all here. But we lost Andy. And no one's seen Rosita."

Shit. Rosita. And Genni. If the half-demon had killed all those who'd accompanied Set beyond the wall, as he'd hinted, then no one else knew we'd found the missing trio. Someone needed to retrieve the bodies. And get Genni some help.

"Where are we going?" I asked Keera as we reached the ground, turning onto a street lined with buildings. Splatters of blood marked the walls and I had to dodge several cracked pieces of stone strewn on the ground.

"Not all the demons left," Keera said.

"What?"

"One of them stayed. We can't get to him."

"Where?" I quickened my steps. My mind was racing. One of them hadn't gone. Why not? Had something prevented them from stepping through that flash of red light?

Keera threw me a disgusted look. I grimaced. Right. That was where she was taking me.

I glanced towards the gates as we crossed the main thoroughfare. The destruction was unchanged. The gates hanging from their hinges, wards defaced around them. I swallowed at the grim sight.

248

Once the demons had entered through the hidden passage Genni had revealed, the wards must have no longer worked on them. Clearly, they were only effective in one direction.

I frowned, my steps slowing slightly. Was that possible? For their repulsion to be directional? If that were the case, I would have expected them to be located on the outside of the wall, facing any potential invaders. I wished I could ask one of the Warders their opinion.

What other option was there? None of those who lived here would have destroyed the wards. Maybe the half-demon had been unaffected by their power. Nate would have been able to prove that if he were here.

Keera turned a corner and a huddle of familiar figures came into view, looking around at our approach. I scanned their faces instinctively. No Andy, no Rosita. Aaron was also missing, as was Warren of course, but the remainder of my students looked relatively uninjured. Jory was closest to us, and he had a wild grin on his face.

"We showed them," he said as Keera and I reached the group. His eyes were overly wide. They matched the instability of his voice. "Took the bastards by surprise, we did." Several of the others nodded behind him, but I couldn't match their enthusiasm.

I moved around them, approaching the alley they crowded around. Steren guarded the entrance, sword held ready in front of her. I tapped her gently on the shoulder. She glanced back, hesitated for a moment, then stepped out of the way.

It was a tiny space, barely three feet across, a strong defensive position for the demon huddled at the far end. There was no other way out.

I paused, examining the demon further. He was hefting a sword that looked far too big for him. He looked barely more than a child, his hair shaved almost to his skull, leaving only a hint of fuzz.

His black eyes flicked to my wards and he bared his teeth. The attempted aggression of the gesture was mitigated by his eyes, darting from side to side.

"What happened?" I asked.

"I kicked his knee in. I think it's broken," Keera said, matter-of-factly from behind me. "But he got in there before we could finish him off. He didn't leave when the others did. Don't know why."

The demon's throat bobbed as he swallowed, flexing his fingers on the grip of his sword, waiting for me to rush at him.

Now that Keera had mentioned it, I could see his right leg hanging limply, forcing him to lean against the alley wall to remain upright.

Young, isolated, and already injured. A combination I could make use of.

The half-demon might not have been willing to give me answers about what he was doing here, but maybe this one could be… *persuaded* to be more cooperative.

"Maybe we should tell Holt," Steren said from behind me as the silence stretched out.

I broke the demon's gaze, turning my head enough to acknowledge the words without letting him out of my sight completely. It would do no good to conceal the truth from them.

"Holt is dead."

The silence shivered. The demon gave no reaction, the name meaningless to him, but his eyes darted past me, watching the reactions of the others. From the corner of my eye, I did the same.

Glances were exchanged, heads hung low. But no one said a word. The silence was perverse. No outcries of anguish or shock. Just the echoing sound of decades of inevitability.

"All hail the king," Jory muttered, his earlier triumph snuffed out. "Set will make it. It'll be okay."

I took a step back, motioning for Steren to resume guard duty, before turning to face them. This time, the words were harder to say.

"Set is dead too."

I'd thought they couldn't look any more horrified than they already did.

I was wrong.

250

The silence they'd maintained for Holt broke. The whispers of denial and indrawn breaths laden with grief were louder than shouts.

Keera's knees buckled and she staggered sideways, catching herself on the wall. She wasn't the only one; several of them reached out to each other to steady themselves, faces stunned and uncomprehending.

"What now?" Miranda whispered.

I pinned her with a hard stare. "Now you give Warren your full support." Turning away from them, I returned to the alley entrance. "And we get some answers."

Steren wasn't so quick to move out of my way this time. Her hands shook as I slipped past her, moving down the alley and stopping a few feet shy of the demon's sword. My wards came to life reluctantly, the pain at the top of my shoulder flaring as the ink began to writhe under my skin.

"You have two options," I said, addressing the demon. "Talk. Or I make you talk. What were you doing here?"

He swallowed again but said nothing. I bared my teeth in an approximation of a grin. I'd been hoping he would choose that option.

"You know they've abandoned you." I took half a step forwards, leaning from side to side, trying to work out the best way to disarm him. I was down to one usable arm, so my options were limited. "All your so-called friends. They're not coming back. You're all alone."

"Zouri will come back," the demon snapped, stabbing forwards with his weapon.

I withdrew before the lunge, watching him wobble precariously, steadying himself on the wall. "Zouri," I repeated. The name coiled insidiously in my chest. I shoved the feeling aside. No time for that now. "Is that your leader? The half-blood?" I clucked my tongue sympathetically. "Oh, he's *definitely* not coming back."

The demon sneered disbelievingly.

"He's dead."

A flicker of uncertainty. Maybe even fear.

"I killed him."

A clenching of his jaw, narrowing of the eyes.

"Made him scream first."

The demon lunged with a snarl, pushing off their one good leg, weapon extended ahead of them, intent on skewering me through the throat.

I ducked, sweeping my right arm upwards, the weapon knocked over our heads. Diving forward, I shoved my shoulder into the demon's chest, stamping down onto his good foot. He wobbled, trying to put weight on his bad leg. It buckled beneath him, and he dropped with a yelp of pain. I ground my foot down onto his wrist, eliciting another cry before he released the sword. Kicking it away, I stepped back, breathing hard as I looked at the pathetic bundle on the ground. The demon was panting, pressed against the wall, braced for the next blow to land.

"What was Zouri doing here?" I demanded. "He said he wanted people to do work; what work?"

The demon said nothing, cringing away from me. He looked so very young.

I lifted my foot, resting it lightly on his ruined knee joint. He flinched, hands snaking towards my ankle. I pressed down harder. With a gasp, he went rigid. "*What work?*" I demanded. Maybe I had been hasty in killing Zouri, but I wouldn't make the same mistake again. I didn't care how long I had to drag this out; I was going to get answers. I increased the pressure further.

"The wards!" the demon screamed, the words almost unintelligible.

I withdrew, taking the weight off his knee. That was easier than I'd expected. Between his youth and isolation, I had hoped he would break quickly, but I hadn't anticipated just how quickly.

"We needed the people to break the wards on the wall," he gasped out.

"Why?"

"I don't know! I swear, I swear," he cried, as my foot twitched threateningly, "Zouri said we could get them to do it, but they wouldn't."

"Why couldn't you destroy them yourselves?"

"We can't. We can't get close enough."

I crouched down, bringing my face closer to where he cowered on the ground. At this distance, I could see him shaking. "Then how did the ones around the gate get broken?" I hissed.

"Zouri! Zouri could get close."

I stood up, looking behind me. The wall was close; I could see it looming above us a few streets over. "Let's test that," I said.

Reaching down, I grabbed the demon's elbows and heaved him upright. My injured shoulder spasmed at the effort. I felt a wave of blood ooze out of the stitched cut. Pressing the demon against the wall, I pulled his wrists behind him, bending them up between his shoulder blades so that I could grip them with one hand. He groaned at the contortion, struggling, but subsided when I shoved him out of the alley. My students fell back, giving us a wide berth, then followed along in our wake.

With his leg unable to support him, I ended up taking more of his weight than was comfortable, especially with my injury. He realised where we were going only a few steps later and struggled in earnest. I grimaced, trying to control him. Wincing, I raised my injured arm and grabbed the back of his neck, squeezing until he cringed and went still.

"No, no, no." His whimpers continued, heels digging into the ground as he tried to halt our inexorable progress towards the looming wall, its intact wards waiting menacingly ahead of us.

We were still a dozen paces away when he gasped, tensing under my grip, his pleading transforming to a high, keening noise that sent a buzzing under my skin. Another two steps and he screamed properly, jerking and writhing. I lost my grip and shoved him away from me, towards the wall.

He fell to the ground several feet away from the base of the wall, bathed in a pool of brightness as the wards along the base of the wall lit up with a smouldering white light. He might as well have been dropped into a pit of fire. The scream that erupted from him tore my eardrums, making me flinch with its intensity. He scrabbled like a crab, heedless of his injured leg as he clawed his desperate way further from the wall.

My wards pulsed under my skin, daring me to draw deeper upon them, to be sucked down, down, down…

The pressure subsided as the demon dragged himself away, his screams subsiding into panting sobs. I ignored him, staring at the wall, at the light from the wards, now fading away, breathing hard.

I'd *felt* the wards upon it activate, just as I felt it whenever there were lots of people using their wards around me at home, but this was much more potent. My eyes roved over the wards, hundreds of them, maybe even thousands, interwoven on the stone. The power here was stronger than I'd realised.

I turned away, feeling the pressure under my skin subside as the repulsion wards deactivated.

We had proved that the demons couldn't have broken the wards themselves. Either the demon was telling the truth about Zouri, as a half-blood, being unaffected, or a human had destroyed the wards. My eyes flickered around my group of students. Was it possible that someone within the city had been working with the demons? I wanted to dismiss the idea as paranoia, but something wouldn't let go of it. The demon could have been lying to protect their hidden ally, whoever they were. And I had no way of knowing.

I looked down at the trembling demon. Shudders swept down his body in waves. His black eyes were open but glazed, and his mouth agape, gasping desperately for breaths. There would be no more answers from him for a while. My students were ranged in a half-circle around him, their expressions ranging from awe to disgust to pity.

"What do we do with him now?" Steren asked quietly. Her face was firmly in the last group.

"Kill him," Keera responded immediately, but I shook my head.

"No. Not yet," I said. "There might be more he can tell us.

Warren might want to question him."

A few hours to stew and reflect upon what he'd just experienced might make the demon more pliable. But he couldn't be left in the open. He was too dangerous, even in this state, and I didn't want any vengeful citizens getting hold of him either. Which meant I needed somewhere quiet and private to stash him, where he wouldn't be discovered.

Ava's warehouse came to mind instantly. No one was going to be snooping in there. And Ava owed me. Or at least—I grimaced at the thought—she soon would. *That* responsibility could be postponed no longer.

"Which of you know which is Ava's warehouse, along the wharf?" I asked my students.

Cautious glances were exchanged. I scowled.

"I don't care if it's a secret or not," I snapped. "Speak up, now."

Jory and Steren both raised tentative hands, then blinked in surprise at the other's response.

"Right," I said. "Take him there. Tie him up and keep watch on him. Don't let anyone know he's there."

"Ava's not just going to let us go in and take over," Jory said cautiously.

"She will for me. Tell her to meet me at the hospital." I turned on my heel, heading along the wall towards the gates.

"Where are you going?" Miranda asked, alarmed.

"To get her reason to cooperate."

16

Among the Dead

Lit by only two torches on opposite walls, the throne room felt small and ominous. The pillars cast long flickering shadows over the floor, overlapping and melding together into a maze of darkness to become lost in.

I sat on the bottom step of the dais and watched my father pace from one wall to the other and back again. Miriam, Ishmael, and Osanna were on duty, but the rest of the Guard shunned sleep as well to be present.

Titan and Hamma stood shoulder to shoulder against the wall. Nate leaned against a pillar close by. The sight of the purple band around his upper arm sent a warm flash of pride through me. His dark eyes tracked my father's restless movement back and forth.

The silence was cloying, sticking in my nose and throat. Osanna seemed to feel it too, her eyes darting often from the closed doors to the others in the room and back again. She hadn't learnt the balance of the situation as the other Guard members had. My father's prolonged deliberations, familiar to the rest of us, were unnerving to her.

"Not that spending time with you isn't our favourite pastime, sire,"Titan said, after a few more minutes of tense silence, "but what's on your mind?"

Father halted, facing Titan with such a cold look that I wondered whether the dark-skinned man had finally overstepped the boundaries he pushed so often.

"Revenge, Titan," he said, his voice as hard as the stone on which he

walked. "Revenge is on my mind."

Titan and Hamma exchanged a look as he returned to his pacing.

"The demons have become more active," Father continued, speaking to the floor. "More attacks on outlying settlements, even on the outskirts of the valley."

"How do you know this?" Osanna asked, no trace of nerves in her voice, despite the twitching of her fingers. "There haven't been any survivors reporting to the watchtowers."

"Sources," my father said shortly, exchanging a glance with Hamma. "This last attack shows a new level of boldness. They entered the city, entered the citadel." His steps slowed, fingers playing over Mercy's hilt, hanging at his side. "I have been complacent," he said quietly, "but no more. This upsurge of attacks is not random, either in timing or targets."

"You think there's a reason behind it?" Nate frowned.

"Yes," my father said. "Something has changed."

"Like what?"

"I don't know!" Father snapped.

Somehow, Nate didn't flinch from his tone.

"So what do we do?" Hamma asked, pushing off the wall and taking a step forward.

Father stopped in his pacing, turning to face the captain of his Guard. "We need more eyes. If there's a pattern to these attacks, we need to find it."

"The soldiers would be more than happy to help. They're just as angry as you are," Osanna offered.

"No," Father said, not taking his eyes off Hamma. "I'd just be putting them at risk. We need something... else."

"Are you sure that's a good idea?" Hamma asked, his face serious. "They have no concept of restraint."

I looked between the two, something tightening in my stomach. The knowledge of what they were talking about curled around me like smoke, tantalisingly out of reach.

"Restraint is not something I'm interested in right now."

Hamma crossed his arms but said nothing more. His eyes darted to Osanna and Nate, then to me. Lips pursed, he shrugged. "It's your decision."

Father turned away from him, looking around the hall. His eyes found mine and locked on. I didn't move, didn't breathe. The pressure built until I was sure it must be a visible thing, crackling the atmosphere into shards of diamond.

"No holding back," he muttered. He looked away, the thread between us fracturing.

I came to my feet. "What are you going to do?" I could feel the answer still, taste it on the tip of my tongue.

"I'm going to wake the Figures."

There was a moment of silence, then CRACK.

I ducked, flinching from the sudden sound. Were they here already? Was it that simple? I looked around wildly, expecting to see grey-skinned silhouettes emerging from the shadows. There was nothing. Another clatter drew my attention to the true source.

A shard of stone, one of the pieces of the carved columns, lay on the floor by Nate's feet. Nate stood rigid, eyes closed, one of his guilty hands visible, clenched onto the stone pillar behind him. His fingers twisted in sinuous shapes, the skin dark with more than just shadows.

Titan stepped away from his post by the wall, striding over to stand in front of Nate, one hand clasping his shoulder, murmuring in his ear.

I risked a glance away, taking in the reactions of the rest of the Guard. Osanna's eyes were worryingly wide as she stared at my father. She didn't seem to be breathing. The more senior Guardsmen were more stoic but I saw Miriam and Edric exchanging doubtful expressions, though they fractured as soon as they noticed me watching. Ishmael was the only one unperturbed by the announcement. There was no joy to disturb the new bleakness of his face, but he was nodding slowly.

Father turned back to Hamma. "The Figures will patrol the outer villages, keep watch for any demon incursions, and alert us to them *before they have a chance to develop. We will meet any attackers out there and make them pay."*

"We?" I echoed.

He met my gaze. "Some of us," he amended.

"That's a lot of ground to cover," I pointed out. The settlements up the valley were miles away, and the ones around the lake to the south and east were even more spread out. There was no way only twelve Figures would be able to keep watch over the entire area.

"They can handle it," my father said.

My lips thinned at his curt reply. Did I not deserve to participate in the quest for vengeance? Then I remembered the sight of the Figures' cold grey bodies, and the muscles through my shoulders and back tightened, ready to shatter. Deserving, maybe, but did I want to be a part of it?

I glanced across to Nate and Titan. The former's eyes had opened, but his face was still pale. Titan was looking at my father, but I couldn't read his expression.

Everyone was silent, feeling the mechanics of the plan solidify around us, the change it wrought on the air. Like something waking up.

Leaving my students to deal with the dazed demon, I strode along the wall, heading towards the broken gates. The story carved into the wall beside me, the transition from intact to destroyed wards, was jarring. Chips of stone littered the ground, crunching under my soles as I passed the defaced wards. According to the young demon, *this* was why Zouri had attacked the city. To annihilate the power held on its wall. But why?

I could understand it as a means to an end - removing the obstruction they represented, to allow easy access to the city they guarded, but what would the demons gain simply from the wards' destruction? Maybe the young demon simply hadn't been allowed to know his commanders' final goals.

A straggled group milled around the splintered remains of the group. Two faces I recognised caught my eye. Bardok and Noah. My eyes narrowed. Excellent. I headed towards them.

"—doesn't matter," Bardok was saying morosely. His black sword was resting against the wall, shining wetly in the sunlight. "Warren was never meant to be King. Those monsters chose right; they killed the competent one."

"That's not fair," Noah objected. He had cleaned himself up since I'd left him in the throne room. Smears of blood still stained his clothes, but his hands and face were mostly clean now.

"Isn't it?" Bardok shook his head, looking past me and squinting up at the palace. "Would've better if they'd wiped out the whole line."

"Has that happened before?" I asked, despite myself.

Noah flinched, spinning on his heel and eyeing me warily.

Bardok nodded. "That's how Warren's grandfather became King."

"Warren will do his best," Noah said, a little firmer, though he was still avoiding my eyes. "He and Set were so close, he'll know what to do."

"Holt only raised one of them to be king," Bardok said bluntly. "Better that than risking them trying to compete over it. Set was taught to lead, Warren to follow."

My stomach twisted. Was that true? Would my parents have done the same if my older brother had survived being born? Then again, they probably wouldn't have had me if he had lived.

"Give Warren a chance," I implored Bardok. "He might surprise you."

Bardok grunted, turning away.

I looked at Noah, who swallowed but raised his chin and met my gaze with determined eyes.

"You and I have a job to do," I said curtly. "Go get your horse, something big enough to transport three people, and several blankets."

"Where are we going?"

"Where do you think?"

260

He glanced out the open gates, hesitating. For a moment, I thought he would refuse, but he seemed to accept this reckoning would have come eventually. With a nod, he turned and hurried away.

Bardok frowned after him, fixing me with a suspicious look.

"Did you mean what you said about Set being the competent one?" I asked before he could question me.

"Yes." Bardok turned to lean against the wall, crossing his arms over his barrel chest as he eyed me. "Set knew his time was coming. He's been making quiet moves for the last couple of years, gathering friends, currying favour."

I remembered the way Set had been approached by people in the mess hall. Like he was holding court.

"I'm not saying he was looking to start a coup," Bardok added, seeing my raised eyebrow, "but he was preparing. Whereas Warren has been playing at soldiers." A significant look accompanied the last few words.

My lips pressed together. "Your boy was pretty eager to join us at that," I reminded him.

"And you turned him down. I understand he didn't take it too well." Bardok's chin lowered and he glared at me from under his brows. "If this is some sort of ruse to get revenge for that, you'll have me to answer to."

"It's not," I said shortly. "And to be clear, I didn't turn him down. It was never my decision. I told him to take it up with Warren. It's not my fault if he didn't."

"Right. Because Warren wouldn't have listened to your suggestion, right?"

The sarcasm was heavy. I looked away. Had Warren's interest in me been that obvious? We stood in silence, staring in opposite directions until the clopping of hooves heralded Noah's return.

I met his gaze, my face impassive, then turned and led the way out of the gates.

Once on the plains, climbing steadily up the rise outside the wall, I looked over Noah's supplies. His horse, dark brown with black mane and tail, stood shorter than I would have expected, given Noah's height. It would be dwarfed by Keera's black mount.

As I'd instructed, several blankets were piled across its back, draping to its belly on both sides to keep them from sliding off. A harness of some sort was fitted around the animal's neck, with straps reaching back under the blankets. Two long poles, at least two inches thick, were lashed tightly to the harness, extending back several feet behind the horse, their ends dragging on the ground. Some type of fabric or leather was wrapped loosely around their length.

Looking forwards again, I squinted at the distant trees, trying to remember where Malcolm's body had been. Having not approached the spot from this perspective, it was more difficult than I'd anticipated.

I could feel Noah's eyes on me as we began to descend the rise. I expected him to begin quizzing me again about where we were going, but he did not. The silence, broken only by the horse's deep, gusting breaths and the plod of its feet on the ground, quivered uncertainly around us.

Halfway down the hill, we found the tracks of many horses, heading back towards the city. The ground was torn by the speed and urgency of their passage. I hesitated, staring at the overlapped hoofprints. One of those horses had carried Set, taking him closer to his death with every step. I should have stopped them and insisted they remain outside the wall. Anything to keep him out of the half-demon's grasp.

His face flashed before me. Zouri.

My hands flexed, knuckles popping with the savage movement. Noah had stopped, his horse tossing its head between us so that I only caught glimpses of his face past its nose. I waited for it to settle, then continued, following the path carved into the ground.

The animal became more restless as we approached the trees, stepping sideways and shaking its head. Noah encouraged it on, clucking his tongue and pulling on its reins. He was several steps behind me when I spotted the ghastly sight of Malcolm's body, still

262

hanging between the trees.

I stopped, staring at it, letting my eyes travel once more over the extensive damage, each wound more brutal than the last.

Noah caught up with me, still wrestling with his horse. He followed my gaze and gasped, releasing the horse's reins as he reeled backwards.

I darted back, drawing on my speed ward to catch the animal before it could flee. My hand firm on its reins, I watched Noah's stumbling retreat. His eyes were huge, his skin pale. A dozen paces away, he came to a halt, knees still visibly trembling.

"This is what the demons were doing when you were stopping Ava from showing me the way out." The edge to my voice was harder than I'd expected, but I made no attempt to soften it. "I wasn't here in time *because you stood in my way.*"

It was probably a lie. The likelihood of Noah's intervention having made any difference to the outcome here was slim. But it wasn't impossible.

Noah's eyes flicked from Malcolm's mutilated body to my face and back again.

"All because you couldn't handle the fact that I didn't ask Warren to let you into our group. Are you pleased with yourself? Happy with the result? *Look at him!*" My shout startled the horse even further. It half-reared, front legs leaving the ground as it pulled backwards. I moved with it, lest the reins break, but refused to release my grip. I didn't look away from Noah.

"Do you want to see Rosita and Genni too, see what was done to them?"

Noah shook his head rapidly at my angry words, going even paler.

"I'm sorry," he blurted out. "I didn't know!"

"You didn't *think,*" I corrected him.

"Sorry, sorry, sorry," he groaned, over and over, his eyes fixed on Malcolm.

"Take your damn horse," I said, holding the reins out towards him. "We're going to get them home."

Genni was still alive but unconscious when I found her. Spreading out the blanket I'd taken from Noah's horse, I rolled her onto it. She stirred slightly, her ruined face tightening with pain, but then slumped again. Using my good arm, I grasped the corners of the blanket beside her head, dragging her back out to Noah. He took one look at her face and turned away, heaving noisily into the grass.

I left him there, returning to the clearing for Rosita. My blade severed the rope holding her aloft cleanly, but the sound of her body hitting the ground was anything but. She was stiffening already, neck rigid where it hung forwards, like some monstrous carrion bird, jutting its head out to rip scraps from a carcass.

By the time I'd dragged her into the sunlight, Noah had mastered himself. Though still pale and shaky, he was fiddling with his horse's harness, adjusting the two long poles, which were now attached to either side of the horse. They crossed behind it, fanning open to form a large triangle, covered with the supple leather I had seen wrapped around the poles before.

Malcolm proved to be more complicated to retrieve. The death-paralysis had taken complete hold of him, his arms held stiffly out to his sides even once I'd cut him down from his suspension, a cloud of insects rising from his body at the movement. I glanced at his ankles, wondering if I could pull him out by them, as I had with Rosita, but the flesh up his feet and calves was charred and black. I didn't want to test the strength left in those bones. Instead, I turned my attention to his upper body. Gleaming black flies crawled over his torso and arms, buzzing when I waved a hand over them, flitting away only to settle again moments later. It took me a few moments to bring myself to take hold of his lacerated arms and work them loose. Dried blood stuck to my hands when I was done, flaking off and fluttering to the ground like autumn leaves. Bringing his wrists above his head, I gripped them tightly in my good hand and began to pull.

In the meantime, Noah had rolled Rosita onto the leather frame behind the horse. I deposited Malcolm beside her, covering them both with a blanket. Folding two more blankets, I made a pad on top of the sledge before transferring Genni onto it. I covered her with the final blanket. Fatal or not, her injuries were not something people should be forced to witness.

I stood for a moment, looking at the three bodies, rolling my sore shoulder. Even though I hadn't used my left arm, it still ached.

Noah stood beside his horse, stroking its neck and taking deep breaths. I walked over to stand next to him, waiting for his eyes to dart to mine, his hand tense on the horse's hair, before speaking.

"I saw you in the throne room. You fought well and you probably could have kept up with the group. I'm sorry for not asking Warren to give you a chance."

"Thanks." The muttered word was dull, its edge blunted by contemplation. "I'm sorry too. For how I reacted. It wasn't your call. And I'm sorry for… y'know." He didn't look back at the bodies behind him, but the hunching of his shoulders and the slight jerk of his chin illustrated his apology eloquently enough.

"Let's just get them home," I said. He nodded.

Genni stirred a couple of times as we made our way back to Leydford, muffled whimpers of pain reaching my ears. Powerless to help, I tuned them out, merely walking a little faster, letting Noah match my pace. Bardok was waiting inside the ruined gates, helping clear the space of rubble from the ruined wall. He took half a step towards us, but Noah shook his head jerkily, continuing to follow me in silence through the city. His muteness was contagious, infecting all those we passed, who fell silent at the sight of the smothered shapes being dragged behind the horse.

At the base of the winding path to the hospital, Noah brought the animal to a halt, stroking its nose absently. With a glance at the blank look on his face, I retreated to crouch beside Genni, twitching the blanket aside to check on her. Her ruined face was slack, but her arm, when I touched it, was still warm.

She was alive, for now, but I had to somehow get her up the

winding path to the hospital. The horse wouldn't be able to traverse the tight switchbacks with the sledge behind it. Either I would have to carry her—not a prospect I relished with my injured shoulder—or I needed help.

I stood up again, looking around. There were several people around, but they were all hurrying about their business. Two youths, a couple of years younger than Noah, caught my eye. One of them met my searching gaze and held it.

"Hey!" I beckoned them over.

"Saviour," said the one who'd been watching me as they approached, a touch of reverence in the word.

The word threw a jagged knot into my throat, cutting me as it never had before. I hadn't been much of a saviour to this city. Still, it was a mask I could don if it would help.

"I require your assistance," I said.

The warier of the pair, hanging back, opened their mouth to make an excuse, but their companion spoke first.

"Of course." They stepped forwards eagerly. "What can we do?"

"I need to get her to the hospital," I said, gesturing at Genni's covered form.

"Who is it?"

"Of course." My helper glared at their friend, who scowled but shuffled forwards in reluctant submission.

I glanced at Noah. "Can you get them where they need to go?" I asked, nodding at the two remaining bodies.

He swallowed but nodded.

"Alright," I turned back to the other pair as I drew upon my wards. "You two take that end. Gently now…"

Ava was waiting just outside the cavern, her hand clenched on the head of her cane. When the three of us shuffled awkwardly into view, her eyes snapped at once to the hidden shape in our arms. Her face paled, her mouth gaping open.

"She's alive," I said in a low voice as I passed her.

She gasped, a shuddering inhale of half-articulated prayers.

Inside, I headed right, towards the area where the more serious injuries were still being tended to. There was even more activity than when I'd left. The medics who had been treating the minor injuries earlier were now assisting here. I stepped into the path of one of them, hurrying between beds.

"Need some help here," I said.

She hesitated, glancing around, then stepped towards me, reaching for the blanket covering Genni.

I shook my head. "I wouldn't do that. Not here. Is there somewhere private?"

The woman scowled, flicking her hair as she sneered at me. "We don't have time to mess around," she snapped. "We're rather busy, in case you hadn't noticed." She turned away and found her path blocked by Ava.

"You're going to see to her right now, or I'll tell everyone about you and Darius," she snarled, leaning in close to the other woman, who blanched, flushing bright red.

She looked around, checking to see who might have heard, her eyes lingering on my helpers, then jerked her head at me, leading the way to the edge of the room, where an archway led to a smaller room beyond. She pointed me to a raised bed at the end, where a large window let light spill into the room. With some more shuffling, we deposited Genni gently onto its surface.

Retreating, I let the medic approach, dismissing my assistants with a smile and a murmured thanks.

I caught Ava's arm as the pair left.

"Where's Warren?" I asked.

Ava's face twitched, though I couldn't read the expression upon it. She turned, pointing back through the archway to the other side of the hospital. "With the dead," she said.

I nodded and released her, fleeing rather than have to watch her examine her daughter's injuries.

The archway Ava had indicated, on the opposite side of the hospital, was set deeper into the mountains. There were no windows and no lanterns inside. The second-hand illumination that filtered inside did not reach the edges. The space was small compared to the cave where people were being treated, yet I imagined it would normally be adequate for its intended purpose. Not today.

There were no beds; the dead were laid out in rows on the floor, more than I wanted to count. As I stood in the archway, two men shuffled past me, carrying another of the deceased between them. Soon there wouldn't be room for any more. They laid the young woman beside her fellows, then backed out in silence. A familiar face not far from hers caught my eye. Andy.

Keera had told me he had died, but the sight of his body still twisted something inside me, an aching, tearing sensation. Swallowing, I forced myself to look away, drawing upon my sight ward to penetrate the darkness at the edges of the cavern.

At the back of the cave, three motionless figures were separate from the rest. Set and Holt were lying together in front of the others, leading their people even in death. Warren sat beside his brother, knees drawn up to his chest, his face streaked with tears as he stared at them, as still as any of the dead.

I picked my way towards them. Warren made no indication that he'd registered my approach as I sat beside him. Holt looked peaceful, his face calm and serene as I'd never seen it in life. Set was less so. Blood spattered over his chin, and the gaping wound on his neck drew my eyes when I looked at him.

Don't look, don't look.

But just like before, I had to look. I couldn't take my eyes off him. I'd thought he was the future of this city. Had been counting on it. Holt would die, and Set would have remained, his calm, steady strength opening the way for a new alliance. A chance to learn more about the ward. He would have understood. But the dream had died with him.

"Why did this happen?" Warren asked dully.

My heart ripped a little further.

"I don't know," I said.

268

If he'd asked 'how', I might have been able to give him an answer. But 'why'...

"He knew you." Warren's voice was sharper now, cutting. "The one who did this. He knew your name."

I met Warren's red-rimmed eyes. The suspicion simmering within them felt like a jab in my stomach. Unexpected. Painful.

"I'd never seen him before," I said honestly. "But he killed my father."

"How do you know that if you'd never met him?"

"Things he said. And someone who saw it happen told me it was a half-blood."

"Half-blood?"

"Half-demon. You saw his eyes? They're white around the edges, like ours."

Warren made no response to that, looking away from me. "So he was here for you?"

"I don't know why he was here."

"You provoked him though! Why couldn't you have just not said anything?!"

"I never meant for this to happen!" My voice rose, my anger rearing to match his.

We were both silent for a few seconds, the dead crowding around to judge us.

"But it did," Warren said, his tone bleak once more.

I said nothing. It didn't surprise me that he was looking for someone, anyone, to blame. I couldn't even deny the possibility of truth within the accusation. I stood up, careful not to jostle my arm.

"I'll keep watch at the gate tonight," I offered quietly. "In case any of them come back."

Warren scoffed. "It doesn't matter. They can't get past the wall."

I hesitated. Surely he knew... must know... must have put it together. "Warren," I said, "the wards around the gate have been destroyed."

He looked up at me, incomprehension written across his features.

"What?"

"The wards are broken," I repeated. "That's how they got into the city."

Warren ran both his hands over his head, tugging at his hair, eyes blank and staring. "Set was right," he said, seemingly more to himself than to me. "We should have left." His eyes closed, his knuckles turning white. "It's not fair," he whispered. "This shouldn't have happened."

"Lots of things shouldn't happen," I said quietly. "But it did. So mourn them. Then make them proud."

He said nothing, so I left him there, one of the dead.

It was later than I'd expected when I emerged back outside; the sun was already sinking towards the horizon. I tried to account for all the hours of the day and failed. The streets were quiet as I made my way toward the gates. The only people I saw were sat in open doorways, watching me pass with dull eyes.

Stopping under the archway, I stared across the grassy plain, stained golden by the late afternoon sun. I was instantly reminded of when I'd emerged onto this same plain only days ago before I'd found—before I'd *killed*—the Figure. It had the same peaceful serenity I'd experienced then too. At least this time, I already knew it for the lie it was.

"Leaving again?"

I jumped at the voice, whirling around. Keera was watching me, eyes narrowed. I scowled, irritated at myself for getting so lost in my thoughts.

"No," I said. "I told Warren I'd keep watch tonight, given…" I gestured to the broken wards before turning away.

"Oh."

At the sound of retreating footsteps, I glanced back. She was walking briskly away. Shaking my head, I turned my attention back to the plains. It was going to be a long night. Tiredness was already prickling at the back of my eyes, hanging heavy on my limbs. With a sigh, I brushed the debris off a patch of ground and sat on the cold stone, bracing my back against the wall.

This time yesterday, I had been sitting in my room, dwelling on the welt on my arm and the storm raging outside. Thorns's guidance had been incomprehensible, I'd been stuck inside the city, and Set had still been alive. Would I change things if I could? Trade my freedom for his life?

I thought I knew the answer to that uncomfortable question. What would Father have thought of me, that I would delay my return home for one life?

I smiled painfully. Here I still was, my freedom right in front of me, no one stood in my way, but instead, I was playing watchdog. I had no qualms about it either. This was where I needed to be. Maybe tomorrow, things would be different. But for now, I was staying. And, for the first time, that was my choice.

New footsteps brought my attention back to the city again. Keera was back, and she wasn't alone. I stared as she made her way to the other side of the archway where the gates should have been and flung herself down to sit opposite me. She was armed, a sword with a worn leather grip at her side.

The group that had accompanied her milled around in the courtyard, finding spaces for themselves and settling down. Half of them wielded close-combat weapons - axes, swords, a double-ended spear. The rest were archers, propping up small quivers of arrows, stroking their bows nervously as they eyed the open gateway.

I looked back to Keera. "What's this?"

She shrugged. "Steren is… you know where. Aaron and Jory will take the next shift."

"And them?" I nodded my head to her cohort.

"Our city. Our responsibility."

I blinked, stunned. Were these really the same people who, only days before, had fled from the sound of the gates opening? I looked over them again. Some of them looked terrified, their hands tense, sweat visible on their foreheads. They would break easier than ice if the demons returned. But they were here.

"Thank you," I said.

Keera stared out at the plains. "Didn't do it for you," she said brusquely.

"Right." I eyed her. "Why do you hate me?"

"I don't hate you." She shot me a look that said otherwise. But, after a moment of silence, she continued. "I was the one who was sent out to confirm Noah's story after he brought you back here. And in case you hadn't noticed, that's pretty bloody dangerous."

The image of Rosita's body flashed before my eyes. I swallowed.

"Plus, I had personal plans I was rather looking forward to that I had to put off to do so," Keera continued. "So, yeah, I resented you pretty heavily. And haven't had any reason to change my opinion since."

I stared, her face slightly harder to pick out now as the shadows began to gather.

"So," she said briskly, glancing back at the group, "what did Warren have to say about… our new friend?"

I grimaced, turning away, out across the plain. The sun had truly set now, casting everything into purple and grey. With a long breath, I drew upon my sight ward. The world instantly became visible again, the details picked out in red hues to my eyes. The grass swayed like a carpet of fire, flaring with each movement. Nothing would be able to approach these gates without me seeing. I would have a cracking headache by morning though.

"I haven't told him," I said in response to Keera's question.

"But you spoke to him."

I didn't answer. How could I try and explain that it hadn't been the right time?

Keera gave a dark chuckle at my silence. "So much for giving him our full support. Or did that apply to everyone except you?"

Nate's angry words from years before echoed in my ears. *He's not my king.*

It was more accurate for me now than it had been for him then; I wasn't a citizen of Leydford. Warren had no authority over me. But I didn't say the words.

272

"I'll tell him tomorrow," I said. "Give him time to mourn for now."

Keera said nothing, but I could feel her disapproval and knew she might be right. We couldn't hold the demon captive forever. Warren wasn't going to get enough time to mourn properly, no matter how long I tried to delay.

With a sigh, I turned my eyes back to the empty plain, the burning grass swaying uncertainly. It was going to be a long night.

17

Reunion

Standing atop the East Gate, my eyes swept the landscape. The small, close-packed dwellings of the poorest area of the city spread out below me. Beyond, the road wound carelessly through open fields, punctuated by small fences and huts, until it disappeared into the trees carpeting the foothills of the mountains. High above, I could make out the dip in the peaks where the pass sat between them. Somewhere out there, my father was hunting, along with most of the Guard. With a sigh, I shifted my weight, my arms crossed tightly.

"Having fun?"

I glanced around as Nate climbed the steps to join me. His eyes scanned the horizon just as mine had. The strip of purple cloth stood out against the skin of his arm.

"No," I replied sourly.

He smiled softly. "They'll be fine."

"If they were fine, they would be back by now."

It had been seven days since Father left in a flurry of frenzied activity. He hadn't told me where they were going or what information the Figures had uncovered to cause their sudden departure. I expected them to be gone for a few days, but not a whole week. When I'd returned to my room at the end of the third day, a note had been left on the bed, written in my father's hand.

Making them pay. Stay strong.

Two short sentences. Not enough.

I had no idea how it had gotten there. They had taken no messengers

*with them. Whoever delivered the note made no attempt to
communicate with me directly, just left the note lying on my bed. If
Father had thought his words would calm my nerves, he had been
wrong.*

*"Watching for them won't help," Nate said, turning away from the
view as if to demonstrate his point.*

*After his private outburst to me on the roof after his mother's
funeral, I'd expected him to be angry about being left behind whilst the
others went out to get revenge upon the demons. Maybe he had been; I
wasn't present when he and Miriam were told they would be staying
behind. If he was resentful, however, he hadn't shown it around me.
He might even have been relieved to be staying here, so he didn't have
to encounter the Figures.*

I didn't move. "Do you have something better for me to do?"

"Actually, I do," Nate said.

Frowning, I turned away at last. "Has something happened?"

*"No, everything's fine," Nate reassured me, already bounding away
down the steps.*

*With my father gone from the city, any official business was my
responsibility. So far, the most onerous thing I'd dealt with was
meeting an envoy from Lambridge regarding the upcoming trade
meeting. Mediating a dispute between two farmers over damage to a
fence bordering their lands had been both frustrating and amusing as
increasingly petty historical grievances were thrown back and forth
between the pair, growing ever more irrelevant to the present
situation.*

*A couple of the soldiers at the bottom of the steps dipped their heads
jerkily to Nate as he passed, but most merely frowned at his back.
Their expressions cleared as I followed him down, all of them sinking
into respectful bows. I scowled at their lowered heads but had no time
to berate them as Nate was already striding off.*

"What's the hurry?" I asked as I caught up to him.

"No hurry," he said with forced airiness, slowing his pace.

"They're just getting used to the idea of you being on the Guard,

that's all," I said.

Nate snorted. "It's fine, Mara. They don't bother me."

"Really?"

He shrugged.

I eyed him suspiciously. Nate had been distant over the past few weeks. I'd barely seen him outside of when he was on duty. I'd assumed he was still grieving his mother's death. Still, if he was back to being social, or as close to social as he got, I wasn't going to question it.

He turned off the main road, and I glanced up.

"The armoury?" I frowned. "What are we doing here?"

My hand strayed to one of the weapons at my sides. It still didn't feel quite right, but after Titan and I had started trying much shorter blades, I thought we were at least going in the right direction. Fighting with two weapons at once had been a tricky adjustment, but Titan insisted I try it to counter the disadvantage of having a shorter reach. My progress felt slow, especially when I had Nate to compare myself to, but I could almost hold my own against him. On a good day. A very good day.

Nate didn't reply, shooting me a look somewhere between nervous and excited as he led the way inside, turning immediately to the right. Curiosity piqued, I sped up, trying to see where we were headed. When he stopped, I nearly walked into his shoulder, reeling backwards to avoid a collision.

"Wha—"

He stepped aside before I could finish the question, and I fell silent at once.

In this room packed with racks full of swords and shelves crammed with bows and arrows was an anomaly: an empty table. Or rather, an almost empty table.

"For you," Nate said quietly.

I'd already taken a step forwards, passing him without realising it.

The weapon was beautiful. Simple and elegant. Probably only half the length of Nate's sword, yet perfectly proportioned. The hilt was wrapped in black leather, with tiny hints of gold wound around it. I *wanted to pick it up so badly that it hurt.*

"How... Where..." I breathed.

"I had it made," Nate said from behind me. "Had a hand in making it, actually."

Slowly, I reached out. The first contact hit me like a spark, a fraction of Thorns's power running through me. Stepping closer, I closed my fingers around the hilt and lifted it.

It felt wrong.

It was more right than anything else I'd ever held, but the sheer perfection of its appearance was diminished when it was in my hand.

My eyes were suddenly wet, and I had to take a deep breath.

I was touched Nate had done this for me. No one would deny that it was a beautiful weapon, strangely weightless in my hand, light glinting off the edges. But it wasn't perfect. The balance was wrong. The blade leant sideways in my hand, trying to twist itself out of my grip.

Nonetheless, it was better than the others I'd tried. It would be my honour to wield it.

Fixing a smile on my face, I turned around.

Nate stood there, holding out a second, identical blade to me. I swapped the one I was currently holding from my right hand to my left and forgot it was there.

Reaching out, I accepted the second blade and was made complete.

I closed my eyes, revelling in the feeling. They were there, ready to respond to the slightest twitch of my fingers, but they weren't there because how could they be separate objects? Surely, they had been joined to me all my life, a part of me forever. Hadn't I just set them aside for a second and now reclaimed them, unable to be separated for more than a few seconds?

When I opened my eyes again, Nate was watching me with a small smile.

"Don't cry."

I blinked, more tears coursing down my cheeks.

"I... Thank you," I said. "They're... I..."

His smile widened. "You're welcome. Titan helped with the design."

I just stared at him, shaking my head, trying to find the words.

"They're... I feel invincible," I breathed, blinking away the last few tears so that I could see him properly. "It feels like I could take on anything." I flexed my fingers, feeling the malleable grip and hard metal underneath, the weapons light and eager. "Like I could beat you," I said, grinning.

"Oh, please," he snorted. "That'll never happen."

I drew myself up, feeling the movement in my bones, in my soul, as I never had before. "Who is part of who's Guard?" I barked.

Nate didn't take his eyes off mine as he sank to his knees, tilting his chin back, baring his throat to me, a shine playing in his dark gaze. "Forgive me," he said.

Dawn crept across the sky like a deer venturing into an open clearing, tentative and wary, ready to flee at any moment. The residents of the city who had turned out to stand guard had long since fallen asleep. I longed to join them. My eyes were sore and dry, my limbs heavy. Every heartbeat sent a fresh throb of pain through my head, where the predicted headache was sitting like an iron band, squeezing my skull from all sides.

I was pacing back and forth in the gateway, attempting to stave off the exhaustion hounding me, when I heard people beginning to shift behind me. Releasing my sight ward, I blinked at the sky. The rising sun, though still hidden behind the mountains behind me, had stained the clouds pink, the bright colour heralding the new day.

Dropping my gaze, I blinked at the open plain, just as empty as it had been all night. After so long using my sight ward, it was a shock to see the natural golden colour of the grass, rather than the reddish hues I'd been staring at for hours. Rubbing my stinging eyes and yawning, I considered my next move.

I needed to talk to Warren again. Hopefully, he would have started processing yesterday's events. Then something would need to be done about the demon held in Ava's warehouse. My anger fizzled at the edge of my mind at the thought of him, but in a half-hearted way. The first thing to do, I decided, would be to get some sleep. The people could organise a daytime watch without me.

Turning away from the plain, I stepped back through the shadowed gates, nodding to Jory and Aaron as I passed. They looked as if they would have spoken, but I kept walking, willing my feet to get me as far as my room within the cave system. It felt like an impossibly long journey at that moment. Holding in a sigh, I plodded on.

Halfway to the path up to the caves, I saw Warren walking toward me. My heart sank. So much for getting to sleep before being faced with this conversation. Before he reached me, however, a horn cut through the silence, blaring its nasal tone out over the city.

We froze, our eyes locked.

I'd heard that sound before. Not so loud, but just as unnerving. It had rolled out across the plain to where Set and the others had found me. That horn had summoned them back here, to their deaths. Because they had known what it signalled. Now I knew too. And I hated it, hated the realisation, hated seeing the same horror spread over Warren's face.

The demons were back.

I spun around, sprinting back towards the gate. Warren shouted something behind me but I didn't slow down. I wasn't even sure I wanted him to catch up. If I was heading towards danger, I wanted him to be as far away from it as possible. But at the same time, how could I protect him if he wasn't with me?

The courtyard was a completely different scene from how it had been when I'd left only minutes before. The sleepiness was gone, painted over with confusion and terror. The fighters were clustered around the open gates, weapons held in shaking hands, fumbling fingers setting arrows to bows. I slipped through them to the front as another horn blast deafened me, drawing my weapons as I did so. I thought I was ready to face whatever was waiting on the other side of the gates.

I was not.

He stood alone, dark hands empty of weapons. He was *cautious*, the word embodied in every line of his figure. His stance whispered it, his open hands spoke it, his face shouted it. The glances he flashed at the wall from his dark eyes proved it. Cautious.

I knew him instantly.

"What's he doing?" a voice behind me hissed. "Is it a distraction?"

"Who cares? Shoot the fucker," another replied. I knew the voices, the faces that went with them, but they didn't matter now. Irrelevant.

The creak of a bow broke my reverie.

"Stand down," I said, forcing the hoarse words up my tight throat.

"But—"

"Stand down," I barked, rounding on the archers. "Anyone fires an arrow, I will personally return it through their eye."

They drew back, unnerved by my sudden aggression. I didn't care. Turning away, I shoved my blades back into their sheaths and, for the second time in the space of a day, left the city. This time at a run.

Nathaniel came to meet me, his steps slow and measured. We were still some way from the wall when we met, my sprint slowing before I ploughed into him. For a moment, we stared at each other. I couldn't take my eyes off his face.

He dropped to his knees, tilting his head back to bare his throat to me. "My Queen," he murmured.

I swallowed down a lump in my throat, choking at the sight. It had only been days since we'd last seen each other, but it felt far longer.

"Rise, my brother," I replied, my voice shaking, and he did as I directed. My eyes roved over his face, drinking it in. He was here. Real, solid, present. A knot in my chest loosened, and I could

280

finally breathe again, my constant suffocation lifting. How many times had I wished for his company, to watch my back, to talk through my ideas? And now he was here.

His black eyes darted over me at the same time, catching on the dried blood visible on my shoulder. "Are you alright?" he asked, his voice sharp.

Tears welled suddenly in my eyes. My physical pains had become insignificant the moment I saw him. But there were deeper hurts that not even his presence could fix.

I shook my head because it was true. I was not alright.

I stepped forwards, dropping my forehead to rest on his shoulder. It was presumptuous and hideously inappropriate, but I couldn't stop myself. I needed to feel him, to know he was there, that I wasn't alone.

He swayed at the unexpected contact, hesitating for a moment. Then I felt his arms come up around me, light pressure on my back as he returned the contact.

I closed my eyes and just let go.

It was over too quickly. Nate made no move to disturb me, but the minutiae of reality circled around me, pecking like birds at the bubble of my bliss, plucking it away one shred at a time. Eventually, I could ignore it no longer.

With a suppressed sigh, I pulled back. Nate let me go without resistance, his face unreadable.

"What are you doing here?" I asked. "How did you find me?" *Again*, I added mentally, aware that this was the second time he had appeared in the exact place I was, with no obvious way of knowing my location.

He looked over my shoulder at the city behind me. He was still standing with his hands held slightly away from his body, the pose catching my attention. I looked down. His arms were streaked to the elbow with a wet black substance, almost like...

"Nate," I breathed, staring at his blood-encrusted hands. "What happened?"

Nate raised his hands in front of him, staring at them as if he'd forgotten they were attached to his body.

"There was an attack here, wasn't there?" he said, looking back up at me.

"Yeah, yesterday," I said, frowning. "How do you know about that?"

"I heard about it this morning. The ones who came back were talking about you."

"Came back where?" There was a twisting feeling in my stomach, the tension that had just been released ratcheting up again. "Nate, where have you been?"

"On the other side," he said cryptically. He wasn't looking at me anymore, his gaze focused over my shoulder.

I looked back. In front of the ruined city gates, a crowd of people had gathered, the boldest of them spilling out onto the plains. I recognised the one at the front, shrugging off the hands trying to hold him back. I grimaced. Warren would have to wait.

"That's not an answer," I said, turning back to Nate.

He blinked, dropping his gaze to mine. "I needed somewhere the Figures couldn't follow me. I tried to throw them off your trail, leaving false paths, but then I needed somewhere they couldn't go."

I knew what he was saying but didn't want to admit it. I had to drag the words out of my throat. "You've been with the demons."

Nate nodded.

I stared at him.

Part of me wanted to back away. Nate had been with the demons. How long had he known where they were and hidden the knowledge from me? What else might he be hiding? What if he had gone there not, as he said, to escape the Figures' pursuit, but because he'd wanted to?

The other part of me forced those doubts aside. This was *Nate*, it reasoned. The boy I grew up with, the man who had sworn an oath to protect my family.

Nate said nothing, his eyes flicking between mine, waiting in trepidation to see what my reaction would be.

It was this recognition that settled the turmoil within me, letting my shoulders relax. I knew Nate, had trusted him for years. And I wasn't going to stop now. Not when I could read the fear of that outcome in his expression.

"It's true then," I said, as if I hadn't been doubting the very foundation of our relationship. "They have a base? Hamma always said they must. But the Figures have never found it?"

Nate's face softened, his gratitude evident as he nodded. "Yes, they have a home," he said, giving a pained smile at the mention of his former companion. "But it's not a case of *finding* it. It's… elsewhere."

"Elsewhere how?"

Raised voices reached my ears. I glanced back again. Arguments were breaking out at the entrance to the city. I could see red faces and wildly gesticulating arms. I was running out of time.

Nate followed my gaze, observing the deteriorating situation. "It's like… another world," he said hurriedly. "And the Figures can't get there."

"But you can."

He nodded. "I can."

My teeth ground together but I'd made the decision to trust him and I wasn't going to go back on it now. "I've got some things to finish here," I said, "and then we're going home."

Nate raised an eyebrow. "Good."

I turned towards the city, unsurprised when he fell into step beside me. "This could get nasty," I warned him, as we made our way towards the gate. "They've just been attacked, and it wasn't the first time."

Nate merely nodded, his dark eyes fixed ahead.

The crowd fell silent as we approached. Most of my students stood behind Warren, their faces tense. Warren's expression was cold.

"What happened to his face?" Nate muttered before we were within earshot.

"Demons," I replied out of the corner of my mouth. That seemed to be the answer for every atrocity committed here.

Warren wasn't looking at me. His gaze locked on Nate, his face tightening as we got closer to the gate. But he couldn't lie to himself forever. As he realised what walked next to me, he took half a step backwards and drew his sword.

Instantly, the crowd boiled around him, leaping forward to defend the king who had been the subject of so much doubt.

"Warren…" I began, but he shook his head, his expression grim, and I fell silent.

"No," he said, his lip twitching in anger. "I don't want to hear it. I trusted you."

I looked at him for a second, emotions warring with me. Anger won out over hurt.

With a flash of speed none of them could match, I darted forwards, twisting his sword from his grasp then stepping back again.

They all flinched at my sudden movement, Warren clutching at his fingers.

"And I have done nothing to betray that trust," I said, tossing the sword to the dirt at his feet.

He stared at me but made no move to pick it up.

"This is Nathaniel," I said, taking advantage of his silence. "He's my brother in all but blood, and I trust him completely."

"How nice for you," Warren sneered. "He's not setting a toe inside my city."

"How do you think those wards got broken?" I hissed, stepping closer to him and lowering my voice. "The demons can't get near them, so who did it?" I took a breath, trying to keep my tone even. "They said the half-blood destroyed them, but what if they lied? You need Nate to prove he can touch them because if he can't, someone else broke the wards."

"You think—"

"I don't want to. But wouldn't it be better to be sure?"

It was a minimal possibility, but I didn't want to trust anything the demon said without proof. Plus, it might be the reasoning I needed to get Nate access to the city, at least whilst I tied off some loose ends.

Warren's gaze shifted back to Nate, looking him over with obvious distaste. "What's that?" he demanded, nodding at Nate's hands.

"Demon blood," Nate replied, perfectly calm.

"Dark strength on his arms…" Aaron whispered from behind Warren, his eyes wide.

I resisted the urge to roll my eyes, ignoring Aaron as I watched Warren's face, waiting. To his credit, he didn't react to the quote, his gaze flicking from Nate to me and back again.

"Fine," he said eventually, snatching his sword from the dirt before shoving his way through the crowd, stalking back into the city.

Nate and I exchanged glances, then I stepped forwards, following Warren's path. The crowd fell back, withdrawing from Nate's silent presence at my side.

Inside the wall, I turned right. The destruction didn't extend far from the gate in this direction so we wouldn't have to walk as far to find a surviving repulsion ward.

Nate let out a low breath, almost a whistle, as he looked at the expanse of carved stone. His reaction made me smile, remembering my awe the first time I'd seen it.

Stopping at the first stretch of unblemished stone, I turned to face Nate. The fact he could stand so close to the wall made me think the demon had been telling the truth, but I had to be sure. I met Nate's eyes, nodding towards the spiralling ward carved between us.

His eyes traced the swirling trails coming off the main spiral, like tongues of fire spreading outwards. He reached out a hand, fingers sliding towards the ward.

When he made contact, the reaction was instant. Light flared from the ward, blinding me. Nate let out a cry of pain, snatching his hand back. At the same time, I felt sucking pressure under my skin again, my wards responding to the activation of the larger one. It wasn't as intense as when I'd dragged the demon to the wall, but the feeling was unmistakable.

I shuddered as the sensation faded, blinking away the afterimage of the ward's illumination.

"Are you alright?" I asked, taking a step toward Nate. "What happened?"

He held his hand up, examining it carefully. The black blood was gone, the skin underneath slightly red but otherwise clean. "I think it burnt off," he said, twisting his arm to check all sides. He reached out again, pressing his hand against the ward.

Nothing happened.

"Hmm," he said, frowning as he stepped closer.

"What is it?"

"I can feel it," he said, staring intently at the stone. He lifted his other hand to the surface again. Light flared again, the blood burning away from his other hand.

"Feel it how?" I asked, once I could see again.

"It's like… it doesn't like me."

"It…" I sighed. "Come on, Nate. It's a ward. How could it feel like it doesn't like you?"

"Spoken like someone who's never walked down a street past people who wish you didn't exist," Nate shot back, stepping back from the wall.

My mouth snapped shut. I couldn't deny Nate's experience in that area far outweighed my own, but I couldn't resist the urge to glance back at the crowd who had followed us. Keera was at the front, her arms crossed, the familiar scowl present on her face. After my week here, maybe I did understand the feeling of being watched with suspicious expectations wherever you went a little better than I had before I arrived.

Nate looked back along to the wards that had been shattered. "What happened here?" he asked.

"People died."

I jumped. I hadn't realised Warren had shadowed our movement.

He was standing almost right behind me in the dark alley between two buildings.

Nate ignored him, looking at me.

"Those wards repel demons, keep them out of the city," I said, keeping my voice low. "They found a way around them and then did this so that others could get in. There was a half-blood with them. I think it was the one who killed my father."

"Zouri," Nate murmured, his eyes drifting back to the wall.

I froze. "You know his name." It wasn't a question. My heart shuddered, its beats faltering.

Nate nodded, oblivious to my sudden tension. "They all knew about what had happened, what he'd done. They all talked about it when they thought I wasn't listening." His face hardened, his eyes snapping back to mine. "Is he dead?"

"Oh yes," I said softly. "Yes, he's dead."

Nate nodded again, a single slow bob of his head. "And you're sure it was him?"

"How many half-bloods do you think there are?"

He opened his mouth, then closed it again. "Do you have the body?"

I turned back to Warren, raising a questioning eyebrow. I had no idea what had happened to the bodies of the demons. They hadn't been in the little cave with the rest of the casualties.

"Can I have a word?" Warren asked.

Biting back a sigh, I nodded, shooting Nate a glance before following Warren into the shadowed alley. With the morning sun still hidden behind the mountains, the whole city was damp and chilly, but between the looming buildings, the cold was more pervasive, trailing icy fingers down my arms.

In the gloom, Warren rounded on me. "Are you going to tell me who the fuck you are now?"

"Excuse me?" I took a step back from the vehemence in his tone.

"Who. Are. You?" Warren repeated, each word cracking the air. "Who was your father, that Zouri killed him and then came after you as well? And why did he—" he jerked his head back towards

287

Nate "—kneel to you?"

Pressing my lips together, I glanced back at Nate to give myself some time to think. I had told Holt the truth. Did I not owe Warren the same honesty?

"My father was king of my people," I said, looking back at Warren.

I didn't say anything more. The rest could be inferred.

Shaking his head, Warren drew in a short breath then let it out. "Why didn't you tell us?"

I snorted. "I did tell your father."

"What? When?"

"The evening after our first lesson. You remember I asked you to see if he would give me another audience?"

"But he said no."

"I snuck in anyway."

Warren's eyes widened. "That's why the soldiers were suddenly keeping such a close eye on you! You slipped away from them."

I nodded.

"What did my…" Warren checked himself and started again. "What did Holt say when you told him?"

"He said I was lying and accused me of working with the demons. He thought it was a ploy to gather information on your defences and that I would pass that knowledge onto them if I was allowed to leave."

Warren raised an eyebrow. I grimaced, realising that, from one point of view, it could be construed that that was exactly what happened. I had left, and within hours, the demons were inside the city.

"I'm *not* working with them," I said.

"I know," Warren said.

I blinked. After endless suspicion from Holt, it was a shock to have someone accept my word on the subject so freely.

"And what about him?" Warren asked, looking at Nate again. "Do you trust him?"

I glanced back at my friend. The man who, by his own admission,
288

had been living among the demons for the past few days. Who had known Zouri's name. Who had known there was an attack on this city and had immediately been able to find it.

"I do," I said, turning away from him. "Completely."

Warren's jaw tightened. "Fine," he said. "The demons' bodies are at the end of the wharf closest to the mountains."

"Thank you."

"What are you planning on doing with the demon in the warehouse?"

I blinked. My thoughts instantly went to Keera, though it could have been any one of my students who had told him about the captive demon. "That depends on how much he tells us."

"Fine," Warren said again. He turned and began to walk away.

"That's it?" I called after him, shocked. I'd been expecting to be admonished for not telling him about the demon myself.

He looked back with a weary expression. "What else is there?"

"I… Do you want to question the demon?" I asked.

"I'll be there," he replied, still walking away.

So I let him go because he was right. What else was there to say?

18

Questions

I danced and leapt and spun. Every slash, every stab, every lunge was effortless. The air itself parted before the edge of my new blades. They whirled around me with alarming speed, jumping to guard against imagined attacks, ripping through fictitious enemies. Even my wards were more responsive, the power flowing easily through my limbs at the barest hint of desire.

With a final pirouette, I came to a dizzying halt. My balance ward countered the sensation almost before I could register it. Lowering my weapons, I looked up, met Nate's eyes, and grinned. His answering smile was feral, a predatory baring of teeth as he stepped forwards.

"So... you were saying you thought you could beat me?" he said, drawing his own, significantly longer, blade.

I eyed him cautiously as he rolled his shoulders, raising the weapon in front of him. Baring a misstep or stumble from Nate, I'd never beaten him. If he didn't make a mistake, I was outmatched, and always would be.

Then I remembered the two blades I held. They darted through the air like fishing birds, gone as soon as you looked for them, springing to action without needing me to direct them. And they were mine. Mine.

I stepped to meet Nate, my confidence held firm in my grip. Our eyes met.

Mine.

Neither of us attacked, just watching the other, waiting for the twitch, or glance, or breath, that would give away their intention.

Watching for weakness, finding none. Nate's bottomless eyes were constantly moving. From my face to my hands to my feet. Back again.

I tensed my legs, thinking to trick him into expecting an attack. He dropped one shoulder, preparing to turn out of the way, but aborted the movement before following it through. A smile curled carelessly over his face at my feint. I smirked back.

He took a step forwards, closing the distance between us. I moved sideways, feet brushing over the ground as I circled him, moving even closer, watching him turn on the spot to follow.

We were so close now. If he'd reached out with his weapon, it could have pierced my chest, straight through to my thudding heart.

But he didn't. In fact, his blade dipped towards the ground, leaving nothing but empty air between us, taut and trembling.

"Tamara!"

I spun, my blades springing back up to a guard. The woman drew back, hands raised placatingly.

Straightening, I lowered my weapons quickly. "What?" I asked, trying to hide my embarrassment, determinately not thinking about exactly why my cheeks were full of heat.

"Apologies," she bowed briefly. "The king has been spotted, approaching the East Gate."

My breath caught in my throat. "Thank you."

She dipped her head and retreated.

I whirled around, a grin already plastered across my face. "They're back!"

Nate gave a tight smile at my excitement, sliding his weapon away. "How wonderful."

As Warren departed, I made my preoccupied way back to Nate, who was waiting beside the wall. He took in my expression and didn't comment. My students, along with those who had been brave enough to stand firm against the prospect of another attack, had been joined by others, the bold and curious swelling their ranks. Whispers spread amongst them like ripples, infecting the group. As I watched, a few of them edged forwards, Keera's suspicious face and Aaron's unmasked awe prominent among them.

Irritated, I turned away. "Let's go," I said shortly to Nate, drawing on my speed ward and taking off at a run, following the wall.

Caught by surprise, it took a moment for him to catch up. I glanced back as we reached the harbour, turning towards the mountains.

Aaron's expression lingered in my mind. Had there been other people before me who had been labelled as the Saviour, or were they simply being overzealous with the label now?

I didn't slow my pace until we reached the end of the wharf. There, in the shadows, I found what Warren had directed us to.

It wasn't like the bodies of the fallen defenders — laid out in neat, careful rows in the caves. There was stark hatred in the way these corpses had been dumped, sprawled on top of each other. I spotted the half-blood at once. His head was towards us, bent back at a sharp angle over the chest of one of his companions, his hair brushing the ground. Dry blood ran across his cheeks from his ruined eyes.

Nate's steps faltered as I stopped a couple of feet away, his gaze following mine. I hung back as he continued forwards, crouching beside the half-demon.

"Was it him?" I asked, the words harsher than I'd intended.

"Yes," Nate said. I couldn't see his face, but his hands, resting on his knees, were balled into fists. "It was him."

"How did you know him?"

"What?" Nate swivelled on his heels, frowning at my tone.

"You knew his name. Earlier. I didn't tell you. How did you know it?"

"Oh." Nate relaxed, the offence fading from his expression as he stood up again, gazing at Zouri's body. "The others all talked about him. Some of them thought he was a fool, that Rygorn's death would bring retribution. Others said it was an opportunity."

"They," I repeated. "The demons."

"Yes."

"But you didn't see Zouri. Didn't come face to face."

Nate turned slowly towards me, the frown back on his face. "No, I didn't. And if I had, I would have killed him. No matter what it cost."

I looked away, ashamed of myself. "I know that," I said swiftly. "What else did they say?"

"That Zouri had influence, a lot of it." Nate's frown deepened, his gaze sliding away from me as he thought. "The demons are… divided. There are lots of different factions, all pushing for power, trying to convert others to their cause, thinking they have the right way of doing things. Zouri seemed to be a fairly new player in the game, but he was doing well for himself, gaining lots of followers very fast. But I never found out how he did it or what his mission was."

I glanced behind me, up the wharf. The warehouses all looked the same, but I knew one of them held a dark secret. "I might have a way we can find that out," I said.

Unlike my last visit, the entrance to Ava's domain was unguarded but the splintered surround of the door frame made it easy to identify. Pushing the door open, I stepped inside, Nate close behind me. The space beyond was much as I remembered, full of empty barrels and boxes but devoid of the people that had been present last time. Instead, a single man raised his head, the sudden tension in his body dissipating as he recognised me.

"Alright?" I asked Jory.

He shrugged and nodded, his eyes lingering on Nate curiously. "Any trouble here?"

He shook his head, glancing back over his shoulder. "No," he elaborated. "All quiet. Steren is back there, watching it."

I nodded my thanks, moving past him in the direction indicated, wending my way through the towering maze. Quiet murmurings reached my ears just before I found them in the back corner, underneath one of the high windows.

They had followed my instructions to tie up the demon, though with some unexpected adjustments. He was sitting against the wall, legs out in front of him. His arms were crossed in front of him, each wrist meeting the opposite elbow, his forearms wrapped in several strands of coarse rope. His ankles were bound together as well.

The part I hadn't anticipated was the fact his injured leg was splinted, two thin planks of wood lying along his knee, bound above and below the joint.

He had been sniffling. The light from the thin windows above reflected off the smears of snot across his face where he had tried ineffectively to wipe them away. It made him look even younger.

Several feet away, Steren sat cross-legged on a table. She was the one who had been talking but fell silent as Nate and I stepped into view, unfolding her legs and sliding off the table.

"Mara," she said, then seemed unsure of how to continue. She looked from me to the demon and back.

"Go and wait by the door," I told her. "Warren is on his way; show him here when he arrives."

She hesitated for a second, then seemed to shake herself and hurried away.

I sauntered over to Steren's perch, leaning against the table. The remains of an empty crate lay at its feet, broken into pieces. I cast an assessing eye over the thin planks making it up, understanding where the splint had come from.

Nate hadn't moved, and the demon's eyes were locked onto him. Black and black.

I crossed my arms as I watched the pair, waiting to see what would happen.

"Please." The whisper quivered in the air, resonating with hope. The demon leaned forwards a little, desperate face still focused on Nate. "Please…"

The word sent a shiver through me, but I suppressed it.

Nate turned towards me. "Explain?" The request was seasoned

with understandable confusion. We had never kept demons alive as prisoners in Alderth.

"Brother—"

"Stop," Nate snapped, glaring at the younger demon.

He cowered, hunching back into the wall, and began weeping again.

"He was injured in the fighting and left behind," I said to Nate. "He got himself into a defensible position and was able to hold everyone off but didn't leave for some reason."

"He wouldn't have been able to cross with an injury like that," Nate nodded, his eyes lingering on the demon's splinted leg.

"Zouri…" the demon whimpered between sniffles. "Zouri will come back."

"How old are you? You think you're important to him?" Nate asked impassively.

The demon lapsed back into silence.

"When they told me, I came and pulled him out," I continued.

"And?" Nate raised an eyebrow.

"And I had questions," I said simply. "Zouri was already dead, the others had gone…" I shrugged.

"Liar," the demon hissed quietly.

I ignored him. "He said that Zouri was able to get close to the wards because he was half-blood, and he destroyed them so the rest could get into the city."

"So he was telling the truth," Nate said.

I frowned. Why was he pointing that out?

"What we *didn't* get around to discussing," I continued, overlooking Nate's comment, "is exactly *why* they were here in the first place."

The thud of a sharply closed door, followed by approaching footsteps, made me pause. Nate took a step to the side, closer to the demon, as Warren strode into the space where he had been. The new king glanced around, taking in the three of us.

The demon, the half-blood, me. The fearful, the wary, the tense.

"Having fun, are we?" Warren's eyes lingered on the demon, but

295

I sensed the chill words were directed at me.

"We were just talking about how someone could justify their continued existence."

"Zouri's going to kill you," the demon spat. Warren's arrival seemed to have woken new hostility in him.

"Slow on the uptake, aren't you?" I said.

"Zouri won't be coming back," Nate said softly.

The demon's face hardened. "Traitor," he snarled.

Nate huffed with laughter but made no other reply.

"Are you quite done?" Warren snapped.

I raised an eyebrow but desisted, leaning back against the table.

"This city, *my city*, has been attacked by you creatures for years," Warren said. His legs tensed, as if he wanted to take a step toward the demon, but restrained himself. "You're going to tell me why."

The demon swallowed, eyes darting between the three of us. Maybe he had thought Warren, eyes vivid blue, arms bare of wards, was the least dangerous of us. Warren's tone disavowed him of that notion.

"Zouri said he could get inside, that he would find a way past the wards, to open the path for the rest of us. He said he would clear the way for glorious victory…"

"I don't care *how* he did it," Warren snapped, cutting off his propaganda. "I asked *why*."

The demon subsided, flushing slightly at the dismissal of his misdirection. Jaw working rebelliously, he flashed another calculating glance between us.

"We can take this outside if you'd prefer," I warned him. "Go back to the wall…"

"We had to destroy the wards," he bit out.

"Yes, to get inside, but you needed people to do it for you. You've said that," I said, my patience waning now.

"No. All of them. That's why we came. To destroy all the wards on the wall."

There was silence in the warehouse. Out of the corner of my eye, I saw Nate glance at me, but I couldn't look away from the young

296

demon. Warren seemed just as speechless as I was.

"All of them," I repeated. The words were sour on my tongue, leaving a painful tingling behind. "How? Zouri was the only half-blood. He couldn't have done all of them by himself."

"He said we would get the people here to break them once he had got us inside. We tried, but no one would do it."

"That's why Zouri came looking for your father," I said, glancing sideways at Warren. "That's the 'work' he wanted doing."

Warren's face twitched slightly, but otherwise, he gave no response.

"Why?" I asked, switching my focus back to the demon. "What did you gain by destroying the wards? What's so important about this place?"

"I don't know!" the demon cringed away as I stood upright. "It was Zouri's plan! He said we would be heroes!"

"How long have you been following him?" Nate asked.

The demon hesitated, eyes dropping to his lap.

"How long?"

"A couple of weeks." The mumbled words were barely audible.

I shook my head, my jaw jutting forwards with frustration. After deciding Zouri was too dangerous to be left alive, the demon I *had* spared was useless.

Nate turned to me. "A word?" he said, tilting his head back towards the exit.

I nodded, moving across to the passage leading back towards the door. Warren hadn't moved.

Nate stepped between him and the demon. "Please."

Warren let out a deep breath, then gave a tight nod. Turning on his heel, he led the way swiftly back through the maze of boxes.

We passed Steren and Jory by the entrance, the former coming to her feet at once. Warren jerked his chin, indicating she could resume guard duties, but I caught her arm before she could pass me.

"Don't talk to him," I warned her in a low voice. She blushed before hurrying away, head bent.

I followed Nate and Warren outside, squinting in the sunlight. Nate walked to the harbour edge, his steps fast and nervous, before rounding on us.

"He doesn't know anything," he said bluntly. "He's too young, and if he has only been with Zouri for a little while, he's irrelevant."

I nodded. It was the same conclusion I'd come to inside. "You think we should just kill him now," I said.

"No," Nate shook his head. "*Use* him to get to someone who can get you answers."

I frowned at him. "Like who?"

"One of the leaders of the other factions. You say the attacks have been happening here for years," Nate glanced at Warren, "that means they pre-date Zouri. So there must be a bigger motive. Whatever the reason why they wanted to destroy the wards, others should know what it is. Release the kid back to them as a sign of good faith, and set up a meeting to find out why they are attacking in the first place."

I gaped at him. "You want to let him go? Are you mad?"

"We gain nothing by keeping him here. If I take him home, think of what it could accomplish."

Take him home. Of course. Because you couldn't deliver a message without a messenger. Nate wasn't just suggesting we release the demon. He was offering to accompany him. To accompany him *home.*

I drew back a little, staring at Nate, taking him in as a whole. He looked just the same as always. Those earnest eyes, despite the darkness they held. His *bare* arms, free of ink but holding their own strength nonetheless.

I blinked. His bare arms.

"Where is it?" My voice shook. My pulse was deafening in my ears, drowning out all else. "Your Guard's band. *Where is it?*"

Nate's hand twitched as if it would reach up to the place on his arm where the purple cloth should have been, the place where my father had tied it. There was nothing there.

The sight of the bare skin sent a thrill of fear through me.

"I left it behind," Nate said, his voice softer now, eyes downcast. "Rygorn gave it to me. It seemed right that I should give it back after I'd failed him."

Fuck.

I searched my memory, trying to recall whether or not he'd had it when he told me of my father's death. But I couldn't remember. I'd been so overwhelmed with the news that I hadn't paid attention to much else.

I stared at him helplessly as my racing heart struggled to return to a calmer rhythm. "You only just got out of there," I reminded him. "And you had blood up to your elbows when you did. Are you sure it's a good idea for you to go back in? And for what? A parlay? The demons will never agree to that."

"Yes, they will," Nate insisted. "Zouri had enemies. This kid might not know anything useful to you, but he might be of interest to the other factions. And it would be a sign of goodwill."

"You can't have it both ways," Warren said, speaking for the first time since we'd come outside. "Either he knows things, in which case, he'll tell them to us, or he doesn't."

"And you're willing to limit yourself like that, are you?" Nate snapped. "What if you could be the one to stop the attacks here for good?"

Warren looked pensively back over his shoulder at the warehouse.

Nate rounded on me. "You too. The demons know what's going on back home. Djet is an unknown factor to them, just as much as he is to us. They don't like having him on the throne. Make them an offer and they will take it."

"Offer? An offer of *what?*" I said, exasperated.

"Peace."

I stared at him. "Peace," I repeated. "You want me to make peace with the ones who killed my father? Killed my mother? And yours! Not to mention all the others." My voice was rising, the words sharp in the air between us, slivers of anger searching for blood.

299

"I think we should do it," Warren said.

My jaw dropped. "You what?" He didn't even trust Nate. Now he was willing to go along with this insane plan?

"He's right," Warren frowned at Nate, who held himself immobile as their eyes met as if any sudden movement might scare away Warren's compliance. "What do we have to lose? And it would be worth it if it means no one else has to lose their brothers."

My jaw snapped shut. He was right, but he was also wrong.

I had something to lose. Someone to lose.

Two faces turned to me, waiting. One filled with quivering eagerness, the other a resigned hopelessness.

"You fought your way out," I said. It wasn't a question, and Nate didn't try to deny it. "If you go back in, they're going to try and kill you, no matter the circumstances." I shook my head. "I can't lose you too."

"You won't," Nate said. "You know I can handle myself."

I looked up at the sky, but it was a dull, murky grey, with the occasional patch of low cloud hanging under it. There was no guidance to be found up there.

"Swear you'll come back."

"I swear it," Nate said at once. "By name, by blood, by honour."

I looked at him, his black eyes steady and bright, and nodded. "Alright. How? You said he couldn't cross himself with his leg like that. Can you do it for him?"

Nate looked away, face creasing with concentration, before letting out a gusty breath. "I might be able to cross from here, but not with him as well. We need to get him outside the wall first. Then I'll take him across."

His casual tone made my lips press together, but I voiced no objection.

"Let's get on with it then," Warren said.

Inside the warehouse, a small group had gathered. I blinked at the presence of most of my students, having not seen them arrive. No doubt Ava had other, less obvious, entrances to this place. They didn't hang back as we strode purposefully through the cramped space but hurried along in my wake, pressing curiously forwards.

I came to a halt as the demon came back into view. His wide eyes darted between the many faces, breath quickening. I could almost see the scenarios flashing through his mind. What would happen if I stood aside and let those behind me claim their vengeance with blood and fists? I'd had my revenge. I'd ripped it from Zouri's face. Why should I deny the same satisfaction to others?

I took a breath, reining in my bloodlust.

"Nathaniel?"

He stepped forwards at once, striding towards the helpless demon, who cringed from his approach, writhing desperately as he attempted to flee.

"Traitor!" he spat, trying to shuffle away.

Nate gave a brief laugh. "To whom?" he countered. "My loyalty remains the same as it has always been."

"To your blood!"

Nate stopped at that, going still as he loomed over the demon. "My blood?" he repeated, his voice colder now. He dropped suddenly to a crouch, his hand hovering over the demon's injured leg in silent threat. "My mother was raped as her family burned. Should I be loyal to the one who did that? Or to the ones who would have stood by and watched it happen?"

My shoulders tensed at the harshness of his words.

The demon made no response, shifting uneasily, eyes lingering on Nate's threatening hand.

"Now, do you want to get out of here, or are you so unafraid of death that you want to keep antagonising people?" Nate continued, in a somewhat calmer tone.

The demon bared his teeth. "Look around you! Didn't you see what we did here? We *are* death."

"And yet you're afraid," Nate shot back.

"Death shall know fear."

The hushed words made me look around. Aaron was standing

just feet behind me, his eyes wide.

"It's you," he said reverently, staring at Nate. "It's you."

"Nate, time to go," I said. The last thing I needed was for him to be caught up in a maelstrom of pious fervour.

Nate nodded without looking back. He slashed through the bonds around the demon's ankles with one sharp motion, then reached out, pulling him to his feet. The demon hissed in pain, hopping a little, but conceded to put some of his weight on Nate.

I spun on my heel, stepping up to Aaron, who was blocking the path out, his face still lit with intense devotion.

"Move," I ordered. "Now."

He stumbled aside as I shoved my way past, forging an opening through my students.

We made an odd procession through the city. People stopped to watch, backing out of our way, or fled from the pair behind me. Warren's steady presence at my side deterred any attacks, but I kept a hand on my blades every step of the way, just in case.

Nate's head was up, his gaze intent when I glanced back. The demon hobbled along with his assistance, shooting nervous glances at the looming wall. I hesitated as the broken gates came into view. The wards were still just as broken, so I hoped they wouldn't prevent the pair from leaving.

As I paused, Nate surged forwards, his grip on the demon tightening as they plunged through the archway.

The wall rippled with light, and I felt the same dragging pressure on my wards as they passed through the portal. The demon let out a ragged cry, then slumped. On the other side of the wall, Nate glanced back over his shoulder, his dark eyes fixing on mine.

His mouth quirked up slightly in a reassuring smile then he turned away and, with a flash of red light, was gone.

19

Answers

We raced through the city as if we had wings, soaring past the crowds, lifted high by the wind. The twin blades flapped at my sides, already a part of me, adding to my elation.

Nate followed in my wake, his footsteps heavier and surer than mine, the sounds darting around each other, layered but never touching. The steps leading to the carved citadel doors loomed ahead. Drawing on my strength wards, I tensed, gauging the distance, then leapt, clearing the height in a single bound, skidding to a halt on the top step and turning.

Nate had stopped at the bottom of the steps, laughing at me. He climbed each step with deliberate care, the grin never leaving his face. I laughed back at him. Joy boiled inside me, frothing out of every pore, infecting the very air around me. They were coming home.

Trembling with excitement, I scanned the streets, trying to guess where they would come from. Finally, finally, they were coming home.

Only a minute later, a moving tide of shouts and cheers rippled across the city from the east. My grin widened, anticipation coiling in my stomach.

Then they were there, all of them, walking up the street as if returning from a short stroll. My cheeks ached from smiling. Though it tested my resolve, I held my place, watching Father climb the steps.

I bowed. "Sire."

"Tammie," he smiled, arms open.

I hugged him eagerly. "How did it go?"

He laughed, but it was an unfamiliar sound. "Shall we at least go inside first?" There was a tension in his voice that didn't belong. The smile fixed on his mouth didn't reach his eyes.

I nodded, my joy evaporating, the grin sliding from my face like melted butter.

Father moved past me, leading the Guard into the citadel. Most wore expressions like his; tense, worried, unsure. Two of them, however, were different.

Hamma and Titan stood rigid, faces hard as they stared straight ahead, neither daring to glance at the other. I stepped back, letting them pass in silence, turning to watch their stiff backs retreating. I felt as if my stomach had disappeared. Nate, flanking the other side of the doors, looked back at me with equal unease.

Something was very, very wrong.

All I could do was stare at the spot where Nate had disappeared and doubt. For a single instant, I'd had a plan, a way home, with Nate at my side. Now he was gone, far too eagerly, to a place where I couldn't follow, with no guarantee he would return.

Warren remained for a moment then turned away and he too was gone, leaving me alone. At least, until another figure took his place, Aaron gesturing at the point where Nate had been.

"Who is he?"

I glanced sideways, noting the fanatical light in his eyes and far more disturbed by it now than I had been when it was directed towards me. "A friend. A good one."

"A demon?"

"Half-blood. His mother was one of my people."

"A child of two worlds," Aaron murmured.

I scowled. "Do you have scripture mentioning that as well?"

"No."

I managed to swallow my snort of derision.

"Even you can't deny the signs."

"I'm not looking for them."

"Regardless, if these talks work out, it could mean the ending to *years* of death."

I looked sideways. I hadn't realised he had been eavesdropping on that debate. How many of the others had been listening in? "And you think that 'ending' could be the 'light'?"

Aaron shrugged. "He shall come from the darkness, bringing the light, dark strength on his arms. Death shall know fear."

"If it's 'he' then why was everyone giving *me* looks?"

"It's a gender-neutral term."

"So you just twist the words to fit whomever you want."

Aaron turned to face me at last, his face dark. "I don't have to twist anything. Dark strength on his arms. Come from the darkness. Death shall know fear. It all fits!"

"*So what?*" I snapped, rounding on him.

He took a step backwards, instantly calm again. "Nothing. It's simply an observation."

I shook my head, frustrated. "Look, Aaron, I—"

"You don't believe," he cut across me. "That's okay. But you can't make other people stop believing either. Look around you! Do you think this is difficult for you? We've lost *everything*. We thought these walls kept us safe, that while we were inside, we were protected. Now we have to find new ways to sleep at night.

"We thought Holt would lead us through anything like this, and even if he didn't, we knew Set would step up and take his place, and we had faith in him to do it well." His voice cracked a little. "We've lost that too. So if some of us have a little bit of hope that these talks could bring something good, or if we choose to look for omens, maybe you shouldn't judge us for it."

We stared at each other in silence for a few seconds. He nodded decisively as if he'd just proven some major point, then turned and left.

I looked back out at the empty plain. Aaron said the people knew Set would have stepped up, and he was right. That, at least, I believed in. What would he have thought of Nate's proposition? How would the two brothers have reacted if they'd still had each other? I would never know. I would never get to experience them together without their father's influence.

The memory of Set's eyes, so fierce and strong, wrenched the knife inside me a little deeper.

I'm sorry, I thought. Warren was right to blame me. I should have saved him, should have done *something*.

Set was dead, and there was nothing I could do about it. But maybe I could do something else, in his memory. Warren and I would meet with the demons if they agreed to it. We would get answers about why they were attacking this place, why they attacked my people, but that was it. Nate could dream all he liked. I was never going to make peace with those monsters. Never.

I wanted nothing more than to curl up and go to sleep, but I couldn't risk Nate returning to receive another reception like the one this morning. So I hung around the gates instead, doing whatever I could to assist those clearing the area. Drawing heavily on my strength ward to counteract the fact that I only had one working arm, I helped a group of men lift the felled gates, propping them against the outside of the wall, providing a partial barrier in the city.

That done, I assisted Bardok and Noah in clearing chunks of rock from the base of the wall, where Zouri's destruction had littered the streets with debris. It was there that Nate found me.

Bardok saw him first, lunging to grab his black sword—never more than an arm's reach away—as he stared at something behind Noah and me. We turned to follow his gaze.

Nate's black eyes followed the chunk of rock that slipped from my grip and to the ground, cracking in two.

I stared at him, torn between relief and horror. True, he was alive and back, but there was blood on his face where his lip was split and a bruise was forming around his right eye.

"I take it back," I said, staring at his injuries. "I don't want to talk to them. I want to kill them."

Nate grinned as he walked toward us. There was a slight hitch to
306

his steps. "They'll meet."

The air suddenly seemed too thick to breathe.

"When?" I croaked.

"Tonight. Before sunset."

I let out a long breath. Were we really going to do this? Cautiously, I reached out a hand towards his battered face, but he pulled away before I could make contact.

"It's fine," he said, almost exasperated. "You know I've had worse."

"It's different," I groused. He gave me a withering look. "I don't have to like it," I amended, and this time he smirked. "We need to let Warren know," I said, still shaking my head at him.

"I'll tell him," Noah piped up from behind me.

I looked around, watching him lean to the side to get a better view of Nate.

"Hi."

Nate returned his gaze without a flicker of emotion. "Hello."

"I'm Noah."

"Nathaniel."

"So, you know Mara?"

I rolled my eyes. "Noah? Warren will need to know quickly."

He just hummed, still staring at Nate.

Bardok reached out and cuffed his shoulder. "You've got a job to do," he said gruffly. "Get to it."

Noah shot him a mutinous look before trotting off, heading towards the path to the palace.

"Thanks," I said with a grimace.

Bardok shrugged, turning away from us.

"What's that?" Nate asked, looking at his black sword.

Bardok frowned, giving Nate a suspicious look. "A sword. What does it look like?"

"It's been blooded."

"Of course it has," Bardok said, his frown deepening. "Look around you. It's had plenty of opportunities to be—"

"No," Nate cut him off. "It was made with blood. Demon

307

blood."

There was a moment of silence.

"And how could you know that?" Bardok asked, suddenly brusque, letting the dark metal swing down to his side as if to hide it from view.

"I can feel it. I've seen one before," Nate said, eyeing Bardok with an expression I didn't recognise.

"It's nothing to do with you," Bardok growled, giving us one last look before stalking away.

"How could it have demon blood on it?" I asked, watching him leave. "He takes it around the city. The blood on your hands burned when you got close to the wards."

"It's not coating the blade, it's part of it." Nate frowned. "I don't imagine they would have let one go easily."

"Do you think they know it's here?"

Nate grimaced. "If the demon whose blood is in it is still alive, they would be able to find it, but that wouldn't help them cross the wards. If they were dead, the other demons probably wouldn't know what happened to the blade. But if they know it's here, it could well be the reason why they've been attacking. If they don't... Best not to let them know about it."

"They would be *that* bothered by it?"

He nodded. "It's quite an investment, on many levels, to make one. They're highly valued."

I looked after Bardok and doubted, yet again, whether these talks were a good idea. "You know a lot about a lot of things, all of a sudden," I said, not looking at Nate, but he just laughed.

"Our sword-smiths know about them," he said. "They can make them."

I snorted. "What use is that? It's not like we've got demon blood lying around by the jar. What's the point of them anyway?"

"It makes the metal stronger, harder to break or chip. Supposedly makes them move faster as well, but no one seems to have been able to prove that."

I looked around at him, eyebrows raised. "You looked into this, didn't you?"

He shrugged, looking away, an odd expression on his face. Almost guilty…

I narrowed my eyes. "Nate?"

"Hmm?"

"Would it work with demon blood that wasn't pure?"

"What do you mean?" His tone, the innocence laid on just a little bit too thickly, gave it away.

"Nate."

"Mara."

"Have you made one?"

"No," he said, too blunt to be lying now.

For a moment, I relaxed.

"I made two."

I stared at him, waiting for the glint in his eyes to show he was joking, but it wasn't there. He was staring straight ahead, determinedly not looking at me. My fingers brushed the two blades at my sides, weapons *he* had given me.

"Are you angry?" he asked after several seconds of heavy silence.

"Angry?" I was stunned, of course, but not angry. "Why would I be?"

Nate hesitated. I held my tongue, waiting.

"Lots of demons blood their own weapons," he said slowly, "because it means it's difficult to lose them. If they are misplaced or dropped during a fight… they can find them again."

"You can find these?" My voice had risen alarmingly.

Nate nodded, still refusing to look at me.

"That's how you found me," I said, connecting the pieces. "When I was on my way back. East of Alderth. You weren't searching randomly for me. You knew where I was."

"I knew which rough direction you were in, relative to me," Nate corrected me. "It's not very specific."

"And when you found this city too."

He nodded again.

I let out a disbelieving breath, shaking my head.

"Are you going to stop using them?"

"No. But you should have told me."

"I told you I had a hand in making them."

I fixed him with a level look. "You should have told me." He ducked his head in chastised acknowledgement. "What would you have done if I hadn't liked them?" I asked.

"Destroyed them," Nate said at once. "Too distracting to leave them hanging around," he explained at my startled expression. "And what else would I do with them? They were for you."

"How did you know that Bardok's sword was blooded if it's not from your blood?" I asked, curious now that I had gotten over the shock.

"Once it was so close, I could feel it," Nate said. He shivered slightly. "Also, the colour is fairly obvious."

"Why aren't mine black?"

"I didn't put much blood in them. Also because I'm not a pure demon, I expect."

Abandoning the broken rocks on the ground, I wandered towards the harbour, thinking about the revelation. Nate fell into step beside me, limping slightly.

I gestured to his face. "I'm guessing they weren't overly pleased to see you again?"

Nate huffed in agreement. "I think that was partially the situation, what with the kid and how I left, but... yeah."

"What happened when you left before?" I asked. "All that blood…"

"It wasn't as bad as it looked," Nate said hastily. "All the time I was there, they kept saying they trusted me, and how I was finally in the right place, and all this nonsense. They were watching me the whole time. As soon as word got around about the attack, enough for me to know it was you, I think they guessed I was going to try and leave. And they tried to stop me." He shrugged. "I didn't let them. That was that."

"I'm sorry about earlier. I… I doubted you."

"Yeah, I noticed." Nate came to a halt as we stepped out onto the wharf, turning to face me. "I might have left the band behind when your father died, but I didn't forget my oath. I'm still part of the Guard if you'll have me."

"Technically, the Guard would serve Djet now."

"That's nonsense, and you know it," Nate snapped. "*You* are queen, no matter who sits on the throne."

I smiled sadly. "Then yes, of course I'll have you. As if I'd let you go." I walked on and Nate followed me, just as he always had.

"No ships?" he remarked, looking out across the empty harbour.

I shook my head. "They've been attacked a lot here. They're suspicious of strangers. They don't trade at all."

"A port town with no trading. That sounds sustainable," Nate shook his head. "How come they let you in?"

I snorted. "It wasn't exactly a unanimous decision. Or one I had a say in. A couple of days after we split up, I got into a bit of a fight. And afterwards, I accidentally released my growth ward."

"Titan always warned you about that."

"Yeah, with good reason. I sort of… blacked out."

"You *fainted?*"

"Stop laughing."

"Sorry." He didn't sound sorry.

"It's not funny!"

He cleared his throat, clearly trying to stifle his chuckles.

"I think I have a pretty good excuse for forgetting," I snapped. "Given I'd just killed a Figure."

"You *what?*" Nate yelped, all trace of mirth gone as he stumbled, staring at me with wide eyes.

"Or at least, I thought I had," I continued. "The body disappeared."

"Body…" Nate repeated weakly. "Wait a moment. What *happened?*"

"I don't know. It found me, we fought, I stabbed it, it fell down. I blacked out, got brought here, and was told the body wasn't out there anymore. I haven't seen any sign of them since."

Nate ran a hand through his hair, clearly trying to process the stream of events. I still didn't understand it myself.

"I'm sorry," he said eventually. "I should have been there."

I shook my head. "It was my idea to split up."

Nate let out a long breath. "So much for throwing them off the trail," he muttered.

I shot him a questioning look.

"I tried to lead them away," he elaborated. "Went back and forth, putting down false trails. Before I…"

"Before you crossed over," I finished for him. He had mentioned that earlier, I remembered.

He nodded.

"That's what the red light is, isn't it?" I asked, remembering the flash when he had disappeared outside the gates. "It's not just a fast way of travelling. It's them crossing over to their 'other world'."

Another nod.

"You said the demon wouldn't have been able to do it when he was injured."

"Yeah. I mean, a couple of cuts, or anything like this—" he gestured to the injuries on his face, "—wouldn't stop them, but a broken bone… I can't imagine it would be possible to focus enough to cross in that much pain."

Having reached the end of the wharf, I led Nate across the grass, past the sandy circle where I had held my lessons. We sat just beyond it on the open grass, me looking out towards the sea, Nate facing back towards the city.

"Why didn't you say anything before about being able to cross?"

"Because I didn't know what it was, what it meant. It's like this… pressure, always pulling at me. But I never mentioned it because I thought it was something everyone felt. And no one else ever talked about it, so I didn't either."

I looked away from him, remembering the pressure I felt dragging at my wards when the web of wards on the wall activated. Was he describing something similar?

"I only worked out what it might be after the attack on your

312

father, when the demons were leaving all at the same time. I felt them do it and I knew I could have followed."

"But you didn't?"

He shook his head. "I wasn't sure if anyone else survived. I had to make sure. And then I came to find you."

We sat in silence for a minute.

"What's it like over there?" I asked. "What are *they* like? What are they going to want?"

"I don't know what they'll want," he said, staring out across the water. "They're... divided. All loyal to their own leader, whoever they think that is, but it changes so fast, different factions fighting, or allying, or absorbing others. It's nothing like home."

The word sent a thrill of warmth through me.

"They were more welcoming, in some ways," he said. "As I said, they kept trying to integrate me. I got some strange looks sometimes, but there was no open animosity. It was almost like they were trying to prove something." He shook his head. "They're willing to talk though. That has to be a good sign."

"I guess."

He frowned at my hesitancy. "What is it?"

"Nothing. Just... I've been thinking about it. Anatoly, Petra... all the old monarchs, their reins had times of peace, or what's presented as peace in the records. I always assumed they were just quiet periods, that the demons were more focused on attacking elsewhere but if they're willing to talk to us now... maybe it really was peace."

"And?"

"And I don't want that to be true."

"Why not? It would prove that it could be done."

"But what if it is?" I said. "What if we could theoretically have worked out a deal with them years ago? Think how many lives would have been saved. My mother might still be alive."

"As would mine," he said, meeting my gaze without flinching. And you might never have existed, I finished silently.

"We can't change the past," he said quietly. "But think of all the

313

lives you could save in the future."

"You want this to work. Why?"

"You need more of a reason?"

"Back when you were persuading Warren… you were desperate. So yeah, I need a reason for that."

Nate grimaced as he looked away. "I can imagine what that must have looked like," he acknowledged. "Thank you, for not doubting me."

I snorted. "Believe me, there were lots of doubts."

"For trusting me, then."

"You weren't making it easy." I sighed, remembering the icy terror that had clamped around my chest like a vice when I'd noticed the absence of his Guard's band. "But I do trust you. Just don't ever make me regret it."

His mouth quirked upwards. "I won't," he promised.

"Good. Now, you haven't answered the question."

It was his turn to sigh now. "When I was over there, I just… They're not all evil. They're not consumed by hatred, plotting to wipe us out. They're rational, reasonable. They're just… people. Which means there must be a reason *why* they are attacking us. They don't go to Lambridge, or Charhelm, or any of the other places without wards. It's only us. So there *must* be a reason."

"You think it's something to do with the wards?"

"The two places the demons are attacking are the two places that have wards. Does it seem like a coincidence to you?"

I grimaced but couldn't deny it. My tattoos felt suddenly heavier on my skin. The warmth where I maintained a steady pull on my growth ward was now a burning. It didn't seem like mere chance. Not at all. And the young demon we'd interrogated had said they came here to destroy the wards. But why?

"There's something else as well."

I cocked my head at Nate, a silent invitation for him to continue.

He hesitated, hands flexing on his knees in the silence. "How many other half-bloods do you know of?" he asked.

I frowned, thinking. "There was Elissa, the one who killed
314

Nicholas's family. Before that…"

"Not them. I mean ones that are alive now."

I blinked at him. "Just you. And there was Zouri, if he still counts. Why?"

"I met four on the first day I was over there."

"What?" I gaped at him.

"I think they—*we*—are more common than we realised, and the demons are deliberately keeping it that way."

"How would they do that? And *why*?"

"Because we're dangerous. Look at what happened here. I can get past those wards, and I can cross over to their world too. I can go to both places, the way neither side individually can."

"But how could they hide so many half-bloods? That doesn't make sense."

"Doesn't it? I was eleven when Rygorn found out about me," Nate said. "My mother moved us around constantly. If she kept me hidden from him, maybe she inadvertently hid me from the demons as well."

"And you think they were looking for you?"

"Imagine how it would have been if they had," Nate said grimly. "I would be on the other side. Like so many others are."

"*Thorns*," I breathed, horror-struck. "It's deliberate."

Nate nodded, his jaw set. "Exactly. Attack a small, isolated group, maybe even just one family, choose a suitable… candidate," he faltered over the word, looking sick. "The mothers are too scared or ashamed to say what happened. The demons wait, then come back. Kill the mother, take the baby. Or even if they had told anyone what happened, once they disappear, people would just assume the women went elsewhere, to escape the memories. Or worse." The darkness in his tone scared me, but I understood; this was personal for him.

"Now I really don't want to talk with them," I said.

"But what if it could stop it from happening?" Nate pointed out. "Or we could just kill them all."

He snorted with laughter, seemingly relieved to be moving away from the subject. "Or that," he agreed.

I grinned as well, but the expression slipped away. That was what we'd been doing my whole life, and before, with no success. It was impossible to win when they could retreat to places we could never reach.

Suddenly, Nate's point about the half-bloods being dangerous made a lot more sense. He could take the fight to them.

I shoved the thought away. At the very least, I owed it to him to try and make peace before asking him to embark on a one-man war.

Looking away from him, I remembered my promise to Set's ghost. I remembered my mother, my father, the rest of the Guard. I thought about Nate's mother, his theory of what had been done to her and, apparently, to so many others. Peace felt less like an unlikelihood, more an impossibility.

"We've got company," Nate said suddenly.

I twisted, looking behind me.

A young girl stood there, hands clutched together in front of her, staring at us with wide eyes.

"The, umm… the king has requested your presence," she said.

Beside me, Nate stiffened.

"Thank you," I said. "Where is he?"

"In the hospital. He said to tell you that she's awake."

"Alright. We know the way."

She backed away several paces before turning and running off.

I looked at Nate, raising an eyebrow in a silent question.

"The king," he repeated softly.

I recognised the pain in his face. "I know," I said. The words brought the image of my father to my mind too. "But he *is* their King, and it's been thrust upon him when he didn't expect it. When no one expected it. He's not doing such a bad job, everything considered."

"Is that your way of telling me to go easy on him?"

I stood up, grinning. "Maybe. If I thought you could."

The hospital was calmer now, though still full. The noises were lower, whimpers and soft weeping, rather than the raw, ragged screams from earlier. I glanced across at the dark cavern of the dead as I led Nate through the beds. A woman sitting against the wall drew my eye. Rhianna was staring blankly ahead, eyes unfocused, face frozen in horror.

Swallowing, I hurried towards the small room where I deposited Genni earlier and ducked inside. The young woman was propped up on the bed, a blanket covering her legs, bandages wrapped around her head, obscuring both eyes. Ava sat by her side, clutching her hand with a white-knuckled grip. Warren stood by the window, eyes on the ground.

Nate drifted away from me, melting into a shadowy corner. I stopped at the foot of Genni's bed but said nothing. Warren had authority here; it was his place to speak.

For several long moments, I didn't think he would be able to do so. Eventually, he looked up, his face hard and shadowed.

"Genni…"

Her hands clenched on the blanket, twisting it into painful lines.

"We need to know what happened. Please."

The breath Genni took was more like a gasp, an inhalation of agony. I dropped my gaze, staring at her feet. Asking her to relive the horror she had gone through was cruel, but Warren was right. We needed to know exactly what happened out in the forest and how the demons gained access to the city.

"We… I…" Another shuddering breath. "I told Rosita that I was going to go back outside the wall, to look for Malcolm again. I was the one in charge when we went out before. I was supposed to bring everyone back, but I didn't. I… I left him behind. We got separated, and we couldn't find him, and it was getting light. So I got the others back. And I left him out there."

Her hand, visible at the top edge of my range of vision, had relaxed, no longer wrenching at the blanket, but stroking it with a single finger, back and forth. The motion was hypnotic.

"Rosita said it was a bad idea, but I was going to go without her,

317

so she…" Genni's voice dropped to a whisper. "She came with me." She gulped, her breathing ragged. "I shouldn't have… I should have stopped her."

"You couldn't have known what would happen," Ava murmured, her hand still clutching her daughter's.

Genni shook her head. "I knew it was dangerous. So *stupid*."

"So you went outside the wall," Warren prompted, his voice cold and empty. I looked across at him, wondering how he could be so unfeeling. His expression betrayed the truth of it. It was a maze of tortured lines. It looked like he was about to break down and scream in anguish. His eyes burned with pain. How he kept his words steady, I couldn't even guess.

"Yes," Genni said. "We searched all day, but we didn't find anything. Then… then…" Her hands convulsed. "They found us."

I glanced at Nate, unmoving in his shadowed corner. Only his eyes betrayed his stillness, darting to meet mine.

"There were so many of them, I couldn't keep track, and one of them… his eyes…" Genni paused, breathing hard. "His eyes were different, not like the others. They looked normal… until you got up close. It was like his irises were black. Just this gaping pit of emptiness." She shuddered. "They… they took us to Malcolm."

Her mouth twisted, teeth bared as she remembered.

"You saw his body?" I asked

Her grimace smoothed out, her voice going flat. "He wasn't dead."

"He *what*?"

"He was still alive," she said tonelessly. "At least…" She faltered again. "At least he knew we came back for him."

"What happened?" I prompted her.

"The one with the different eyes, he said they didn't need Malcolm anymore, not now they… now they had us—me and Rosita. He told the others to do what they wanted. Then they took us further into the trees. It was already dark. We couldn't see what they were doing. We could hear it though." Another shudder wracked her body.

I risked another glance at Warren. His eyes were closed, his hands clenched into fists and trembling.

"It felt like *hours*," Genni whispered, seeming unable to stop her story now that she had begun. "And when it was… over, when he was quiet, they came to us and offered us a deal." She took a deep breath. "If one of us told them where the other entrance to the city was, they would give the other one a quick death. Then they…" She gulped, trying to force out the words. "They… my legs."

I cringed, hands flexing convulsively at the thought.

"Rosita… she was so brave. She told them she would never tell. Spat at them." Genni swallowed, her voice going flat again. "That's when they cut her tongue."

I lifted my gaze to the ceiling, willing myself not to vomit. Seeing the aftermath had been one thing. Hearing about it, reliving the night through Genni's words, feeling it play out in horrific detail, was somehow much worse.

"I… they… I couldn't see. But they… did things. And she was screaming. So much. And I…" her voice dropped to a whisper again. "I told them. I told them where the entrance to the tunnel was. I'm sorry. I tried not to. But I had to. I had to tell them."

There was utter silence.

"Please don't be angry," Genni begged. "I'm sorry. I tried."

There was another pause. I looked at Warren, but he seemed incapable of words, his jaw clenched tight.

"Set was angry," Genni said. "He hasn't come. I let him down. I let everyone down." She began to weep, loud sobs that shook her shoulders despite the lack of accompanying tears.

Warren moved at last, striding jerkily across the room and out the doorway. Ava watched him go before looking at me. Our eyes met briefly then I turned away. Maybe I was a coward, but I couldn't bear to break that piece of news again. I followed Warren outside, Nate shadowing my steps.

I caught up with Warren in the sunlight outside. He stood just outside the cave, hands on his hips, breathing hard as he surveyed the city with narrowed eyes. I stopped beside him, waiting in silence. He would probably call off the evening's talks, and I wouldn't blame him. How could anyone make peace with the beings who had done *that*?

"This has to work, Mara," he said, the words hard and clipped. "This can never happen again. Never."

I glanced over my shoulder. Nate lurked a few steps behind us. I met his black eyes, thinking of how Genni had described Zouri's. Empty pits. Nate's eyes would never be empty to me. They were full. Full of emotion, of history, of potential.

"I know," I agreed, turning back to Warren. "We're not going to let it."

20

Enemies

Inside the throne room, with the doors closed behind us, I waited for an explanation. My eyes flicked restlessly between Hamma, Titan, and my father.

Sitting down heavily on his throne, my father tilted his head back, eyes closed. "It's been a long journey," he said. "You're dismissed."

The Guard exchanged glances.

"Sire," Hamma began cautiously.

"Get out," Father snapped.

I flinched. My hands shook at his tone. I clenched them tightly behind my back as silence smothered the room.

Titan was the first to leave. The rest of the Guard trailed behind him towards the door.

"Nathaniel," my father said as the half-blood moved to follow his comrades. "Stay."

He did so, exchanging a glance with me.

"What happened?" I asked as soon as the door closed behind Ishmael, my voice shaking just as much as my hands.

My father sighed, his eyes still closed. "The mission was successful," he said. "Using the Figures let us get close enough to turn back a couple of attacks. The demons withdrew soon after. So we came back."

"Father..." That wasn't what I wanted to know, no matter how important it was.

He opened his eyes, gazing at me sadly. "I have no idea. Hamma and Titan fought, and neither of them will tell me what it was about.

They've barely looked at each other since."

"They fought?" I gaped at him. It was unheard of for two members of the Guard to raise a weapon against each other outside of training. And for it to be those two...

"It didn't come to blows," my father said, "but it might have done if the rest of us hadn't woken up. They were on watch together, next thing anyone knows, they were shouting like they wanted to kill each other. We didn't hear enough to work out what it was about but..." he paused, looking across at Nate. "Your name was mentioned. Anything you want to tell me?"

Nate went stiff, his face pale. "What? No. I don't know anything about it!"

My father sighed. "I didn't think you would. I'm not blaming you. I thought you should know before any of the others start asking questions though."

Nate didn't respond, dropping his gaze to the ground, his brow creased.

"So, what now?" I asked.

My father spread his hands helplessly. "We just have to hope they work it out."

"Why don't you ask them what happened?"

"I have. More than once. Neither of them would tell me. And believe me, I wasn't asking nicely by the end."

I looked away. Titan and Hamma, arguing? It didn't seem possible. And what could the disagreement have been about, for them both to refuse to answer my father's questions?

They'd always been so close, the three of them always in sync. And now what? We had to hope they would work it out? 'Hope'? I didn't like the sound of that one bit, and my father's face wasn't doing anything to reassure me.

In the interest of privacy, Warren led us to the palace, taking us to a chamber just down the hall from the throne room. A small window looked out along the cliffs towards the sea, but Warren turned away from it, lighting candles on a cluttered table.

He gestured carelessly to a stone shelf on the side of the room, laden with food - a basket of rolls, strips of smoked fish, some type of root vegetable.

"Help yourselves," he said, without looking at the food. "They still bring enough for three."

I eyed the offering, much more interesting fare than I'd ever seen in the mess halls in the city below, but held back. My growth ward could sustain me, though the constant burn under my skin had reached the point of discomfort.

"I'm sure there are others who need it," I said gently.

Warren shot me a glare. "In case you hadn't noticed, we've just had a substantial decrease in population. You might as well eat it."

I dropped my gaze but acquiesced and began to eat. Nate remained by the door, hands cushioning his lower back as he leaned against the wall.

"I haven't poisoned it," Warren said sourly.

Nate gave a humourless smile. "I don't eat," he said.

"What?"

"I don't eat."

"Of course you don't," Warren muttered, turning away and falling into a chair, rubbing his face.

I dropped my gaze to the roll I'd been tearing to pieces and stuffed some into my mouth.

"So, this evening," Warren said, dropping his hands as he changed the subject, looking between us. "What's the plan? Where are we meeting them? How many will there be?"

I looked to Nate, ceding the questions to him.

"It'll be outside the wall, obviously," he said. "But we should stay relatively close, so you can get back inside if things go badly."

"Are we expecting things to go badly?"

"Better to be prepared."

"How very reassuring," Warren said wryly. "You didn't bother to arrange a specific place then?"

"They'll know where we are."

"Great. So they might be able to spring up *between* us and the wall then? Fucking fantastic."

"They've agreed to talk," Nate reminded him. "Doing that would be… counterproductive."

"Unless this is all a trap."

Nate had no response to that.

"Who will it be?" I asked. "You said there are different factions, different leaders. Which one is coming?"

"Madina. She's in charge of the largest faction and has a reputation for integrity. I'm sure she wasn't aligned with Zouri, at least. She said she'll talk, so she'll hear us out. And she has a lot of influence. If you want things to change, she's the one to start with.

"She'll have her second with her and… and some others." He looked at Warren, continuing quickly. "You don't want to seem too scared, so don't bring too many of your people. Maybe three or four. Ones you trust to fight, and fight well."

My eyes narrowed slightly. I hadn't missed Nate's hesitation. Who were these *others* he was expecting to turn up?

"Three or four? That's it?" Warren's eyes were wide with dismay.

"We'll be there too," I reminded him.

He grimaced. "Fine. What do we want from them?"

Nate and I exchanged a glance, but I knew this was a question I had to answer myself. The problem was that Warren's agenda and my own weren't necessarily aligned. I had my own people to think about, whether they were present or not.

"Well," I said slowly, playing for time. "We want to find out why they're attacking, both here and at home. Without knowing that, there's no way to move forward." I looked at Nate again.

"You two already have a theory."

I jumped slightly, staring at the man sitting in the chair, reminded eerily of Set and his uncanny ability to read me.

Warren slapped his palm on the desk, punctuating my silence. "Well?" he demanded. "You can't expect me to go into this half-blind. Are we going to stand together, or should I be expecting you to turn your back on us if they ask it?"

"If they offer to leave *us* alone in return for me turning a blind eye to what's going on here, then I'll tell them to crawl back into whatever hole they came out of," I snapped, furious.

"You were quick enough to abandon us a couple of nights ago!" Warren shot back.

We stared at each other, angry blue eyes meeting shameful brown ones.

"I came back," I said.

"Right."

The cold word hung between us, surrounded by all the other things he could have said. How it didn't change the fact that I'd left in the first place. How I was too late. How it wasn't enough.

"I'm here now," I said. "I will stand beside you in this no matter what they offer. I'm not going to abandon you again." Maybe it was too late. But it was all I could give him.

Warren slumped in his chair, closing his eyes briefly. "Thank you. And... sorry. I'm not... I wasn't meant for this." His eyes opened again, gazing hopelessly at me.

"I know. But you're all your people have." I took a breath, trying to push the swirling emotions back down inside me. "We think it's the wards," I explained. "It's the only thing linking us. And the demon said they wanted to destroy them all. We need to find out why."

Warren nodded jerkily. "What about the others?" he asked, looking back to Nate. "Even if we can get this Madina on board, how can we stop another splinter group from attacking, like Zouri did?"

Nate grimaced. "To put it simply... you can't. But as Mara said, if we can find out why they are attacking, it might allow you to remove the motivation for them doing so." He glanced out the window. "We should go."

"Already?" I followed his gaze. The sea was tinged slightly orange and the cliffs shone golden in the afternoon sunlight. Turning away, I shoved another roll into my mouth, chewing furiously.

Ignoring Nate's smirk, I swallowed with an effort, then cautiously released the draw on my growth ward. My head spun slightly but my vision remained clear and focused. I blinked a couple of times to make sure the solidity wasn't temporary, then nodded to the two men.

"Okay. Let's go."

Warren sent a messenger ahead to seek out those who were to accompany us, and gather volunteers as a secondary line of defence at the wall. We walked in silence along the path, watching the boy scamper away down the slope at a reckless pace. At a fork, I paused, glancing up the cliffs. Above us, I could just about make out the entrance to the cave where the prophecy was carved.

"I'll meet you at the gate," I said, making an impulsive decision.

Both men looked like they wanted to object, but I strode away before they could, bounding up the mountainside. By the time I reached the small plateau in front of the cavern, I was out of breath. The sinking sun was shining directly inside, but the space was devoid of people.

Frowning at their absence, I stepped in, watching my shadow slide over the sheet of metal set into the back wall. It winked at me, reflecting the sunlight. Looking away, I headed to the side, where the long swatches of purple fabric I'd noticed on my previous visit hung down the walls.

Pulling out one of my blades, I cut a long strip free, wadding it up in my fist before heading back outside.

There was quite a crowd gathered at the gate by the time I arrived. Warren was moving among them, giving instruction and encouragement.

Nate stood in the open threshold, arms crossed as he stared intently out at the empty plain.

"How long do we have?" I asked him breathlessly.

"A few minutes," he said.

"I…" I hesitated, suddenly unsure.

Frowning, he turned to face me.

326

Holding out my hand, I let the purple fabric unravel, swaying in the breeze.

Nate's body tensed at once, his eyes widening. He nodded, trembling, eyes fixed hungrily upon the fragile strip of fabric.

He dropped to his knees.

I took a breath, trying to remember the wording of the oath required of him. It tumbled through my mind, twisting and snaking back on itself, the specific order eluding me. Nate had no such apprehension.

"I swear to protect the throne, the city, and the people, against any threat," he said. "I swear to stand against any foe, to risk any injury, to sacrifice my life if necessary. By name, by blood, by honour, I so swear it."

My breath caught in my throat at the surety of his voice, the complete lack of hesitation. The words coiled their way into my heart, smouldering there like a fire. Reaching down, I wound the cloth around his upper right arm, tying it off in a knot with shaking fingers.

He rose slowly to his feet, a reverent look on his face as he touched the band, as if reassuring himself it was real.

"It's yours. As it always has been. You didn't fail my father," I said firmly. "Will you stand with me now?"

Nate's back straightened, his face hardening. "Always."

I smiled, feeling the new warmth in my chest burn a little brighter.

"Moment over?" Warren asked crisply, brushing past us onto the plain. "Excellent."

Nate and I exchanged a rueful look as our backup hurried after their king.

"Ready?" I asked him.

"No," Nate grinned nervously.

"Tough." I turned and followed Warren.

We'd barely caught up to him when Nate stopped, throwing out an arm to stop me.

"Wait," he said, eyes wide.

Warren shifted slightly closer on my other side.

"Right there," Nate pointed ahead of us. "They're coming."

Even though I expected it, the flash of red light still made me flinch. Seven demons stood in front of us, their numbers matching ours.

At the front stood a girl of middling height. Sheets of black hair hung to her shoulders, framing her round face. She was thin, with slender wrists and legs, but I could see strength in the lines of her shoulders and waist. My eyes returned to her face and I amended my initial assessment. Her circular face gave an impression of youth, but this was no child.

Close by her side, half a pace behind, was an older man. There was grey speckled throughout his scraggly hair and the short beard covering the severe lines of his chin. Five other demons ranged behind them in a rough arc.

Seven pairs of inky black eyes. My hands twitched, itching to reach for my blades. I flexed my fingers and resisted the call.

"So," Warren said.

I didn't begrudge him the authority to speak first. Standing outside the wall of his city, it felt right.

The girl, who I assumed must be Madina, looked at him for a moment, then raised her black eyes to the wall behind us. "It certainly is impressive," she said, her voice deeper than I'd expected.

"It's a bit of a mess at the moment," Warren said stiffly.

"So I've been told," Madina mused. Her eyes flicked across to Nate, a slow smile oozing across her face. "Nathaniel."

"Madina," he acknowledged her.

"There are several people who will be disappointed at the path you have chosen," she said.

One of the other demons snorted loudly. "Understatement." He glared at Nate from under a wide forehead, his square jaw set. His short, sandy-coloured hair stuck up in angry spikes. "That's it then?" he demanded. "One strip of colour and you run straight

328

back to them. Like a whipped dog."

I bristled, barely restraining myself from snapping back.

Nate just sighed again. "Come on, Benas," he said. "It was three days. What did you expect?"

"A little loyalty would have been nice."

"I'm loyal to the same person I always was."

I tried not to smile, but failed, dropping my eyes.

"What about blood?" the demon, Benas, snapped. "What about loyalty to your family?"

"Don't go there," Nate said, and there was a warning in his tone.

I glanced sideways at him and he met my questioning gaze.

"My half-brother," he muttered by way of explanation.

I felt my eyes go wide and he grimaced in response. Had he expected this? Was that why he'd faltered when mentioning the 'others' he had said would be accompanying Madina?

I looked back at the demon, Nate's half-brother. Other than their matching hair colour, I saw no other familial resemblance.

"Enough," Madina said. "This is not why we are here."

"You're right," I said. "So why don't you tell us why we *are* here?"

Madina's eyes narrowed slightly. She spread her hands, cocking her head slightly to the side. The sheets of her black hair remained perfectly vertical despite the movement. "You requested this meeting," she pointed out. "Maybe you should be telling us why we are here?"

"I was led to believe you would be open to the idea of peace."

"Do you expect me to truly believe you want peace?"

"It wouldn't be the first time it has been done," I said, watching them closely.

The gamble paid off.

"Never openly," the older demon, close behind Madina, said whilst she raised a conciliatory eyebrow.

I fought to keep the grin off my face. The admission was proof my suspicion had been right. "Maybe that was the issue," I said, battling to keep my voice level. "Perhaps it is time for a more open approach."

There was a ripple of laughter amongst the demons.

Madina gave a tight smile. "And how would that have been received?" she asked. "Do you think your people would have listened to us if we'd walked through the streets and asked for a cessation of hostilities?"

I pressed my lips together. No, that would not have been met with an amicable response.

"We have tried for peace," Madina continued. "Over and over again. It does not last. Within a decade, your monarch changes, and we are right back to the beginning. Each time we approach a new king or queen, we put our lives at risk. And all we are ever offered is compromise and broken promises."

"You didn't approach me."

Madina laughed now. "You claim the title of queen? When you have never sat on the throne?"

"I do."

She stilled, her eyes calculating.

"The throne *will* be mine," I declared.

"If you say so."

"And Djet?" The demons shifted, their expressions tightening at the name. "I assume you approached him?"

"He was… unreceptive to our emissaries."

"Meaning?"

"He killed them."

"I see. Well, maybe you should reconsider who you recognise as the monarch."

Glances were exchanged, black eyes narrowing.

"So what will it take? What is your cost for peace?" I pressed.

Madina never looked away from me, despite the flutters of movement from behind her. I held her gaze, waiting.

"Give up your wards."

"Excuse me?"

"You heard."

It was my turn to laugh now, a burst of derision escaping me before I could stop it. "Is that all?" I scoffed. "Sacrifice our capability to stand against you, leave ourselves to your mercy? I don't think so."

Madina turned aside, raising her eyebrows at the demon just behind her. Clearly my response was exactly what she had expected.

"Well then," she said. "We have nothing further to discuss."

"Yes, we do," I snapped, stepping forward. Nate shadowed my movement. "Why? Why do you want us to stop using the wards? Why did Zouri try to destroy the ones here?"

"Because they are killing us."

The simple words made me draw back, frowning. Yes, the wards allowed us to fight against the demons, but we couldn't get to their home. They would be safe if they just stayed there.

"Only when you attack first."

"No!" Madina punctuated the shout with an angry slash of her hand. "You think your powers come for free, that there is no cost to them? You're wrong! There is a price, and we are the ones who pay it!"

There was a moment of silence.

"Explain," I said.

"Those wards funnel energy. They do not create it," Madina hissed, jabbing a finger at my shoulder. "They simply draw it from elsewhere, channelling it to your purposes. That power comes from our world. Every time you draw upon a ward, you steal energy from *our* realm, energy we require to live. The more you draw away, the less is left to sustain us. We starve as you grow stronger. Already the effects are intensifying. Another hundred years or so... we may cease to exist."

I stared at her, searching for the lie, the deception. It could have been there. But if it was, she hid it well. I glanced back at Nate, gauging his reaction. The wideness of his eyes spoke to his shock, but the grim set of his mouth told me he believed the story.

"If that's true, why have you never said anything before?" I asked.

Madina snorted. "You think we haven't?" She took a step forwards, eyes fixed on me. "It used to be that most of us wanted to spread the word, to sue for peace and understanding. And sometimes we were even believed. Your monarchs would say, 'prove your good intentions, don't attack for five, ten years,' however long they liked. So we wouldn't. But when that time was up, there was always a new monarch, and we had to start over. And with every failure, every new start, it became harder to remember why we were bothering.

"You ask why we never said anything before? Because fewer and fewer of us believe it's worth saying anything at all. So we look to other, bloodier options. Why do you think Nathaniel came to *me*? Because there is not one other leader among the demons who would have listened or welcomed the idea. They think it's too late for that. I had started to think the same."

She fixed me with a sharp look. "I was there when we explained this to your father. Do you want to know what his response was?"

I swallowed, unable to speak, unable to look again.

"He said he would do everything he could to find a way to give his people more wards each, so that we would be exterminated faster."

Powerless to hold her accusatory gaze, I dropped my eyes.

The demons weren't innocent though, I reminded myself quickly. All the attacks, all the deaths on their hands…

Yet, if what Madina said was true, the deaths were not their intent, merely the removal of the wards. My shoulder jerked suddenly as the words registered.

Could it have been a demon, that foolish night six years ago?

Between one breath and another, I was back there.

Trudging back to the citadel alone after sunset, thoughts preoccupied with the admonition I was inevitably going to receive for my lateness, I hadn't been paying attention to the dark street. Not that it would have made a difference. There wasn't enough time.

I heard the sudden footsteps behind me, had the fleeting impression of movement. I turned. Too late.

332

Something hit my shoulder blade, jerking across my back.

Pain erupted, disproportionate to the wound itself, the same level of agony coursing through my body at the destruction of my strength ward as I'd felt at its activation, sending me crashing to my hands and knees. Gasping, blinded by tears, I had barely been able to raise my head enough to see a distorted pair of feet approaching. They halted abruptly, then fled, leaving me crippled on the ground.

I blinked, pushing the memory away. What if that had been some new strategy of the demons? To ambush lone children in the dark and eradicate the wards from our skin before we even learned how to properly use them?

Yet I'd never heard of others suffering the same fate. Unless they too had hidden it, ashamed of their vulnerability.

I squeezed my eyes shut, trying to drag myself back to the present, but it was no good. I'd lost the thread of our conversation. Swallowing, I looked back. Nate was right behind me, his face tight with concern. My diversion had not gone unnoticed. My eyes flickered down to the purple band around his arm and I took a deep breath, drawing strength from his presence.

Right. The wards.

Turning back to Madina, I shook my head. "I cannot give up my wards, even if what you say is true. Djet holds my throne. I cannot take it back from him without them. Afterwards..." I took another deep breath. "Afterwards, we can talk again."

The demon behind Madina scoffed again. "More empty promises," he muttered, but Madina waved a hand, and he subsided.

"Wards or no wards," she said, "it will take more for you to reclaim your throne."

My eyes narrowed. "What do you mean?"

"You have many miles to cover between here and Alderth, and then you must enter the city to reach Djet. Do you think you will be able to do so unaided? What if the people stand against you? This is why you really sent Nathaniel to us, is it not? You want our help." Madina smiled indulgently. "I am willing to give it. My people will ensure you get to Djet. You will stand with them, making our alliance public, and afterwards, as you say, we will discuss the matter of the wards again."

I shook my head slowly. "That's not what I want."

"No?"

"No!" I said, louder this time. "I would *never* be accepted if that were to happen."

"You don't have another plan. How else will you succeed?"

"Another way. *Any* other way. My people will not stand against me. I *will* get to Djet, and I *will* kill him. But it would be better if I failed than if I succeeded because of your help."

Madina shook her head in disgust. "Very well. If you want to risk it all... so be it."

"One more thing."

She raised an eyebrow in a sarcastic invitation.

"This city is not to be touched. There will be no attacks on the people here. No more attempts to destroy the wall."

Madina glanced up at the wall behind us, then shook her head. "I cannot promise that. There are many who believe direct action is the only option left to us. They do not answer me."

"Then make them!" I snapped. "Zouri is dead. I carved his face open myself. If there are still those who believe he was going about things the right way, convince them otherwise."

"Why do you care? You have no ties to this place."

"I care," I said softly, taking yet another step closer to her. "Do not misunderstand me. If there is one more death in this city because of your people, it won't just be the end of talks between us. I will come after you with everything I have. You won't have to worry about your world dying because I will end every single one of you before that happens."

Madina bared her teeth, a deep snarl reverberating up her throat, echoed by those behind her. "As if you could," she spat.

I looked sideways. Not directly at Nate, but close enough that the implication was obvious. "Actually, I think I could."

Several pairs of dark eyes refocused on Nate. The snarling grew even louder.

Beside me, Nate shifted his weight. The growl he sent back rose louder and louder. It was a physical effort not to flinch away from him. Then the terrible sound faded away, leaving nothing but silence.

"Very well," Madina said. "I will do what I can."

Inclining my head, I stepped back again, glancing at Warren. He gave a tight nod of approval.

"But there is something else I want as well."

I looked back at Madina, waiting.

She hesitated before continuing, as if unsure of how to phrase her request. "One of my people, my second, is missing," she admitted eventually.

"There are several bodies in there," I said, jerking my head back towards the city.

She shook her head. "Sornath would never have joined Zouri," she said. "You say you will return to Alderth, take the throne. When you do, I would *appreciate* it if you would keep an ear open for word of him."

From her tone, it was clear that her appreciation was not something to brush aside.

"You think he may be there?"

"No one knows where he is. I have people searching, but they've been unsuccessful so far. Do not misunderstand me. Even if he is passed from this life, I *will* bring him home."

I met her gaze and nodded. "I understand. If I hear anything, you will know about it."

"Good. Then I look forward to our next talk," she said.

There was a flash of red and she was gone, quickly followed by the others, except for one. Nate's half-brother remained, arms crossed as he stared at his kin.

I glanced sideways at Nate, who shifted slightly, eyes darting between us. I gave him a quick nod, turning to Warren as Nate moved towards his half-brother.

Warren wore an unreadable expression.

"Well, that was —"

I shook my head, silencing him. "Let's get back inside first," I said. The light was fading fast, leaving us in twilight. Shooting Nate and Benas one last glance, I turned, hurrying back to the gate with Warren and his guards. They all relaxed a little as they passed through the gates, glad to be behind the thick stone again, even if the web of protection carved upon it was incomplete.

The crowd gathered just inside had swelled in our absence. Every pair of eyes was upon us, full of tension and expectation.

"Well?"

"What happened?"

"What did they say?"

The clamouring broke out all at once, a wave of questions that threatened to drown us. Warren raised his hands, stemming the tide.

"I will address everyone tomorrow morning. For now, I'm sure there is still a lot of clearing up to do," he said.

Tomorrow morning... My stomach twisted, a decision I hadn't realised I'd made rising within me. The attack was over, Warren was established as King, and we had the beginning of a truce with the demons. I had other things to do and none of them would be achieved by remaining here. My time in this place was up. I wouldn't be present to hear Warren's address tomorrow morning.

The group hesitated, dispersing with palpable reluctance and plenty of bitter mutterings. The four who had accompanied us slipped away too, quickly accosted by the eager crowd. I registered Keera's tousled hair and blinked in surprise. I'd been so focused on the demons, I hadn't even noticed she had been one of those standing behind me.

"Thank you," Warren said, turning to face me. "For what you said at the end."

"It was true. I do care. And if anything happens here, *anything*, you let me know."

"I will." He turned, squinting back up at the wards high enough on the wall to have escaped Zouri's destruction. "Do you believe

336

them?"

I didn't need to ask what he meant. "I don't know. It makes sense, in some ways, but... I don't know how they can prove it anyway."

"What if they could? What if it's true?"

My hand rose, unbidden, to grip my upper arm, clutching at the tattoos there. To give them up, to be weak, vulnerable... the very thought filled me with dread. Yet if what Madina said was true, to refuse would be to intentionally cause the demons' extinction, when the animosity between our races might be nothing more than them fighting to survive.

"I don't know," I admitted.

We stood in silence, trying to comprehend the ramifications of the discussion we'd just had.

Jogging footsteps made us both look around to find Nate coming through the open archway. The plain behind him was empty.

"Are you okay?" I asked immediately.

He nodded.

I wanted to question him further, to demand why he hadn't told me about his half-brother, but with Warren there, I held my tongue.

"So..." Warren himself broke the tense silence. "What are you going to do now?"

I met Nate's eyes and knew I could delay no longer. I'd done all I could for the people here. It was time to face my own responsibilities at last.

"Now... I think it's time we went home."

Of course, it wasn't that simple. Much though I was tempted to simply turn and walk out the gates right at that moment, there were things still to be dealt with. I had to fetch my pack from my room, and then I left detailed instructions for how to get to Alderth, though admittedly via a slightly convoluted route. There had to be a reason why our people had never interacted before, beyond the simple reluctance of Leydford's citizens to venture beyond the safety of their wall. Hopefully, if there was some natural obstacle between us, the route I had left would allow them to avoid it.

In exchange, Warren handed over a small shard of slate, a copy of the repelling ward etched upon it. It wasn't perfect, but given the complexity of the ward, it was better than I would have expected. My heart leapt at the possibility that our Warders might be able to engineer its form from the sketch. I tucked the fragment of rock carefully into my pack.

There was a surprisingly large crowd of people to see us off, despite Warren's order for them to disperse earlier. The majority of it was made up of those I'd seen fawning around the supposed prophecy, some with their eyes on Nate, some still focussed on me. Apparently, they were still divided over its meaning. I didn't care anymore and ignored them all.

All my surviving students were there, their eyes holding a fierce hope that hadn't been there when I'd first met them. Even Keera gave me a jerky nod.

Noah hovered anxiously on the outskirts of the group, but I grasped his wrist without hesitation. For the first time, I thanked him, genuinely, for bringing me to the city. He gave an embarrassed grin but nodded.

I turned away, approaching the open archway. Hidden in the shadows, Warren stood with his arms crossed, fingers tapping against his elbows. Nate moved past him first, giving a nod that held more respect than I would have anticipated. Then it was my turn, and I stepped up to the man who had never wanted or expected to be king.

"You're sure you won't stay the night?" he asked, glancing sideways at the dark plains.

Hoisting my pack higher onto my shoulder, I smiled and shook my head. "Thank you, but no. We'll be okay." I gave him a firm look. "And so will you."

He huffed. "So, you're off to fight for your own people now?"

"I have to at some point."

"And it'll be dangerous?"

"No more than this was."

"Liar." His eyes held mine. "Don't go and die out there."

"I'll do my best," I said with a grim but he didn't smile back.

He stepped forwards. I froze but allowed him to embrace me, returning the gesture awkwardly.

"I'll be hearing from you then," he said as we broke apart. "When you're a queen."

"You will. Absolutely. King."

He grimaced, and I laughed softly at the expression.

"Better get used to it," I advised him.

"I'll do my best," he said.

"I know you will." I smiled gently.

"I don't blame you," he blurted out as I stepped backwards. "For any of it."

My shoulders dropped a fraction. A breeze kissed my face, like Set's shade passing by. "I know you don't," I said softly. "Just don't blame yourself either. Make them proud."

He nodded jerkily.

With one last gentle touch on his elbow, I turned to where Nate waited for me, leaving Leydford for the final time. Together, we broke into a jog, abandoning ourselves to the night, on our way home at last.

21

The First Guard

To say that things were uncomfortable would have been a gross understatement. Hamma and Titan were constantly on different shifts and did everything they could to avoid being in the same room when off duty as well. Any time they were forced into close proximity, the air turned icy. The sheer intensity with which they ignored each other was a physical force, sizzling between them.

I couldn't imagine a disagreement that would have caused such a deep rift. I desperately wanted to know what was wrong but had no idea how to ask or who to approach first. If they refused to talk to my father, I doubted either one would be receptive to my inquiries.

Nate seemed even more off-balance by the change. After my father's revelation that he was, in some unknown way, involved, I couldn't blame him. For all our theorising and discussions, however, we had failed to come up with any substantiated reason for the rift.

The rest of the Guard were constantly on edge and my father was withdrawn and distracted, snapping at the slightest provocation.

A few days after the Guard had returned, I was passing the armoury when I saw Hamma hurrying inside. Frowning, I came to a halt. Titan had been training this morning. There was a good chance he was either in the armoury or would be coming back soon. No doubt that was why Hamma was in such a rush, trying to avoid the other man. But what would happen if they encountered each other?

With only a mild twinge of guilt, I turned and followed Hamma, ducking inside the armoury and looking around. He was nowhere in sight. I set off into the maze-like room, padding between two sets of shelves, peering through them, trying to catch a glimpse of his wild hair. Footsteps from behind made me jump. I darted around the edge of the shelves into the next row and froze. The steps continued without pause, passing the spot where I crouched.

It was Titan.

I waited a few seconds for him to get further ahead, then prowled after him as quietly as I could, hoping he wouldn't realise he was being followed.

Less than a minute later, Titan's steps came to an abrupt halt. I crept closer, listening. For a moment, there was nothing but silence, then a new pair of feet tapped out a rhythm, moving swiftly away.

"It wouldn't kill you to be in the same room as me," Titan said, a definite sourness to his tone.

The other pair of feet stopped, but nothing was said for several seconds.

"You're—" Hamma began eventually.

"It's not contagious," Titan snapped, moving forwards again, and there was a clatter as he dropped something. "I'm the same person I always was."

"No, you're not," Hamma insisted. "You don't belong here."

There was another loud clatter. "It's funny you should say that because I thought this might be the one place it wouldn't be an issue," Titan said angrily. "No one is interested, no one cares, no one is going to ask, so why would it matter?"

There was a moment of silence.

"It matters," Hamma said, but his voice was quieter now.

Titan scoffed in disgust. "I've been driven out of one place for this. Are you going to drive me out of here as well?"

"No one is driving you out."

"Oh, really? Because you're the only one who knows and look how you're reacting."

Another pause.

"So Nathaniel—"

341

Titan's growl drowned out anything more than Hamma might have said. "Don't," he snarled. "We've been over that."

"You've been lying to me," Hamma said. "To everyone."

"Only by omission."

Another long silence.

"So what now?" Titan said.

There was a faint sigh.

"I guess... I guess I just have to figure out how to deal with it," Hamma replied. His footsteps resumed, fading away.

"And if you can't?" Titan asked the empty room.

I remained perfectly still, waiting in silence as I listened to Titan finish his business and leave.

Alone, I stood up, thinking hard.

So Titan had told Hamma something, something about himself that no one else knew. And Hamma was... What? I couldn't make sense of his responses. Was he afraid of Titan?

The pair of them, along with my father, had always been so close, like brothers. What secret could Titan have revealed that would break such a bond? And without knowing that, how could any of us even attempt to fix it?

We ran for hours without speaking, my mind racing as fast as my legs. My wards of speed, balance, and strength burned under my skin, but their familiar warmth was accompanied by an uncomfortable tightness in my chest. It felt like guilt.

Perhaps it was my imagination, but the draw felt different now. I could almost sense the power flowing from that other realm, wicking out around the spirals which shaped it to my needs.

I wondered if Nate was dwelling on Madina's revelation as much as I was. He kept pace with me easily, his blood granting him enhancements to match my own. Or maybe he was thinking about his half-brother. Did he have more siblings I didn't know about? Or that *he* didn't know about?

The moon rose, giving enough light to see by, though the ground was smooth enough that it wasn't an issue anyway. A different problem swiftly began to make itself known, however. Though my heart ached for me to continue, to carry on all the way home without stopping, my head was spinning with exhaustion. The adrenaline brought on by the meeting with the demons was wearing off and left in its wake was the realisation that it had now been almost two whole days since I slept. I couldn't keep going any longer.

Nate didn't ask questions when I began to slow but followed me silently into the trees. Keeping my weapons within easy reach, I lay down, expecting to fall asleep instantly. I did not. Every rustle of wind made me twitch, eyes snapping back open again. I had become accustomed to sleeping inside again. Or maybe it was just the memory of what Set and I had discovered within these same trees that kept me awake for so long.

When the sun rose, we rose with it, though I felt distinctly unrested. At mid-morning, we left the plains behind, turning north away from the coast to enter the forest. After only half a night's sleep or less, we were both on edge, tension creeping into paranoia. By the time we stopped for the evening, I had a crick in my neck from looking over my shoulder. Yet there hadn't been a single glimpse of silver-grey skin all day.

It was inevitable. I knew, and I was sure Nate did too, the odds of us getting back to Alderth undiscovered were pitifully low. I was convinced something about Leydford's wall had prevented the Figures from attacking me there. There was no other explanation for their conspicuous absence. Now we were out in the open, surely it was only a matter of time until they found us.

The Figures had, literally, been created to keep Alderth safe. Their purpose, when they were awake, was to remove threats, whatever they were told those were. Djet had no doubt directed them to recognise me as such a threat. The throne had a power of its own; if I could lay even a single finger upon it, I could counter Djet's orders, but until then, I was powerless to do anything.

Except I had killed one. And yet, I hadn't.

Sighing, I poked at the small fire we'd started. What had happened that day? My blade definitely pierced the Figure's skin. I hadn't imagined it. Even that was a marvel. But afterwards... Had the Figure been *pretending* to be dead for some reason? Or had someone else come along and removed the body?

On the other side of the fire, Nate was methodically shredding dead leaves, flicking each piece into the fire before ripping off a new one. Head down, jaw set, he barely seemed aware of what his fingers were doing.

Seeming to sense my eyes on him, he looked up, letting the rest of the broad chestnut leaf fall to the ground. He grimaced, a cocktail of sympathy and self-consciousness on his face. His eyes flicked away from me, over my shoulder, and widened. He leapt to his feet, drawing his sword.

I spun on my knees, my weapons jumping to my hands. What had he seen?

A pair of glowing white eyes hovered just beyond the ring of light cast by the fire.

I lurched to my feet, raising my weapons in front of me. I had hurt one of them before. I would do it again. It wasn't just my life at risk this time.

The Figure ghosted out of the trees, moving soundlessly forwards. I gripped my weapons tighter, reading to spring. Then a second one stepped into sight, emerging from the trees on my right. And from the left, a third.

Icy fear crept up my limbs, making my hands tremble, inching closer to my heart.

Nate leapt over the fire, at my side in an instant, putting his back to mine. I could feel him shaking too.

We were surrounded. More silver-grey bodies emerged on every side, the firelight flickering off their metallic skin.

"Well," Nate said, his voice unsteady, "this is probably going to make me the worst member of the Guard in history. Has anyone ever lost two monarchs before?"

"You give up on me now and I'll kill you myself," I said, raising my blades higher.

"Oh yeah?" he laughed, the shrill sound wavering in the air. "You might have to get in line!"

I leaned back a little, feeling him return the pressure, and was inexpressibly grateful. I might have failed my father and my people. I might be ruining the budding alliance with the demons. I might be abandoning Warren. But at least I wasn't alone.

I wanted to say something, to tell Nate how grateful I was to have had him as a friend, how there was no one I would rather have had with me right then. I wanted to tell him everything. But the words wouldn't come.

The Figure ahead of me advanced a step and I tensed, the shaking in my hands intensifying.

"Tamara."

I froze. Behind me, Nate did the same, his elbow suddenly stiff and unyielding where it pressed into my side.

The voice was smooth and even, empty of any infliction. Empty of life.

"Tell me that was you," Nate said quietly.

I wished I could. If I hadn't seen the jaw move, the mouth open, I wouldn't have believed it myself.

"Seriously, because I didn't think you had *that* big of an ego. If you want your own name to be your last words, I guess that's fine because otherwise—"

"Shut up!"

He lapsed into silence, but I could still hear him breathing, fast and shallow, and knew he was listening intently.

"Tamara."

I inhaled sharply. Even the inside of its mouth was grey, lips blending with teeth and tongue. Swallowing at the disconcerting image, I tried to formulate a response.

"Yes?" I croaked. Clearing my throat, I tried again. "What do you want?"

The Figure cocked its head to the side. It blinked, the luminescent white eyes vanishing for a brief second.

"To protect the monarch," it said, in that flat, empty voice.

My hands tightened on the hilts of my blades. Was this something they did? Announce their intentions to all their victims?

"To protect you," it continued.

I stared at its expressionless face.

"I… but… what?" I shook my head, trying to throw off the shock that had me struck dumb. "But Djet…"

The Figure shook its head too. "Djet is a pretender. You are your father's heir. Blood doesn't lie."

"That's not true!" I blurted, heedless of my words. "It's not about blood. What about the Claiming?" This had to be a trick, some cruel joke. I glanced back over my shoulder. Nate met my gaze with wide eyes.

"It's *about* what is best for the city. And right now, that is you."

"But *how*? How can you support me?" I turned back to the Figure again. "Djet has Claimed the throne. I thought…"

"The throne does not control us," it said. "It never did."

I let out a breath of stunned laughter. How many more facts I'd thought irrefutable were they going to destroy?

"I don't… but…" I clamped my mouth shut, trying to find other words. *But, but, but.* "You tried to kill me."

"Tried to talk to you."

The words came from my left this time, my head whipping around to find the one who had spoken.

"You didn't give us much of a chance," it continued.

My eyes dropped to its chest, where a faint white line was visible, marring the wards carved there.

"I killed you," I said.

"Indeed. That hurt, by the way."

I stared at it, my incomprehension rising. Was that meant to be a joke? Were they *joking*?

"Then how…" I flicked one of my blades towards it, indicating its presence. "How…"

Its white eyes followed the blade, but it said nothing.

"Enough," the first one spoke again. At least, I thought it was the

346

same one. They were indistinguishable.

My eyes flicked around the circle, from one to the next, all staring at me with the same inanimate expression. Was it merely a more sophisticated mask than I could have imagined? How could such creatures as this have intelligence?

"What are you?" I demanded.

The Figure ahead of me shook its head and gave a disconcerting smile. The expression didn't fit its face.

"Wrong question."

"Then what's the right one?" Nate spoke up for the first time. His voice was almost steady. Almost.

The Figure's smile widened, and I realised why it looked so strange. Its cheeks didn't move. There was no visible shifting of the skin there, no creasing around the eyes. It was as if the mouth just stretched outwards, consuming anything in its way.

"*Who* are we?" it said.

My swords tumbled from my grip, dropping with dull thuds to the ground. I saw them fall from a great distance. There was a rushing sound building in my ears, the ground tilting beneath my feet. I staggered and would have fallen if Nate hadn't caught me. I saw his hand on my shoulder but couldn't feel it. He was speaking, unintelligible noises tickling at my ear. The Figure just stood there, its glowing eyes never leaving mine.

"You should sit down," it said, its words somehow cutting through to my brain. "We have a lot to discuss."

I nodded vacantly, staggering again when Nate relaxed his hold on me.

The Figure looked away, moving around to the other side of the fire. The others did the same, all coalescing into a single group, some crouching, others remaining standing behind them.

No longer fixed by their horrifying gaze, I gulped in a breath, pressing a shaking hand to my stomach. With Nate's assistance, I sank to the ground, legs curling underneath me. Reaching out, I pulled my blades back towards me, clutching at the cold metal. I risked another glance at the one who'd made them for me. His

347

expression was slightly nauseated, jaw clenched tight.

We weren't dead. I forced myself to focus on that fact. I could deal with this. I had to.

Taking a breath, my head swimming with the influx of oxygen, I turned back to the Figures. I'd lost track of which one I'd been speaking to before. They all stared at me with identical eyes. I picked out the one I had encountered before by the wound on its chest, crouched on the far right, but otherwise could find no differences between them.

Who are we, they'd prompted me. The implication was inconceivable, the words ringing over and over in my head.

"You're… people?" I asked, the hushed words barely audible over the crackling fire.

One of the Figures in the middle smiled again, that strange widening of the mouth without any bunching of their cheeks.

"Originally, yes," it allowed.

"Originally?"

"We do not really qualify as such anymore."

I shook my head. "How did you… get like that?"

In answer, they moved, every single one raising their right hand to trace over a swirling white symbol carved into the centre of their chests.

"*Thorns…*" Nate swore from behind me, jerking backwards.

I couldn't help agreeing. Seeing them all move in such perfect synchronicity was disturbing.

"The wards did this to you?"

The one they'd touched was unfamiliar to me, as were most of the wards they carried. My eyes skated over their bodies. Every inch of their silver-grey skin was covered with spirals of varying designs, from the immobile skin of their cheeks and foreheads to the tips of their fingers.

"You get power from yours," the Figure pointed out, as they lowered their hands. "We get power from ours."

I resisted the urge to glance at Nate. If Madina was to be believed, that wasn't the whole story. We didn't *get* power from our

348

wards. We stole it. Why had Madina not mentioned the Figures in our discussion? They had more wards than I could count. If the demons wanted to destroy all the wards, surely the Figures would be a part of that?

"That doesn't explain how you became…" I gestured at them. Smooth grey skin, white eyes.

"Let's just say there were consequences to having so many wards," they said.

"And you were just people before?"

"Not quite *just* people," it said, and I thought I could hear amusement in that flat tone. "We were, we *are*, the First Guard."

"But there's only seven on the Guard, not twelve," I blurted out as if their number was the only shock in that announcement.

They just stared at me. Warmth rose to my cheeks at their silent, judgemental observation. Nate's hand suddenly clamped onto my arm. I looked around, taking in his pale face and wide eyes. His mouth worked soundlessly, unable to form words.

"Count them," he finally choked out.

Turning back, I did. Then I counted again.

Both times, I came to the same number.

Thirteen.

There were thirteen of them. Not twelve.

"But… I saw you," I breathed. "When you were sleeping. There were twelve of you."

Thirteen pairs of white eyes were fixed on me. The silence stretched on, pressing around me, ripping everything I'd known to shreds.

"We don't actually sleep," the one with the scar on its chest said.

My world lurched sideways again.

"I knew it!" Nate snarled, leaping to his feet.

I threw out a hand, steadying myself where he'd knocked me. "What?"

"I *knew* it!" he repeated. "They… I…" He was spluttering, incandescent with rage as he glared across the fire. "I hid down there once, early on. And I kept seeing them move, but when I looked again... they weren't. I kept trying to tell myself it was my mind playing tricks, but every time I did, I would see another one turning towards me, reaching out."

"That's why you were always so scared of them."

His scowl deepened. Chuckles rippled from the Figures, the sound cold and icy.

"It's not funny," he snarled, a note of real danger in his voice now.

"Yes, it was," the scarred one said. It was grinning, but unlike the other one, its cheeks were engaged with the movement, the wards on its face creasing, wrinkles visible around its white eyes.

"I was *eleven*!"

"You were covered in blood. And we were curious."

"Curious!" Nate tensed, about to spring, but I seized his arm, holding him back.

"Don't," I said. I had no idea what would happen if he attacked the Figures. Would they strike back? It wasn't worth finding out. "You will not tease him about this," I commanded them.

There was utter silence, none of them offering any further jibes. But they didn't apologise either.

"Why," I began, changing the topic as I pulled Nate down, "if you were so desperate to talk to me, did you then disappear for a week? Where were you when I was in Leydford?"

"You were safe," one of the Figures said. "Behind warded walls."

"Oh really? You think she was *safe* when she got hurt?" Nate snapped.

White eyes fixed on me, sharpening. "You're hurt?"

"I'm fine."

"You weren't so intent on '*protecting the monarch*' then, were you?"

"Nate, that's enough!"

"Where are you hurt?"

"I'm fine!" It was mostly true. The wound on the top of my shoulder was aching fiercely, but as long as I didn't lift my arm, it was bearable.

"We couldn't have gotten to you anyway," the First Guard tried

350

to defend themselves. "There were too many people around. And given your previous response to us, we doubted you would have been quiet if we had managed to corner you."

I pursed my lips in disbelief as I looked across the fire at them. Surely there had to be more to their absence. "Was it the wall? The repulsion wards?" I asked.

"No. We're not demons. Suffice to say, we were willing to wait."

"But you're in quite the hurry now. Why didn't you come to me in Leydford?" I pushed.

"That's irrelevant right now."

"Tell me."

"No."

Their simple refusal hung in the air between us. There was no malice or anger in the word. Just immovability. My mouth thinned. They were not going to back down over this. This was not a fight I was going to win.

"Why didn't I know any of this about you before?" I asked instead. "It could have saved a lot of time. Why are you only telling me now?"

"Because you weren't Queen. Only the current monarch and Guard know the truth about us."

"I'm on the Guard," Nate said stiffly. "I didn't know."

"You would have been told after seven years of service. As it stands, you are the only member of the Guard left. Consequently, you are also Captain of the Guard and therefore exempt from the time limit."

Nate went still beside me. I was equally frozen. Captain of the Guard... Technically, it was true. But I hadn't thought about it in those terms.

"But now that you know..." It turned its eyes back to me. "You're needed. Alderth is starting to fall apart. We're going to help you take back the throne."

"You've been inside the city?" I asked, leaning towards them eagerly.

"A little. There are limits to the places we can go and not be seen.

We cannot move freely without causing panic."

"Why does that matter? Why haven't you gotten rid of Djet already if you support Mara?" Nate demanded.

"And then what?" the speaker countered, turning their gaze onto him. "There would just be another Claiming. Djet spread the word that he had awoken us once he discovered we were gone. We could not murder him when people believed we were under his control."

"Couldn't you have made it look like an accident?"

"No," they said flatly.

"What *have* you managed to find out?" I said, exasperated.

"People are going missing," the Figure said. "Children."

Children. A chill ran down my arms. The terror they must have felt. And without wards, unable to defend themselves…

My heart went out to their parents. To lose not only someone you love but also the investment, the sacrifice they represented, given what the parents had to go through to conceive them. I forced the image away.

"What's being done to find them?" I demanded.

"Not enough. Djet has no interest whatsoever. He has no interactions with the people at all, from what we can observe," the Figure said. "It has led to a lot of uncertainty. Some soldiers have tried to organise searches but as soon as one of them takes charge, Djet has them killed."

"He's not *that* disinterested then," Nate muttered.

"Does he not care? Doesn't he want them found?" I asked.

"He doesn't want anyone to be a rallying point for resistance or to gather enough support to challenge him."

The silence hung for a few seconds, the implication of their words clear.

"Does anyone know I'm alive?"

They shook their head. "No. Some of them hope it, but only quietly. And that hope dwindles every day, which is why you must return. People are afraid to defy Djet, but given his apathy towards ruling, they are beginning to think they don't need a monarch at all."

352

"Is Djet so much of a threat?"

There was a moment of hesitation. "Too many have stood against him and fallen. There may be something else at work, but we have been unable to find out what."

My mouth twisted downwards. I had assumed that once I made it home, it would be a fair fight. Me against Djet, and nothing else to matter. The possibility that he might have some unknown advantage made my heart pound with trepidation.

"We can get you into the city," the Figure continued, oblivious to my internal nerves. "With us escorting you, there will be plenty of support, too much for Djet to deny. He will have to face you. We won't be able to intervene openly in the challenge but if you can get Djet close enough to us, we may be able to assist you."

I stood up, my heart pounding at their nonchalant words. "You mean cheat?" I gave them a moment to reject the accusation. They did not. I turned and strode away.

It only took a few seconds for a pair of hurried footsteps to catch up. Nate walked beside me, not saying anything until I stopped.

"Oh," he said as I began to pace back and forth. "I sort of hoped we were leaving them behind."

I shot him a glare. From the grin on his face, he wasn't serious. Not completely anyway.

"It's going to be okay," he tried to reassure me. "With the Figures behind you, no one will even think of standing in your way."

"Exactly!" I spat, and Nate recoiled from my venomous tone. "That's all anyone can think to offer me. The demons, the Figures—they're both the same. '*Here, we'll walk you in, and then people won't have any choice but to accept you whether they like it or not*!'"

"But they do want you."

"Do they?" I spun to face him. "You heard them. The people don't think they need a leader at all. Djet has shown them that much. And if I have to threaten my way in, then what's the point?" I took a deep breath, trying to calm myself. "People *should* have the right to stand against me if they want. If the only way for me to get the throne is by scaring everyone out of my way or by cheating, then I don't want it. It will mean nothing. I'll be no better than Djet. Don't you understand that?"

Nate was silent for a moment before he answered. "What I understand," he said, his voice flat, "is that you're going to throw everything away for your pride."

"Excuse me?" I glared at him.

"You're going to risk your father's legacy just because you won't accept help!"

"That's not the point!"

"Isn't it?" His voice rose as well. "Refusing the demons, I could understand. They're the enemy. But the Figures, First Guard, whatever you call them, they aren't. Even if people are scared of them, they know which side they are on. That's not threatening people; it's just them declaring their support. If we get there and normal people want to stand beside you, would you turn them away?"

"Of course not, but—"

"You don't have to do this alone."

I met his gaze, letting the quiet seep into me with each breath. "I didn't think I'd be alone."

He sighed. "Mara, I'm not enough. And we both know having me next to you isn't necessarily going to gain you any support."

"What if it wasn't just you?"

Nate frowned.

"They said you're the last member of the Guard. They're wrong."

Nate's face closed off instantly. "I was there, Mara. They're all dead."

"They are. But what about the ones before them?"

His eyes went wide. "You mean…"

I nodded. "People don't trust the Figures any more than they would the demons. They're horror stories told to children. If the demons walked me through the gate, people would hate me. If the Figures walk me in, they won't trust me. But if the Guard, *the real Guard*, with faces they know… if they stand behind me, that's when people will think, not judge."

354

Sighing, Nate rubbed his face. "Why can't it be easy?"

My mouth quirked into a smile. "The easy path isn't always the right one." I hesitated, eyeing Nate calculatingly. "You know where he is, right?"

Nate's mouth thinned, but he nodded. "Yeah. I know where he is."

22

Titan

The doors to the throne room closed behind the last petitioner, and my father leaned back in his chair, closing his eyes.

"Jenna," he said, and she looked up, somehow managing to continue scribbling notes at the same time. "Remind me to follow up on the situation in the library, and I want to tour the fields in the next few days to see how things are out there for myself. And find out where the party from Lambridge is; they're late and I don't want them here when the group from Charhelm arrives. We don't need them snarling at each other over this stupid salt argument while they're here."

I looked up from my seat on Father's left, watching Titan and Edric walk the length of the hall towards us. With Nate and Hamma also on duty, standing on either side of the throne, I'd expected the atmosphere to be frosty. Other than an initial awkwardness, however, there had been no indication of anything awry between them. Maybe that 'hope' my father had mentioned might be coming to fruition. Then again, having the length of the hall between them probably helped.

"Excellent," my father concluded, standing up. "Well then—"

"Sire," Titan called, stopping a few steps away. "There is another matter."

My father frowned, pausing. Edric was looking at Titan in surprise as well.

"Of course," Father said, pushing the rest of the way out of the throne. "Walk with me."

"Actually," Titan said, without moving, "I would prefer to address this here."

There was a moment of silence. Every pair of eyes was upon Titan now, but he wasn't looking at any of us. His eyes were fixed firmly on my father's feet. My heart began to race. What would Titan need to talk about that would have to be done in the throne room?

I glanced sideways at Hamma. He was watching Titan with a guarded expression.

"As you wish," my father said, returning to his seat.

Titan took a deep breath, his eyes still fixed on my father's feet. "You and your mother have been good to me over the years, far better than I deserved. I can never express how grateful I am to you both for having taken me in. It has been an unparalleled honour to serve your family, and yourself." He took another breath. "But I feel that time has come to an end."

I stood up. This couldn't be happening.

But he kept talking.

"I have protected you and your family to the best of my ability, but I no longer feel I am the person best suited to be occupying a position on your Guard. I would ask that you release me."

There was a ringing silence. I shook with the desire to speak but had no idea what to say. When I glanced sideways, I found Father to be just as lost for words as I was. On his other side, Hamma looked shocked and, perhaps, a little guilty.

"Titan," my father said eventually. "Taking you in was one of the best decisions my mother ever made. You're one of the best fighters I've ever seen, and you've been an even better friend. None of that has changed. Please, tell me what's going on."

Titan closed his eyes at Father's tone, but when he opened them again, his face was hard. "This decision has been a long time coming," he said. "I know what you are thinking, but this is unrelated."

I certainly knew what I was thinking; Titan was lying. There was no way this wasn't about the argument with Hamma.

My father stood up. "This is—"

"Please," Titan interrupted him, finally looking up and meeting his gaze. "Rygorn. Release me."

There was a moment of silence, then my father glanced sideways. "Leave us."

There was a moment when no one moved. Then Jenna gathered her bundle of notes, clutching them to her chest as she rose shakily to her feet. Edric took a hesitant step to the right, echoing her.

I didn't move. My eyes were fixed on Titan, but he refused to meet my eye. I could practically feel Nate behind me, his stare equally intense.

"Tammie."

I flinched, meeting my father's steady gaze. Surely he wouldn't accept Titan's resignation. He must just want us to leave so that they could talk alone. Maybe he would finally be able to get Titan to reveal what the disagreement with Hamma was about.

The words I'd overheard between them returned to me.

'I've been driven out of one place for this. Are you going to drive me out of here as well?'

I swallowed. That couldn't happen. This was Titan. He'd always been there for me, for as long as I could remember. Always on hand to distract or entertain me when Father's duties became too heavy or Mother was unavailable. Always willing to give up his time or effort or energy to help me master my wards.

"Tammie." The word was soft, gentle.

Of course, Father had a much longer relationship with Titan. If anyone could talk him out of this madness, it would be him. And he wouldn't want witnesses when he did.

Slowly, I nodded, taking a reluctant step backwards and following Jenna and Edric across the room to the door out onto the hall that led to the Guard's rooms.

Nate was even slower to move, every step dragging across the floor.

Hamma hadn't moved, still staring at his comrade. Titan turned his head, looking away. Eventually, Hamma turned, walking briskly across to where the rest of us waited. The door swung closed behind him with a dull thunk.

In the silence, all eyes turned to Hamma. I was ready to demand the truth from him, to use any means necessary to get it, but the look on his face made me stop. There was pure shock written across his pale skin and wide eyes. His mouth, though half-hidden behind his wiry beard, was in a thin line.

"What did you do?" Edric snarled, rounding on his fellow Guard member, seemingly uncaring or oblivious to Hamma's surprise. "Enough with the lies—this has gone far enough. What happened between you two?"

Hamma's face hardened, a little colour seeping back into his cheeks. "It's none of your concern."

"To Thorns, it's not!" Edric took a step closer, their faces inches apart. "This affects all of us."

Hamma seemed to grow before my eyes, drawing himself up. Edric, one of the smallest members of the Guard, was several inches shorter than him, and Hamma used that to his advantage now, towering over his subordinate. "It's not my place to tell," he said. "This is his decision."

"And you're the one who—"

"That's enough!" Jenna snapped. "This isn't helping."

Edric took a step backwards, shaking his head in disgust before turning and striding away.

I felt a brief flash of shame. I should have been the one to stop them. In my father's absence, it was my responsibility. They answered to me. But Father wasn't absent. Not really. He was right behind that door, discussing who knew what with Titan. And I was out here. Excluded. Clueless. Helpless.

I took a stumbling step towards the door but held back. Barging in would achieve nothing. But how could I stand here without doing anything? Without knowing anything.

Dropping my gaze, I thought hard. No matter what the outcome of their discussion, they would both have to leave the throne room at some point. Knowing Titan, he wouldn't come out this door, where he knew

Hamma might be waiting. But there were three doors into the throne room. Which of the others would he choose?

Turning on my heel, I strode away, getting faster and faster, until I was running, the corridor lost in the blur on either side of me.

Jenna called something after me, but I didn't hear. Didn't care.

At the end of the corridor, I yanked open the door and barrelled into the main hallway past the throne room. The large doors towered to my left, solid and unyielding and firmly closed. One of the kitchen boys had been walking past and spun around at my sudden entrance. I ignored him, striding over to stand in front of the doors. Waiting. Waiting.

Nate had followed me. We exchanged a glance as he took up a spot beside my right shoulder. His jaw was clenched, eyes tight.

If my father yielded, if Titan managed to convince him, this was where Titan would emerge. He had too much respect for the rituals to do anything else. All I needed was for this door to remain closed.

To my surprise, Hamma had followed us as well. He stood by the wall to the left of the doors, leaning on the stone. In the absence of the earlier vulnerability of his expression, my anger began to coil again.

"You're excused," I said coldly.

He held my gaze. "Think I'll stay."

I didn't look away. I could order him to leave. Something that would take him out into the city, far away, where he wouldn't get to know the outcome of the issue he was responsible for. But I faltered under the steady weight of his eyes. I was the one to turn away.

The doors remained closed.

Nate paced restlessly along the wall. Seen out of the corner of my eye, there was a prowling quality to his movements that did nothing to ease the tension in my chest.

Someone walked past, throwing us a confused glance. I barely registered them. My vision was starting to waver, my head spinning. But I couldn't force myself to move. I couldn't leave. What if...

But the doors remained closed.

With every passing second, a spark of hope burned brighter inside *me. Maybe they had already left together through the side door. Maybe I would see Titan later that day, standing at my father's side, where he belonged.*

Maybe I should have sent someone to watch the other door as well. How long would I stand here, waiting, when the best outcome might have already happened? I wasn't going to ask Nate to leave though. Not from this. Would it be cruel to send Hamma, to potentially force Titan to come face to face with him? Then again, if Father had convinced Titan to stay, maybe it would be the right time for him to also persuade them both to reveal the truth of their disagreement. I looked across to the Captain of the Guard, considering.

The doors opened.

Titan stepped through, his head down as he pulled them closed behind him. He turned to face us.

Blood dripped down his left arm, oozing from a shallow vertical cut along his bicep.

The purple band was gone.

I fell backwards, my hands colliding with the wall as I let out an unintelligible sound.

"No," Nate growled, hands clenched into fists.

Titan looked at us with red-rimmed eyes.

Unbidden tears filled my eyes, spilling down my cheeks as a keening sound ripped through my chest.

"No."

"It's done."

"No!"

"Nate—"

"It's not... You don't get to..."

Titan looked down, having no response to give, and Nate's litany of horror abated.

"I'm sorry, Nate," Titan said, and his voice shook. "But it's done."

Nate shook his head wildly.

Titan closed the gap between them, seemingly fighting more tears of his own. He reached out a hesitant hand, gripping Nate's shoulder.

Nate shrugged off the light touch, launching himself at Titan and throwing his arms around him.

Titan returned the embrace, dropping his head onto Nate's shoulder. A terrible sound rose from the pair as they clung to each other, putting my own keen of grief to shame. It rose to a peak, a caustic groan that cut at my chest, before falling away.

It was the sound of something permanent shattering into pieces.

When Nate had fallen silent, Titan raised his head, whispering something in his ear. I didn't hear what he said and didn't want to. Nate seemed to shudder all over, his grip loosening. His hands dragged down Titan's arms, unwilling to let go, as Titan stepped away and turned to face me.

I had no idea what to say. We stared at each other, not quite eye to eye. He'd told me I would be as tall as him someday.

It seemed we'd both fallen short of the other's expectations.

"It has been a privilege," Titan said seriously, "to know you. To have been able to watch you grow. Don't ever forget yourself."

"I hate you," I forced out the words, my voice cracking.

He gave a shocked chuckle and raised an eyebrow.

I stood my ground, feeling the anger build in my chest, turning me to stone, to ice. But the ice cracked as quickly as it had formed, falling away, leaving nothing but sorrow behind.

"I don't—"

"I know," he cut across me.

"Thank you," I whispered. "For everything."

"I'd do it all again," he promised.

"What now? What are you going to do?"

Titan forced a smile. "It's a big world, Mara. There's plenty of it left to see."

"You're leaving?" The tightness in my chest sharpened, claws of panic digging in. "You'll come back, though? You'll visit?"

His smile faded a little. "We'll see."

I stared at him uncomprehendingly. He held my gaze for a moment, then turned away.

At the sight of Hamma standing stiffly against the wall, he froze. There was a horrible pause when Hamma just kept staring straight ahead. Shoulders dropping, Titan stepped forwards, moving past him.

"Titan," Hamma spoke softly, but in the grief-filled silence, the word carried. Titan paused, looking sideways at his former Captain. "Don't..." Hamma hesitated, trying to find the words. "Don't ever believe this is what I wanted."

Titan looked at him for a moment, then shook his head. "Don't forget who I was. Who I am. All of it."

Hamma nodded, and Titan walked away. His footsteps echoed back, leaving a burning imprint on my soul. He stepped out of the main doors into the gloomy day and was gone.

The space he left behind stretched out, glaring accusingly at me. I should have done something differently, should have said something more.

Surely this had been avoidable.

Unable to bear the sight of his absence, I turned away, back towards Nate.

He was staring down at his right hand. There was blood on his fingers from Titan's wound. As I watched, he wiped it off onto the band around his arm, the red staining the purple.

When I first saw the cabin, I was sure Nate must have brought me to the wrong place. There was no way anyone could be living in a place so dilapidated. The window facing us was missing a pane of glass, and the little section of roof jutting out over the doorway was sagging precariously. Weeds crept up the walls, infecting the wood with veins of green. A water barrel stood beside the cabin. Its rusty pump dripped water steadily, a monotonous plunk-plunk-plunk that matched my heartbeat.

There was a whole network of such cabins scattered through the foothills of the Baerston Mountains, prime territory for beaver and mink trappers. Now that autumn had taken hold, I would have expected them all to be occupied. Though, given the state of this one, it wouldn't be unreasonable for it to be overlooked. We were also relatively close to Alderth. The likelihood of foot traffic would discourage any animals from lingering.

I glanced sideways at Nate. His injuries from his return to the demon realm looked worse than ever in the late afternoon light; the cut on his lip was scabbed and dark, and the bruise around his eye had spread to his temple.

"Are you sure this is the right place?"

"I'm sure," Nate said, though there was a slight frown on his face, eyes tight with worry.

Briefly, I wondered if he had come here before. Was he surprised by the state of the place because it had changed from the last time he saw it or because he hadn't been here before? Four years was a long time. He might have visited. Then again, I hadn't.

Glancing over my shoulder, I scanned the trees behind us for any sign of the Figures but could find none. With them on our side, there had been no further need for caution. Nate and I had pushed ourselves to the limits of our abilities, covering the distance from the plains to the mountains in a single day. The Figures kept up with ease, ghosting out of the trees at regular intervals to report on the path ahead, or advise me on which route to take. Their capacity to simply *appear* beside us unnerved me. I could still barely get my head around the concept that they were here, verbal and intelligent.

Whilst on the move, they weren't so loquacious, but every word they said was enough to make me marvel.

Now though, they were hanging back. Nate and I were alone. Or so it seemed.

The door to the cabin jerked open, catching on the step outside, and a man lurched out.

I drew in a sharp breath, my eyes widening.

Titan had let his hair grow, dark fuzz clinging to his scalp and cheeks, but his face was just as I remembered it. What I did not remember was the stagger in his walk or the bottle in his hand.

I watched in silent shock as he swayed, barely staying upright as he wobbled his way around the back of the cabin and out of sight.

364

Glancing sideways, I found Nate's mouth twisted into a grimace, mirroring my own. He moved first, slipping out from the trees and crossing to the door, still jammed on the stone step. He glanced inside, then turned back to me, shaking his head. Titan was alone.

I pushed my way out from the trees but had barely taken two steps when there was a hoarse shout.

"Whoss there?" Titan's voice was slurred and wavering, all the strength I remembered gone. "I warn you. I'll gutchoo..." There was a pause and then a thud. "... like a fish," he finished weakly, before staggering back into view. He was still holding the bottle, brandishing it like a sword. At the sight of Nate standing in front of the door, he stopped, blinking blearily.

"Well, if tisn't the puppy," he said, stumbling over the words. "Come to howl at me some more, have you? What happened to your face, puppy?"

I took another step forward. "Titan," I began.

He swung around, almost losing his balance. "Oh good, the candle as well. Just a bit burned out." His face went blank, his mouth twisting as his eyes dropped to the floor. "All burned out," he muttered.

I edged closer, but his head snapped up as he staggered back a step.

"No," he growled. "Just leave me alone!" The bottle flew from his hand as he gesticulated, smashing against the ground a few feet away from me, spraying clear liquid over the dirt. Titan stared at the broken glass with empty eyes. "Look what you made me do," he said, his voice oddly childlike. He turned and lurched back into the cabin, Nate jumping out of his way, and slammed the door behind him.

"Well, that could have gone better," Nate said.

I stared at the shards of glass, sparkling with the sharpness of its broken edges. "He's been drinking," I said blankly. I'd never known Titan to drink. It was forbidden to the Guard whenever they were on duty anyway, but even outside of that, Titan had rarely partaken. Certainly not to this extent.

Nate sighed. "Excellent." Turning, he pulled the door open, peering inside. "He's asleep," he announced with disgust. "Or unconscious. What was he thinking?"

I shook my head. "He must have thought we were dead. You, me, Father, the Guard. And this is how he chose to cope."

"This isn't coping."

"I know." I sighed. "So what now?"

We woke Titan with half a bucket of cold water thrown over him. He coughed and choked, flailing around wildly. I jumped backwards, out of reach. Eventually, he sat up, wiping off his face and squinting up at us.

He flopped back onto the now-wet bed, one arm thrown over his eyes, with a groan that hitched, turning wheezy. Concerned, I took half a step forward before I realised he was laughing, a breathy giggle that didn't sound like him at all.

"We're *all* wet now," he gasped out, between the giggles, rolling onto his side.

I threw up my hands, turning away. "This is useless," I snapped. "How are we meant to talk to him like this?" I'd hoped the rude awakening would help. Clearly not.

I looked towards the doorway. Only one of the Figures had come inside, now standing like a silent sentinel beside the door.

"How long will it take him to sober up?" I asked them.

In lieu of a response, it moved forwards, stepping past me and Nate to approach the man still floundering on the bed, now humming idly to himself.

With snake-like speed, the Figure lashed out, grabbing Titan's arm and pinning it to the bed.

"Huh?" Titan raised his head bemusedly.

The Figure made a swiping motion with its free hand over Titan's retrained arm. A cut opened under its touch, blood welling red and viscous from the wound.

"Hey! Ow!" Titan's weak protests were ignored.

The Figure slapped its hand over the cut and went still.

366

Titan lapsed into silence as well, his eyes drifted closed, face spasming in pain.

It was over in seconds. The Figure straightened up, stepping backwards. Titan groaned, but it was a lucid sound.

"Fuck," he swore, eyes opening. He glared up at the retreating Figure. "That hurt, you bastard."

The Figure made no response, and Titan's eyes swung over me and Nate. He sat up, eyeing us for a moment, wary but sober.

"You're really here?"

"Yep," I confirmed and threw the rest of the bucket of water at him.

Titan turned his head to the side and spat before looking back at me. "Thanks," he said sourly.

"Awake now?" I asked.

"Getting there," he said, wiping the residual moisture from his face. "You're not dead."

"No. I'm not."

We looked at each other for a long moment.

He looked away first, pushing to his feet and walking across the small room. "What are you doing here?"

I raised an eyebrow and glanced sideways. Nate hefted the second bucket.

"If you throw more water over me, I'll kill you," Titan said without looking back, and Nate hesitated.

"With what?" he challenged. "You seem to have lost your sword."

"I lost everything," Titan said, so quietly that I almost missed it, before raising his voice. "I don't need a sword to take you apart, Nathaniel, in case you'd forgotten."

"Once, perhaps," Nate allowed. "You're not the man I remember."

"No," Titan agreed, "I'm not." He sank into a chair beside the small table, pulling another bottle towards him.

I strode forwards, taking it from his hand. In one sharp movement, I smashed it on the corner of the table. Titan whined, dropping his face into his hands.

"What are you doing?" I growled.

"I was hoping to keep drinking. What are you doing?"

"Not going to happen," I said. "I need you."

I slapped my hand onto the table in front of him. Pinned beneath my fingers was a strip of purple cloth. I didn't know where the Figures had got it and didn't much care. I'd asked, and they'd delivered.

Titan looked at the scrap of material, then reached out and pushed it away. "You don't need me."

"Wake up!" I growled, frustrated. "Do you even know what's happening?"

"Rygorn is dead. The Guard is dead, present company excluded," he rattled off dryly. "Djet is on the throne, doing no one knows what. You and puppy are here to fight the good fight and restore balance to the world. With some added support, apparently." He gestured at the Figure, now back in their spot by the door. "Trust me, they're all the backup you'll need. Just get on with it."

"I don't want them," I said shortly. "I want you."

"Then you're an idiot."

"Really? I asked. I swung an arm.

His hand came up faster than I could track, catching my wrist before I could connect.

"Even half-drunk, you're still faster than me," I said. "There's no one I'd rather have at my back."

"Not drunk anymore," Titan muttered, dropping my arm and glaring towards the door.

"So, is that your plan? Just sit here, in the middle of nowhere, and drink yourself into oblivion?"

"Pretty much, yeah."

"What happened to you?" I asked, disgusted.

"Nothing!" Titan roared, slamming his hands onto the table, and I finally saw the man he used to be. "I sat here while everyone else was off dying without me!"

"And are you going to let it happen all over again?"

He raised tortured eyes to meet mine.

With a sigh, I slid into the seat opposite him, leaving the strip of purple cloth between us. "You protected my father for years, and you were good at it. Then you retired." I pulled a face. "I'm not going to get into that now. The point is, you did your part, and it's not fair for me to ask you to come back, but I am because *I need you*. I can't just walk away. So, please. I'm asking you to come with me. Or would you rather stay here?"

Titan looked away. I knew I'd hit him where it hurt, but I didn't take the words back. He was a fighter, down to his bones. Being out here while others had fought and lost their lives... he might as well have died himself.

Slowly, he reached out and pushed the fabric back towards me. "Keep that," he said. "You'll want to give it to someone else later."

"I want you to take it now," I said bluntly. "You can think of it as temporary if you want to."

His fingers closed on the purple cord.

I stood up. "We leave before dark." I walked out without a backwards glance.

The sun had sunk low when Titan emerged from the cabin, Nate and I both turning at the sound of the door shutting. He'd shaved, returning to the bald look I remembered, and his sword was once more hanging at his hip. I hadn't seen it inside the cabin. Where he'd hidden it, I wasn't sure, but I didn't plan on asking. He had kept it, and that was what mattered. He walked up to me without meeting my gaze and dropped to his knees.

"My Queen," he said, and I heard everything in those two words. There was still a conversation that needed to be had about his drinking, but I was willing to put it off for now.

Reaching down, I pulled the fabric from his fingers, tying it around his proffered arm, right over the scar where my father had cut his previous one off. Without saying a word, I pulled him to his feet. He met my gaze, and I nodded once before turning and walking away, hearing the two members of my Guard fall into place behind me.

"So…" Nate said. "Since when do you call me 'puppy'?"

Everything was quiet, the only sound that of the whispers of a distant wind. I stood alone, looking down from the ridge to where the distant lights of my city twinkled and danced between tree branches. Behind me, Nate and Titan were sleeping, as I should have been. The First Guard roamed unseen through the trees around us, guarding us while we slept. Some of them had slipped away into the valley, checking the path ahead and the situation inside the city. There seemed to be no need for them to report back. It was as if they all knew what the others were seeing instantly. Another thing to add to the list of things I didn't understand about them.

I had laid down with the other two as darkness fell, but my mind refused to switch off. Random thoughts coiled around my brain, from reviewing the layout of the city and the best route to take to the citadel, to all the things I would need to do if we got through the next day victorious. Number one would be to send out messengers. If Djet had left my people to their own devices, no doubt our trade agreements would have suffered similar neglect. There would be a lot of amends to make. Hopefully, I would also be able to spare a messenger to go back to Warren as well.

"You should sleep," a metallic voice said, its grey-skinned owner gliding up to me.

I shook my head. "Can't."

For a moment, we were both silent, looking out over the valley. "You should let us come with you."

I closed my eyes briefly, too tired to face that argument again. Nate, Titan, and the First Guard had all joined forces earlier that evening, trying to persuade me against my course. It wasn't until I'd pulled rank and reminded them, rather forcibly, which one of us was trying for the throne that they had lapsed into unhappy silence. I'd expected further arguments tomorrow but hadn't anticipated it tonight.

"No," I said flatly. "I've already agreed some of you can come if you stay out of sight, but that's as far as I'm willing to go."

The First Guard turned their head away without responding. I hadn't told them that I'd received an almost identical offer from the demons, or about my truce with them. I hadn't told Titan either.

"How's it looking down there?" I asked eventually, nodding into the valley in an attempt to change the subject.

"Quiet."

I bit back a sigh. "Wake us if anything changes," I instructed, then turned and walked back to where the other two lay on the ground. Looking across, I found Nate's eyes open, watching me. I rolled over, putting my back to him, and tried once again to go to sleep. It was a long time coming.

23

Home

*We ran in silence. Once, there would have been jokes, laughter,
teasing comments. Not anymore. The source of our merriment was
gone.*

*Father led the way, setting a brisk pace as we turned off the Eastern
Road, pushing through low branches and bracken. He was flanked by
Edric and Hamma. I turned my eyes away from the bushy ginger hair.*

*I wasn't the only one who could no longer look at Hamma. The
dissension amongst the Guard was tangible. Hamma refused to talk
about the argument between himself and Titan. Even Father wouldn't
talk of it, though I was convinced Titan must have told him before he
had left. There was no way Father would have let him go without
knowing the reason. But he wouldn't even speak of the former
Guardsman.*

*A branch whipped me across the face and I flinched, swatting at it
too late. No one said a word.*

*Nate kept pace on my right and the other one, the new one, was on
my left. I couldn't look at him either. I hadn't attended his initiation,
though Father had invited me. The thought of standing there and
listening to them speak of Titan's service, of hearing Hamma say that
he would be remembered, was too much for me to bear. Instead, I'd
shut myself in my room and drawn upon my wards until I was sure
my skin would blister from the heat and I could pretend my tears were
from the pain.*

Rian was young, with a slim face that drew down to a pointed chin and long, pale blond hair that was constantly escaping its tie and wisping around his head. He was stoic and serious.

He was everything Titan was not.

I hated him for it.

I made all the right faces and noises. I smiled and welcomed him to the Guard, listened intently on the rare occasion he chose to speak, and pretended that every word didn't make me want to scream. The silences were even worse.

Ahead, Father slowed to a walk. I blinked as we followed suit, seeing brighter light ahead. I didn't recall any other roads or dwellings out here. It must simply be a natural clearing.

But when we stepped out into the sunlight, the space was anything but natural.

Father kept going, picking his way over the debris, but I remained frozen, staring.

The destruction was absolute. Entire trees had been ripped up by the roots, leaving huge depressions in the earth. The trunks were shattered, branches stripped and left scattered on the ground. And lying among them... other things.

Limbs, twisted beyond recognition. Stubby-ended hands, every finger ripped off, tattered skin left as a testament to the deed. Broken bones pierced through skin, the white gleaming in the sunlight against black blood. A torso was propped against the remains of a tree trunk, attached to neither legs nor head.

Silent, I moved forwards, torn between a desire to close my eyes and the total inability to look away from the horror. My foot scuffed over something on the ground and it rolled away from me. A finger, this one cleanly severed.

Shuddering, I moved on, eyes now fixed firmly on my feet. Behind me, I heard Nate and Rian following with equal care.

Only when I found the ground in front of me clear did I look up. I recoiled instantly.

Here was the head of the torso I'd seen earlier. And the heads of every other body strewn in pieces around me. They sat upright on the ground, all facing east in a neat line. Unlike the rest of the bodies, they were pristine, untouched. Every pair of black eyes was wide open. Demons. They were all demons.

I glanced back at the killing ground I'd just crossed. The wounds jumped out at me again. Black blood was everywhere. How had I not noticed it?

Swallowing, I looked forwards again, and my breath caught in my throat.

One of the Figures strode across the open space. One of its silver-grey hands was clenched in the hair of another decapitated head. Blood still dripped from its neck. The Figure placed it down in line with its fellows, rotating it until it aligned with the others. Then it turned away, its white, staring eyes passing straight over me, and headed back in the same direction it had come from.

"Enough."

The word made me flinch. Father was standing to my right, his face impassive as he looked around. One of the Figures was already beside him. As I watched, another emerged from behind them, moving to stand beside its companion. The one who had just brought another head to the line had turned on its heel, converging on them as well. In seconds, six of them stood there, identical glowing white eyes staring vacantly ahead.

Only six of them, to have done all of this. I wondered where the other six were.

Swallowing again, I moved slowly around the line of heads. From behind them, Father didn't have to see their wide black eyes, their slack expressions. But I looked. These were the creatures who had killed my mother.

I turned slowly, surveying the carnage once more, and didn't know what to feel. My eyes fell on the Figures and I halted.

Hamma's words from before Father had woken them came back to me.

They have no concept of restraint.

I now understood what he'd meant.

"I think it's time," Hamma was saying, his arms crossed as he stood beside my father. "This is too much."

Father's eyes swept the unnatural clearing, meeting mine and lingering. He nodded slowly, the movement stiff. "Yes, I suppose."

Something moved behind me.

I spun, my hands jumping to the twin blades that I was now never without. Nate, already beside me, had also reached for his weapon. He took a couple of steps towards the noise, then went still.

Curious, but sure he would have reacted if it was a threat, I strode over to him, following his gaze.

A pair of black eyes blinked back at me, wide with terror. She was young, with long dark hair splayed out around her. She was missing an arm, as well as the lower half of both her legs, but her other hand still stretched imploringly out towards us.

"Kill me." The words were a whisper, barely audible, hoarse and twisted with pain.

I stood an instinctive step backwards, glancing at Nate as I did.

His expression was dark. That was the only expression he wore now, brow lowered in a perpetual scowl. Titan might have been the one who had left, but he wasn't the only one I'd lost.

"Kill me," the demon pleaded again.

I was still backing away, my face hardening now the shock of seeing her alive had passed. Why should she deserve mercy? Just as the thought formed in my mind, Nate drew his sword and, in one swift movement, drove it through the demon's chest.

She shuddered, then went limp as Nate withdrew his blade. Without saying a word, he turned back towards me, that glower still on his face. He didn't meet my gaze.

I turned back towards Father, who was watching. He made no comment, merely turning to the Figures.

"Go home," he ordered.

They turned away at once, disappearing through the trees.

"Let's go," Father said to the rest of us.

I hesitated as the others moved away, looking out once more over the *bloodshed and butchery.*

When we'd rounded a corner to find a Figure standing in the middle of the road, my initial reaction had been shock, perhaps tinged with fear. Father had ordered us all to wait while he approached the lone creature, walking past it along the road. The Figure turned and followed him briefly, both of them stopping, facing away from us. I'd frowned at their backs, wondering what was going on. When Father returned with news that there had been demons in the area and told me to continue on home, I had refused. I'd wanted to know what had happened, to see what had gone on, to understand what the Figures were doing out here. Now I did.

As I turned away and began to follow the others home, I fervently wished I hadn't insisted on accompanying them off the road.

I opened my eyes to the grey of dawn and the sound of voices. If they had been any others, I would have leapt to my feet immediately, fearful of an attack. Not with these voices. They were as familiar to me as my own.

"—didn't think it would go quite like that," Titan was saying, to smothered laughter from Nate. "So there I am, *dripping* wet, and this beaver is just sat there staring at me, with the *smuggest* expression on its face."

"Did you get it?"

"Are you kidding? I couldn't feel my toes! I was coming home! Besides, I think that one deserved to get away."

Nate continued to chuckle, the sound fading into a soft silence. "I'm glad you're here," he said after a few moments.

"Missed me that much, huh?"

Nate snorted. "Oh no, not at all." Another moment of silence. "Things were different after you left."

Titan didn't respond.

"Why did you go?"

I froze, my ears straining. I hadn't brought up the subject again and hadn't expected Nate to either. But now he had... I found myself shaking with the effort to remain immobile. I wanted to turn over so I could see their expressions. More than that, I wanted to jump up and shake the answer out of Titan myself.

"It doesn't matter."

"Ty…"

"Leave it, Nate," Titan said, a bite in his voice now.

This time, the silence was heavy. Full of bitterness and empty of truth.

"Besides," Titan continued, though the levity in his tone was forced, "you had Mara."

Leaves crinkled as someone shifted.

"Ut-oh. What's that face for?"

"What face?" Nate said quickly.

My heart stuttered, eyes sliding closed as I listened harder.

"That one," Titan said, deadpanned. "Come on, what's on your mind?"

"What, 'cos you're always so honest with me?"

"Nathaniel. Spit it out."

"It's just… she changed too. Or maybe I just noticed it more."

"Noticed what?"

"She's… cold. When I told her about her father, she barely even blinked. Five seconds later, it was as if it was nothing. Just an inconvenience."

There was an icy sensation slipping down into my chest. I *had* blinked. I had nearly fallen apart. Surely he'd seen that. Hadn't he?

"If she doesn't feel anything, is that the sort of person we want in power?"

"Do you really think that?" Titan snorted. "She feels. She just does it deeper than you, Nate. Think about how she was brought up. Everyone always watching her. Is it any wonder she learned to hide it?"

"That's not what I meant. It's like… how do we know she's hiding emotions, not putting them on? Is she faking the control, or is she faking the feelings?"

It was true that I kept a tight hold on my expression most of the time, but I had always thought he was able to see through it. Or so I'd thought.

I'd heard enough. Making as much noise as possible, I pushed to my feet.

They were facing away from me, sat side by side in identical poses, arms resting on their knees. Titan had turned at my movement, but Nate remained staring forwards.

"We should get going," I said. "Nate, go find the First Guard."

He obeyed at once, rolling forwards to his feet and heading off into the trees without looking back. Titan stood up more slowly, coming back towards me. I avoided his gaze.

"He doesn't mean it," he offered. "He's just worried."

"How nice for him," I snapped. "But it's not my fault he has no self-control."

"He's scared. He doesn't want to lose you."

I nearly gave another sharp retort but stopped myself before I could. "Let's just go," I said, turning away and moving to pack up my things. Titan said nothing more.

"Mara, this is madness."

I gritted my teeth. Titan's silence hadn't lasted long. Now, looking out across my city, his endless advice to delay was wearing my patience thin. Wood and thatch and flashes of dark stone, my home was close enough to touch. From our vantage point at the edge of the trees, just about the outermost fields, I could make out people moving around below us, tending to crops and herds.

"There's no other way, Titan," I said. "I'm going to have to face him. It's inevitable."

"You've heard what the First Guard have been saying. He's not normal. Taking on three challengers at once? No one is that lucky."

"Maybe he was just better than they were."

"And you think you're better than that? Better than him?"

I pressed my lips together and said nothing. My time at Leydford had been wonderful for my ego, but it was not an accurate comparison. I was a good fighter; I'd been trained by the best. But

378

there were plenty of others who could match or beat me.

"Isn't it worth looking into it?" Titan pleaded. "Just in case there is something, some advantage he has, that we can mitigate?"

"People are going missing, Titan. *Children*. We don't have time for that."

"We can do *something*. Talk to some people. Maybe someone already knows something about him."

"And if we talk to the wrong person, Djet will know I'm coming. He's going to have allies and supporters. None of us can walk down there without being recognised. What if his 'advantage' is something he needs to prepare? What if catching him off guard could be what I need?"

"And you're willing to take that risk?"

I turned, finding Nate behind me. "What do you think?"

He met my gaze. Titan was right about him; I could read every emotion flickering across his face. Surprise at my addressing him, a hint of guilt about what he'd said this morning, the stubbornness that he wouldn't take it back, but neither would he abandon me. Then it cleared, leaving nothing but loyalty, simple and pure. He looked away, following my earlier gaze towards the city.

"I think Titan's right," he said eventually. "We don't know enough about Djet, but everything we *do* know makes me think it's a bad idea to go at him blind. We don't have to wait around for days, but surely we can afford to look into it a little."

Watching his face, I was surprised to find I felt no betrayal at his verdict against me. Instead, it seemed to calm something inside my chest.

"Okay," I nodded.

I looked left to where one of the First Guard was standing silently. There was no casualness to the pose. They never slouched, shifted their weight, or crossed their arms. They just stood, straight and immobile, as if carved from metal.

"Is there a way to get in without being seen?" I asked.

White eyes turned to look at me. "We can. You three… probably not."

Gritting my teeth again, I turned back to stare down into the city.

"That's how it's meant to be," they pointed out.

"Who is there that we can talk to?" Nate asked. "Most people have been avoiding Djet, right? And he's been avoiding them."

The First Guard nodded.

"We might be able to bring you one of his supporters, but it would be risky."

I remembered the young demon, the way he had screamed as I'd dragged him closer to the wall.

"No. Not unless there's no other option," I said. "Someone must have been paying attention, watching Djet. What about the ones you were talking about earlier? The soldiers who had been trying to organise searches."

"Possible," the First Guard allowed. "But there's no guarantee, and if we choose the wrong one, they might be a spy for Djet."

I sighed, tapping my fingers on my arm, thinking. "How much were you aware of?" I asked them. "When my father was ruling."

Their face twitched, the metallic skin above one eye quirking up. Without an eyebrow there, it was a strange thing to watch. "Most things. You were listening to the part about how we weren't actually asleep, right?"

Behind me, Nate made an unhappy noise in his throat. "I still can't believe you didn't tell me about them," he muttered to Titan.

"Thinking that just proves you weren't ready to be told. They're not just any old secret." He stepped closer, addressing me now. "Why does that matter anyway?"

"Jenna," I said simply.

Titan hummed speculatively, but the First Guard was shaking their head.

"Not a good idea. She approached Djet almost as soon as he Claimed the throne, offering her services. He turned her down, but they might have a more private arrangement."

"I don't believe that," I said. "She was too loyal to Father. She might just have gone to Djet as a ploy, an attempt to get more information. Did she know about you?"

380

The First Guard quirked their non-existent eyebrow once more. "Does the concept of a secret mean nothing to you?"

"She's our best chance," I declared. "Even if she doesn't know anything herself, she will be able to tell us who is the best alternative to speak to."

"That still doesn't help us get to her," Titan pointed out.

I turned to Nate. "Do you know any other ways in? Ways people might not know are there, or might not be watched?"

"Plenty, but I doubt any of us could fit through them anymore. And I don't know how we would get close enough to use them anyway."

I grimaced. So much for that idea. "You said you could get into the city," I turned back to the First Guard.

"We already are," they said, giving that disconcerting smile again.

"Could you pass a message to Jenna and get her to meet us outside the city?"

The smile faded. "We don't talk to people. It's better if we're not seen at all."

"What about a note?" I asked, then frowned, diverted by a sudden thought. There had been a note. When Father was away, hunting the demons with the First Guard... a note had been left in my room. Had it been them who delivered it?

"Jenna wouldn't believe it," Titan said, shaking his head. "She'd think it had been left by Djet or one of his people as a trap. It would be too risky for her to act on it."

"Then we have to go in." I looked around at them all. "There's no other option."

"We'll be seen," Nate warned.

"So give me another suggestion!"

"Jenna is living on the outskirts of the city," the First Guard said. "We might be able to get one of you to her without being seen. But it could only be one of you. And it might not work anyway."

"Alright then," Titan said, finally uncrossing his arms. "I'll go in with them, find Jenna, and arrange for her to meet us out here."

Nate began, "It would be better if I—"

"No," I cut him off. "It has to be me."

"No way."

"Absolutely not."

Nate and Titan spoke together, their voices intermingling.

"That's too risky," Titan said. "If you're caught, that's it. It's over. If I'm seen, it would be unusual, but if word gets to Djet that either of you are in the city…"

"If you go, it doubles the chances of something going wrong. You have to get in, and out, and then Jenna has to sneak out without being followed, and then she would have to get back in as well. I go in, I talk to her, find out what she knows about Djet, then I get out. Simple."

Titan shook his head at me. "You still have to get in and out. Same amount of risk, with a much higher stake. It doesn't make sense."

"I'm going," I said. "That's final."

Two jaws clenched, two pairs of eyes glaring at me, but I glared right back and neither of them argued any further.

With the decision made, all that was left to do was wait. The First Guard had nodded and declared they would be ready soon before turning away. I stood at the edge of the trees, arms crossed, my fingers tapping out a busy rhythm.

Another of the First Guard joined us, standing beside their companion. Their utter stillness was unnerving. Glancing over at them, I found myself believing at last that they had never really slept at all.

Nate stepped up beside me, blocking my view of the silent, grey-skinned beings, his dark eyes tight as he surveyed the valley below.

"We should come a little closer with you," he said.

"What would be the point? If anything happens, they'll get me out."

He said nothing.

"Unless you doubt their competency?"

The sarcastic question worked, and he snorted.

382

"It just… it doesn't feel right. You going in alone."

He's scared. He doesn't want to lose you.

I glanced sideways. Was this what Titan had meant? Was he afraid of what might happen to me? Or was he afraid of what I, in all my apparent heartlessness, might do?

But it was too late to try and work out which, or even to persuade him one way or the other. The First Guard had broken their ranks, which had swelled whilst I was talking to Nate. Three of the four stepped forwards, all looking at me in the same instant.

"We're ready," one said.

Taking a breath, I nodded, stepping towards them, away from Nate. "I'll see you when I get back," I said as Titan moved up beside the younger man, offering them both a smile before turning away and following the First Guard down the slope. I was going home at last.

The journey down to the city was the strangest hour of my life. I gave myself over entirely to the First Guard until I felt I ceased to exist. My steps echoed theirs, following precisely in the prints of the one in front. Two others remained on either side of me, directing me this way or that, reacting to things their absent companions could see.

In the fields, it was a simple matter to avoid contact with other people. We skirted around buildings or hunched in ditches, sometimes only momentarily, sometimes for many long minutes, until my legs cramped and my back ached.

As the fields began to butt up against the poorest houses, one of them slipped away. The remaining two pressed in closer around me, so close I could feel the chill of their skin behind me as we crept through tiny alleys, sometimes even taking to the rooftops, scuttling insect-like across the uneven canopy. People were more abundant here and in much closer proximity. My shoulders were tight with tension, waiting for one of them to look our way. Yet they never did. The First Guard seemed omniscient, always choosing the deserted passages, hesitating just long enough for heads to turn in another direction before darting out.

At one point, we sheltered in a shadowed ingress for several long minutes. The main thoroughfare was only feet away, and I couldn't see how we would be able to cross it unseen. I opened my mouth to ask if we should try another way when there was a loud bang from the side. Like everyone else within sight, I looked around, realising too late that the First Guard had taken advantage of the distraction to move. They were already halfway across the street before I became aware of their movement. With a burst of warmth from my speed ward, I raced after them but already knew I would be too late. Heads were already turning back towards me, and I wasn't even halfway across the open street.

Something cold and sharp grabbed my arms, yanking me forwards. My feet left the ground, and I was suddenly inside the alley on the other side of the street. I stumbled at the sudden halt, looking back. The First Guard stepped back, but I could still feel the residual chill of its hands on my skin.

Shoving down a wave of distaste, I forced myself to nod in silent thanks. They made no acknowledgement, merely jerked their chin forwards, after their companion. With a shaky breath, I continued on.

I'd expected the wall to be our major obstacle, but when we arrived at the northern gate, having circled further around the city than I'd expected, it appeared deserted. No one stood atop the gate to watch the road, and no one challenged us as we passed underneath it. I looked at the First Guard, about to question where the soldiers were, but they shook their head, pressing a finger to their grey lips, and gestured me onwards quickly.

Pursing my lips, I followed them onto a narrower street, pausing in a doorway whilst a pair of women passed. At the other end, we crossed diagonally between some buildings and entered another back street. Only a few steps along it, the First Guard came to a halt, turning back to face me. I tilted my head quizzically at them, and they pointed silently to the window just above our heads. Looking up, my jaw clenched. So this was it.

384

The shutters were open, but I couldn't hear anything from inside. Nodding to the First Guard, I crouched down, then jumped.

My hands grabbed onto the window ledge and I hung for a moment, waiting for any response from inside. There was no movement from inside. The top of my left shoulder, where Zouri had stabbed me, stung at the strain, but it was a bearable pain. I was reminded irresistibly of the last time I'd hung by my fingertips, when I'd been breaking into the palace at Leydford to talk to Holt. Unfortunately, the window above me was somewhat narrower than I'd expected. This manoeuvre would take more finesse. Setting my toes against the rough stone making up the foundations, I walked them up the wall, my knees sliding between my elbows. When my feet were high enough, I braced myself and straightened my legs, pushing up and out until a sliver of the room beyond became visible.

I could see a closed door and the edge of a table, but nothing else. It appeared to be empty. Shifting my hands to grip the inside of the window, I hoisted myself up, locking my elbows. There wasn't enough room to get my feet up to the window as well, so I simply let myself tilt forwards, slithering inelegantly onto the floor inside.

Picking myself up, I looked around properly. The room was of a moderate size, several paces across in both dimensions. The stone walls were caulked with a pale resin, giving a bright, smooth finish, unbroken by any hangings. A wooden table sat against the wall to my right, its surface bare. It was big enough for four, but only two stools sat on either side of it, one of them pushed up against the wall, out of the way. In the opposite wall sat an open fireplace, kindling already stacked inside, a neat pile of logs beside it. Two doors stood on either side of the fireplace, one of them ajar. Behind it, I could hear movement. Someone was humming as they shifted heavy objects, scraping loudly across the floor.

Straightening up from my crouch, I angled my head towards the door, listening. If it wasn't Jenna… if the First Guard had got the wrong house, or if this was a trap…

The scraping sounds stopped, silence falling. Someone sighed.

My hands crept to my blades.

The door opened and someone stepped through.

Soft hazel eyes met my darker brown ones, both equally startled.

Jenna looked much as I remembered her, a hand or so shorter than me but with thick, light brown hair that added to her height. It was currently tangled and messy, sticking out around her pale face. Dark circles highlighted her eyes as we stared at each other.

"Tamara?" she asked, her voice a hoarse whisper.

I nodded. "Hello, Jenna."

She remained petrified for another second, then finally broke from her trance, taking a step forward and dropping to her knees, her head tilted so far back I thought her neck would break.

"My Queen," she murmured.

"Rise," I said, blinking back the prickling in my eyes, indicative of the rising emotion in my chest.

She did, her eyes searching over my face. "You're here." Her face split into a sudden grin. "I *knew* you weren't dead."

As if you'd die without coming back to haunt me.

I smiled, both at her declaration of faith and the memory of Nate's echoing words.

"No," I agreed, sobering. "But I need your help."

"Anything."

"I need you to tell me everything you know about Djet."

She nodded slowly, drifting over to the table. I shadowed her. Sitting on one of the stools, I rested my elbows on the edge of the table, hands clasped together.

"I will tell you everything I remember and have been able to find out," she began warningly, "but I haven't been able to access my notes from that time, so I might be wrong on some details."

"Your notes?" I frowned, leaning forwards. "Notes from what? Have you encountered him before?"

"Yes," she said. "A few weeks after your mother's death, he was arrested."

My head jerked up, a million questions flooding my mouth.

386

"What for?" The most important one burst out first.

"He tried to break into the Warding House."

"He did *what*? Why?"

Jenna took a deep breath. "Perhaps I should start at the beginning," she said, waiting for my nod before continuing. "A few years before his arrest, Djet was delivering a crate of ore to the blacksmiths. Their apprentices were busy, so he took it into the workshop himself and stepped the wrong way as one of the smiths turned around with a hot poker."

I winced.

"His speed ward was destroyed. Just an accident, but…" her voice trailed off.

I stared down at the table, my fingers clenched, knuckles white. I knew that pain, and the utter devastation that followed it.

"Afterwards, he went to work in the public records hall," Jenna continued. "Kept to himself, wore long sleeves to hide his ward. He also visited the Warders. I spoke to Master Atticus. Apparently, Djet begged him to replace the broken ward. But of course, he was too old, so Atticus refused."

To wear long sleeves was unusual here, rare, even, but with a broken ward, I could understand why Djet had chosen to do so.

"So Djet tried to break into the Warding House to steal the designs," I said slowly. It made sense, in a desperate sort of way. The Warders possessed the only physical copies of the wards. It would be near enough impossible to recreate them without a guide, and if Djet's original ward had been burned, he wouldn't be able to use that one as a reference.

"He was caught before he could get inside though, and brought before your father for sentencing. Rygorn was… Well, this was right after Titan quit the Guard, so he wasn't especially patient."

I winced again, remembering how we'd all had short fuses after that incident.

"I don't remember exactly what happened, but Rygorn sentenced Djet to two years imprisonment. Djet was rather distraught, didn't go quietly, shouting all sorts of things. Rygorn told him that if he tried anything like that again, he would personally break all the wards Djet had left."

"He didn't," I gasped.

Jenna shrugged apologetically. "Like I said… Titan…"

"Yeah, I know." I dropped my face into my hands. Even as emotionally unstable as he had been then, I wouldn't have expected Father to say something quite that cruel. "So after the two years, what did Djet do?"

"Nothing much that I've been able to find out. Went back to working in the records hall. He quit though, about a year ago. I have no idea what he has been doing since then, and no one else seems to know either. He didn't seem to have any particular friends, so either his supporters now are only following him because he's Claimed the throne, or they knew him more recently."

"How did it happen? The Claiming?"

"It… well. I suppose it didn't, really. That night…" Jenna shot me a cautious look.

I nodded, waving her on. I didn't want to think about my father's death right now.

"Well, we knew something was wrong when Rygorn and the Guard hadn't returned after dark. We organised a search, went out after them. I went with them, so I wasn't there, but… Djet walked in before we'd even found the bodies, sat on the throne, and declared himself King."

I stared at her. "He already knew." The words hovered, halfway between question and statement.

Jenna nodded. "I don't know how."

Nor did I. Or maybe I just didn't want to.

Djet might have discovered the bodies first and made use of the opportunity. But the chances of that were minimal.

The alternative, however, sent a chill through me.

Had Djet known about the attack *before* it took place? Even worse, could he have been a part of it or have assisted Zouri in some way? Had my father's threat to him been severe enough for that?

"Of course, there were other people still in the throne room," Jenna continued. "Some of them objected, either with official challenges or... less formal means." She shot me another wary glance. "Their bodies were dumped on the steps. Six of them."

"Six? All at once?"

Jenna nodded grimly. I looked away, across the sparse room. The First Guard had said it was only three. One man against *six*, all of whom would have had their wards. And to oust a pretender, as Djet would have undeniably been at that time, without confirmation of my father's death...

As Jenna had said, they wouldn't have been formal about it. But they were dead, and Djet lived.

"How?" The word slipped out unintentionally. My mind was still inside the throne room, watching the fight through a concealing fog, the details blurred.

Blood spilt in that room again. And not by demons this time.

But if Djet didn't have a speed ward, how could he possibly have defeated them?

Jenna hadn't responded to my question, and I looked back at her.

"I..." She avoided my gaze, pulling her hands back off the table. I could see the movement of her arms as they twisted together out of sight. "I'm not sure about this," she said warningly.

"Tell me."

"I went to him. The morning after. To offer my services. I didn't mean it," she added quickly. "I was just trying to find out more about him."

"And?" I prompted, leaning closer.

"He'd been injured in the fight, and his sleeve was ripped. And I saw... I mean, I think there was..."

I said nothing, waiting.

"He has more wards." The words escaped Jenna in a tumbling rush.

It was no effort to make my face blank now. It felt frozen, stuck in impassivity.

"I'm not certain, they weren't clear. They're not tattoos. It was like… like he'd cut them into his arms. Scars. Lots of them."

The silence stretched on. I needed to say something. But the words didn't come. Djet must have found another record of the wards. And to get them accurate enough, by carving them into skin… the thought made me nauseous.

What was I meant to say? What was I going to *do*? Djet had extra wards. He'd recouped his loss, whilst I still had one less than I should have. How could I stand against him?

I managed to pull in a ragged breath. I wasn't alone. Maybe the First Guard would know how I could counter the inequality. Their bodies were covered with wards; if anyone knew the mechanics of them, surely they would.

"I see," I said eventually.

"I might be wrong," Jenna said hastily. "But I've been asking… he still wears long sleeves. No one has seen him with his arms bare."

"I understand." Silence fell again, pressing down upon my chest, filling my lungs until I couldn't breathe, until I was choking, suffocating, *dying*… "What else?" I asked, forcing the words out before the terror could overwhelm me. "What about the children?"

Jenna blinked. "Right. Yes. Twenty-one missing as of this morning. Plus three adults as well."

Twenty-one. I swallowed. Less than the number of steps it would take to walk from one end of the throne room to the other. Not a big number, really. But when I pictured them… Twenty-one tiny faces. Twenty-one worried families.

"What do we know about them? Is there any pattern to the disappearances?"

Jenna shook her head. "Not that we've been able to find. Some are from the farms, some from the slums, some from inside the city. Ages from nine to fourteen. Only two had begun to get their wards."

I frowned. Had the perpetrator misjudged their ages? Were they deliberately targeting those who hadn't received their wards yet?

"What about the Unmarked?" I asked. "Have any of their

390

children gone missing?"

Jenna frowned at the mention of the community further south. "I don't know."

The Unmarked lived on the shores of the lake. Technically, they were under our rule, but they had been managing themselves for years now. Even if they had problems, they wouldn't bring them to the city. People here held a deep suspicion of those who rejected the wards, and the feeling was mutual.

I remembered Madina's demand that we give up our wards, and suddenly the rarity of demon attacks upon the Unmarked made sense.

"What's been done to find them?" I asked.

"Nothing, as far as Djet is concerned," Jenna grimaced. "Some of the soldiers have been trying to organise searches, but as soon as they do, they turn up dead as well. There's one who has been having some success. He's doing it quietly though. We've been letting people make their own investigations and then report back to him. He collates the information, lets people know what has been done, what still needs looking into." She looked up suddenly. "You should meet with him. He might know more."

"No," I said quickly. "I don't want anyone to know I'm here. If Djet knows I'm coming, he'll have time to prepare."

"Camran wouldn't tell him."

"I'm not willing to take that risk."

Jenna pursed her lips but nodded. "There's something else as well."

My eyes narrowed at her tone. "What is it?"

"Nathaniel."

My jaw clenched, but I said nothing.

"He's missing," Jenna said. "The rest of the Guard were all found with your father. But he... was not. He hasn't been seen since. And... we found an extra band. As if he took it off."

Shit. I'd forgotten Nate had done that. That was going to take somewhat more explaining, but I wasn't going to let Jenna continue with her prejudiced suspicions any longer.

"Nate has been with me," I said, the coldness of my tone inducing a layer of frost over the table between us.

Jenna went still, her eyes darting between mine. "Oh."

"He's the one who told me about Father's death, and about Djet. He's the one who found me." Maybe he hadn't been with me for all the intervening time, but she didn't need to know that.

"I see." Her voice was getting smaller with each word.

"And he will be with me when I come into this city. And when I've killed Djet, he'll be standing beside me because he is a member of the Guard and because that's where he belongs." In contrast to hers, my voice was darkening, growing larger until it surrounded us.

"Of course," Jenna said meekly. "I didn't mean—"

"Yes, you did," I cut across her. "And I'm sure plenty of others have been saying the same thing. Which is partly *why* Nate came to me, rather than staying here."

"And the band?"

I gave her such a glare that she recoiled. "Is not your concern," I said, enunciating every syllable.

Jenna bowed her head and said nothing.

"What happened to my father's body?"

Her head snapped up again, her eyes wide with relief at the change of subject and a hint of pity as well. "He was burned, right under the tree. Along with the Guard."

It was the answer I'd hoped for, prayed for. So why did it hurt?

Seven pyres lit in my absence.

Hamma, gone. Ishmael, finally reunited with his twin. Edric, Miriam, Osanna, gone. Rian, whom I'd never really given a chance. Gone.

Father. Gone.

All of them released into the sky. And I hadn't been here.

"Tamara, I'm so sorry."

I shook my head, clearing my throat as I looked back up at her. "It's a loss for everyone," I said.

Jenna didn't respond, her gaze fixed on the table between us.

I stood up. I wanted nothing more than to be out, to be back under the trees, with Nate and Titan and the First Guard. We needed to work out what to do about Djet's extra wards.

"I have to go," I said unnecessarily. Jenna rose as well, and I fixed her with a steady look. "You served my father faithfully for many years. I would be honoured if you would stand beside me as well."

She dropped to her knees again. "Of course," she murmured, head tilted back. "My Queen."

I nodded.

"When will it be?" she asked, rising back to her feet.

I glanced out the window. The sun was not yet at its peak. The First Guard might need time to organise, to prepare. They would be furious with me. But I was done with delays. Time to get this over with.

"Today. Be ready." I was gone, hopping back out the window before she could respond.

Yes. Today. One way or the other, it would be over.

24

Choices

The wounds left by Titan's departure, whilst deep and cruel, healed. Rian proved to be a capable fighter and carved himself a place within the Guard. He remained quiet and reserved but when he voiced his opinions, they were useful and accurate.

As the days slipped into months, we reforged ourselves. The Guard drew together and eventually, there were days when you couldn't see the hole that had been ripped through them.

Nate took the longest. I suspected he would never fully forgive Hamma. But they could work together and that would have to be enough.

After a year, Nate and I were mostly back to the way we were before, though there were times when I looked at him and still felt Titan's restless spectre looming over us like a black cloud.

On the anniversary of his departure, I made my way to the roof. I'd expected it to be deserted. A quiet place where I could escape. But there was someone already there.

Nate turned as the door opened, gazing warily at me from his perch on the ledge around the roof, then looked away, staring out over the city. I crossed to the edge, sitting beside him and dangling my legs over the drop.

"It just doesn't feel real," he said after a few minutes of silence.

"I know. Sometimes I still expect him to be here."

Nate looked away, his jaw hardening.

"Sorry," I offered. "You know what I mean though? And he could

have visited."

Nate shrugged. "I didn't expect him to. Everyone leaves. That's what they do."

"Ouch."

"It's true." His hand flexed on the stone between us, a trickle of dust slipping out from between his fingers. "I've never had many people," he said suddenly.

"You've still got me," I offered.

"Whoop."

"Hey!" I shoved him, glad to see a smile flash across his face, answering it with a grin of my own.

Our smiles lingered as we returned to our silent contemplation, but the expression felt heavy on my face. 'Everyone leaves,' he had said. And I was going to have to prove him right.

But not yet. Not tonight. Tonight, we sat and remembered, and though one of us could not cry and the other refused to, my heart was weeping. And I knew his was as well.

One year rolled into two, and a different anniversary stole enough attention to keep us from brooding too much over Titan, though I felt his absence keenly in the lead-up to the celebration planned for my eighteenth birthday. Even without him, it was still an evening of mad revelry. People filled the square outside the palace, spilling along the adjacent streets as the crowd swelled. At the top of the steps, I was presented with a hollow glass sphere. It was coloured with swathes of purple, red, and black, and I held it up to admire it in the late afternoon light for a moment.

The superstitious people said you could tell someone's fortune in the manner with which they broke their sphere. Some chose to let it fall and smash on the ground or crush it in their hand, but it was traditional to toss it upwards and then break it with a weapon as it fell. Even the technique used to throw it could be seen to have a meaning. How high it went, how fast it rotated. Too many variables to be able to predict how everyone would interpret them.

Taking a breath, I turned it gently so that the colours were in the right orientation, my hand clutching it tightly from above. With a glance out at the crowd, I flicked it upwards, setting it spinning with my fingers as I did so.

The colours blurred together, making its rotation look impossibly fast as it hung briefly in the air at eye level. Then, it began to fall.

My twin blades flashed as they emerged from their sheaths, whipping through the air to close around the sphere from either side, shattering it into a thousand pieces. Metal rang upon metal as the blades met, and glass rained down upon the stone.

The crowd erupted into cheers, and the celebration truly got underway.

A group of musicians arranged themselves halfway up the steps, and a large portion of the square was given over to dancing. I avoided the area. The musicians were more a source of annoyance, making it harder to hear what the endless crowd was trying to say to me as I moved among them. I recognised faces from the petitions that I now heard alongside Father and from my weekly outings in the city to visit the market and meet people there. I did my best to remember details about those I knew and listened to the new stories of those I did not.

One couple, glowing with excitement, showed me the pair of spheres they had ready for their engagement ceremony the next day. They would toss the fragile balls to each other, the distance between them supposedly an indication of their faith in their love, and then keep them until their wedding day when they would be broken together, the pieces mingled forevermore. Some couples chose their own colours, but these two had gone for the customary design, with wisps of white, grey, purple, and black. I admired them with a genuine smile and wished the pair all the best.

In the weeks following my birthday, another matter I'd been putting off seemed to loom larger every day. I had never discussed the possibility of my pilgrimage with my parents. It was an old tradition, one most had dispensed with. But I knew my father had made the journey, as had my grandmother, and every monarch before them.

No one mentioned it, but now I was officially an adult, I could feel the idea chasing me down every hallway, dragging at my limbs during every training session.

It was more than the tradition, however. More than the expectation.

I wanted out. I wanted to get away from the city and the swirling vortex of memories held captive within it. The chance to leave behind the ghosts of my mother, of Orion and Helena, of Titan, tempted me more with every single day.

There were places in the world where no one would be watching me, where I would be able to scream and no one would hear it.

But even as the itch to leave intensified, so did my desire to put it off. Because for all that I would be escaping, there was more that I would be leaving behind. So days rolled into weeks, into months, into another year.

The time was marked by a vicious demon attack on the outer farms that left three families dead. Father made no reference to reawakening the Figures, who had been sent to sleep after the incident in the clearing, and I was relieved. After the level of savagery I'd witnessed, the mere mention of them was enough to put me on edge. Other than the single, isolated incident, however, there was no sign of the demons.

But even the attack couldn't distract me for long, and my pilgrimage wouldn't be put off forever. There was someone else waiting for me.

The storm hit without warning. The spring weather had been crisp and clear, with no rain for several days. But as the evening drew in, dark clouds gathered in the sky as if summoned.

I lay awake in my room, thinking of my Father. He would be outside somewhere, listening to the rumbling voice that spoke to him.

As a child, I had sometimes tried to listen, desperate to hear even a single word, a tiny glimpse of Thorns's will. But the thunder had never been anything except meaningless noise.

That night, it changed. I listened and I heard.

There were no words, but every flash of light was a physical blow on my skin, every rumble of thunder an angry growl that ripped around me.

I had delayed for too long. Thorns was angry.

Rolling out of bed, I lurched to the window, hands gripping the sill, and prayed for forgiveness, begging them not to punish my people for my mistake.

When the storm faded, I hadn't slept a wink.

Before the sun rose, I packed a bag, then went in search of my father. He was on the roof.

Osanna and Ishmael guarded the door. They said nothing as I stepped between them and ascended.

Father was standing on the north edge of the roof, gazing towards the mountains, where the last wisps of the storm were still visible.

I joined him silently, following his gaze.

"Tamara," my father said, the word both acknowledgement and query.

I took a deep breath. "It's time."

For a moment, he was confused, eyes searching my face. Then he glanced once more at the retreating clouds. "Ah," he said, smiling. Turning to face me, he reached out, grasping my shoulders. "I understand."

"Thank you. For everything."

He shook his head. "Everything you are comes from within you. Don't forget that."

"I won't."

"Go on then," he said, pushing me away lightly. He jerked his head towards the retreating clouds. "They're waiting to talk to you."

Stepping back, I bowed to him, and for the first time, he bowed back.

Though there was a lump in my throat, I smiled, turning away and hurrying down the stairs. My steps were light as I danced back to my room. This was it. I was leaving.

Nate was waiting outside my door. My enthusiasm, which had been building with every second, dimmed. He shook his head in admonishment to see me approaching down the corridor rather than emerge from within.

"*You should have woken me,*" he said, as I ducked inside, grabbing my bag before returning to the hallway. His eyes fell upon it at once. "*Where are we going?*"

My hands clenched around the straps of the bag, and I took a bracing breath. This was going to hurt him.

"*We're not,*" I said. "*I'm going alone.*"

Nate snorted. "*I don't think so. You don't get to run off on your own, in case you hadn't noticed.*"

"*I do for this,*" I corrected him. "*I'm going on pilgrimage.*"

"*What! Why?*"

I frowned. "*Because it's tradition.*"

"*A stupid tradition. Gallivanting off alone for three weeks? No one else does it. Why should you?*"

"*The monarchs do it,*" I corrected him. "*I need to go.*"

"*No. Don't.*"

"*Nate, this is something I have to do.*"

"*Then I'll come with you.*"

It was my turn to shake my head now. "*No. It must be done alone. And your first duty is to Father, who is staying here.*"

"*I didn't join the Guard for your father!*" he snapped.

My heart twisted in my chest. I'd known that, though we had never acknowledged it in the open before.

"*I'll be back before you know it,*" I offered.

"*Whatever.*" He turned away, staring at the wall.

I waited, but he didn't break. "*Is this how you want to leave things between us?*"

"*I'm not the one leaving,*" he said coldly.

I stared at the side of his face. Jaw set, he looked just like the angry boy who had been dragged before my father a decade ago. We had been through so much since then. Surely he would give up in a moment, sigh, and turn back to me and say it would all be okay.

But he did not and I couldn't wait forever. So I walked away and did not look back.

"He's done *what?*"

I couldn't blame Titan for his horror. The revelation burrowed into my bones like ice.

"He's got more wards," I repeated, pacing back and forth across the clearing. "Cut into his skin, or so Jenna thinks."

"That's…" Titan trailed off, lost for words for the first time.

"They would work, wouldn't they?" I asked, turning to the First Guard. The three who had escorted me back out of the city had rejoined their companion, who had remained here to keep in contact with Titan and Nate.

One of them nodded. "It won't be as efficient as a tattoo, but as long as the design is correct, yes."

I'd suspected as much. The story of the two boys who had experimented with charcoal to such devastating consequences came to mind. The fact that wards could activate from other mediums was not news, but I was glad to have it confirmed.

"And whilst we're on the subject of Djet," I said, fixing them with a glare, "you told me it was three challengers he killed. Jenna said it was six."

"Six?" Nate repeated.

"Only three of them actually challenged him," the First Guard said.

I stared at them.

"That was the question you asked," they said.

"And you didn't think the other three mattered? That it wasn't *relevant?*"

"You didn't ask."

I just gaped at them, my hands gesticulating emphatically before me as my mouth opened and closed soundlessly.

"Don't bother," Titan advised me. "That's how they are."

I gave a scoff of frustration but conceded. "His extra wards. Is there a way to stop them working?"

"You should be able to break them, just like any others."

I knew a ward could be broken. The proof of that was evident on

400

my back. And Djet already knew it too. Titan shot me a glance, then dropped his gaze swiftly.

"Otherwise," the First Guard continued, "no."

"Stupid question," Nate said, "but why doesn't everyone have more wards?"

We all looked at him, his arms bare of ink. Of course, having never been eligible to receive the wards, it shouldn't surprise me that he knew less of them than I did.

"Mainly, it's a balance of any benefit they give compared to the ease of actually using them," Titan explained. "It's hard to draw on multiple wards. Having more doesn't necessarily mean they can be put to use."

"There's more than that," the First Guard added. "When you have more wards… bad things can happen."

Nate looked at them, his eyes flicking over their inhuman bodies, every inch of metallic skin covered with carved swirls. "You don't say."

"What sort of bad things?" I asked.

The First Guard shrugged. "That depends how many extra wards he has and how long he's had them for. Initial problems, as Titan said, are mainly physical. The exertion of using them can lead to extreme fatigue and lapses in judgement. Combined with the additional capabilities the wards grant, this can be dangerous in itself. If Djet has managed to master them physically, however, he'll start struggling with his mental capacity."

"He'll go insane?"

They nodded. "Paranoia, delusions, hearing voices, mood swings, struggling with impulse control."

"Sounds like a whole bundle of fun," Nate muttered.

"As we said, the exact symptoms will depend on the extent and duration of his meddling."

"Wonderful," Titan snapped. "So either Mara has to slash his arms to ribbons before he can retaliate, or we have to hope he's so unhinged he won't be able to stand upright. Both excellent options."

I glared at him, but he turned away. His hands were shaking slightly.

"Thank you for your confidence," I shot at his back.

Nate grimaced. "It doesn't sound good," he agreed.

"I don't care how it sounds," I said. "This is how it is. I have to face him. Today."

"Today?" Nate's jaw dropped.

"Where exactly are *your* extra wards?" Titan asked, turning back to me. "Because clearly, you've gone insane already!"

"What's the benefit of waiting?" I snapped. "Twenty-one children are missing, Titan! And the only people doing anything about it have to hide their efforts. What would you have me do, wait until Djet is so demented he starts acting on his delusions, whatever they may be?"

That was if he hadn't done so already. Surely Jenna would have mentioned if Djet was overtly irrational, wouldn't she?

"I would have you *survive*!" Titan snapped. "Not throw your life away on this suicide mission. That's my *job*, Mara, to protect you."

My eyes flicked to the purple band I had tied so recently around his arm. "I thought you said that was only going to be temporary."

"You said that, not me."

We stared at each other.

"I'm going to do this, Titan. I'm not a child anymore, and you can't stop me."

Titan threw up his hands, turning to Nate.

Nate looked from him to me, then dropped his gaze to the floor. Titan turned away, exasperated, but I waited, knowing Nate would speak.

"You know what will happen if you lose," he said quietly.

It was my turn to look away now. Even if seeing Nate by my side was enough to dispel the doubts most people had been harbouring about him after my father's death, Djet would surely kill anyone who stood beside me.

"You don't have to come," I said. "You could... you could go back to Warren. Or..." I hesitated, not wanting to mention the demons in front of the others.

Nate's face tightened but he shook his head. "You can't get rid of me that easily. I'm not going anywhere."

"I'm sorry I left." The words slipped out before I could stop them.

One side of his mouth twitched upwards. He knew what I was referring to. "I'm sorry I let you go."

Titan sighed loudly. "Who's side are you on, kid?"

"The same one I always was," Nate said.

I smiled at him. "Time to go home?"

He nodded. And that was all I needed.

My world was silent. Maybe birds twittered in the trees as we left them. Maybe a herd of goats gave startled cries as we passed. Maybe the people who stopped and stared let out gasps of shock or cries of greeting.

I knew none of it. There was only the swirl of my thoughts and the thuds of my feet hitting the road, every step carrying me closer to home. Even my heart seemed silent.

Chin elevated, I kept my eyes forward. My back felt exposed without my pack, which I'd left in the trees. Either I would be able to send someone back for it, or it wouldn't matter. With every stride, my fingers brushed against the twin blades at my hips. I knew I would only have to turn my head to see Nate and Titan walking behind me, their sharp eyes scanning for danger.

Word was spreading now. I could see it, feel it like a ripple around me. Faces turned towards me from the fields, labourers straightening from their work, some breaking into a run towards the roadside, clambering over fences and leaping ditches. Some reached out their hands, others called out, their mouths moving with silent words. Some I acknowledged with a flicker of my eyes, a brief nod, but I stopped for no one.

Noises returned as I passed from the open fields to the slums, the Eastern Gate looming ahead. Voices echoed around me, from speculative murmurs to cries for friends or family to join us. And join us they did. The ground trembled from the cacophony of footsteps. I daren't look back to see how many had joined the parade. Were they following to show their support or just to witness the outcome? I wasn't sure I wanted to know. Wasn't sure it mattered.

The thin, wide-eyed faces staring at me from the ramshackle houses made my heart contract painfully. Surely these were the ones who had felt the change in monarch more than any others. How many people had been bringing them work or donating food that they didn't need without someone to remind them of the obligation to those less well off? There were no cries of greeting for me here, just silent stares from doorways. They didn't turn away, and I looked upon them without flinching, unable to read their expressions.

The buildings became sturdier as I moved on, clad with thick layers of mud to keep out the weather. More faces peered out at me, shock evident upon them. Then I turned the corner and the gate was in front of me.

My eyes filled with tears. Appalled at myself, I blinked them away, caught off guard by the sudden onslaught of emotion. What was wrong with me? I hadn't been affected like this by the Northern Gate when I'd entered with the Figures. It wouldn't have been so bad then, with no one else to see me. Just as I thought I'd mastered myself, the thought hit me that my father was not waiting for me inside. I had to fight once again to keep my expression steady.

Tilting my face up, I blinked quickly, as if blinded by the sun, my gaze falling on the silhouettes of people atop the gate. They must have seen the procession approaching, but from their stunned faces as I drew closer, they hadn't guessed the source of it.

The Gate wasn't actually a gate at all, merely an open archway of stone, and as I lowered my gaze, I looked beyond it to the courtyard within. An entire company of soldiers was stationed there, fanned out in a semicircle. I scanned their expressions, watching determination turn to surprise. The midday sun flickered on weapons as they trembled, some lowering. Glances were exchanged, uncertainty shared and multiplied.

"Don't stop," Titan murmured from behind me.

I made no response, privately agreeing. To pause would be to grant them power over me, even in their confusion. I needed them to fall back and would push them if I had to.

Before I could force them into a decision, however, someone came sprinting down the road behind them. The soldiers glanced back at the sound of his approach, moving aside instantly for him to come closer. I tensed, hands twitching. Was this Djet?

I dismissed the suspicion at the sight of his bare arms. My eyes rose higher, skating over his wards, the ink around his speed ward blooming out under his skin, and finally to his face as he skidded to a halt.

He had black hair, a touch shorter than Nate's, that stuck up all over his head as if he'd just run his hands through it. Thick eyebrows sat low over grey eyes, and a strong, square jaw was shrouded by dark stubble framing his thin mouth.

He gave a quick wave of one hand, and the soldiers stepped back, weapons lowering as they relaxed. The tension that had just left my shoulders returned. Not Djet, perhaps, but he had enough authority to be a threat if he chose.

Behind him, I saw Jenna waiting a little further up the road, and something clicked into place.

"Camran," I said, slowing my pace as I approached him. Jenna thought this man would be an ally.

"You're alive," he replied, not bothering to confirm my suspicion.

I raised an eyebrow. "So it would seem." We were only a pace apart now, and I stopped, examining his face once again. There was something almost familiar about it. I must have seen him around the city before.

"I assume you're here to…" He jerked his head back towards the palace.

I inclined my head.

He mirrored me, bobbing his head. "Alright then." He glanced past me, to Nate, and something flickered across his face. Fear? Regret? *Guilt?* The emotion was gone before I could identify it, and he turned away.

"Clear a path, lads," he barked. "Step sharp!"

The soldiers scrambled to obey, falling into two lines along the sides of the street. Camran turned back to me and bowed. "Your Highness." He stepped back, sweeping out an arm for me to pass.

I looked along the empty street, waiting for me to walk along it, and my throat closed up once again. Maybe if Nate had been inside my mind at that moment, he wouldn't have doubted my ability to feel was genuine. But Titan was right as well; I held the emotions down inside, letting them warm my chest but with no sign of them reaching my face.

With a slow breath, I walked on.

There was a slight hesitation in Nate's steps as he followed me, but I dared not look back. I heard Camran fall into place behind the two Guardsmen, rattling off orders as we passed through the ranks of soldiers, some of whom continued with us, an honour guard to escort me home.

The closer to the citadel I got, the more familiar faces I saw. Two of the girls who had worked in the palace kitchens. Stallholders from the weekly market. Jaws dropped on all sides. Some called out to me, but I kept my expression grim, acknowledging them only with my eyes. I could not stop again. Not now. Not when I was so close.

I knew every step of the route and could have walked it with my eyes closed, but somehow, the open space before the palace steps came earlier than I'd expected.

My feet faltered as I looked up. It was just as I remembered. The three-story building loomed, its large windows looking down on me expectantly. Below were the carved wooden doors and the broad stone steps leading up to them.

A man sat on the steps, elbows resting on his knees, head bowed.

I continued towards him alone, a flick of my fingers enough to tell Nate and Titan to remain behind. Nate took one final step

forwards as if drawn after me by an irresistible force. I couldn't
think of that, of him, now. Every fibre of my body was focused on
the man ahead of me.

I took a diagonal line up the steps, circling around so I would end
up beside him. My limbs were tense, legs ready to leap backwards
at the slightest hint of movement, but there was none. I was only
two steps below the one he sat on when he finally moved, head
coming up to look past me, staring out across the courtyard.

He was older than I'd expected, at least fifteen years my senior,
possibly more. His long brown hair, streaked with grey, fell
forwards, shadowing his deep-set eyes, which were narrowed into a
squint. Like Camran, he hadn't shaved, the stubble over his chin
greyer than the hair on his head.

As Jenna had said, he wore a light shirt, its sleeves falling to his
wrists. His hands were clasped together in front of him, fingers
intertwined.

"Djet."

He drew in a deep breath, his chest and shoulders rising. Then he
sighed it out again, his eyes continuing to sweep the courtyard
below.

I risked a glance to the side, following his gaze.

Nate and Titan stood at the bottom of the steps. Camran and
Jenna were right behind them. Beyond, the space was crammed
with people. Some huddled back against the buildings as if hoping
to go unseen, but others pressed forwards, staring eagerly upwards.

"Tamara."

The acknowledgement, so many seconds after I'd spoken, made
me jump. I looked back at him. He was slower to turn, eyes raking
up and down me once before fixing on my face.

I couldn't look away. After so much time spent imagining this
moment, when I would finally be face to face with the man who
had stolen my throne, now that it was here, now *he* was here, he
wasn't what I'd expected.

Here was the one person who would, undeniably, understand the
secret I had hidden in the deepest core of my soul, though he

407

didn't realise it. He would know why I had been so desperate to keep it hidden. He had experienced that which I'd fought so hard to avoid; the combined sympathy and rejection that came from having a broken ward. Maybe we could have spoken, could have helped each other.

And he might have been responsible for my father's death.

My jaw clenched, and the fragile thread that had stretched between us, linking our broken wards, shattered.

"I know why you're here," he said, turning away from me again. "But I can't let you do it. I'm sorry." He even sounded it, the words soft with remorse.

"You're *sorry*?" I shook my head. "Sorry isn't good enough. You had a *responsibility*, Djet. The moment you sat on that throne. You were supposed to keep the people safe. Instead, you've done nothing whilst *children* go missing." Unlike him, I made no effort to keep my voice low, letting the accusatory words ring out for everyone to hear.

He was upright without me seeing him move, eyes blazing as he glared at me.

I flinched, feeling my stomach clench.

No one moved that fast. No one.

"What do you think I've been trying to do?" he hissed. "I'm trying to save them! Don't you see? We are *limited*. Vulnerable. And I'm the only one willing to do something about it." His eyes were wild, darting away from me as if distracted by unseen things around us, then snapping back to my face moments later.

The First Guard were right; he was half mad already.

"I think all you've been doing is working to regain what you lost," I said, ignoring the latter part of his ramblings.

Djet didn't seem to notice, tilting his head slightly as he looked at me. "What we *both* lost," he corrected me, so quietly that I barely heard him.

My heart stuttered. "What did you say?"

He didn't know. No one knew. How could he know?

"I was watching," he continued, matching my hushed tone. "You
408

never went to the Warders. I thought you would. I was *sure* you would. They told me it wasn't possible, that it couldn't be replaced. But I knew they were lying; I knew they could do it. It would just have to be someone younger. Someone important…"

I stumbled back, tripping on the next step up. At the edge of my vision, Nate took half a pace forward. For once, I had no idea what my face was doing. Nor did I care.

"But you didn't," Djet continued. He was suddenly closer again, following me up the steps without appearing to move. One moment to the next, we were inches apart. "That was annoying. But I'm not angry. Not at you." He smiled as if trying to prove his point.

The expression didn't reach his eyes.

"I'm impressed. Truly. You've done so well, without anyone ever knowing. You never told anyone, did you?"

He was watching me, watching for an answer to his question. My mind was still reeling, unable to process the implication of his words.

"It was you." The words were a whisper, nothing more.

Djet's face softened, pity seeping from the lines around his eyes. "I'm sorry," he murmured. "But I had to do something. I had to know." He glanced away, head blurring with the speed of the movement.

"*You* did this to me."

Again, that blurred movement as his head spun back around. He gave a jerky nod. "I never told anyone though. I know what it's like." His mouth twisted down. "The looks. People never see *you* again. Even after what *he* said to me… but that wasn't your fault. So I never told anyone."

I launched myself forwards. There was no thought to it, no preparation. One second, I was staring at him in motionless horror, then next, he stumbled backwards with the force of my shove, my angry hands raised between us.

My breaths came fast and harsh, shoulders shaking with each one. I wanted to scream at him, to shout and rage. But I couldn't.

Because there was a whole crowd watching us. And like he'd said, I'd never told anyone. I wasn't going to change that now. So I just stood there, trembling with a fury I didn't dare fully unleash.

Djet, having regained his balance, shot me another sympathetic look. "I *am* sorry," he said. "But you showed me something new as well, so it was worth it!"

I had several choice words for him over that, starting with the fact that he didn't get to decide what his crippling me was worth.

"I hadn't realised until I thought about it, but you had two," his voice dropped lower again, so I had to strain to hear, "so it didn't matter if you lost one. It never held you back; you could still harness the full power, even with only one of them left. Don't you see! They are holding us back. They set limits and don't care for the consequences!"

"They?" I stepped towards him, despite myself. "Who's they?"

"The Warders!" Djet snapped impatiently. "They say we can only have one of each ward, and they're *blind* to the possibilities of setting that restriction aside. Just look at the Figures! They have so many wards, and see what they are capable of! It's not fair that we should be denied our true potential. We have only to dream."

He was rambling again, his eyes fluttering away from me more and more as his voice rose.

"I'm only doing what has to be done, to unchain us, to set us free. It couldn't be done any other way. It's a necessary evil to take them away. If only people would understand, I wouldn't have had to do it, but—"

"Wait," I cut into his endless flow. "Take them? Take who?"

Djet blinked, frowning at me as if unaware of what he'd said.

"Who?" I demanded, and this time, when I stepped towards him, it wasn't unintentional. My voice was louder now, my words ringing around us. "What do you mean 'take them'?"

"I…" Djet shook his head but wildly, as if to shake off a fly, rather than in disagreement.

"The children?" The thought made me sick, but I had to know. I had to make him say it. "Was it the children?!"

410

"I had to!" His shout, even louder than mine, rang around the courtyard.

There was a moment of silence, then a surge of noise from below. Cries of outrage and howls of anger rose from the watching crowd as they pressed in towards the steps.

"It was the only way they would get a chance," Djet continued, though I was sure those below wouldn't be able to hear him over their own noise. "To be free."

I risked a glance to the side. Camran's soldiers were attempting to restore order, but even without them, the crowd hesitated. They shouted and shook their fists, eyes and hands angry. But they didn't dare try to climb the steps. Their fury unable to overcome their fear.

Titan and Nate seemed oblivious to those around them for once, faces fixed on me.

"It was for them," Djet insisted as the people below quietened slowly. "There were too many people looking before, too much suspicion. I had to be able to do it without people nosing around. I would have proved it worked! I just need enough time. An opportunity!"

"An opportunity for what?" I snapped. I was quickly losing patience with his babbling. Trying to prise the meaning from the blather was exhausting.

What circumstances would it have taken to ensure no one would be able to investigate the children's disappearance? What opportunity would he have needed to be able to steal them away without people questioning his actions?

Because that was exactly what he had done. The First Guard and Jenna both told me so. Anyone seen to be coordinating a search for the missing children had been killed. Because Djet wasn't uncaring about their disappearance. Quite the opposite. He had been dedicated to ensuring anyone searching for them was unsuccessful.

Surely there was only one level of freedom, of power, that would have afforded him that.

I'd already had the awful thought, back when Jenna had told me Djet had Claimed the throne before it was even confirmed that my father was dead. Here was more evidence.

The blows kept coming. *Whamwhamwham.* Responsible for my broken ward, responsible for the disappearance of more than twenty children. And now, one more crime that could be laid at his feet. The worst of them all.

"What did Zouri promise you," I asked, my voice somehow remaining level, "to betray my father?"

Djet, having opened his mouth to continue his ramblings, closed it again, his eyes wide as he gazed at me.

"Or did you approach him?" The words devolved into a snarl.

"You know him?" Djet asked, his voice soft with his shock.

It was all I needed. Zouri's name should have been unfamiliar to Djet. It was not. They'd known each other. And there was only one event they had in common.

My blades screamed as they erupted from their sheaths, blazing in the afternoon sun.

"Djet, you are not fit to lead!"

Finally. *The* words.

He stared at me, the surprise draining from his face like sap oozing down a tree, leaving it cold and hard.

"You colluded with our enemies to bring about the death of my father. You are responsible for the disappearance of more than twenty children. You are not fit to lead."

We glared at each other. Me, with my weapons raised, every muscle taut and shaking. Him, impassive and unmoving.

It took another second of silence before I realised that Djet wasn't even carrying a weapon. My arms lowered a fraction. Technically, it was his right to dictate the time and place when he would meet my challenge. Then my face hardened again. No. That right was only for a lawful monarch. He had forsaken that privilege many times over.

His eyes narrowed slightly at my hesitation, his mouth curling up.

I lunged.

412

He was gone before I was even halfway through the movement, vanishing completely.

There was a shout from the crowd, though I wasn't sure whether it was due to my attack or his disappearance.

I spun, searching. He was already there, stepping in close, his arms shoving mine aside.

"Are those the only crimes you would accuse me of?" he hissed, his face inches from mine. "Nothing *else*?"

I bared my teeth. But as I did so, it happened again; his eyes slid away, brow furrowing slightly, focused on something else. Quick as I could, I spun my blade in my right hand, reversing my grip on it. The sharp metal swung towards Djet's arm. I stepped back, dragging the blade down as I did so.

Djet gasped, his other hand leaping to the wound. He hunched over, cradling his arm against his chest, eyes clenched shut against the pain. A far greater reaction than such a simple wound should have caused.

I felt a flare of triumph. I must have gotten lucky and hit one of his extra wards. I lunged forwards again, blade extended to slash across his arm once more.

He saw me coming, drawing back, though without the unnatural speed he'd had before. My weapon snagged on his sleeve, tearing the fabric. My hand came closer, fingers brushing against his forearm. I snatched at the cloth as he stepped away. Something ripped.

Djet stumbled back, eyes turned to me in shock. I didn't meet them, captivated by what I had revealed.

Aided by the slit cut by my blade, Djet's sleeve had torn to the seam at the shoulder, a huge strip of cloth hanging limply from my fingers, leaving his left arm half-bare.

The burn caught my eye first. It was worse than I'd imagined, a wide swath of flesh warped and twisted. More than half Djet's speed ward was unrecognisable, though spots of black ink still sat among the wrinkled white scar. The burn had only missed his balance ward by the barest of margins, the upper edge reaching

413

threateningly towards the delicate design.

Then my eyes drifted downwards, and I forgot about the ward he had lost.

He had replaced it many, many times over.

The intricate speed ward, arguably the most complex of all the wards we carried, was carved into his skin, over and over again, packed so closely together they almost overlapped. I had expected one or two extra wards. Not enough to cover his entire arm.

Two of them were broken, the red line where I'd cut Djet running across them. Not luck at all. Inevitable. But there were so many more. I looked up and met Djet's eyes. Through the fading pain of having two wards broken simultaneously, there was dark fury in his gaze. His lips drew back, exposing his teeth in a snarl, and he lunged forwards.

I danced backwards, drawing on my speed ward as I did so, but he was too fast. I didn't even see the blow coming. The impact to my stomach sent me staggering, the pain like a tidal wave. I tripped on the steps and went crashing down, one hand thrown out to break my fall, bruising my knuckles, the other curled across my stomach, my blade clattering to the step below.

Djet's slow, deliberate steps approached from behind, but I couldn't turn, couldn't stand, couldn't move. Couldn't breathe. Floundering, desperate for oxygen, mouth working uselessly. Through black spots in my vision, I saw Nate and Titan at the bottom of the steps. Nate had jumped forwards, eyes fixed on mine.

A tiny gap opened in my throat and I sucked in air. My stomach spasmed, making me cough, but I could breathe. Another gasp cleared my head and my vision. Something struck my wrist before I could turn. The sword I'd kept hold of skittered away, bouncing down the steps as Djet's foot knocked my wrist out from under me. I rolled away from him, grabbing my remaining blade before jumping to my feet. He was already coming after me.

I retreated, hunched over with the persistent pain in my abdomen. No time to retrieve my lost weapon, I slashed and

414

blocked, giving ground before Djet's relentless onslaught. He was slower than he had been before; his movements were still dizzyingly fast, but they were no longer invisible. If he'd been armed, he could have crippled me in seconds. But for all his excess speed, he wasn't a fighter. Whereas I had been trained by the greatest warrior in a generation.

And Djet was distracted.

His eyes flickered again. His arm, raised to deliver a sharp blow towards my shoulder, hesitated for a second.

I knew what I had to do.

A quick twist and slash, and he cried out, staggering backwards, another ward broken. I pressed my advantage, leaping after him, but he ducked away, one foot lashing out, colliding with my knee. My leg crumpled, sending me crashing to the stone again as he retreated. The impact stung, the steps digging into my shins. Gritting my teeth, I hopped upright. Weight on my left side, I lurched one step sideways. Despite the pain, my knee held. Shaking, but solid.

I looked up and my heart stopped.

Djet stood four steps below me.

He held my other blade in his hand.

How dare he? How *dare* he?

Nate's face flashed before my eyes, the slight smile he'd worn as he'd passed them over to me. He'd bled to make these weapons. Bled for me.

And now the man who'd sent a group of demons to massacre him was holding it.

No.

I leapt.

Djet's eyes widened, his mouth opening in shock at my jump, sailing over every step between us. Then I hit him, knocking us both down, tumbling over the steps. His extra wards were forgotten. I lashed out at him with fist and foot, too close to use my weapon, but not caring. Every impact sent shivers down my limbs, the pain euphoric. If it was hurting me, it was hurting him too.

We rolled to a halt side by side, within reach of the watching crowd. Djet lunged away, scrambling back up the steps. I reared up and thrust my blade down. It pierced through the back of his thigh and struck the stone below.

There was an indrawn breath from the crowd. Then he screamed.

I yanked the weapon up, bringing a gush of blood with it. Djet turned, curling in on himself, his hand going to his injured leg as his face turned towards me. I met it with my fist, still clenched around my blade. There was a sickening crunch. Djet's head snapped away from me. My second blade dropped from his fingers, metal ringing on stone.

Leaping past him, I snatched it up.

Mine.

I breathed a sigh of relief, revelling in the reunion. Behind me, I could hear pained breaths hissing between clenched teeth and the muted shuffling of people pressing cautiously closer.

My people. It was time to prove that.

I took my time turning, letting my head lead the movement, my expression deliberately measured and serious. The mask my father had taught me to wear. Taught me so well.

Djet was immobile, both hands clutched around his thigh, blood pulsing between his fingers. I looked at him impassively. Maybe that was what I should have been aiming for all along. All the speed wards in the world couldn't help him when he couldn't walk.

Raising my gaze, I surveyed the crowd. Every pair of eyes was fixed on me, waiting.

"Something to say?" Djet said, between pants, squinting up at me. "A nice speech to make? Some *secrets* to reveal, maybe?"

I froze, my breath catching in my throat. The threat inherent in his words made me shiver inside. Would he tell them what'd he done, tell them my deepest secret? No one would accept me as queen if they knew about my broken ward. My eyes flicked down. He'd already admitted he'd made the decision to hold his tongue in the past, even after what Father had said to him. But now, I was the one who had broken him. I was no longer blameless, no longer innocent.

He knew my secret. He would always know. And there was nothing I could do to guarantee he wouldn't tell anyone. Except, there was one thing I could do. One way to be certain.

I'd killed Zouri in a flash of emotional misjudgement. Some part of me still questioned whether it had been the right decision.

Djet was responsible for the disappearance of children around the city. Undoubtedly he would be able to tell us where they were now, whatever he had done to them. I needed that information. But I needed to be sure my secret was safe too.

Which did I value more? The security of the lives I was about to take responsibility for, or hiding the trauma cut into my skin?

Even Djet had recognised that having one of my strength wards hadn't held me back. I had no way of knowing if he was right, if I would have been stronger with two or not. But nor did anyone else. My capabilities would be called into question, no matter what I did. I couldn't let that happen.

Djet wasn't looking at me anymore but had turned towards the people who were still leaning eagerly forward, waiting for our next moves.

"You know what you have to do," he said, voice suddenly louder, back rigid as he stared into the crowd. My gaze followed his, but all the faces I could see in that area were confused, glancing around as if to try and identify who he was talking to.

"Spread the word," Djet continued. "Burn it all."

My stomach clenched. I had known he might have allies, but the reality of it hadn't hit me until that moment. Even with Djet defeated, there were still others who might continue his agenda. But they were a problem for later.

"You're right," I said, and my voice was cold. "I do know what I have to do."

I gathered my two blades together, holding them parallel, both hands wrapped around their hilts. I swung them high.

Djet turned back towards me. His head got halfway around

before my blades bit into his neck, severing it completely. His body slumped, spasming wildly on the step. Blood spewed from the sundered neck, pooling on the step and running down the stone. The head rolled a little way before coming to a halt, rocking back and forth, face down.

It was done.

I stood there, blood crawling along my blades, for several moments, revelling in that simple fact.

It was over. My secret was safe.

There was just one last thing to be done.

I looked up. The crowd was silent. No one cheered or cried out. They just waited, the faces in front hiding those behind.

Turning away, I trudged wearily up the steps, feeling my knee ache with every step. Halfway up, I stopped and turned back. Much better. I could see everyone now, all the way to the back, where people packed the streets leading to the square. There seemed to be no end to them.

"You know me."

The words were barely audible, even to me, catching in my throat. I took a deep searing breath and began again.

"You know me!" They rang out this time, clear and strong, and I felt something settle onto my shoulders. It was the tone I'd heard from my father so many times.

Authority. Power. Majesty.

"I have been gone a long time. I do not deny it. I have been to other places, met other people. But everywhere I have been, I never forgot where my home was. I never forgot who my people are."

A parade of faces flickered through my mind. One lingered, sharp blue eyes piercing my soul. I held onto the memory for a moment, then released it.

"I've changed whilst I was gone. I've seen things, done things, that have changed me. I've made decisions, made choices, that I couldn't have imagined making a year ago. But some things have not changed. This is still my home. I am still my father's daughter.

And you are still my people!

"That is a choice I have made. I chose to come home. To you. I chose you yesterday; I choose you today. I will choose you tomorrow!"

The silence quivered, hanging on the edge of something.

"But that's not enough." I lowered my arms, unsure of when I had raised them. "It's not enough," I repeated. "I've chosen you. But now it's your turn. It's your choice. You all knew my father. You chose him. Will you give me the same chance? *Will you choose me?*"

For a moment, the silence held. Everyone was quiet and still.

It began slowly. People glanced at their neighbours. Someone nodded. Then another. Whispers grew to murmurs, to outcries, to screams. The silence shattered, and the roar rose from all sides. It was approval. It was a welcoming. It was a demand.

It ripped through me, vibrating in my chest like thunder, like the very voice of Thorns themself.

I let them scream for a while, basking in the sound, then raised a hand. The sound ebbed slightly, the crowd unwilling to quieten. Then, only a second later, there was sudden silence. The crowd drew back, every pair of eyes widening as they looked above me.

I turned.

The First Guard stood along the top of the steps, twelve of the thirteen of them lined up in a perfect row. Like those watching, my breath caught in my throat at the sight. Even knowing I had their support, the sight of them sent a thrill of trepidation through me.

As one, they dropped to one knee, bowing their heads forwards.

I turned away, back to the crowd.

Nate and Titan were first to follow suit, kneeling at the bottom of the steps, heads tilted back.

Something in my chest twinged at the sight, then ripped completely as the rest of the crowd followed suit, all of them sinking to the floor and offering up their throat to me in the ultimate sign of trust.

It was too much. Finally overwhelmed, I sank down to sit on the broad steps, tired beyond belief. But for all my exhaustion, somehow I knew, this was only the beginning.

Epilogue

On the Other Side

The woman, the *Queen*, sat on the steps and the demon stood up, face impassive. He pushed off the window frame with his left hand, the wound on his arm stinging as if the woman had dealt him the blow only seconds before, rather than almost two weeks ago. But that wasn't important now. He made his way across the room and back to the ground floor. He *could* have crossed from the upper floor, but it might have involved a hard landing on the other side if he didn't judge it right. Far easier to go down the stairs.

As he reached the room below, another swell of noise seeped through the shuttered windows. The demon hesitated, staring at them. Had something else happened? Should he return to his vantage point?

He dismissed the thought with a shake of his head. He witnessed what he was required to. It had been a physical effort to remain concealed when Tamara revealed the sheer extent of the atrocity the other one had committed. So many of their leeching wards, carved over and over into his skin. The demon's lips drew back from his teeth at the mere memory of them. But it was over now. That one was dead. Tamara was victorious.

That was all Madina had wanted to know. It was time to go home and report back. Madina would no doubt nod serenely and add the knowledge to the web of her scheming. As to his other master... there was no way of knowing how that one would react.

The demon stood utterly still, eyes closed as he extended his senses. His soul did the same, writhing in his stomach, eager to return home. With the noise outside, it wasn't as easy as it might have been. But still, just a reach and a grasp and…

The demon stepped forwards and opened his eyes to a familiar red-tinged landscape. It was a hard, barren sight. A light wind swept over jagged rocks and boulders, billowing through the sheer-sided canyons rising in the distance. It picked up streams of dust, tossing them high in the air. There was nothing else moving. No plants. No animals. Just rock and dust. Nothing living.

Pursing his lips, the demon set off, leaping from boulder to boulder with easy familiarity. The desolate place might look cold and inhospitable, but it was home. At least, it had been. Now…

He could already feel the cold leeching at his bones. His soul snarled, pulsing within him, raging against the feeling of suffocation. The demon caressed it with a thought, soothing the distressed creature. It wasn't much further now.

He passed a spot where the wind gusted stronger, but the gateway wasn't his destination. His goal lay a little further on. He came to a stop on top of a large rock, eight feet tall, with a sharply pointed tip. He balanced there for a moment, one foot on either side of the peak, surveying the landscape. Then he jumped down, landing hard on the smaller boulder below. Another jump, another drop. Sand, packed tightly into the crevasse at the bottom, crunched under his feet. Turning sideways, he moved on, twisting sinuously through the narrow passageway.

The opening sat in the shadows between two leaning sheets of rock, hidden from casual glances. The demon moved into the gloom without apprehension, the darkness yielding under his gaze, everything lit up in shades of red.

Inside the cave, the demon breathed a little easier. Already, he could feel the warmth seeping towards him from further down. He broke into a jog, following the gently sloping path, seeking that internal glow. His soul, restless after the crushing weight of the other world, stretched, pressing against him. He shoved it down again, impatiently this time. He still had a job to do. The pressure didn't diminish, chasing him along his descent.

He reached the first level, pausing to glance briefly out at the open space. It was crowded and noisy, but he didn't linger. The ones he was searching for were unlikely to be this close to the surface. Turning away, he continued down the path, following as it twisted into a sharp turn. The heat was like a physical presence as he descended, bringing warmth to his limbs and air to his lungs. Every breath came easier as he dove deeper, closer to the Core.

At the fifth level, he caught sight of a familiar face just beyond the exit from the spiral. If Amanath was here, Madina would be too. In Sornath's absence, his younger brother had stepped quickly into his role as Madina's second, determinately ignorant of the rumours the promotion had sparked. The demon paused, dipping his head slightly in deference to his elder. Amanath looked him over with a sneer, then jerked his head to the side.

The demon moved past him, heading towards the huddle of figures he had indicated, pushing through them. Some hissed at his shoving, but his soul flared within him, staring down theirs until they quietened. At the front of the group, he paused, waiting to be acknowledged. It didn't take long.

Madina called him forward with an elegant wave of her hand. The other one the demon had been searching for sat beside her on a slightly lower stool. Inside his stomach, the demon's soul went silent, retreating into a tight ball. He bowed, careful to encompass them both within the movement.

"Well?" Madina asked.

"It's over. She won. The people seemed to accept her," the demon said.

"And Nathaniel?" The other one leant forwards, his face intent. His brown hair was cut close to his head, and deep-set eyes stared from under a lined forehead, with equally severe lines around a thin mouth.

The demon hesitated. To answer would be to acknowledge the question, which Madina had not authorised. But to ignore it would be an offence he would have to pay for later.

"I expect he was with her, was he not?" Madina asked, saving him.

"Indeed," the demon inclined his head gratefully. "And another one. The Southerner."

"Hmm." Madina's mouth pulled into a grimace. "I see." She was silent for a moment, then nodded. "Thank you. You may go."

With a final glance at the one who sat beside her, the demon bowed again, then scurried away.

"Well," Madina said, turning back to her companion, "there you have it." She shook her head. "Those two are bound closer than you realise. Breaking them apart won't be easy."

"Leave that to me," the man said. "You were impressed with him though, weren't you?"

Madina gave a dry smile. "I suppose I was. I should have anticipated nothing less. He is your son, after all."

The demon gave a predatory smile, displaying every one of his teeth. His eyes gleamed. "That he is."

The End

Mara's journey will continue in book two:

Blood Runs Deep

Acknowledgements

If I were to thank everyone who has helped me with this book, the acknowledgements section would be just as long as the main content. I owe a debt of gratitude to everyone who has shown an interest when I have mentioned this—very long—project. Each question or word of encouragement has spurred me onwards.

Special thanks must be offered to some, however.

Firstly, to all the members of my writers group; Martine, Shanon, Siobhan, Hatty, James, and all the others who came and went, and offered not only a patient ear, but consistently kind criticism whenever it was needed.

Secondly, to J. A. Guynn who was brave enough to not only let me beta read his novel, but to reciprocate in return. Thank you for your two-way patience, and for all you have taught me.

Next, to all the others who have been willing to read over the many drafts of this novel. Maddie, Jackson, Theresa, Abi, Taylor, Ted, Johanna and Will, just to name a few! You were all invaluable in your own way, and I must offer additional thanks to those of you who waded through the earliest and roughest versions.

Last, but not least, to my very best friend in the whole world, Katie. Though we remain separated by oceans, your heart is forever held within mine. I can say with certainty that this book would not have made it to publication if I didn't have you to encourage, console, badger, praise, nudge and love me. I owe you more than I can ever repay.

As always, the very final thanks must go to you, the reader, not only for choosing to read this novel, but for getting to the end! Whether you enjoyed it or not, please consider leaving a review on whichever platform you are most comfortable with and if you wish to contact me, you can do so at: info@armstrongauthor.co.uk

Printed in Great Britain
by Amazon